PI

The Ne

"Deliciously real, modern,
—*New York Times* bestselling author Katy Evans

"Relentless chemistry and sizzling romance make this book a must read!"   —*New York Times* bestselling author Laura Kaye

"A wonderful, sweet love story."   —*Romantic Times*

"If you're looking for a quick, sexy read, this one is definitely for you."   —The Reading Cafe

"Fun, sweet and sexy. . . . Fans of Jaci Burton and Shiloh Walker will enjoy *What You Need*."   —Harlequin Junkie

PRAISE FOR LORELEI JAMES

"Lorelei James knows how to write fun, sexy and hot stories."
—Joyfully Reviewed

"Sexy and highly erotic."   —TwoLips Reviews

"Incredibly hot."   —The Romance Studio

"[A] wild, sexy ride."   —RT Book Reviews

Want You to Want Me

LORELEI JAMES

JOVE
New York

A JOVE BOOK
Published by Berkley
An imprint of Penguin Random House LLC
penguinrandomhouse.com

ISBN: 9780451492760

First Edition: August 2020

Printed in the United States of America
1   3   5   7   9   10   8   6   4   2

Cover design by Rita Frangie

One

—

NOLAN

The *SpongeBob SquarePants* theme blared from my phone. I silenced it right away, but the damage had been done. "Sorry."

"Please tell me you're not watching cartoons while we're trying to have a meeting," my cousin Brady Lund, CFO of Lund Industries, complained.

Cartoons? WTF? Why would he accuse me of that? Like I fucked around in meetings all the time?

Maybe you oughta tell him you were tempted to watch anything to drown out his boring, meandering drone.

"That's Mimi's ring tone. She's home sick today and apparently she's bored."

"That's why my son isn't getting a cell phone until he's responsible enough to use it," Brady retorted.

"Shouldn't be a problem since he's only a couple of months old," Ash said. "Can we get back to business?"

"By all means. What do you propose?" I looked at Brady,

who'd just finished giving his preliminary first quarter revenue report before my phone's untimely interruption.

Brady sighed and ran his hand through his dark, already disheveled hair before his gaze moved between me and our cousin Ash, the COO of Lund Industries. "To be honest, I'm uncomfortable giving my recommendations in present company. No offense, Nolan."

Technically I was the odd man out in this session as I was the CEO . . . in waiting? In training? On deck? In the wings? I wasn't the third power "C" in Lund Industries—yet—I'd step into the role of CEO of Lund Industries when my father, Archer Lund, stepped down.

No one saw that happening anytime soon.

I stood. "Have your admins give mine a shout after you've brought this up in executive session." I headed toward the door, but I paused in the doorframe and faced them. "In the future, I prefer to be excluded when you need a sounding board for your recitation of bad news. No offense."

"No need to get pissy, Nolan."

"That wasn't me being pissy. I just don't want you to present me with a list of problems without allowing me to participate in a discussion of solutions."

I stepped into the elevator and hit the down button. My office wasn't on the same floor as the other executive offices.

Since Lund Industries owned the entire building, each Lund family member was fortunate enough to get his or her own space. As CEO, my father had the nicest office on the highest floor. His brother Monte, who was president of the board of directors, and his brother Ward, who handled corporate accounts, had separate offices but shared their floor with the executive boardroom. As CFO, Brady and the financial department had one entire floor to themselves. Same for Ash and the operations department. My cousin Annika headed the PR department, which shared a floor with marketing. My mother, my aunt Priscilla and my aunt Selka also had their own floor, which was home to the Lund Cares Community

Outreach—LCCO—program, a foundation that funded numerous charities and events in the Twin Cities and across Minnesota.

The rest of the building had the usual sales, legal, acquisitions, international and research and development departments, each with a dedicated floor. We also had an entire floor designated as an employee lunchroom, break room and lounge.

For the decade I'd been working at Lund Industries, I'd spent time in every department. Starting out, I hadn't even merited my own office space. My current office was in the cyber security wing on the IT floor. It wasn't an impressive space, but it did have its own entrance that kept a buffer against the noise from the IT department, as well as a private elevator to the executive parking level. My admin's area was considerably smaller than her colleagues'.

Correction: than his *colleagues'.*

Sometimes my brain reverted and got the gender wrong. My terrific PA, Sam, who'd been with me two years, had started to transition four months ago. My only concern when she told me about the change was that *he'd* intended to resign. But thankfully that hadn't been the case.

I've had a diverse group of friends of all orientations my adult life, but seeing Samantha transition to Sam was a first for me. I was grateful it wasn't a new situation to our HR department. So they were fully prepared to prepare me on handling an unfamiliar situation respectfully.

He glanced up. "How'd the meeting go?"

I paused at the edge of his desk. "Did you ever have a friend who forced you to listen to a presentation or a speech and you realized they were just practicing on you?"

Sam groaned. "Not again."

"Afraid so. I don't know if Brady expected me to tell him that his delivery was too dry or what, but I was too busy processing the information he was spewing out to realize that's what it was. After he reached the end, they couldn't discuss potential solutions with me, so the whole damn thing was pointless. Next time Brady's admin Jenna calls for a meeting? Grill her on specifics of said meeting so I don't waste my time."

"Absolutely, sir."

"Thank you." I looked at the stack of messages next to his daily planner. "What'd I miss?"

"Six calls returned from Friday afternoon. Five were departmental. Chris from IT stopped in to remind you it's Rube Goldberg appreciation week so you might see oddities throughout the IT floor. A woman named Janiece called twice. Once to say she had a memorable time with you this weekend, the second time to leave her number and request you call her."

I frowned. "I don't remember a woman named Denice."

Sam shook his head. "*J*, not *D*. *Ja-niece*. Tall. Long red hair. Sparkly aqua-colored top. You mentioned her reminding you of the Little Mermaid. And before you give me that haughty eyebrow raise, the excess of information came from Miss Janiece herself . . . so you didn't get her confused with someone else."

"Hilarious. But the only place I went this weekend besides Jaxson and Lucy's was my buddy Baylor's birthday bash, for like an hour. This Janiece chick . . ." I racked my brain. "Might've been the one I talked to briefly as I stuffed my face with chicken wings. Or maybe the one I chatted with as we waited for our drinks." I sighed. "I don't remember." I shot him a look. "Not because I had women lined up like I used to."

Sam smirked. "Ah, now we're talking about the good old days."

I rolled my eyes.

"I'm just relaying the message, boss."

"Much appreciated. Let's hope she gets the message when I don't call her back." My gaze dropped to his skinny tie, an understated purple with modernist cubes in shades of black and gray. "Great tie."

His fingers moved to fuss with the knot. "Thanks. It's vintage. Givenchy."

"Stop dressing better than me, Sam."

That earned me a full-on grin. "That's the ultimate compliment coming from a guy with a personal stylist."

"A stylist who is currently annoyed with me."

"Why is he annoyed?"

"Because I haven't expressed an interest in anything from the spring lines."

"Poor Nolan . . . facing the wrath of Jacques Andres." His lips twitched. "He'll probably put you in lime-green gingham to teach you a lesson."

"Don't even joke about that." I shuddered. "So is there anything else?"

Sam fiddled with his tie again. "Yes. It's about your Lund Cares Community Outreach project. Have you come up with an idea yet?"

I fought a groan for many reasons, the biggest one being that my mother—one of the three Lund matriarchs—had asked me this exact same question yesterday at brunch. "Who called to get you to nag me about this?"

"Your aunt Priscilla. First thing this morning. Fair warning, boss. She said if you don't have a solid plan delivered to the LCCO office by tomorrow, she's setting up a bachelor auction for next month."

Fair warning, my ass. That was straight-up a threat. I had half a mind to tell her to go ahead and do it. See if she'd really force the last two single Lund men—including her son Ash—into strutting our stuff for charity.

Sam held up his hand to silence my retort. "All joking aside, sir, a bachelor auction might've been all the rage in the 1990s, but now it'd be seen as LCCO being woefully out of touch."

"As I'm aware, Sam."

"Which is why I have a new idea. If you're interested in hearing it."

"Of course I am." I gestured to his fingers, still messing with his tie. "Stop fussing. I'm not that goddamn scary to bounce ideas off of."

He smiled. "True. But my idea for your project is a bit unconventional and maybe controversial."

"Hit me with it."

"An event for LGBTQ youth. It wouldn't necessarily have to be a fund-raiser, but more along the lines of a mixer for LGBTQ kids from various schools in the Twin Cities."

That immediately piqued my interest. "What age group are you thinking?"

"It'd be geared toward high school students."

"Where would we hold the event? Would there be a group activity?"

"Jax's bowling alley was the first place that popped into my head. The activity would be team bowling, with the teams of four drawn randomly to truly make it a mixer. We could kick around the idea of adding a speaker, but then the event becomes less normalized, if that makes sense." He blew out a breath. "While attitudes toward LGBTQ kids have come a long way, this would be another avenue to show support."

"Sam. That is a grand idea." I grinned. "And I'm not just saying that because you're saving me from being bachelor number two."

"You really think so? I mean, I was worried you'd think I was creating a personal platform—"

"Which you are, but not in a bad way. This is how community outreach is supposed to work—funding great ideas, promoting them and getting involved." I rubbed my hands together. "Turn on the answering service and come into my office so we can get this started."

The last place I wanted to go at nine P.M. on a Monday was Lakeside, the ice rink Jax owned. But he'd left the paperwork for renting the bowling alley for my LCCO project on his desk and I needed physical proof to turn in tomorrow morning that I actually had an event lined up.

I timed it so I could briefly pop into Jax's office, grab the envelope and go, since Margene, the rink manager, usually closed up on Mondays.

But Margene's car wasn't parked up front. Instead I saw Gabi's Toyota Tundra.

Gabi—"the" Gabriella Welk, Olympic athlete, superstar women's pro hockey player—who coached at Lakeside. The woman I'd (mistakenly) accused of having a crush on my brother, which turned out to be totally untrue, which made me look like a complete dick.

Unsurprisingly, I wasn't Gabi's favorite person. She called me Mr. Fancy Pants. If there weren't students around, she'd slip up and call me dickhead.

I, in turn, called her by her full name—Gabriella. I knew it annoyed her, but hey, it *was* her name.

As I sat in my car, debating on whether to just go home and stop back in the morning, another vehicle zipped past me and parked near the front entrance. A guy jumped out and strode into the building.

Although I'd never officially met him, I recognized him as Gabriella's boyfriend. His appearance would distract her, so while they played grab-ass or whatever, I'd sneak in, get what I needed and get out.

As soon as I walked in, I knew there'd be no quick grab and go. An angry voice echoed down the hallway, from her office, which I'd have to walk past to reach Jax's office.

Her tone immediately put me on alert when she yelled, "Jesus. You scared the piss out of me."

I could see his shadow, just inside the doorway. He said, "I need to talk to you."

"And you think now is a good time? Dammit, Tyson. You can't just show up where I work—"

"You've left me no choice but to track you down since you're not returning my calls."

"Because I'm busy."

"It's an excuse. Avoidance. Whatever. This can't go on any longer."

Not good. I didn't want to listen in on what sounded like a serious conversation, but Gabriella was here alone with her pissed-off boyfriend and I wouldn't let her fend for herself.

"Fine. Spit it out," she retorted.

"I'm in love with your sister," he blurted. "We didn't mean for it to happen, it just did."

Silence.

"Say something," Tyson demanded.

"If you and Dani are in love, why isn't she here with you right now sharing the happy news?"

"Because she's scared of you, Gabi."

"She should be. How long have the two of you been sneaking around behind my back?"

"It's not like that," Tyson protested.

"Oh, so you two aren't currently fucking?"

"For your information, no, she and I haven't been together like that."

She laughed. "Then how could you possibly know if it's love?"

Ooh. Good one, Gabriella.

"Because it *is* love. Just because you don't understand it—"

"Omigod, spare me! If you say something lame like your love transcends intimacy"—she snorted—"I swear I will brain you with my goddamned hockey stick."

That one was even better.

"We haven't been intimate because we knew it would hurt you. This is a screwed-up situation, but the last thing either Dani or I want to do is cause you any pain, Gabi." A pause. "You introduced us, for god's sake."

"This is why I don't do nice things. They always come back to kick me in the ass," she retorted.

Another pause.

"Will you knock off the sarcasm for one minute and listen to me?" Tyson asked.

"Fine. Say what you need to."

"Things haven't been great between you and me for a while."

"You aren't seriously thinking about blaming *me* for the fact you're lusting after my little sister, are you?"

"No, but your response to this conversation is proof of why you and I don't work. After Dani left for Florida to train for the Olympics, you pulled back from her, from me and from your former teammates—teammates who resented the hell out of Dani because she was there instead of you. Dani had no one to talk to but me. So we spent a lot of time together. All of it platonic, all of it that getting-to-know-you stuff that you and I never bothered to learn about each other."

"So because I have no clue what your favorite color is—"

"Will you stop interjecting your personal regrets into this conversation? Because we both know you preferred hookups to a relationship for this very reason, Gabi."

Ouch.

He sighed. "Believe it or not, I didn't come here to fight with you. I came here to break it off in person and to ask you to not be too hard on Dani about this. She worships you. The fact her feelings changed for me has been eating her alive."

Silence.

"What happens after you leave here, Ty?"

"We both move on."

She mumbled something I didn't hear.

Then Tyson stepped back and Gabriella barreled past him. She'd almost reached me lurking in the corner, when Tyson said, "Wait."

She whirled back around. "What?"

"I wasn't done talking to you."

"Tough shit, because I'm done talking to you. I need to finish closing procedures, so feel free to let the door hit you in the ass on your way out." She threw open the inner rink door with such force it juddered against the concrete and slammed shut.

Tyson ran his hand through his hair and exhaled. He gave the arena door a long look, almost as if he was stupidly considering going after her, before he turned and spotted me.

I spoke first. "Sorry. I stopped to get some paperwork and I didn't want to interrupt your conversation."

"Calling it a *conversation* is putting a positive spin on it," he muttered. He studied me. "Who are you that you're stopping by this late for paperwork?"

"I'm Nolan Lund. Jax's brother."

"Did Gabi know you were here?"

"Are you kidding? I've been on the receiving end of infuriated Gabriella and my first thought was to flee." I resisted telling him it'd be wise for him to do the same before she stormed back here.

His gaze sharpened. "I take it you two are friends?"

"We're acquainted. Why?"

"Could you stick around for a little longer and make sure she's okay?"

Was this dude for real? I scrutinized him and realized he was truly concerned for Gabi's well-being. Still, he was an asshole for dumping her for her sister. "Sure."

With a muttered "Thanks" he shot out of there like his ass was on fire.

Not that I blamed him.

I probably should've done the same thing—then it was too late. She stomped out of the rink, demanding, "What the hell are *you* doing here?"

Two

GABI

An awkward moment followed, where neither of us said anything.

Nolan Lund, that good-looking bastard, broke the silence first. "Stopped to get some paperwork and saw a guy rush in here. I figured you were alone, so I thought I'd check and see if everything was okay."

"I'm peachy keen, jellybean."

He raised one arrogant eyebrow. "Quoting Rizzo from *Grease*? I'm shocked."

I shrugged. "I identify with the mouthy ones."

His intense blue eyes searched my face. "What happened?"

"Is that why you're here? Hoping to catch me messing around on your brother's dime?"

"Jesus. No. And indignant deflection won't work, Gabriella."

"I can't believe you're surprised I don't want to talk about my feelings when it comes to my boyfriend. Or should I say *ex*-boyfriend."

"Your ex? Since when?"

"Since about two minutes ago."

"Wait? You broke up with him here? Tonight?"

"Don't flatter me, slick. We both know you overheard *him* breaking up with *me*. And if you stuck around to watch the train wreck, you'll be sadly disappointed that I'm not about to go off the rails."

"Your ex might've been thinking you'd have a breakdown."

"Why?"

"He asked me if we were friends."

"What did you say?"

He bestowed the sexy, smirking grin that had me dreading his answer. "I told him the truth."

"That we're enemies?"

"You think we're enemies?"

"Don't you?"

"No. Frenemies, maybe."

My eyebrows rose in surprise.

"I said we knew each other since my brother owns this place. Then he asked me to make sure you were all right."

"Of course he did. Because he wants to come off as the good guy."

In the entryway, Nolan reached for the lighting panel the same time I did, and his rough-skinned fingers brushed mine.

I jerked my hand back, surprised he didn't have soft, white-collar hands, since he held a soft, white-collar job. "Thanks for your concern, but I got this."

Outside the front door, he said nothing while I dug out my keys.

"Look. I appreciate you sticking around, but as you can see, I'm perfectly fine."

"Then explain to me how you planned to lock up the building with a can opener."

I glanced down. Sure enough; I'd clutched the carabiner with my random mini tools in my hand, not my key ring.

Goddammit. What was wrong with me?

You're not invincible. This breakup has *affected you.*

After I locked up and set the alarm, I turned around and Nolan was right there. Nearly nose to nose with me. No sarcastic smirk on his too-perfect lips. No mean glint in his mesmerizing laser-blue eyes.

"Just because you're not currently sobbing over the breakup doesn't mean you're not distracted by it. Get pissy with me, Gabriella, but I'm not letting you get behind the wheel to drive home when you're acting like this."

"Like what?"

"Like the poster girl for road rage."

Girl. As if.

But you are a little ragey, Gabs, admit that.

"Well, lucky for you, ace, I'm not headed home."

"Doesn't matter where you're going. I'll drive you."

I blinked at him. "Did you seriously just offer to drive me to the bar?"

"Which bar?"

"Buddy's."

That gave him pause. "You sure you wanna go there?"

"No, Nolan, I'd rather go to Flurry," I retorted. "That's your usual hangout, isn't it? But since I don't *own* the type of clothes that'd pass their snooty dress code, I'm going to Buddy's. Plus, half-price happy hour drinks started at nine. Some of us have to stick to a budget."

"Then Buddy's it is." Nolan gestured to his car.

His sleek, two-door sportscar, painted a gorgeous bright blue with glossy black accents, hogged two parking places. Just as I opened my mouth to call him out on his assholish parking behavior, a series of beeps sounded, and the car doors moved.

Up.

Holy shit. It had doors similar to the DeLorean in *Back to the Future*. It might've been the hottest car I'd ever seen.

Not that I'd tell him that.

But my awe must've been apparent because I heard him snicker.

"Admit it. The doors are wicked cool."

"They do have that alien spaceship vibe, Chewie."

"Chewie?" Nolan laughed again. "I'm definitely more Lando Calrissian than Chewbacca."

"Dream on. So is this a new toy? I've never seen you drive it."

"It's not a new car, but it's new to me. I bought it to celebrate after I was named future CEO. It's not great in the snow, so it's been stored. Today looked decent so I took it out."

Winters in Minnesota were brutal, but we'd had above-average temps the past week as we drifted into spring. "What kind of car is this?"

"Bugatti Veyron."

"Never heard of that brand."

He shrugged, not surprised I wasn't familiar with a vehicle that probably cost over a million bucks.

"Get in."

It was cool watching the doors slide shut. The flashy blue leather interior and knobs and buttons in weird places gave it that exclusive vibe. This vehicle most likely cost more than I'd earn in a decade. Or a lifetime, the way my career had gone of late.

Nolan pulled out of the parking lot. "Buddy's. You're sure?"

"I'm sure it's no surprise to you I like dive bars with cheap booze."

Buddy's was only two miles down the road from Lakeside Ice Arena. But a mile across the wrong side of the tracks, so to speak. I'd started hanging out here after my first night working at Lakeside more than a year ago. I'd needed a drink after dealing with my boss at the time, a little troll of a man with an inferiority complex, who, thankfully, was no longer employed at the rink. I still dropped in occasionally, but not nearly as much as I used to.

Nolan eyed the parking area with distaste, choosing to

parallel park beneath a streetlight. As soon as he opened the doors, I bounded out of the car and headed to the front entrance.

Being at Buddy's soothed me, the knowledge that some things resisted change. Rusty metal siding formed an entryway. The bullet holes in the scarred metal door were from an incident years past between a jealous girlfriend and her cheating boyfriend. The door hadn't been replaced, since it still served as a badge of honor for the owners and a helluva conversation piece for the regulars.

Inside the doorway, I scanned the space. With only about a dozen customers, it was a slow night.

"Gabi!" a voice boomed from behind the bar.

My gaze winged to the bartender and I grinned. "Rico."

"Been a while, champ."

"Yeah. Well, I've been busy."

"Haven't we all. I missed that smiling face. Have a seat." He yelled at the guy sitting in "my" chair to make room for Buddy's most famous customer.

Famous. Right. I crossed the sticky linoleum and mouthed *Thanks* to the gray-haired dude who'd relinquished his wobbly barstool for me.

Rico leaned across the shellacked bartop. "First one's on me. Margarita rocks, right?"

"Aww, you remembered. You really did miss me."

He smiled. "None of these assholes know anything about hockey. I missed arguing with you."

Then the bar went quiet.

No surprise as to why.

Nolan Lund.

A beautiful billionaire dressed to the nines was an oddity at Buddy's.

To Rico I said, "He's with me." Rather than releasing an ear-piercing whistle to get Nolan's attention, I waved my hand over my head. I did have some class.

"With you?" Rico said. "As in—"

"He's my DD."

"Ah. That explains it. That suit is too damn nice for him to be your parole officer."

"Hilarious."

Nolan took the seat beside me, next to the wall.

Rico set a full glass in front of him.

"What's this?" Nolan asked.

"Coke. Unless you'd prefer *diet.* You're her DD, right?" Rico didn't wait for his response. He returned to making my drink, presenting it with a flourish.

I took a long sip and sighed. "Perfect as usual, Rico. Thanks."

"Lemme know if you need anything else, champ."

Nolan and I sat in silence for several long minutes. From the corner of my eye I watched him take in the space. The limited selection of top-shelf booze reflected in the faded mirror. The scuffed wooden bar spread out in a long, blocky C shape. The TVs suspended from the ceiling. The lone pool table, currently unused. The throwback jukebox, also quiet. The plastic molded bar signs—Hamm's, Grain Belt, Olympia, Schlitz, Pabst Blue Ribbon—beer brands straight out of the 1960s. The customers, a mix of biker-looking types, eyes on the TVs, and couples sharing laughter over pitchers of beer. The lone cocktail waitress, Brenda, a well-preserved sixtyish woman and also Rico's mother, loaded glasses in the undercounter dishwasher.

After Nolan pulled his phone out, I expected he'd start scrolling through it. But he set it aside, reached up and loosened his tie.

"Aren't you worried about someone stealing your car?"

"It's insured." He sipped his Coke. "It's also got an alarm system that'll wake the dead and alert the cops."

He'd said that loud enough so anyone listening in the bar knew not to fuck around with it.

I stirred my drink, a million other thoughts racing through my brain.

We must've sat there awhile, because finally, Nolan said, "Are you going to talk to me? Or do I have to wait until you've had several of those before you loosen up?"

"Fine. I'll spill my guts. Have you ever been dumped?"

A beat passed. "No. I haven't."

Of course he hadn't. "It sucks."

I drained my drink and signaled to Rico for another. "It'd be easier to pretend this breakup blindsided me. But the truth is . . . I deserved to get kicked to the curb."

"Why?"

"Besides the fact I'm a shitty girlfriend? Before Tyson showed up and confronted me, I hadn't seen him in over a week. And in that week, he'd texted me twice. Which is two more times than I'd texted him."

"That answers my next question."

"Which is?"

"If you missed him, which would be no, since apparently you forgot all about him."

I tossed ten bucks at Rico when he served the fresh drink.

"How long were you with Tyson?"

I licked the salt off the rim of my glass and took a sip. "Nine months. I knew him from University of North Dakota—UND. A bunch of us displaced hockey players who'd relocated to the Twin Cities hung out regularly. He and I usually ended up together, so we started dating. A few months in, he took leave from his assistant coaching job at a private high school to be a third-level assistant coach for the U.S. Olympic Women's Ice Hockey Team." I scowled. "Never occurred to me *not* to introduce him to my little sister, Dani, the newest member on the team, since he'd be part of her coaching staff. To be honest, I was relieved that Dani would have someone to look after her." I sighed. "It's my own fault. Out of sight, out of mind. Literally. Both of them. They talked about each other to me all the time, and I thought it was cute they were so friendly. Since returning from the Olympics, both Dani and Tyson went silent on me."

"So you truly didn't know about them sneaking around behind your back?"

I looked over at him. "If you were there, then you heard Tyson's claim that nothing physical had happened between them."

He studied me. "And you believe that?"

"Yep. Tyson is the good guy that all women want to be in a relationship with. Dani is the stereotypical good girl that all men are looking for." I refocused on stirring my drink. "It's like some code of honor thing for them. Neither of them would purposely hurt me, which is why this situation will be awkward as hell for a while."

"You're not in the wrong here."

"Aren't I?" Maybe that's why I wasn't bawling my eyes out. And maybe—just maybe—a small part of me felt relieved. Ty and I had always been better friends than lovers. Sex hadn't been lousy between us, it just hadn't been a priority. I'd chalked up the lack of lust to conflicting schedules and then physical distance after he'd temporarily relocated to Florida.

"What's going through your mind right now?" Nolan asked.

"That I need to find a great rebound ASAP."

Nolan choked on his soda.

Rico grinned at me as he reached into the cooler. "Just say the word, champ, and I'll jump through all the hoops to be your rebound man."

Laughing, I shooed him away. My phone vibrated and I pulled it out.

Three missed calls from Dani. I shoved it back in my pocket and let the current call go to voice mail.

"Was that your sister?"

"Be interesting to see how many times she'll call to try and explain."

Nolan's eyebrows lifted. "To explain? Not to beg your forgiveness?"

I shrugged and knocked back another swig.

Neither of us said anything for several long minutes. I'd

started to tell him he could take off and I'd find my own way home, when he spoke.

"You play pool?"

I kept my expression bland. "Sometimes. Why?"

"Table is open. Let's have a game."

"Sure." I motioned Rico over. "A shot of Cuervo and some quarters, please."

Rico poured two shots; one for me and one for him. He winked. "This way you're not drinkin' alone."

Lick, salt, shoot, squeeze. A little moan escaped when that burning warmth spread down my throat, followed by the sour tang on my tongue. God. I loved tequila shooters. I couldn't remember the last time I'd had one. And that's why I always limited myself to *only* one.

"Another?" Rico asked.

"Shot? No. Margarita? Yes, please." From the corner of my eye I saw Nolan open his mouth, probably to warn me to slow down, so I held up my hand to stop him. "I'm entitled to drown my sorrows, Lund. You volunteered to be here as my DD, not my liver monitor. Feel free to leave anytime you've had enough."

"Whatever. I'll rack." He sidestepped me and headed to the pool table.

I watched him walk away, wondering if he'd leave his snappy suit jacket on the back of the barstool like a regular joe, or hang it up on the deer antler coatrack I'd never seen anyone use.

Of course he hung it up.

Then Nolan crouched to insert the quarters and push the mechanism that released the balls. I chose my stick, a short one with a heavier bottom.

He sauntered over to pick his own cue. "You want to rack or break?"

"Rack."

"Fine. I'll break." He rolled up his shirtsleeves.

I might've made a smarmy remark about him getting

serious about beating me, but my gaze had gotten stuck on his forearms. With that kind of muscle definition? The man did more than push pencils all day.

Damn him. I didn't want to notice that.

The balls cracked and scattered across the green felt as he broke.

We both watched as the 11-ball dropped in the far-left corner. "Looks like I'm stripes." He moved around for his next shot . . . and the cue ball followed the ball into the side pocket.

I plucked my fresh drink from Rico, keeping my game face on as I snagged the cue ball and positioned it. I sank two balls before I scratched.

Nolan called the 9-ball in the corner and missed.

"Ooh. Almost. Those rebounds are a bitch though."

Now Nolan didn't look nearly as out of place with his tie askew, his sleeves rolled up and his hands wrapped around his cue stick as he leaned into it with his feet braced apart.

After sinking three balls, I banked the cue ball off the side rail and it barely tapped the 7-ball, but it somehow dropped in. "Sorry. That was slop. Your turn."

"I'm not taking a turn out of pity, Coach Welk."

I shrugged. "Suit yourself." I focused on the 1-ball and nailed it. Then called the 8-ball in the corner pocket and nailed that one too. I glanced over at Nolan.

He narrowed his eyes at me. "What just happened here?"

"I beat you." I finally allowed a smirk. "Go ahead and practice since most of your balls are still on the table."

"Like hell. Let's go again. I'll rack 'em this time."

Like that would make a difference.

I felt Nolan's eyes on me as I sipped my drink. I wasn't anywhere near drunk, but I did have "I'm tipsy" talkative tendencies. "What?"

"Is this when you suggest a bet for the next game?"

"If I'd wanted to hustle you, I would've let you win the

first game. Besides, I'm guessing you're the one who grew up with a pool table in your house, whereas I didn't."

He drained his Coke. "Quit stalling."

After paying for game two, I sauntered to the opposite end of the table, chalking my cue as I walked.

Before I could line up, two bar regulars showed up. Upon seeing me, they immediately walked over.

"Heya, champ! Long time no see."

"If it isn't Matt and Jeff." I allowed myself to be hugged awkwardly. Then I gave them each a once-over. "All of the hunting seasons must be done if you two are here."

Jeff shoved his hands in his pockets. "No huntin', but ice fishin's been good up until last week."

His brother Matt added, "Real good."

Their gazes followed Nolan as he moved to stand beside me. "We still playing?"

"Yes. This is Matt and Jeff, a couple of regulars. They're brothers—"

"Twins," they said in tandem.

"I see that," Nolan said with annoyance.

Then they just stood there and stared at one another.

Which I blamed on Nolan. I smiled at the brothers. "We'll catch up in a bit, cool?"

"Cool."

After they were out of earshot, I whirled around. "Asshole much, Lund?"

"What did I do?"

"You were rude."

"*I* was rude? They're the ones who interrupted our pool game. Besides, I wanted to make sure you didn't invite the regulars to play doubles with us."

"Aww. How sweet that you want me all to yourself." I broke, knocking in two stripes and one solid.

Then I ran the table—five shots in a row. Finishing with a hard bank to the 8-ball, neatly putting it into the side pocket without scratching.

A little over the top, but I took a victory lap around the table anyway.

"Now that you've thoroughly kicked my ass at pool—twice—tell me how you got to be so good."

"You're assuming I spent all my formative years on the ice and had no time to develop other skills?"

"I don't need to assume anything. My brother was a pro hockey player too, remember?"

"And you consistently beat him at pool?" I prompted.

"Yes."

"What other games did the little Lund brother win?"

He flashed me a cocky grin. "Most any game where brainpower was involved."

I snorted.

"On the physical side, I've always been able to outrun him—distance and sprints. We're evenly matched in basketball. Sparring and grappling . . . I'll admit he usually wins, even now that we're adults, but it is different when we're not wrestling because we're pissed off at each other like when we were kids."

"At least you got to fight with him. I wasn't allowed to even look at Dani wrong." Why had I told him that?

Those baby blues of his turned shrewd. "Is that why you're not confronting your sister now? Out of habit?"

I returned my pool cue to the rack on the wall, wishing I would've kept my mouth shut.

Then Nolan was right there, prodding me. "Gabriella?"

"I don't want to talk about this, Nolan."

"I get that. But I think you *need* to talk about it."

"Why you gotta be so nosy?" I growled at him. "Can't I just drink and pretend everything is—"

"Peachy keen, jellybean? Because I'm one hundred percent sure that's not true."

The way he studied me had the opposite effect to my usual response of adding another coat of steel to my already

WANT YOU TO WANT ME 23

tough outer shell. The idea of him chipping away at the chink in my armor didn't fill me with dread.

I dropped into the closest chair and he didn't miss a beat; he plopped right down beside me.

"Why weren't you and Dani allowed to fight like normal siblings?"

"We didn't have a normal childhood together. I'm twelve years older than her. My parents tried to have another baby for years and couldn't, so I got the full scope of their attention. I won't claim I showed above-average hockey prowess from an early age, but I did love hockey more than it just being something I did for fun. Anyway, my parents didn't make a big deal about what I wanted to do for my twelfth birthday, and I secretly hoped it was because they'd signed me up for club hockey in Fargo. I wanted that more than a party or presents and I knew it was a big expense. But on that birthday, they told me I was going to be a big sister.

"This is where, in a Hallmark Channel retelling of my life, I'd be overjoyed by the news, I'd promise the unborn sibling all the love and protection my preteen self could imagine. But the truth? I knew that baby would change my everything. And she did." I smiled. "Don't get me wrong, I loved her immediately, but I didn't want my life to change to accommodate hers."

"Your parents expected that?" Nolan asked.

"Not until Dani turned two. By then I was playing club hockey. At that point it was apparent I had skills above the norm. It was also at that point my parents wanted me to quit club hockey and just be satisfied with playing on the local high school team."

"Can I ask . . . was their reasoning for that suggestion financial?"

I shook my head. "The issue was the travel time between our farm and Fargo, which was forty-five minutes one way. No other kids in my rural area were players, so ride sharing wasn't an option. The wonky weather in North Dakota in the winter was always an issue too. The solution was to have me move in with a widowed woman in Fargo, a hockey patron, who lived close enough to the rink that I could walk to team practice and I could ride the bus to the high school."

"So you went to hockey boarding school."

"Basically. But I wasn't around much in the summer either because I attended hockey camps. I'm pretty sure my dad was against me living in town because he wanted my help at home. My mom . . ." I could stop the story there.

"What happened with her?"

Just say it. "She told me I was selfish. That Dani deserved better than a sister who preferred hockey to her. That there'd come a time when they'd expect me to step up and be there for Dani, for whatever she needed. Mom made me promise and she's held me to it ever since."

"Jesus, Gabriella. You were what . . . fourteen when you made that promise? Do you really think it applies now? That you have no right to be upset that your sister stole your boyfriend?"

"I'm saying it's just another thing, in a long line of things, that Dani gets because I let her. And this one, it's one of the easier things to let her have."

Nolan frowned.

"So to answer your question, I got good at pool because the ice rink where I spent a good chunk of my life had a pool table for kids like me, who were dropped off early and were the last to leave as we waited for rides. Even when I lived a five-minute walk away, it became a habit to stay and play after practice as a way to wind down." I stood. "I'm ready for another drink."

I'd told him way more than I'd ever intended.

To lighten my mood, I wandered over to Matt and Jeff's table. They bought me a margarita and I learned more about pulling an ice fishing house off a lake than I ever wanted to know. But the conversation and the drink loosened the tight feeling in my chest, so I was able to offer Nolan a genuine smile when I returned.

He slid his phone into his pocket.

"Checking your stock prices?"

"No. Just catching up on a game I play."

"Please tell me it's *Candy Crush*."

He laughed.

"*Angry Birds*?"

"Are those your favorites?" he said curiously.

"Nope. I'll tell you when I get back." I snagged my purse. "I'm going to the restroom."

The bathroom was hidden in the very back of the bar behind the storage room.

I hadn't been gone long, but before I turned the corner to go into the main bar, I noticed Rico had moved out from behind the counter and stood by my chair with his arms crossed. I couldn't see Nolan from this angle and neither of them could see me.

"Why are you flirting with Gabi?"

"What? I wasn't flirting with her."

Leave. Right now. Return to the bathroom because you don't need to hear this.

Problem is: I wanted to hear it.

Rico kept pushing. "Admit it. You're more than her DD."

"Don't be ridiculous."

"I saw you eyeballing her ass during the pool games. I saw the 'back off' looks you gave the regulars who just tried to say hello to her. If you're into her, dude, just say so."

Nolan chuckled.

A strange feeling tightened my insides; throat, chest, gut.

"I'm not into her *at all*. She's not my type."

Yep. Totally should've left.

"I really am just her DD. That said, I definitely expected more than her macho 'man this sucks, I need to get drunk and get laid' attitude after her boyfriend dumped her tonight, which is exactly what I hear from my *guy* friends after a breakup."

Rico said, "You don't know Gabi at all if you thought she'd be crying in her tequila."

"You're right. I *don't* know her at all. I get that she's tough. But I suspect that's all there is to her, regardless if she's in her hockey uniform."

Oh that stung.

But mostly because he wasn't wrong.

Given the craptastic day I'd had, that comment shouldn't have been what brought me to tears, but it was. I wheeled around, nearly knocking the cocktail waitress over. "Damn. Sorry, Brenda."

"What's wrong?"

"Nothing. I—I just need to get out of here." *Right now.* "Can I go out the back?"

Brenda looked concerned. "Are you going to be sick?"

"No. It's just . . . everything I shoved down today is starting to surface and I don't wanna be in public when the meltdown happens." Not a lie; I barely kept my voice from shaking.

"Honey, that I can understand. You go on."

"Thank you." I handed her a twenty. "This should cover what's left of my tab. Tell Rico I'll see him later."

She nodded. "What should I tell your DD?"

That he can go fuck himself.

When would I learn that a man like Nolan Lund—charming, wealthy, gorgeous, well-connected—would never look beyond the surface of any woman, let alone me? I had no issue admitting that my outer shell had none of the slick, glossy veneer he required. Most days I was perfectly fine with that.

However . . . today was not one of those days.

"Gabi?" Brenda prompted.

"If he asks, tell him I got a ride home."

I already had the Uber app open as I slunk out the delivery exit.

Two minutes until the car arrived.

Enough time to chastise myself for thinking for one moment that Nolan Lund and I could ever be friends.

Three

GABI

Bang bang bang.

I pulled my pillow over my head and tried to sink deeper into my mattress.

The banging continued.

Jerking the covers back, I stumbled out of bed. It was the first Sunday in months I didn't have to be up at the crack of nothing to be at the rink, and dammit, I deserved to sleep in.

I didn't bother checking the peephole before I twisted the deadbolt, slipped the chain and threw open the door, bellowing, "What!"

"Good morning to you too, sunshine." Liddy, my pesky neighbor/pain-in-the-rear friend, breezed past me carrying a covered plate that smelled heavenly. She disappeared around the corner and called out, "I'll just put on the kettle."

Yawning, I made my way into the kitchen. Liddy looked every inch the English rose with her smartly styled strawberry-blond hair, her flawless ivory skin, her knee-length floral dress topped with a formfitting pale pink cardigan and ending with nude-colored kitten heels.

When she spun around, I half expected to see a string of pearls around her neck, white gloves on her hands and a designer pocketbook tucked in the crook of her elbow. She scowled at me. "Bloody hell, woman. You actually answered the door in shambles? You're lucky I didn't bugger off at the sight of you."

So much for my comparing her to an English rose; she was more English bulldog. "*You* woke me up. And you would've kept beating on the bloody door if I'd ignored you."

"True. But you will forgive me, when you see I brought scones. Thoroughly English, freshly baked blueberry scones with real clotted cream and lemon curd."

I curtsied. "Did you bake them before you headed off to church, milady?"

"Piss off, puckhead. Not only don't I go all British Bake Off, I refuse to step foot in any of the fifth-cousin-removed churches here in the colonies that blasphemes the glorious Church of England."

I laughed. "I thought you were an atheist?"

She sniffed. "Darling, I'm agnostic. True atheists don't celebrate Christmas and I just can't imagine a life without presents, eggnog and plum pudding." She gave me a once-over. "Speaking of presents . . . I have a delicious morsel of news to accompany the scrummy scones, but you'll have neither until you hit the loo and look less knackered."

"Oy. Just get off the telly with yer mum? Because blimey, you've gone full-on British slang first thing this morning, mate."

Liddy rolled her eyes. "Wanker."

"You love me."

"I do. Which is why, ever since our conversation Wednesday night, I've been thinking of ways to help get you out of this slump."

My face got hot. After a couple of glasses of wine during

our weekly Whine Wednesday and Liddy's urging, I'd voiced my dissatisfaction about my personal and my professional life. I didn't regret opening up to her even when I should've known that Liddy—a "fixer"—would obsess about helping me. Maybe that's what I'd secretly wanted. "Liddy—"

The teakettle whistled. The interruption allowed her to shoo me off, promising my tea would be the perfect temperature after I exited the shower.

I shuffled off to the bathroom after snagging a Red Bull from the fridge. While I liked tea, it didn't provide me with enough of a caffeine kick.

Under the lukewarm shower spray, my thoughts drifted to my friendship with Liddy and how important she'd become in my life.

Liddy and I had met months ago when I'd moved into Snow Village.

Snow Village was like any other gated community in that it was comprised of three connected apartment buildings with separate parking garages, a fitness facility with a large multipurpose room, a fenced pet park and a playground. The unique aspect? Most of the residents were athletes—current and former—who competed in winter sporting events. I'd been lucky to score a two-bedroom apartment due to the fact my boss, Jax, and Jensen Lund, the owner of Snow Village, were cousins, not solely because I played hockey.

Other than having my new furniture delivered, I'd opted to move myself in, since my boyfriend, my sister and most of my hockey buddies were in Florida at USA Olympic training camp. It'd felt wrong asking my colleagues at Lakeside for help, so there I was hefting boxes onto a handcart, hauling them out of my truck bed and up the elevator to the third floor in building three.

On the second-to-last trip, I heard a very annoyed, very British female voice yell, "Are you daft? Moving all those bloody boxes by yourself? Just wait a minute."

Then I found myself looking up at the lithe, lovely Liddy

Eldridge, who I'd soon discover was the former national ice dancing champion from Great Britain. Not only did she help me drag up the rest of my belongings, she assisted me with assembling my IKEA furniture. Between the cursing over missing hardware, sharing two bottles of wine as I unpacked, and her gentle teasing about my sports-themed decorating style, we became fast friends.

I also learned that Liddy had retired from professional skating after an ugly breakup with her skating partner/husband, and after a few years touring the world with Disney on Ice, she'd become a freelance ice dancing choreographer as well as a representative for a London-based athletic apparel company. She, in turn, heard about my assorted hockey triumphs, from winning back-to-back state championships at Fargo North High School, to accepting a full-ride hockey scholarship to UND with hopes of bringing a women's hockey Frozen Four title to my college, to playing on the U.S. Women's National Hockey Team, winning three world championships and two Four Nations Cups, to winning silver medals in 2010 and 2014 playing with the U.S. Olympic Women's Ice Hockey Team, as well as my short-lived honor of being named the first female assistant coach to a college men's hockey team at UND, only to resign in protest a few months later after that same college—my alma mater—eliminated the women's hockey program entirely.

With Liddy, I could be honest about everything going on in my life, when I'd taken to editorializing it for everyone else. After I'd blurted out the incident with Tyson and my sister, she'd kept pouring the wine while I'd detailed my fears about lack of direction and cohesion in my professional life. My position at Lakeside was supposed to be temporary, and as a part-time coach I wasn't making much money, so I had to supplement my income by refereeing with the Minnesota Youth Hockey League. When I considered playing hockey professionally again, I had to weigh it against searching for a full-time coaching gig that'd pay the bills, but wouldn't restrict my ability to travel and run hockey clinics. As if all of that "I'm not reaching my potential" wasn't angst-inducing enough, Nolan Lund's comment added another blow to my self-esteem.

I wasn't looking forward to revisiting that conversation even when I felt relief that Liddy understood those issues had not only become stumbling blocks for me, but were rapidly becoming a wall I couldn't get past.

Showered, hair combed, clothed, and pepped up from the Red Bull, I exited the bathroom.

Liddy beamed her sunny smile at me. "There's my lass. Fresh as a motherfecking daisy." She pointed to the chair across from her. "Have a seat."

I fought a smile at seeing the "proper" way she'd staged the table. A yellow ceramic teapot was centered between two delicate teacups patterned with sunflowers, which were perched on matching saucers, then placed above and to the left of butter-colored dessert plates that each held a circular scone (no triangular imposters here), loaded with cream and curd. A tiny dish of sugar complete with a miniature spoon, a small silver pitcher of cream and a few lemon curls on another mini-plate rounded out the setting.

I hadn't owned many pieces of fussy dishware before meeting Liddy. And I could admit, looking at all of this, I felt sophisticated. Like a grown-up.

"Now, while you eat, I'll dash off a few observations."

"About?"

"Everything."

I bit into the scone and moaned. These were nothing like the dry, tasteless cardboard scones I'd had previously.

"First, I think you need something bold on that wall above the loveseat. The room came together so beautifully, it won't do to have that area look barren. Even mirrored tiles in shades of rose gold would fancy it up."

Liddy had helped me personalize my space, banishing sports memorabilia to my office. She'd added shades of burgundy and blush pink to the gray, silver and black furnishings I'd chosen. While the room appeared softer, more feminine, it'd retained the comfort factor I wanted. And the best part? We'd done this shabby chic upgrade on a shoestring budget.

She ignored her scone and studied me over the rim of the teacup.

"What?"

"You have great posture."

I blinked at her. "Uh. Thanks?"

She snickered. "I meant you carry yourself well. And knowing that, I went online and watched some of the interviews you've done over the years. You're very confident with a camera shoved in your face. In fact, you seem more personable, which I wouldn't have believed if I hadn't seen it. Luckily, that widened your scope of options."

I licked lemon curd off my finger and took a sip of tea. "Options for what?"

"Your career." Liddy leaned forward. "You're knowledgeable and you're intensely devoted to hockey, which are the two biggest plusses. The rest can be learned."

"What are you talking about, Lids? I'm lost."

"I've realized there are so many paths open that you haven't considered, that I fully expect you to smack yourself in the head with a 'why didn't I think of that?' when I suggest them."

I made the "get on with it" gesture as I shoved another bite of scone into my mouth.

"I thought about this—and you—all day Thursday and Thursday night. How to get my talented American friend to a happier place in her professional life. Friday rolled around and I continued to be distracted. I wasn't really thinking about where my appointment was when I dropped off the requested set samples for an upcoming promotion, until I started yakking with a mother of one of my former students. As she's conveying her frustration with her daughter Maddie changing her major from performance to journalism . . . it hits me. That's what Gabi needs to do; leave the performance aspect of hockey behind and get into the broadcasting booth."

I choked on the scone, quickly grabbing my tea to wash it down. "That dry English humor. I bloody love that about you, Liddy."

"Gabi, I'm not joking. Not in the slightest."

"Okay. Let's back up. This woman you talked to. She indicated she's upset with her *own daughter* for wanting to get into broadcast journalism. And yet you somehow took that as a sign *I'd* be better suited for that kind of job? When I don't have a degree in journalism or mass communications?"

"Precisely. Because you have life experience. You're a seasoned hockey veteran. A revered coach. And you do have a bachelor's degree."

"In kinesiology," I retorted. I didn't tack on that I had a double minor in men's and women's coaching because she'd probably consider that irrelevant, as well as the fact I'd never done anything outside of hockey with my kinesiology degree.

She waved off my response. "You're missing my point. This woman is in the world of sports broadcasting. Her daughter mistakenly believes that because she skated on her high school team, won a state championship and competed for two years on the college skating level, that would give her a leg up over her peers in the job market."

"Might also give her an advantage because . . . oh . . . her mother *works* in the business."

"That's where Maddie the major jumper—and you—are both wrong. Some cutesy twenty-two-year-old with a newly minted degree is no competition for a woman like you, with the accolades, experience and passion for the sport. That's what they're looking for."

"Who is looking for that?" I demanded.

"Wolf Sports North."

My jaw dropped. "What the hell, Liddy? You didn't tell

me that your appointment was at Wolf Sports North! They're the biggest independent sports reporting network in the Upper Midwest."

"I didn't?"

Count to ten. "No, you did *not*. And yes, you absolutely should've led with that."

"See?" Liddy beamed. "You tossing out an official word like *led* just proves my point that you'd be a natural in the world of broadcast journalism."

"This person—what's her job at Wolf Sports North?"

"She used to be in PR, but now she's production associate for *Minnesota Weekly Sports Wrap-Up*."

"Production associate," I repeated. "For one of the most popular programs in their lineup."

"Yes, but she and I both agreed that subject matter is too broad for someone like you. She'd rather see you focused on the college hockey scene. According to her, her boss, head of all programming at Wolf Sports North, is looking to diversify the male-dominated commentator roster, specifically for winter sports." Liddy cocked her head. "I know you, Gabi. You can hold your own with any of them. So please seriously consider it, okay?"

"Consider what?"

Breezily, she said, "Applying for the sportscasting job opening."

"What opening?"

"The one we've been talking about. You *do* need to pay attention, darling."

Calmly, I lifted the lid off the teapot and peered in. Sniffed it for good measure.

"What are you doing?"

"Checking to see if you brewed cannabis tea, because clearly we're both high right now since nothing you've said is making any sense."

Liddy snorted. "I don't know which I dislike more, you questioning my tea-making skills or you questioning my method in finding an opportunity for you to advance your career."

"I'm not questioning you." Yes, I was. I inhaled and exhaled slowly. Then I reminded myself that conversations with Liddy could read like CliffsNotes; she touched on the important points but left me to fill in the pesky details.

But if what she'd alluded to was true . . . this could be the clichéd career "game changer" for me.

I offered her a sunny smile when I noticed the pinched look setting in around her mouth. "For my own clarification, please let me start from the beginning. On Friday you dropped off promo at Wolf Studios North and ended up in a conversation with a production associate for *Minnesota Weekly Sports Wrap-Up*. She told you the entire cable broadcast company was looking for sportscasters, preferably women sportscasters with real athletic experience, to apply for an open position in their collegiate sports division. Specifically their collegiate winter sports division, with an emphasis on hockey."

She rolled her eyes. "Bloody hell, Gabs, isn't that what I said?"

Not even freakin' close. "My next question is: What—if anything—did you tell them about me?"

"Give me some credit. I didn't call you out by *name*. All I said after learning about the job opening was that a neighbor of mine from Snow Village had been considering a career change. I might've mentioned you were a former Olympic athlete, currently coaching hockey at a private facility." She smirked at me. "My friend's eyes positively lit up when I leaked that little factoid. Then she urged me to urge *you* to start the application process."

"Process?"

"Oh, you know how corporations are these days. You fill out a basic application. If you make the first cut, then they'll share the rest of their hiring process, which likely will involve multiple steps as they eliminate potential candidates throughout each stage." She drained her tea. "You'd better get started since the application deadline is tonight at midnight."

"No pressure."

"No, darling, more like 'no guts, no glory.'"

"Thank you, Liddy. This is . . . above and beyond."

"You'd do the same for me, I'm sure." Then she shooed me off. "I'll clean up here. You go clean up your résumé."

Then I became so engrossed I didn't hear her leave.

There weren't many changes since I'd submitted my résumé to Lakeside Ice Arena more than a year ago.

Except now I could list Jaxson Lund, former NHL player with the Chicago Blackhawks, three-time winner of the Stanley Cup, as my boss and mentor.

I just hoped they'd keep the application confidential. While I doubted Jax would fire me over applying for another job, I didn't want to put either of us in the awkward position of admitting I needed to explore other career options, even when technically, I hadn't signed an employment contract with him.

After I finished the résumé, I tackled the actual online application. That took several hours but I managed to submit everything by nine P.M.

I'd just settled in to watch an ESPN sports highlights show when my phone buzzed. I glanced down at it to see a message from my sister.

DW: Can we talk?

What was I supposed to say? I didn't intend to let this silence go on forever, but she could give me longer than five damn days to deal with my thoughts and feelings.

So I simply responded: Not yet.

Four

NOLAN

"Did I see Gabi flip you off?" my brother Jax asked after he plopped beside me in the spectator seats at Lakeside Ice Arena.

"You win our conversation starter contest this week," I said dryly.

Jax shoved me with his shoulder. "Not everything has to be a competition. Anyway. What's up? Surprised to see you here."

"For some reason I thought Mimi's game was tonight. I got here and realized I had the wrong day. Meems saw me so I can't bail until she's done with practice or she'll text me a dozen times to ask if I'm mad at her." As if I could ever be mad at my crazy-sweet niece.

"True." Jax propped his elbows on his knees. "You've been scarce."

I shrugged. "Happens when I'm working seven days a week."

"That much? Why?"

"Acquisitions, potential acquisitions, oh and more potential acquisitions."

"In other words . . . just another day at the office for you LI bigwigs."

"I am *so* not a bigwig at LI."

Down on the ice, Mimi volunteered to go first for skill training and I actually saw Coach Welk send her an amused smile.

Had Gabriella ever given me anything close to a smile like that?

Have you ever deserved it from her?

"Nolan?" Jax prompted.

I looked at him. "Sorry. What did you say?"

"Is everything all right at LI? I thought the eighty-hour, seven-day workweeks were in the past for all the top executives."

"Ash and Brady both did their time getting up to speed in their departments, so I'm just following their lead. Wouldn't want LI employees to think 'the Prince' is a slacker." The Prince. I hated that nickname.

"Speaking of our cousins . . . do they know how much you're working?"

"Doubtful."

"Does Dad know?"

"It's because of Dad that I'm in the office so damn much."

The coach blew her whistle and all her little charges gathered around her, attention rapt on her, which was a feat for a dozen nine-year-olds.

"That didn't answer my question, bro."

I blew out a slow breath. "No. Dad doesn't know. During office hours I'm dealing with a million day-to-day things. It's only when everyone is gone that I can take a deeper look at proposed acquisitions." I kept my gaze on Mimi lining up for a skating race. "I absolutely don't need another monumental fuckup, Jax."

He sighed. "No one blames you."

"*I* blame me. My half-assed research into Digi-Dong cost Lund Industries five million in legal fees and settlement costs. If I would've taken the time to dig deeper, I would've discovered that Digi-Dong didn't own the tech they were pitching." Still burned my ass every time I thought about it. Our subsidiary, LuTek, was set up to be a software manufacturing arm of LI, so we could've just bought out the other partner and taken the product to market ourselves, but it was cost prohibitive.

"From my understanding, it could've happened to any investment group. A partnership goes bad and partner one files for a patent before partner two. Partner two was out to punish anyone who did business with Digi-Dong." Jax laughed and nudged me with his shoulder again. "Come on. Admit part of the reason you recommended investing in Digi-Dong was because you snickered every time you heard *dong* in that stupid name."

"Yes, I believed that people in the market for security-based doorbells would get a kick out of the name, especially if our amazing marketing department put the right spin on it. We were projected to clear millions of dollars on that tech item in just the first year." I sighed. "Instead it cost us money and face."

"And that was the final gong for the Digi-Dong corporation. May their dong finally be at rest."

I laughed. "Smartass."

"Feel better?"

"Some." But it wouldn't stop me from doing my due diligence after hours on potential acquisitions.

"Here's what'll put a skip back in your loafers. Saturday night we're having a preview party for the barcade."

"Already? They got that done fast."

"Seems like a lifetime ago that Dallas brought me the concept. The speakeasy is still months out from opening for business. Annika believes having one 'high-concept' space open while building mystique around the second bar will be to our advantage."

Our younger cousin Annika was a PR wiz, so I didn't doubt she had it all mapped out. "What's the dress code for the barcade?"

Jax groaned. "Of course that's the first question you asked. It's on the official invite; they went out today. All I've been told . . . it's supersecret, super VIP. No kids. No cameras."

Mimi skated up and leaned on the railing. "Uncle Nolan! Didja come to see me practice?"

"Yes, I did. You're looking good out there, short stuff."

"Didja see I won my race?"

The whistle blew and Coach Welk skated behind Mimi. "Lund. This is not a social hour. Get back with your group."

"Yes, Coach Welk." Mimi skated off.

Gabi looked at Jax. "Was there something specific you needed, boss?"

"Nope."

"Then with all due respect, sir, you and Mr. Fancy Pants are welcome to take your gossip session elsewhere. You're distracting my class."

My eyebrows rose. So I was back to being Mr. Fancy Pants.

"We were just leaving, Coach Welk," Jax assured her.

I followed him out of the arena.

Once we were out of earshot, he whirled around. "What did you do to Gabi to piss her off?"

"Nothing! In fact, last week we even went out for drinks."

Jax's eyes narrowed. "Jesus, Nolan. Did you hit on her?"

"No. I wasn't drinking."

A loud harrumph sounded and then Margene, the rink GM, sauntered out from behind the front desk. "Of course a man like you would have to be drunk to hit on a woman like her, isn't that right?"

I looked at Jax, who stared back at me with the same puzzled expression.

"What did I miss?"

"You're smart. You'll figure it out. Or you won't." Margene shrugged. "I kinda hope you don't. Be fun to see how it plays out. I wouldn't want to tangle with her."

We watched Margene storm down the hallway to the bathroom and slam the door.

Jax said, "I'm confused."

"Join the club."

"You really didn't hit on Gabi? Because if you did, she'd tell Margene since they're tight."

"I swear I didn't. We played pool. That was it. I didn't even drive her home, although I was there as her DD."

"Then how'd she get home?"

"No idea. She disappeared for twenty minutes and when I went looking for her, the cocktail waitress said someone else had picked her up." At the time I'd figured she'd barfed in the bathroom from too much tequila and had bailed on me to save face. Which was why I hadn't contacted her.

But what if I'd been wrong? What if there'd been another reason she'd left?

Jax poked me in the chest to get my attention. "Whatever you did, you'd better fix it."

"Even if I don't know what it is?"

"Yep. Come on. Let's finalize the dates for the youth bowla-thon."

Five

GABI

"And go!"

I skated backward as I watched my 14U girls team work on rebounding. So far, I'd barely convinced them that knowing how to rebound was just as important in hockey as it was in basketball. The puck was already by the net. Move in, move out, constant movement on the puck forced the opposing team into defensive mode. If they came forward with the intention to steal, that's when high shots were magic. A wrister BOOM. Nothing but net.

The arena is a noisy place, so I usually found myself yelling over the din. At times I wondered if I'd forgotten what a normal tone of voice sounds like.

"Keena! Don't hug the wall. Move in." I'd finally gotten these girls to listen without having to look at me and that had improved their playing by two hundred percent.

I blew the whistle to signal a line change after Parker whizzed the puck past Kari, who hadn't been paying attention, resulting in icing for Team A.

Anna, my co-coach, used a different-pitched whistle to signal her players to switch lines. In truth, I'd gotten hired as Anna's assistant coach, but I stepped into her position during her maternity leave. She'd struggled after her C-section and I'd agreed to finish out the season as the head coach.

"Jacie," Anna shouted, "watch your line, you're offsides."

I sent Anna a thumbs-up; somehow I'd missed that. This team would progress even more if I had a ref on the ice during practice skirmishes. Being rec—recreational hockey— rather than club hockey, meant many of these girls were only playing for fun, so not all the rules and subsequent protocol and penalties were firmly cemented in their heads. Unlike club players, like I'd been, who memorized hockey rules and regulations as catechism at a very early age.

"Face off, ladies."

Just as they got into position and I crouched down to drop the puck, the buzzer sounded, signaling the end of class. Rather than skating off to the dressing room, all the players, including those on the bench, skated to me.

"All right. I saw excellent hustle out here today from everyone. Be proud. You're more than ready to face the Raptors on Sunday. We'll meet here, ninety minutes before the game. That'll give us time to drive to Rosewood Arena, get suited up and warm up. If something changes in your schedule, and you're not able to make the game, text me or Anna as soon as you're aware of the conflict. Anna will pass out family game passes in the dressing room after you fill out the transportation sheet for game day." I paused. "Any questions?"

"Gotcha, Coach Welk."

"Have a good weekend, ladies. Rest up, stay out of trouble and—"

"Wash your gear!" they shouted in unison.

I laughed. I'd at least drilled that much into their heads. "Dismissed."

While Anna dealt with the paperwork, I moved the nets off the ice, picked up the pucks and checked the players' benches for any trash. Usually the girls helped clear the ice since their class was the last one on Friday nights. But I'd worked them hard and I would've been anxious to get away from me too at their age. Besides, there was something cleansing about ending my workweek the same way I'd started it—alone on the ice.

"Gabi."

I looked up into the face of my sister. I'd zoned out so much I hadn't noticed her standing in the front row of the spectator seats.

A week and a half had passed since Tyson had broken up with me. During that time I'd avoided talking to Dani. Not because I was mad at her, but because I really didn't know how to respond to her without coming across as A) insincere, B) nosy or C) bitter. And really, did she want to deal with the questions foremost on my mind?

Am I supposed to congratulate you?

Have you slept with him yet?

Do I have to beg you not to ask me to be in the wedding?

What did Mom and Dad say?

Awkward situations freaked me out, which is why I avoided them. Case in point, when Nolan showed up for Mimi's practice on Wednesday, smiling at me as if he hadn't insulted me on the one day my female ego needed bolstering . . . I oh-so-maturely had flipped him off instead of talking to him.

Seeing Dani's miserable face, I knew I couldn't retreat to that brusque demeanor. "How long have you been here?"

"Since their team practice started. I stayed in the top level so I wouldn't distract you. I love watching you coach. You're amazing."

Being this close to Dani just reminded me that we looked nothing alike. She had flaxen blond hair, whereas mine was basic light brown. Her eyes were a golden amber, mine were boring blue. Her lanky appearance of delicacy belied her athletic strength, while I was shorter and sturdier with more obvious muscle mass. On the ice, she was grace with instant adaptability. Whereas I embodied a freight train; scarily fast, my focus on one track.

"Why are you staring at me without saying anything? Figuring out where to punch me first?"

I gave her another purposeful once-over. "You know I only hit you when we're on the ice. So if you wanna suit up . . ."

She laughed. Then covered her mouth with her hand. "Sorry. I just—"

"Tell me one thing, okay? Are you happy with Tyson? The I-found-my-other-half, giddy-over-the-moon, crazily-in-love-with-him type of happiness?"

"Yes. He's . . . everything." She sighed.

She motherfucking *sighed*. Dreamily, no less.

Jesus. Had I ever sighed like that over any man, say nothing of sighing like that over Tyson?

Nope.

In that moment I finally understood what I'd been struggling with. I wasn't jealous that Dani had found that kind of sigh-worthy love with Tyson. I was envious that my little sister had found it *first*.

I smiled at her—a genuine smile. "I'm relieved to hear it. And I am happy you're here."

"You don't hate me?"

"Sis. I could never hate you. But I've gotta be honest. It'd be better for you, me and Tyson if we didn't hang out for a while. So don't feel guilty for throwing yourself into couple-hood."

Her brows furrowed. "You don't want to see me at all?"

"If it's just you? Sure. But it'd be weird if the three of us sat around and watched movies like we used to."

"I get it." Those honey-flecked eyes searched my face. "Will you be okay, Gabs?"

What she was really asking? If I'd be okay alone. What she didn't understand, what I'd only started to grasp myself, was I'd felt alone even when I'd dated Tyson. When I'd dated anyone, actually. "I'll be fine. Lots of irons in the fire."

Dani leaned in. "Have you heard anything else about the new team?"

"How'd you hear about it?"

She rolled her eyes. "Remember that hockey players are the worst gossips. Natt and Viv wouldn't shut up about it until JR snapped that not everyone had gotten the call."

"Meaning JR didn't get a call?"

"I don't think so. Amylin didn't chime in either."

Shit. Two of my former teammates on the national team, same age as me, had been bypassed.

Or maybe they just passed on this so-called opportunity because they're ready to have real lives and real jobs and are done chasing pucks.

I zeroed in on my sister. "Did you get a call?"

"Yes. Did you?"

"Yes."

She squealed. "We might be playing on the same team? That would be the tits."

"This is your big sister warning you not to get your hopes up. Many people have tried to expand the league. No one has succeeded. It's always just talk."

"Gotcha."

Loud voices echoed from the locker room.

"I know you've got stuff to do, but can I get a hug before I go?" Dani asked.

"C'mere." I squeezed her tightly. "Thanks for showing up."

"I couldn't let it go on another day." She whispered, "I love you, Gabs."

"Love you too, Dani. We'll talk soon."

Saturday morning had been busy with hockey classes, but I'd left the rink by two. By three I'd showered, eaten and retreated to my home office to check my email.

Monday morning I'd gotten an email from Wolf Sports North indicating they'd received my résumé. The remainder of the email was the standard "don't contact us, we'll contact you" and their disclaimer about misdirected emails. I'd figured I wouldn't have a response from them either way for two weeks.

So it shocked the hell out of me to see an email from an assistant to the production manager. I clicked on it.

Personal and Confidential

Gabriella Welk:

Congratulations! After reviewing your application, you've passed to the next round.

You are invited to complete Step 2 in the interview process, which is to submit an audio and video recording that showcases your game calling expertise. The details were sent in a separate document as an attachment.

We're also including the following weblinks as reference points to clarify our submission expectations.

Also attached is a more in-depth questionnaire, which should be filled out in its entirety and returned with your AV file. Both are due 5 (five) days from receipt of this notification.

Best of luck. We look forward to your submission.

Sincerely,

Dahlia Switch
Wolf Sports North

I must've reread the email ten times before I actually believed I'd made the first cut.

Holy shit.

This was definitely worth celebrating.

Six

—

NOLAN

The Lund family members—aka the Lund Collective—were tasked to arrive at Full Tilt Barcade an hour before the official pre-party started.

I wandered into the first room. Jax and his wife, Lucy, were in deep in conversation with some guy I didn't recognize, so I scanned the area for other familiar faces.

When my cousin Dallas saw me, she squealed and bounded over for a hug. "Nolan! You're here." She made a show of looking around me. "Where's your plus-one?"

"I'm flying solo tonight."

I checked out her attire, first noticing the neon-green headband and her high ponytail dangling to the left side of her head. My gaze moved to the bright orange and vivid blue geometric earrings that brushed her bare shoulders and matched the six chunky strands of necklaces circling her neck. She'd donned a *Flashdance*–style oversized black T-shirt dress with FULL TILT spelled out across her chest in sparkly purple letters. Below that on the T-shirt was a blocky, stylized version of the Minneapolis skyline in vibrant primary colors. She'd wrapped a wide fluorescent pink leather belt low on her hips, probably to hold up the purple mesh skirt that resembled a tutu. She'd finished the ensemble with white high-top sneakers laced with lime-green, Day-Glo-orange and pink laces. She'd layered so many bracelets up both of her arms she actually jingled.

"Somebody raided her mother's closet for that straight-from-the-'80s garb," I said with a grin.

Dallas beamed. "The T-shirt dress is new, but my mom lent me everything else. Isn't it gnarly?"

"Totally gnarly. But I wasn't aware this was a costume party."

"If it was, you'd lose, dude. Where are your Vans? Your pastel T-shirt paired with a sports jacket? Your T&C board shorts? Your fanny pack?"

"What's wrong with what I've got on?"

She assessed my outfit; from the hip-length sleek-cut gray wool jacket, worn over a mustard-yellow mock turtleneck sweater, to the oxblood-colored belt that held up my gray, yellow and maroon plaid slacks, and ending with the burgundy leather sneakers that tied the look together. Her gaze met mine and she grinned. "Nothing. Your ensemble is one hundred percent on point, as usual."

"Thank you."

"I dressed this way to have some fun with the pre-opening *par-tay*goers since I've been super stressed. Plus my horoscope said to indulge my whimsy tonight."

"Well, from what I've seen, you've certainly outdone yourself."

"Would you like a tour of Full Tilt?"

"Only if you're not too busy."

Hooking her arm through mine, she said, "I'll always make time for you, cuz."

I'd seen the layout for the space, but I'd been skeptical that a barcade—an '80s arcade gone upscale bar—could be realized. Pinball machines and tabletop games were scattered throughout. While technically this was one enormous room, the alcoves with the half walls separating the space and the low ceilings relayed a more intimate feel. Add in the seating arrangements, from high-top tables and chairs to couches to groupings of lounge chairs, no two areas were alike. There were three small bars spread out, rather than just one large bar, which would keep the place from feeling crowded. One thing I'd noticed too was the extra room between each pinball machine. If a customer arrived with friends, they could stand around the machine and egg on the player.

Arcades weren't a thing in my younger years. We didn't need a specific place to meet and hang out; instead we played Xbox, Wii, PlayStation at friends' houses. But seeing the arcade wars shown on TV and movies from that time period had made me nostalgic for the loss of something I'd never had.

"So this is the rock 'n' roll section," Dallas said. Then she pointed to the corner. "That Metallica machine is rare, so it'll be popular."

I ran my hand over the Kiss pinball machine—one of five, all different.

We passed a half wall and Dallas said, "These are our classic arcade games. There are several here I've been practicing on in my downtime."

"Which ones?"

"*Tempest. Space Invaders. Asteroids. Ms. Pac-Man. Tetris. Centipede. Donkey Kong.*"

"Got it going on like—"

Dallas placed her hand over my mouth. "Do *not* get that song stuck in my head tonight, Nolan." She whirled around, taking several long strides, and turned a corner.

This area resembled a home theater with four big-screen TVs arranged in a rectangle. "This room is our crown jewel, with the exception of the *Medieval Madness* pinball machine we bought that cost as much as a new car."

"What's so special about this area?"

She literally bounced on her toes with excitement. "It's our cell phone games area. If you're used to playing *Angry Birds* on your phone, you can log in to our server and play it on the big screen. And you don't have to switch to a handheld controller, which is usually why some players can't level up on a gaming system, when they're used to playing in app format."

"Dallas. That's genius."

"I know, right? It's set up for singles and multiple players. We'll debut an original Full Tilt game app every other month that newsletter subscribers can download. They can practice the game on their own time or come in and try it out on the big screen and we'll host tournaments with prizes." She beamed. "No one else has even thought of doing this. Lucky for us, we have our own software developer who did."

My eyes narrowed. "Is he developing just phone apps?"

"*She*"—Dallas emphasized—"is also an engineer who's going all MacGyver on swapping guts and parts out of old pinball machines and busted-up arcade games to create something unique to us. That'll be in development for a while yet."

Then she led me through the car-themed and TV show–themed areas. The largest, most open area housed games that fell into the fantasy realm.

Dallas took me back to the bar where we'd started. "Sorry if that was more of a drive-by than a blow-by-blow. I'm sure I'm forgetting half of what I'm supposed to showcase."

"No, it was perfect. I don't know how you're keeping this all straight. My head is spinning."

She swiped two flutes of champagne off the counter. "Here's to keeping that smart brain of yours offline all night as you get ready to play the game."

"What game?"

A devious little smirk deepened her dimples. "Telling you would just spoil the fun."

"What are you up to?"

"Not me, blame the cosmos."

I blinked at her.

"Anyway. Cheers!"

We touched our glasses together.

After we sipped, I said, "I'd envisioned this place more like—"

"Dave and Buster's," my cousin Ash said behind me.

I turned and faced him. "Exactly what I was thinking."

Dallas said, "That comparison sort of works. Except no one under twenty-one is allowed. We give out tokens for free or reduced drinks instead of paper tickets for cheap-ass toys. Oh, and there's no food." She paused. "Although, that may change once the other club is open."

"Everything is top-notch . . . I'm so damn proud of you, sis." Ash hugged her. Then he stepped back to give her outfit the same perusal I had. "Interesting fashion choice. I'm hoping the music here isn't '80s themed."

Dallas patted him on the cheek. "Don't worry. I'll request some Backstreet Boys and NSYNC to keep you happy."

"Don't know why you'd do that," Ash scoffed. "I never listened to that stuff."

She and I exchanged a look. Then I said, "Uh, *yeah*, you did. I was there. Remember?"

"But *she* wasn't." Ash nudged Dallas's shoulder.

"But you left evidence of musical choices where a snoopy baby sister could easily find it. And you weren't around to tell me to *keep out* or *go away*."

Ash kissed the top of her head. "I never would've done that anyway, brat."

Dallas handed him her empty champagne glass. "Duty calls. I'll catch you guys later."

We anchored that corner of the bar for the next hour as the place began to fill up. Ash and I didn't make small talk beyond commenting on the arrival of specific guests.

While Ash and I had always been close outside of work, things had changed between us after my father had named me the future CEO of Lund Industries. I didn't know if it bothered Ash that when I took the reins, he'd have to answer to me. And I hadn't nutted up to ask him.

Then he looked at me oddly. "It's weird that you're still chilling with me. Is that because your date isn't here yet?"

"What date?"

"Come on. You always have a hot woman hanging off your arm at events."

Not lately. But since he and I hadn't been hitting the clubs after work he wouldn't know that. Nor would I tell him that because I'd been putting in extra hours at LI, I couldn't remember the last time I'd gone out with a woman.

Wait. I had gone out with Gabi, but that hadn't been a date.

"Shit, there's my mom," Ash said and turned away. "Cover me."

"What? How am I supposed to—"

Aunt Priscilla waved at me, then her gaze zeroed in on her son. She fought the tide of people—politely, of course, because she was a southern woman.

"Is she gone?" Ash asked.

"No. She's still headed this way."

"Dammit. Did she see me?"

"Yes, she saw you. Ash, you're too old to try and ditch your mother. Not to mention you're too damn big to fit under the counter."

"Piss off."

"Fine. I'll leave."

Ash grabbed my arm with enough force to keep me in place. "Sorry. Please stay."

"What is going *on*?"

"You're the youngest in your family; you wouldn't understand. And you never have an issue finding a simple damn date." Ash straightened and downed a glass of bubbly before he turned around.

Aunt Priscilla glided toward us, dressed in art gallery–

patron chic: flowing black pants, a loose-fitting white silk blouse unbuttoned at the neck to showcase her jewelry—lots of large sparkling diamonds in a silver setting—and finishing the look off with a fire-engine-red jacket that matched her lipstick and her heeled boots.

I kissed her cheek. "You look incredible, Auntie."

"Thank you. Wear enough diamonds and no one will notice other flaws."

Then it was Ash's turn to buss her cheek. "You are radiant tonight, Mom, and it doesn't have a thing to do with the ice."

"Charmer."

"So what do you think of this venue?"

Her eyes swept the room and returned to her son's. "I think Dallas found her niche. She did an outstanding job not only on the concept for this place, but on the execution. I'm beyond thrilled for her. So proud. Both your dad and I are."

"Where is Dad?"

"Playing pinball. As soon as he and his brothers saw the Elvis machine, they were all about the King." She smiled charmingly. "So that's why I came lookin' for you."

Here's where I could run interference. "Why aren't you plinking quarters and hitting those flippers as the King gyrates his hips? Place like this has to be your jam, Aunt Cilla."

"Well, I sure played a mean pinball . . . back in the day."

I snickered at her reference to the Who.

"I might give it a whirl later." She pinned Ash with a look. "After I meet your date. Where is she?"

That's what Ash needed my help with? And . . . I was out.

But Ash blocked my escape. "She's running late. That's why Nolan and I have been waiting at the bar since we arrived. I've been watching the door for her."

I bit back a derisive snort. Ash and I had had our backs to the door for the past half an hour.

"Is that so?"

He gestured to the crowd. "Lotta people, as you can see. I wouldn't want to miss her."

Dude. You are so full of shit that your mama could smell it from across the room.

"Now that, I can understand. So y'all don't mind if I pull up a chair and sit a spell while we wait? We *are* closer to the champagne here. Jax sure didn't skimp on serving the good stuff."

Ash smiled at her—all teeth. "That'd be great. I'll get another chair."

I stopped him from escaping. "Oh no, you stay. It'd be my pleasure to grab one."

Not that I hurried in procuring a chair. No surprise that no one else had joined their little two-person party, given the tightness on Ash's face.

As soon as I settled next to Priscilla with a fresh glass of champagne, Ash's body went rigid. He tossed off, "Finally. I see her by the door. I'll be back."

He cut through the crowds like a warrior on a mission.

Aunt Priscilla leaned closer to murmur, "Fifty bucks says that's the last we see of him tonight."

I laughed. "Hard pass on that sucker bet."

She harrumphed. "How about wagering on what lie he'll tell to cover up his original lie?"

"You're so sure he's lying?"

"*Please.* I'm his mother. I've never been able to read Dallas, but that boy is the spitting image of his father and that man cannot lie to save his life. At least not to me."

I loved seeing this side of my aunt . . . and putting the screws to my cousin would be fun. "You're on. Fifty bucks says he claims his date felt nauseous before she arrived, but she bucked up and came to the party, only to suffer a drastic relapse as soon as she walked through the door, resulting in Ash having to leave immediately to drive her home."

"My my, Nolan. That is plausible. But I disagree. Too predictable. Ash will go for the drama. He's more like Dallas in that regard than he'll admit. I believe he'll claim to be annoyed that she'd showed up so late, they fought about it, which resulted in her absolute refusal to attend the party. They left to sort things out in private, rather than causing a scene on Dallas and Jax's big night."

I held my fist out for a bump.

But we both lost the bet because Ash did show up with a woman on his arm.

Gabriella.

What the fuck?

Ash maneuvered Gabi beside him after they reached us. "Here she is. Better late than never."

Neither of us responded. Mostly because yelling BULLSHIT would be frowned upon.

"Anyway, Mom, you remember Gabi Welk. She works for Jax at Lakeside."

Priscilla offered her a genuine smile. "Gabi. Of course. It's nice to see you again, darlin'."

"Nice to see you too, Mrs. Lund."

Not only did Ash not acknowledge me, Gabi didn't either. Again . . . WTF?

"How did this date come about?" Priscilla asked. "It just seems . . . out of nowhere."

Gabi peered up at Ash—total deer-in-the-headlights look.

"Gabi lives in Snow Village. She helped me out when I moved Dallas in. We got to talking, realized we were both invited to this party and agreed to meet here first and have dinner afterward." He wrapped his arm around her and squeezed her shoulder. "Isn't that right?"

This is where a real date would give Ash a smile or nod.

Not Gabi. She looked ready to clock him.

Why that made me near giddy? No clue.

"This is totally off topic," Priscilla inserted, "but after seeing how spectacularly this space turned out, I cannot understand why Dallas is dragging her feet in finishing the interior design of her own home. Her house sits empty while she moves into yet another apartment."

"Mom. Stop nagging her. This project was a massive undertaking. I can't blame her if after expending her creative energy for someone else that she needs a place to recharge at the end of the workday that doesn't require anything from her."

Priscilla blinked as if a need for downtime hadn't occurred to her.

Just then a tall blond woman sidled up to Gabi. "Oy. This place is posh, innit?"

Gabi said, "This is my friend Liddy. We're neighbors at Snow Village. Liddy, this is Mrs. Lund, Dallas and Ash's mother."

"Happy to meet you, ma'am. That girl of yours. She's got brains and heart, doesn't she? Brings a ray of sunshine wherever she goes. But I have 'alf a mind to kick her arse for keeping her work on this club on the down low."

"Nondisclosures are a fact of life these days. But I am glad she invited you to the party."

Liddy frowned. "Dallas didn't invite me; I tagged along with Gabi girl."

Priscilla raised both her eyebrows at Ash. "Liddy tagged along on your *date*?"

Busted.

Heh heh.

"Excuse me."

My gloating vanished as my mom entered our bizarre circle. "I need to steal Cilla for a moment, Monte is looking for her."

As soon as they disappeared, Liddy snagged two glasses of champagne, handing one to Gabi. Before she drank, she glared at me. "While we haven't been formally introduced, I know all about you. Bit of a preening peacock, aren't you, just ruffling feathers all over the bleeding place."

"Liddy," Gabi warned. "Behave."

"Bollocks. Why can't I rip this tosser a new arsehole?"

"Because the carpet is brand new and blood is a bitch to get out."

She sighed. "You are lit-er-al-ly no fun."

WANT YOU TO WANT ME 59

"I'm loads of fun," Gabi said dryly. "This is my fun face."

I snickered.

Gabi sipped her champagne and looked everywhere but at me.

Dallas bounded over, inserting herself between Ash and Gabi to hug Gabi. "You made it! There are so many people here I was afraid I'd missed you. And Liddy came too." She elbowed Ash out of her way to hug Liddy. "I had no idea you were Ash's mysterious date."

"I, um—"

"Explain later. Right now I need you to come with me. I'm supposed to round up two more warm bodies for a photo op." She dragged both of them away.

Leaving me and Gabi alone.

"It amazes me that Dallas has so much strength for her small stature."

No reaction.

"I also find it interesting that Dallas believed Liddy was Ash's date. While Ash himself told his mother something different."

Gabi didn't respond.

I stepped in front of her, forcing her attention to me "So you and Ash, huh?"

"Why are you surprised?"

"I'm not half as surprised as *you* were, Gabriella, that you and Ash are on a date."

She scowled.

"Just admit that you're not dating him."

"Because that would be so hard to believe? A man like Ash Lund would find a woman like me attractive?"

This wasn't going the way I'd expected. I wanted her to complain about Ash's high-handed behavior, I'd agree he acted like an ass and then we could rip on him for using her to lie to his mother.

"Just because I'm not *your* type, Nolan, doesn't mean you speak for all other men."

Then she aimed those pale silvery eyes at me, eyes sparking with hurt, and I understood I'd fucked up.

Majorly.

"Gabi—"

"Don't you 'Gabi' me, Lund." She invaded my space. "After we'd first met, you'd made up your mind that I was this femme fatale homewrecker out to seduce your brother. Which we both know was a wrong assumption on your part. But did you apologize for that? No."

I opened my mouth to say sorry and she pressed her champagne glass against my lips.

"Zip it. I'm not done."

Okay.

"I let go of my anger over your complete misjudgment of my character—which could've cost me my *job*—because I knew I'd continue to have to deal with you since you're the rink owner's brother. Thankfully we didn't cross paths that much . . . until I had the misfortune of you being there the night Tyson broke up with me. Imagine my surprise when you showed me a different side of yourself at Buddy's. I'd started to think maybe I'd misjudged you too." She snorted. "Then you proved me right again."

"How?"

"You know *how*. So I bailed instead of staying there and pretending everything was peachy keen, jellybean and that you hadn't kicked me when I was already down." She threw her shoulders back. "I've had some time to think, and maybe I've got liquid courage tonight, but I wanna tell you, *bud*, that you're wrong, wrong, wrong because I can't be both."

Jesus. Was she drunk? Because she wasn't making sense. "You can't be both what?"

"Both the tempting kind of woman with the power to make a man stray, and . . . I'm paraphrasing here . . . the kind of woman who isn't the slightest bit feminine, not your type." She paused and took a long sip of champagne. "Ring any bells yet?"

Why was she studying me with an intensity that sent a spike of fear through me?

My brain rewound to the night at Buddy's and my discussion with the bartender. Him asking if I planned to make a move on Gabi and me answering . . .

She's definitely not my type.

Gabi hadn't been there during that conversation.

But that didn't mean she hadn't overheard it.

Fuck me.

That's why she'd left.

In that moment I felt myself shrinking—smaller and smaller to the size of a cockroach.

A vile bug that deserved to be squashed and wiped off her shoe as she walked away.

Which Gabi was currently doing; strolling off after the ultimate mic drop.

Oh, hell no.

Rather than putting hands on her, I outmaneuvered her, ending up directly in front of her again.

"Move," she said crossly.

"No. You've said your piece now I'm saying mine."

She tilted her head back, skepticism apparent on her face and in her posture.

"I'm sorry this apology is long overdue. I was wrong to suspect you had a thing for Jax and you'd act on it. I'm sorry that my misplaced concern for my brother caused problems for you at Lakeside."

Her only reaction was to cross her arms over her chest.

"And I'm truly sorry I said hurtful things when you were already having a bad night. I shouldn't have added to it, but I did, and for that additional hurt, I'm sorry."

Gabi blinked at me. "That's it?"

"Ah, yeah. Why? Is it not enough?"

"Where's the mansplaining? The 'I didn't know you could hear me.' Or the 'I only said that to clear the way for Rico to hit on you.' Or the 'I knew you were listening, and I was just messing with you' or the 'it's not my fault you can't take a joke' kind of excuses?"

"Gabriella. There's no excuse for my dickish, hurtful behavior. What's worse is I didn't know you'd overheard." I cringed. "No, it's definitely worse that you took off and I didn't check in with you to make sure you were all right given the shit day you'd had. And to add further insult to injury, this past week whenever I saw you, I couldn't figure out what I'd done to piss you off." I ran my hand across the back of my sweaty neck. "Christ. I always know how to smooth things over and this time . . . I'm at a loss. I'm not a purposefully mean guy. I don't get off on being an asshole. I'm just so fucking sorry. I won't ask for your forgiveness because I don't deserve it."

I walked away.

Seven

___

GABI

In less than five minutes Nolan Lund had wrecked me again.

This was why I hadn't wanted to come to this party, but Liddy had strong-armed me into attending to celebrate after I told her I'd made the next level for the job interview.

Too much bubbly resulted in too much information from me, giving Nolan a piece of my mind. What he'd done was wrong. No doubt about it.

But the way he'd owned up to it and apologized?

That had set everything to rights with me.

I cooled my heels and my temper with another glass of champagne.

Then I went looking for him.

I wasn't sure where he'd gone, but I suspected he'd be by himself. I dodged and weaved through the patrons clogging the hallway. The crowd thinned when I'd reached the last semiprivate gaming area and I caught sight of him, playing an arcade game in the corner.

Now what?

I paused in the threshold, debating my options.

Sidle up next to him and toss off a pithy comment as if we were cool now?

Approach him with caution and thank him for his apology?

Return to the bar, snag two flutes of champagne, come back here and toast to new beginnings?

In my usual fashion, I decided to wing it.

I marched up to him. "So here's the thing, Lund. I'm guilty of doing the same thing you did."

Without looking at me, he said, "Being an asshole?"

"Yeah, that too. But I've said stuff that could've hurt people if I'd been overheard. It's just . . . that comment hit me where it hurts because I've spent most of my life fighting back against incorrect assumptions."

"I wish you would've fought back against me and mine."

"In a way, that's what I'm doing tonight. Only because I've been drinking. I confronted you—when I could've let myself be pissed off at you forever. So, I accept your apology."

A beat of silence passed between us.

"That's it?"

"It's not enough? You want more?" I teased.

His lips quirked, even when he kept his focus on the game. "I never would've pegged you as funny."

"I hear that a lot. Along with Crabby Gabi."

The machine made a tinny sound and Nolan smacked the button on his left. "Being called Crabby Gabi bothers you."

A statement. "That's what sticks in people's minds. It's hard to overcome."

"Tell me about it. In college I was known as Trollin' Nolan. I didn't go to college here and thankfully that nickname stayed there after I graduated."

"Wait. You didn't go to U of M like everyone else in your family?"

"I went to NYU."

My mouth dropped open. "Why?"

"Because at the time I figured I'd be stuck in Minneapolis the rest of my life, so I wanted to live somewhere else when I had the chance and didn't have a dozen relatives looking over my shoulder." He paused. "You little fucker. Stay put."

"Excuse me?"

"Talking to the game."

I sighed. "I'll leave you be then. I should probably find my date anyway."

The *whomp whomp whomp whomp whomp* sound of him losing followed me as I walked away.

Not that I got far before Nolan spun me around. "Ash isn't your date any more than I am."

"You're right. But you're here, and I'm here, and we just bitched and made up, so let's find a game we can play together and make everything all better."

"Last game we played, you kicked my ass. Twice."

I offered him a sunny smile. "Which is why I'm offering you a chance to redeem yourself."

"Ha. You just wanna sucker me."

"If you're saying no . . ." I stood on my toes as if peering over his shoulder. "I'm sure there's *someone* around here who'd be interested in losing to me."

"Jesus. You're impossibly cocky. Fine. I'll play with you." Nolan loomed over me. "One game, Gabriella. One game of my choosing."

"Unless I win and then you'll demand a rematch. So, it has to be three games." I looked around at the possibilities and rubbed my hands together. "Now what'll it be?"

"*Space Invaders*, *Ms. Pac-Man* or *Pac-Man* are the only dual-player games I've seen. Come on." Nolan placed his hand in the small of my back to direct me. We didn't stop to chat with any of the people he'd smiled at, said hello to or greeted by name. Seemed he knew everybody here.

Seemed he didn't want to introduce me to anyone he knew.

Because he's embarrassed to be seen with you.

I must've stiffened because he came to a full stop. "What?"

"If you'd rather hang out with someone else, it's fine. I can track Liddy down."

He narrowed his eyes at me. "I'd rather hang out with you, even if you're pissed off at me, because the rest of these people are here for the bragging rights of being invited to an exclusive event thrown by the Lund family and for the free booze. They're not even interested in the games."

That explanation made me feel better.

He tilted his head at a rakish angle that was utterly charming. "Or . . . are you getting cold feet because you're afraid you'll lose to me?"

"Now who's being impossibly cocky?"

"Come on, let's go."

A couple had claimed the *Space Invaders* game.

He said, "Ladies first," and directed me to the *Ms. Pac-Man* table.

After sitting down, I leaned forward to read the instructions printed on the outside of the glass. Either they'd replicated this feature, or this was an original machine.

"What are you doing? Don't you know how to play?"

"It's been a long time since I played," I lied, "so I'm refreshing my memory."

He placed two stacks of tokens on the edge of the table. "Ready?"

I pointed at the tokens. "I thought you said we were only playing three games."

"I lied. And I'm picking competitive mode."

"What does that mean?"

"We don't alternate turns. We play our own sides. High score wins."

Then he shoved the tokens in and the machine flashed and beeped.

Shit.

I managed to last, oh, maybe one minute before I was run through by a ghost.

Nolan kept playing.

And playing.

So I started dropping tokens in every time I lost and restarted with a new game.

I had improved, but I wasn't anywhere near Nolan's level—the man was still playing on that first token.

After I dusted all the tokens in both stacks, I stood. "I'll grab us champagne."

He might've grunted a response.

Thankfully I didn't have to venture far to find a cocktail waitress. I downed a glass, then carried two flutes back to the room. The other couple had left, so I parked myself in one of the *Space Invaders* chairs. I read through the instructions on that one so I'd be prepared.

Nolan said, "Are you fucking kidding me? I got through that vortex. The damn handle stuck. Stupid machine."

"Having trouble with your joystick, Lund?"

He smirked, but he didn't move his eyes from his game.

Then the familiar sound of the game ending came from his side of the table.

"I'm out. Next game." He pushed back and loomed over the table, then peered over to check the floor. "Where are all the tokens?"

"It's a ghost in the machine."

"What?"

"The ghosts in the machine have them." I sipped my champagne. "I kept losing to them."

"That was twenty bucks' worth of tokens! That should've lasted us all night."

"What can I say . . . I was a little quick on the trigger. It'd been a long time for me."

A moment passed and Nolan granted me that panty-dropping grin.

Good lord. If I had any more champagne, I might do just that.

Simmer down, Gabi. You're still not his type.

"I brought you a glass of champagne."

Nolan picked it up, studying the bubbles before he drank. "I should save myself the headache tomorrow and stop drinking now."

"Or you could pop four Excedrin before bed and enjoy the free booze."

"Is that your trick?"

"Yep." I tilted my glass at him. "Although, I'll probably pop four more when I get up since I'm coaching and refereeing tomorrow."

He took a sip. "Do you take any days off?"

I couldn't afford to. Instead of sharing that tidbit with the billionaire heir, I deflected. "What about you?"

"I'll probably go into the office and catch up on a few things." He frowned at the game console. "Not feeling *Space Invaders*."

"Great!" I jumped up. "I found a better game anyway."

"Lemme guess. Air hockey," he deadpanned.

"*Ding ding!* We have a winner. I have two tokens left so I'll even pay."

"Generous of you, Coach."

I practically had to drag him to the machine.

Maybe it was bad form to crack my knuckles before we started.

We went back and forth a few times. I scored first.

And second.

My joy was short lived because he scored seven times in a row.

Seven times.

He beat me.

Me: a professional hockey player.

Nolan's brash grin had me growling at him. "Don't feel bad, Welk. I beat Jax all the time too."

"But . . . how?"

"You're focused on offense. You leave your slot open."

"Excuse me?"

He laughed. "I didn't mean for that to sound dirty."

"Sure you didn't," I teased back. "We need more champagne."

We found two seats at the bar. I looked around as the bartender refreshed our flutes. I hadn't seen Liddy in a while and Nolan's family were gathered across the room. "You don't have to sit with me if you're supposed to be with the Lunds."

"Still trying to get rid of me?"

"Well, you *are* hopelessly annoying with that beating-me-at-games thing tonight."

He leaned in. "We're tied. You beat me at pool twice. I beat you at *Ms. Pac-Man* and air hockey."

The waitstaff got busy and neither Nolan nor I felt like talking as we waited for service.

Until he felt like jumping right in. "Earlier, after you accepted my apology, you said it wasn't the first time you'd been on the receiving end of assumptions. What did you mean?"

"Nothing."

"I'm calling bullshit on that."

I groaned. "Maybe I was talking out my ass in a show of camaraderie and commiseration and hoped it'd just float right over your head."

"God, woman, you baffle me."

"Honestly, Nolan, there's nothing baffling about me not wanting to share some of the shitty things people have said to me that haunt me way longer than they should."

He poked my arm. "That's *exactly* why I want to talk about it. After talking to you—really talking—I suspect we share some of the same misperceptions other people have about us. Let's throw the fragments of our broken egos out there and run those motherfuckers over."

"But . . . I have a happy buzz from the bubbly," I whined. "I don't wanna focus on negative stuff."

"I have an idea." Nolan upended his champagne and set the empty glass on its side on the counter. Then he set it to spinning like a top.

"Dude. I am *not* playing spin the bottle with you."

He laughed. "You sure? We're getting along so great now."

I whapped him on the arm.

"We can put our own spin on talking about negative assumptions."

"Such as?"

"Describing them with a positive result from them."

"Sounds good. You go first."

For the second time tonight I saw a raw vulnerability in Nolan's eyes, and I had the urge to protect it—and him—from anyone who'd see it as a weakness and use it against him.

Spontaneously, I wrapped my hand over his and squeezed. "Let's run this shit over and never look back."

Nolan propped his elbow on the bartop and his head on his hand. "I've always put extra effort into my appearance, and I enjoy keeping up with fashion trends. It's become somewhat of a hobby. I understand my good fortune at being born into a situation where money to maintain a certain style isn't an issue. And my family gives me grief about my metrosexual fashionista ways, but it's never mean-spirited."

My exhale caught in my chest because I suspected what was coming.

"But they were the only ones who weren't cruel. Everyone assumed I was gay. I had to be, right? Because I cared about how I looked. Trying to justify it just created worse problems for me. So I stopped defending or explaining myself."

"What's the positive result?"

"It has given me a different perspective on how difficult any marginalized groups can find things. Anytime I can step up and show the general populace that the LGBTQ community deserves the same rights and respect as everyone else, I do." He sighed. "The negative . . . I became a manwhore at age eighteen if only to prove to myself I was hetero and realized I fucking loved women and vice versa, hence the 'Trollin' Nolan' moniker."

"Only negatives as positives, remember?"

"That was the positive."

I felt him studying me but didn't look at him, half-afraid of what I'd see, or worse—what I hoped to see.

"Now it's your turn, Gabriella."

"But I don't wanna . . ." I mock-whined.

"Woman up and share with me, sista."

I rolled my eyes. "I'm not being flip but . . . it's been that same tune different dancer for me since high school. Girls who played sports competitively were butch. Therefore, as a hockey player, I had to be a lesbian. If we slapped each other's asses after a great shot? Lesbians. If we hugged after a game win? Lesbians. No one ever assumes men on any other sports teams are gay if they do those exact same things."

"True."

"Conversely, if we didn't wear makeup off the ice we enjoyed being seen as butch. But if we wore makeup to games, then we were vain, or trying too hard to look feminine to get men to notice us." I snorted. "No one considered that we liked getting dressed up when we went out as a group after a game because it was a relief to get out of the sweaty uniforms we lived in. I'm not saying there aren't lesbians in professional sports—I'm just saying it shouldn't matter."

"Amen."

"I love my sport. I love showing skeptics that female hockey players are just as talented and fun to watch as any men's team. Not just during the Olympics but all the time."

"You are an amazing coach, Welk. The kids at Lakeside worship you."

"Thanks." I forced myself to list a negative aspect of the assumptions, since he'd done it. "As far as negatives . . ."

"Only negatives as positives, remember?"

"Fine. Years spent fighting to prove I'm tough and talented on the ice gives me a chip on my shoulder that's easier to take with me off the ice than it is to leave it there."

Why had I told him that?

Too much champagne.

Nolan's knees bumped mine when he turned on the barstool to face me. "Thank you for showing me off-the-ice Gabriella."

Relieved he'd given me an out, I said, "She's usually not this tipsy."

"So is tipsy Gabriella in a place where she's willing to exchange digits with her former frenemy?"

"Yep." I whipped out my phone and said, "Hit me." Right after I typed in the numbers, I sent him a rainbow unicorn mermaid vampire emoji text.

He laughed. "I'd expected a middle finger emoji."

On a whim, I gave him a tiny head-butt. "Another thing to remember about me, Lund? I live to defy people's expectations of me."

"You've certainly defied mine."

"Same."

With our faces this close, I could see the turquoise flecks in his eyes.

"Can I ask you something weird?" he said softly.

"Sure."

"Do you smell cookies?"

"Uh. No. Why?"

"Every so often I get a whiff of cocoa and vanilla and it's . . ." He frowned. Leaned closer, sniffed my neck and said, "Jesus. It's you."

My chest tightened. "Are you saying I smell, Lund?"

"Christ. Are you kidding me? I fucking love cookies. That scent has been driving me crazy. Why do you smell like cookies?"

"Probably my cocoa butter lotion. I use a vanilla sugar body scrub too."

"It's making me hungry."

We stared at each other.

A half-shouted, "Hey, Gabi," had us breaking apart.

We both turned to see Jensen jogging over to us.

Nolan said, "You must be having fun since I haven't seen you all night."

"It was a blast watching the three Lund pinball wizards trying to outscore one another."

"Who won?" he asked. "Your dad or mine?"

"Neither. Uncle Monte kicked both their asses." Jensen looked at me. "I wanted to say if you're ready to go, you and Liddy can ride to Snow Village with me 'n Rowan."

"Really? You have room in your sportscar for two more?"

"I didn't drive the Corvette. We hired a car service since we knew we'd be drinking."

My eyes lit up. "Is it a limo?"

"Nah. Just an Escalade."

Liddy and I had Uber-ed to the party, so having a ride home was too good to pass up. "Sounds great. Thank you. I haven't seen Liddy in a while."

"She's up front. She got cornered by my mom and sister when she mentioned an upcoming trip to Sweden."

"Cool. I'll be right there." After Jensen jogged off—did the man run everywhere?—I looked at Nolan.

He stared back at me. Neither of us knew what to say.

Then he said, "So we're good?"

"Yeah. We're good. See you around, Lund."

"You've got my number. Lemme know if you need help with your air hockey slap shot."

I flipped him off.

Eight

GABI

ME: How does the moon cut his hair?

  NL: How?

ME: Eclipse it.

NL: 😄 Where did you hear that joke?

ME: One of my students. I thought you'd appreciate it.

NL: I do. Thanks.

ME: You're welcome. Carry on, Lund tycoon.
Don't forget to let your minions out to play once
in a while.

NL: Nah. If I'm chained to my desk, so are they.

ME: You're still working?

NL: It's not that late.

ME: Dude. It's 9:00!

NL: Huh. Time got away from me. I was just about to leave anyway.

ME: Good. I'd tell you that you work too much, but you'd just throw it back in my face that I do too, so I'll save us the argument and remind you to eat something decent that will replenish the energy you've expended today.

NL: Got suggestions?

ME: Meatloaf, mashed potatoes, corn.

NL: Are you being that specific because you have leftovers? Great! I'll be right over.

ME: Ha-ha. No. That's what I would buy if I had to stop someplace on my way home from work.

NL: It does sound good. Thanks for the rec. 🌹

ME: No prob.

TUESDAY NIGHT

ME: I FOUND A GAME WE CAN PLAY TOGETHER!!

NL: Stop shouting at me.

ME: Sorry. Just excited.

NL: What game?

ME: Download Friendly Fire. It's a word game app.

NL: Oh. I already play that one. Challenge me to a game. My screen name is Nolansland85.

ME: My screen name is GWellikers47.

NL: 👍

WEDNESDAY NIGHT

ME: How the hell did you get all the letters to play QUAVERS? That was a 127-point word! Are you cheating?

NL: Aww, that's cute, Welk, that you thought I'd have to cheat to beat you.

ME: 😦

NL: I've been playing this game for five years.

ME: Brag much?

NL: Hey, you're the one who challenged me.

ME: Because I thought it'd be new to both of us. That we'd be evenly matched.

NL: You just hate losing.

ME: You'll know how it feels next game, Lund.

NL: Bring it.

Nine

NOLAN

ME: Great word, Gabriella! See? This is how you lose gracefully. Take notes.

GW: ☝

ME: How have you had time to finish a game a day with me?

GW: Same question back atcha.

ME: Bored at work.

GW: Samesies!

ME: 😊

GW: If I have time to dick around on my phone, I usually pick single-player games. Trying to best my own high score. You?

ME: I've always been a sporadic player on other apps. For FF, I've never played with real people I know. So now that we've gone head-to-head . . . it's fun. The other games are a huge time suck.

GW: I hear ya. I don't have extra time during playoff/championship season—except for when I have nothing to do between games. So this has worked out.

ME: I stopped in to watch Mimi's practice last night, but you weren't there.

GW: Refereeing in Stillwater. I swear I could ref games 24/7 this week. They'd have me do it too, if they could get away with it.

ME: But you enjoy it?

GW: Not as much as coaching.

ME: Are any Lakeside teams good enough to play in any championship games?

GW: No. But I'm prepping my teams for a consolation tourney that all teams that didn't make the finals can play in. If Jax wants club teams that are competitive, he'll have to make some staffing decisions. Soon.

ME: Can you help him with that?

GW: If he asks. He's got other things on his mind. And I just work for him, Nolan. I've got no skin in the game at Lakeside.

ME: That sounds ominous.

GW: It wasn't meant to. I'm just tired.

ME: Of hockey?

GW: Never. Okay. That's a lie. Some days I wonder where I'd be in my life and my career if I would've taken a job outside of hockey after I graduated from college.

ME: Gabi, babe. You wouldn't be you.

GW: Maybe that's not such a bad thing.

ME: Rough day?

GW: Yeah.

ME: What can I do?

GW: I don't suppose you own a beachfront house in Hawaii I could rent out?

ME: Nope.

GW: Story of my life.

ME: Seriously, are you okay?

GW: I am, Nolan. And thank you for asking. I'm just a little punchy tonight.

ME: For what it's worth, everyone questions their
career choices.

GW: Even billionaire tycoons?

ME: ESPECIALLY offspring of billionaire tycoons who
aren't 100% sure of their place in the family biz.

GW: Does it make me a jerk if I admit I'm happy
to hear that it isn't always I LOVE MY JOB with you
either?

ME: No. It makes things real between us. So when the
time comes that we need to vent, or even discuss
changes, we both know we've got someone we can rely
on for an honest opinion.

GW: I concur.

ME: Hilarious since that's the word you beat
me with.

GW: 😄

ME: Get some rest.

GW: Back atcha.

FRIDAY NIGHT

ME: I'm home, mindlessly flipping through channels,
when I land on one of those bachelor/bachelorette-type
reality shows. I never watch them. Not even secretly.

GW: Okay. And you're telling me this . . . why?

ME: Patience, Welk. So these two characters go on a date and the topic question they pull from the magic coconut is . . . Tell me something about yourself that nobody knows.

GW: Umm, coming from someone who watches those shows without apology, that is a standard question.

ME: I've dated a lot, like more than is healthy probably, and I've NEVER had a date ask me that. So I don't get the reasoning behind it. To build drama?

GW: No, I think it's an exercise in trust.

ME: But if I haven't told anyone about it, why would I be inclined to tell a stranger . . . in front of a camera . . . on TV? That is the opposite of trust.

GW: What I'm getting from your confusion is that you have a deep, dark secret you've been dying to tell someone, and you're wondering if I'm interested in being your confessor.

ME: I am not.

GW: R2

ME: D2

GW: Dork

ME: I hate shorthand texting.

GW: You can't mean emojis because we both use the shit out of them.

ME: Bet your middle finger emoji is your most used.

GW: That one and the booze ones. Especially tonight.

ME: Getting your drink on?

GW: Made myself a vodka cranberry when I got home and I went a leeeeettle heavy on the V.

ME: So you're my drunken confessor?

GW: You're really gonna tell me a Nolan nugget no one knows?

ME: Eww. That sounded gross.

GW: I'll rephrase.

Nothing for two minutes.

ME: Welk, you there?

GW: I had to pee. Now where were we?

ME: I was about to sign off and leave you in your cups.

GW: No! I wanna know your secret. Pleeeeeaaassseeee?

ME: Strictly confidential?

GW: Scout's honor.

I seriously doubted she'd been a Girl Scout.

ME: In seventh grade I took a zero on an algebra test after the teacher caught me "cheating" looking at Amber Mahoney's paper. I never told anyone that I wasn't looking at Amber's paper, I was looking down her shirt.

GW: BWHAHAHAHAHAHAHAHAHA

ME: There you go.

GW: Feel better?

ME: No. I'd feel better if you told me something you'd never told anyone.

GW: Oh, you mean like me passing on trying out for the national team so my sister had a shot at making it? And then they win the Olympic gold?

My jaw dropped. I couldn't even think of how to respond to that.

Turns out, I didn't have to think about what to type. My phone rang.

Gabi started talking as soon as I hit answer. "Please, please don't tell anyone that I said that, okay? Jesus. I can't believe I told you."

"Sounds like you needed to tell someone." I paused. "So it is true?"

"Yes. There's the chance I wouldn't have made the team if I would've tried out, but I opted not to be considered for a spot so Dani would be. There's also the fact that if I would've been on the team, they might not have won the gold. So it's fucked-up logic, but everyone thinks I opted out because I believed I was past my prime."

"Dani believes that's why you walked away?"

"Yes."

"Goddammit, Gabriella. She should know about your selflessness."

"No. That's the thing with selflessness, Nolan. You don't expect anything in return. She did great in the games and she earned something I'll never have. But I've gotten to experience so much in my career that she never will. On the balance side, the scales are tipped much higher in my favor."

I thought back to the night in Buddy's when Gabi talked about things she'd given up for her sister. I should be even more pissed off on her behalf that Dani ended up with Tyson too, but Gabi deserved better than him.

"Nolan. Please promise me this stays between us."

"Of course I promise. It's a trust-building exercise, remember?"

"Building toward what?"

"You tell me, Gabriella."

Silence.

Then, "Can we table my answer since this is basically me drunk dialing you?"

I laughed. "Chicken."

"Definitely."

"Sleep it off, Welk. We'll talk soon."

Ten

GABI

'd been home maybe five minutes when my phone rang.

Dammit. I wanted quiet time to reflect on my day.

Don't you mean worry and pace?

Sighing, I flipped over my phone. Caller ID read: Liddy.

If I didn't answer she'd show up at my door anyway and ask why I hadn't picked up.

Forcing a smile into my voice, I answered, "Liddy! What's up?"

"My hopes rather than my blood pressure for once."

"Har har."

"We have margaritas, a bowl of gourmet popcorn and chocolate salted caramel gelato."

I only managed to get out, "Who's we—" before the knock sounded on my door.

Liddy and Dallas Lund crowded into the doorframe, Liddy juggling the popcorn and quart of gelato, Dallas clutching an enormous crystal pitcher.

Dallas sang, "Oh yes, it's ladies' night," and hip-checked me as she walked past.

Liddy kissed me on both cheeks. "Happy Thursday night, darling."

"What's the occasion?"

"That's the beauty of it! We don't need one," Dallas said gleefully. She shook the pitcher and the ice rattled. "I even made my famous margaritas. Break out the glasses."

"Already done," Liddy said from my kitchen. "And none of this 'I'm tired' nonsense, Gabs. It's almost been two bloody weeks since the pre-party at Full Tilt. Remember we all agreed to try to get together *because* we're all busy. This is us sticking to it."

I leaned against her and sighed. "Thank you."

"My pleasure."

"You too, Dallas."

She smiled as she filled the margarita glasses. "I'm just happy that y'all think I'm cool. No one besides my BFF Mac-Guyer and my cousin Annika ever wanna hang out. 'Odd duck' is the nicest term that's been used to describe me."

"Y'all? Girl, where'd that southern drawl come from?" I teased. "You're a Minnesota native."

"My mom is from North Carolina. After spending a few hours with her, I slip a *y'all* in here and there."

"Did you say your best friend's name is MacGyver?" Liddy asked.

Dallas laughed. "That's an easy mistake to make, but no. Her name is Ann-Mackenzie Guyer. Her parents call her Annie-Mac, which is too close to my cousin Annika's name, so I call her *MacGuyer*, because like MacGy-*ver*, she is the cleverest person I know. We've been BFFs since first grade. You'd love her." She pointed to the drinks. "Grab one and let's toast."

We held our glasses aloft and I braced myself for that awkward moment when everyone thought a toast to be a good idea but no one knew what to say.

Not so with Dallas. "Here's to those who've seen us at our best and seen us at our worst and can't tell the difference."

We touched glasses and drank.

My eyes widened at that first sweet, tangy, crisp, cold, citrusy, spicy, boozy taste. "Omigod, Dallas." I glanced over at Liddy and her amazed expression matched mine. "This is . . ." I took another drink and groaned. "Hands down the most fantastic margarita I've ever had."

Dallas bowed. "Thank you. It's a secret special recipe. Takes forever to make but well worth the effort."

"I agree." Liddy raised her glass. "To Dallas, for sharing her labor of love with us."

Another clink of our glasses.

"Let's sit in the living room." I connected my phone to my speakers and picked a favorite playlist. A little Sheryl Crow, Liz Phair, Katy Perry, P!nk, Taylor Swift; sisters in girl power.

"Have you had a chance to relax since the official grand opening for Full Tilt?" Liddy asked.

Dallas curled her feet beneath her in the chair. "I promised Jax I'd be on-site for the first two weeks and I've reached the end of that. It'll be bittersweet to move on to the next project."

"Which is . . . ?" Liddy asked.

"Nothing I'm allowed to talk about," Dallas said, miming locking her mouth and tossing away the key.

Then Liddy focused on me. "You have to have overheard something working for Jaxson."

"It's a miracle I hear anything to do with my job when I'm on the ice, say nothing of overhearing something that I'm not supposed to."

Liddy blasted me with an arch look, a reminder that I had recently overheard things I shouldn't have.

But I didn't take the bait. Nolan had apologized and we'd both moved on.

The fact I'd been texting with him regularly . . . not something I wanted to share. She might read the wrong thing into it.

Or maybe the right thing, which scares you even more.

"Is there anything else we should be celebrating?" Dallas asked Liddy. "I'm seeing . . . a bit more skittishness in your aura. BT-dubs, it doesn't appear to be causing anxiety, so good news?"

"We landed a corporate gift account and I'll be the liaison between the client and the graphics team."

"Congrats! Are you happy you'll be spending more time in London?"

I looked at Liddy. "You didn't tell me that's part of your promotion."

"Only because I just found out this morning." She focused on Dallas. "Dallas, sweetheart, you know I adore you, but it is spooky the way you just toss it out there like I'm wearing a sign."

She shrugged. "You are to me. I can't unsee it."

"Is that hard for you?" I asked her. "The always-seeing part?"

"Sometimes. This . . . sense that I have? It's ever-changing, so even I don't know what to expect most of the time."

"Please explain," Liddy said after taking a drink.

"I'll try." Dallas looked across the space and gathered her thoughts. "If I run into you in the hallway next week, I won't get the same reading from you that I got today, even if your mindset is the same and nothing externally has changed. When I get emotional impressions I can't . . . bank them, for want of a better term." She glanced up. "My perceptions freak people out. They act like I'm a mind reader, but the more I try and explain the less people listen. I've had to make adjustments to *myself* based on other people's random reactions to me, which sucks because I feel less true to who I am. But I've come to accept it'll never become easier."

"You do realize that we are amazed by the whole of you,

Dallas, not just the reading auras and making kick-ass margaritas skills."

Dallas grinned. "I realize I'm not everyone's cup of tea leaves—ha-ha—and I've had to stop talking about the *woo-woo* stuff even when it's a constant part of my life."

I leaned in. "Tell me who's being mean to you and I'll beat them up."

"It's not just people." She sighed and reached for the pitcher of margaritas. "Never mind. Who needs a refill?"

Both Liddy and I raised our glasses.

Even though Dallas and I had little in common, I felt a pull toward her. In this moment my gut was telling me to dig deeper. "So what is the deal with your mother?"

She froze. Then her eyes narrowed. "Are *you* reading *me* right now?"

"Uh. No. Why?"

"How'd you know to ask about my mother?"

"Because you mentioned her earlier."

She relaxed. "You caught me off guard. But ask away about my meddling mama."

"That's why I'm curious. Why did your brother ask me to play along as he tried to convince your mom that we had a date the night of the Full Tilt party? Then while she was genuinely thrilled about your success with the barcade, she also seemed concerned you weren't working on your own house."

"Good lord, Dallas. Does she constantly meddle?" Liddy asked.

"Yes. And no. What mam conveniently forgets? I've told her *exactly* why I can't live in that house."

"Why not?"

"Because it's haunted." Dallas held up her hand. "Normally that shit doesn't bother me. I've been dealing with ghosts since I was like three years old and she knows that. But this ghost? He loves to play dead—in a manner of speaking—meaning, he loves to prank me. He pranked me so well that I bought the damn house *because* I believed it was spirit-free.

Smarmy fucker had just been lying in wait until I showed up alone. Then he pulled the typical ghost tricks . . ."

Never in my life would I have thought I'd have to keep a straight face when a friend mentioned *typical ghost tricks*.

"He had a serious chuckle-fest about the fact he actually scared me." She growled. "No wannabe clown magician gets to make *me* scream in fright in my own damn house. So now, whenever I've had a bad day? I go into the house and shriek out all my frustrations. Then I leave. It's been therapeutic."

This girls' night was therapeutic for me.

I'd been fretting since I'd heard back from Wolf Sports North. They'd loved my game calling submissions and had scheduled an interview for the end of next week. Yes, it was thrilling to make it to the third round. But I was leaving tomorrow for an out-of-town hockey clinic and wouldn't return until Sunday night. Luckily, Liddy had promised she'd help me get into "tip-top" shape for the in-person interview, so I gave in to the pleasant tequila buzz and becoming invested in someone else's dramas.

"As far as Mom meddling in Ash's life?" Dallas said. "All he would have to do is tell Mom to quit nagging him. Personally, I think he should take a page out of Nolan's playbook."

My stomach jumped at the mention of his name.

"For years, Nolan had a different woman on his arm every time we saw him."

Nolan's issues with being called Trollin' Nolan . . . I hoped Dallas wasn't about to get snide about it because then I'd have to defend him.

"Anyway, when Nolan stopped being that guy, that's when Ash should've taken up the mantle. Instead Ash's got Mom convinced he's secretly nursing a broken heart. And I worry . . ." Dallas stopped. "Never mind. I shouldn't be sharing Lund family gossip."

"You know anything you tell us doesn't leave this room, Dallas," Liddy assured her.

Dallas drained her drink and poured herself more. "I've

never said this to anyone. Not to members of my family. Not to any of my friends."

I wasn't sure I wanted to hear it. For Liddy this was juicy gossip—not that she'd repeat it—but for me . . . it was a trickier situation since I worked for Jax. I didn't need to hear the Lund family intimacies they'd be unhappy a member of their own family had shared with acquaintances.

As I debated on pulling a Cowardly Lion and sneaking off to the loo, Dallas spoke.

"Ash is avoiding relationships because of *my* broken heart, not his. A few years ago I met Sasha Igorsky, a Russian hockey player, and we fell in love. He had to return home to Russia for a funeral and no one ever heard from him again— including the NHL. After a few weeks, I hired investigators to track him down, if only to reassure myself he was fine, freed from the gypsy curse and living his best life. But there's no trace of him. It's like he ceased to exist."

Liddy and I exchanged a look. Gypsy curse? Then she said, "You think your brother might've done something to make him disappear?"

Dallas seemed shocked. "God no. I suspect Ash might've secretly given him money to help him out of a weird international immigration legal issue because he knew Sasha was important to me. When that failed . . . Ash felt like he'd failed me. Then Ash avoided me for months afterward. And when I did see him, guilt lit up his aura like a neon sign. Although he's never admitted it to me, I know he refuses to let himself be happy until *I* am. Everyone in my family already thinks I'm flighty and overdramatic. If Mom finds out why Ash is on self-imposed exile into the dating dead zone? She'd freak out at *me*. So once again, my big brother is lying to save *my* skin."

Peculiar, but plausible, because essentially I was doing the same thing with Dani and Tyson. "You haven't dated anyone?"

She shook her head. "I've been too busy bartending, designing business concepts, implementing makeovers and avoiding the ghosts of my past. Literally." She shivered. "Good lord. Talk about being a Debbie Downer."

"No worries. Gabi has her own tale of woe. She was recently dumped. For her younger sister, no less."

Thanks for that, Lids.

"What? Gabi that's awful. Are you close to your sister?"

"Yes."

"Then that's even worse. Did you cry for days?" She held up her hand. "Wait. You're more the 'take his stuff into the parking lot and set it on fire' kind of chick."

"Now I wish I would've gone the gas-and-match route."

"What did you do to get back at him? Sleep with his brother? Throw a dead skunk in his car?"

"Not our Gabi. She's too bloody nice," Liddy complained. "She didn't even get a 'you're shagging my sister I'll prove I'm hotter than her' makeover."

Dallas blinked at me. "You didn't?"

"No."

"Not even a bikini wax for all that hot rebound sex?"

"Nope."

"Eyebrow threading after a facial?"

I shook my head.

"Mani-pedi . . . ?"

"Big fat no on that too."

She gasped and stood. "Then *this* is the celestial sign!"

"Uh . . . okay. The sign for what?"

"Of why I made my famous margaritas. I only whip them up when the mood strikes me and usually it's a sign from the universe that I need to take action."

"Take action on what?"

"Take action on you."

That's when I realized Dallas was studying me like a lab rat. I mustered a smile. "While I appreciate your help—"

"A highlight will release that gray ring of gloom around your aura." She squeezed my shoulder. "Trust me. No drastic changes. Just a little cosmic fine-tuning, yes?"

Say no.

But I always played it safe. What would it hurt to mix it up?

Not a damn thing.

I smiled at her. "You're on."

"Yay!" Dallas jumped up and clapped her hands. "I'll just run to my place and get my supplies."

And she was gone.

Liddy stood. "I'll make more margaritas." After she'd reached the kitchen, she popped her head back out to say, "I'd change into grubby clothes, if I were you. Celestial signs can be messy."

Since I had a break, I sent Nolan a quick text.

ME: Getting my drink on with your cousin.

NL: Tell her hi.

ME: No. I'm warning you not to text me the next few hours so I don't have to explain.

NL: Explain what?

ME: Why you and I are texting.

NL: Embarrassed about that, Welk?

ME: Ha.

NL: Besides, we haven't been texting as much this week.

ME: True. I'm still kicking your ass in FF this week though. 👊

NL: Also true. Everything okay?

ME: Just busy. You?

NL: Same.

ME: That's what I figured. Anyway, I'm headed out of town tomorrow for a hockey camp.

NL: Feel free to forfeit FF if you don't have time to devote to it.

ME: You wish. Later.

Dallas returned with an IKEA shopping bag of "accoutrements"—her word, which she murdered in a bad French accent that sent us into fits of giggles.

We were an odd threesome, proper English Liddy, ghost and aura seer Dallas and me, but I couldn't remember the last time I'd laughed so hard.

My nerves reappeared when it came time to reveal the results of the goop Dallas had slathered all over my hair. I wasn't allowed to look—not even at the reflection in the sliding glass door—until Dallas had dried, combed and fluffed me properly. I managed to keep my eyes closed even after I heard the *snip snip* of scissors.

Liddy and Dallas herded me into the bathroom between them and said, "Ta-da!" in unison.

I opened my eyes.

At first glance I didn't see any differences besides the lighter sections framing my face. But when I tossed my head, I noticed the variances in color. The boring brown was slightly darker . . . and yet shone a coppery blond beneath the lights. She'd chopped maybe an inch off all around, but now the ends curved in the front, toward my face.

"Well? What do you think?" Dallas demanded.

"It's exactly what you promised. Me . . . but better. I love it!"

She and Liddy bumped fists. "Now let's celebrate with gelato."

After I'd suggested a movie to go with our popcorn, we didn't part until nearly one A.M.

As I'd lain in bed, I felt that maybe the universe had intervened tonight. I'd never been a lone wolf. From my earliest memories I'd always been surrounded by friends and activity, even if that was hockey practice and games. I'd missed the camaraderie of my teammates in the past year and a half—ironic given the fact I now lived closer to most of them than when I lived in Fargo.

I realized earlier, watching my players at practice, that I'd settled for the easiest option for my career. My coaching time at Lakeside was supposed to be temporary. I'd accomplished what I'd set out to do: coaching Dani into earning a slot on the Olympic team, watching her compete for our country.

Dani. I missed her too. We'd exchanged texts, but I still wasn't ready to see her and Tyson in a social situation—just another example of how I'd isolated myself.

Maybe if I didn't get this job, I should consider rejoining the hockey life—for fun. Try out for the new pro women's team organizing under the Minnesota Wild banner. The pay was shit, but by sitting out, I wasn't doing anything to help change that mindset.

Eleven

NOLAN

G W: You around?

ME: S'up, my texting buddy?

GW: So say you're in a hotel room. You don't want to go down to the bar and drink. You've already eaten. Your teaching plan for the next day is done. You want to watch a movie, but don't want to dick around with figuring out which one to watch. What do you do?

ME: Watch porn.

GW: LUND

ME: Oh, I wasn't supposed to be honest? Because that's totally what I'd do.

GW: Is that what you're doing now, alone on a Friday night?

ME: Nope. I need both hands to text.

GW: Geez. Why did I text you?

ME: Good question. Why did you text me?

GW: I hoped you'd tell me your comfort movie.

ME: 😳 Why didn't you just lead with that?

GW: Fine. Tell me your go-to movie when nothing else looks interesting.

ME: Guess.

GW: Ugh. I hate this.

ME: I know. That's why I'm making you do it.

GW: If I do it you have to do it too.

ME: No prob. You still have to go first.

GW: 👆

ME: 😄

GW: Your go-to movie is . . . Devil Wears Prada.

ME: For christsake. Seriously, Welk?

GW: Come on, that was funny!

ME: Try again.

GW: The Greek Tycoon?

ME: GABRIELLA

GW: 😊 You'd be annoyed if I said Wall Street, wouldn't you?

ME: Not as annoyed as if you'd said Magic Mike.

GW: Hey, that's MY go-to movie!

ME: It is not.

GW: Fine. It's not. While I'm trying to figure out your movie, you try and guess mine.

ME: Miracle on Ice.

GW: OMIGOD NO!

ME: Slap Shot?

GW: 😮

ME: The Mighty Ducks?

GW: NOLAN

ME: Kidding. It's gotta be Fargo.

GW: I seriously hate you right now.

ME: No you don't. It's why you texted me at 9:30 on a Friday night. You knew I'd respond.

GW: Why did you reply? Why aren't you out clubbing?

ME: Done my share of that and I'm done. I wasted a lot of years on nothing. How's the hockey camp going?

GW: Great. The girls are actually paying attention. I don't have any parents grilling me on whether their daughter is good enough to make the Olympic team. It's heartening to see such a well-run club.

ME: They know they're lucky to have you.

GW: Flatterer. But thank you.

ME: Do you always do these camps by yourself?

GW: I get to be 100% in charge. And keep 100% of the camp fees.

ME: That doesn't surprise me at all.

GW: 😜 Are you working this weekend?

ME: I might sneak in Sunday for a bit. Mimi will be here for a sleepover tomorrow. I plan to exhaust her at Trampoline World so she's not up until midnight demanding more games/movies/food.

GW: The solution for that is to let her invite a friend along to your house. They'll entertain each other.

ME: 😵

GW: What? That's a great idea.

ME: I'm sure you'll get a laugh out of this, but I'm not crazy about having people at my house. I can handle Mimi for a night. Any longer than that . . . she goes to my folks' place.

GW: You don't like kids?

ME: The issue isn't kids. My house is my sanctuary. Everyone else in our family is happy to have football parties, barbecues, hockey parties, and holiday parties, and I let them. There are enough people in the Lund Collective to rotate places to go. No one has said, why haven't we been to Nolan's place?

GW: Does it bother you that they haven't seemed to notice?

ME: No. I'm actually relieved.

GW: Well, at least you don't have to take down the pleasure swing in the living room in anticipation of company.

ME: Hilarious.

GW: Seriously, though. None of your family pops by? Not Jax? Not even your mom and dad?

ME: Nope. They've been here, obviously, but they don't ask to drop in and I don't offer to host them.

GW: Is it because you see them enough at work?

ME: Partially.

GW: What about sexy times with your lady friends?

ME: Happens elsewhere.

GW: That's why there are hotels?

ME: Bingo. And I caught the sarcasm in that, BTW.

GW: 😊

ME: Mimi is the only female that's had an overnight at my house.

GW: Ever?

ME: Ever.

GW: Huh.

ME: What? You think I'm a freak?

GW: No. I think it's insightful that the your-house-is-a-sanctuary thing is an absolute in your life. You are fortunate to have that.

ME: I know.

GW: We totally got off track as far as comfort movies.

ME: I like that we can talk about anything.

GW: Me too. I'm better at texting than talking on the phone.

ME: With me? Or with everyone?

WANT YOU TO WANT ME   103

GW: Everyone. Calling someone it's like . . . is this a bad time? And then I feel guilty when that person says yes, and they have to call you back. Whereas with a text, people can respond when they get time. Or we can get caught up in epic texting sessions.

ME: We've had a few of those this week.

GW: Yes. And I'm confident that if my texts were bugging you, you'd tell me to bugger off.

ME: 😊 Liddy is rubbing off on you.

GW: So is Dallas. I actually checked my horror-scope today.

ME: And what did it say?

GW: That a tall, dark, handsome, sort-of-stranger would . . . TELL ME HIS FAVORITE COMFORT MOVIE.

ME: 😄 😄 😄 😄 😄

ME: Fine. Here it is: Talladega Nights: The Ballad of Ricky Bobby.

GW: Okay. Why?

ME: It makes me laugh. Every time. Now, are you going to psychoanalyze me for that choice?

GW: Dude. No way. I love that movie. It's in my all-time top 5.

ME: 😔 Spill your comfort movie.

GW: Ladyhawke.

ME: Really? Why?

GW: What's not to love about a young Rutger Hauer?

ME: GABRIELLA

GW: All right, besides the animal-crossed cursed love, a stranger who's never had that kind of love believes in it to the point he makes it his goal to break the curse for them.

ME: Confession time. I've never seen it.

GW: 😨 We can't be friends until you watch it.

ME: What? That's not fair.

GW: ✋ Talk to the hand, Lund.

ME: Is it appropriate to watch with Mimi tomorrow night?

GW: No. It's PG-13. Watch it tonight. Or else you'll never hear from me again.

ME: Are you seriously threatening to boycott our burgeoning friendship over a movie?

GW: Yep.

ME: Harsh.

GW: 🙆

ME: Then I guess I'll win our Friendly Fire game. Good thing you're not competitive and don't care that this is the tie-breaking game this week.

GW: Oh, I'll still challenge you there. It is your turn, BT-dubs.

ME: I'LL WATCH IT OKAY?

GW: Yay! You won't regret it.

ME: You owe me a movie night. A movie I get to pick. And we have to watch it together.

GW: Deal. But not at your house, right?

ME: 👆

GW: Ha—you deserved that. Go make some popcorn and settle in.

ME: Bossy much?

GW: 😜

ME: Later—

Twelve

GABI

Monday morning, after a long weekend and not hearing from Liddy at all, the text from her sent me into a panic.

LE: Sorry, love. Major crisis here and I'll be in London at least another week.

She was in London? But she'd promised to take me shopping for interview clothing tomorrow. My interview at Wolf Sports North was on Friday!

LE: Don't freak out, darling. Call Dallas. She did an outstanding update on your hairstyle. I'm guessing she'd love to help you out. Let me know how the interview goes . . . but I'll not wish you luck because you've got this! XOXO

No, I didn't have this.
Rather than texting Dallas, I called her.

She answered on the second ring. "What's up?"

"Dallas! Please, please, please help me—"

"You've reached Dallas Lund." A giggle. "Gotcha. It's my voice mail. I'm on sabbatical until whenever. Leave a message."

I might've laughed at her dickish sense of humor if I wasn't completed screwed.

Okay. Think, Gabi.

I started to pace.

Could I just go to Nordstrom Rack or T.J. Maxx and hope I'd find something decent?

No. Liddy pointed out that my attire for this interview had to be spot on. Nothing too sexy or too dowdy. Style with an eye to fashion trends but not a slave to those pieces that might be considered too haute couture. Hadn't she said that classic styles were the kiss of death? But what was considered classic? Did that include a little black dress? Because that'd definitely been on my must-have list after I realized I'd taken *dressed down* to another level when I'd worn a T-shirt and jeans . . . to a society-column-worthy grand opening event for the billionaire businessman I worked for.

Head thunk.

Next option.

What if I pinned half a dozen possible outfits from Pinterest, showed them to a saleswoman at the designer showroom at Macy's and asked for help assembling those outfits? That would be similar to having a shopping assistant.

But it still isn't like having an advocate like Liddy, who knows fashion, knows you and is an expert on dressing for success.

No, to pull this off I needed professional help.

And then he popped into my head.

Nolan Lund.

He had impeccable style, regardless if he was in business attire or weekend wear, or that sweet spot between formal and casual. He was comfortable discussing his love of all things fashion related.

Surely a man that dedicated to outer appearances would be happy to show off his knowledge to a neophyte like me?

He could be Henry Higgins to my Eliza Doolittle.

The kindhearted concierge to my Pretty Woman.

He could be Victor and give me the *Miss Congeniality* moment.

He could also get your ass fired. His brother is your boss. You really think he'd have no qualms about helping you land a job that would put his brother in a bind?

Well . . . technically I didn't know if I'd have to quit *quit* at Lakeside, but my role and time spent there would change drastically. So there wasn't any way I could leave that factoid out.

Before I lost my nerve, I texted him.

ME: How's mogul life treating you?

Keep it casual. Don't let him sense your panic—save that for the face-to-face meeting.

His phone must've been close by because he answered quickly.

NL: My minions are misbehaving.

ME: LOL, Lund.

NL: Alliteration again?

ME: Absolutely.

NL: 😵

ME: JK.

NL: What's up, buttercup?

ME: Need some advice. The in-person kind. You at the
office today?

NL: Yes.

ME: Great! I'll be in the neighborhood. I'll swing by.

The dialogue bubble started and stopped three times before he figured out how to respond.

NL: Sending a request for your visitor's pass.

NL: Main level security will direct you where to go.

ME: Thanks. CU soon.

It was tempting to change into the black skirt and blazer
set from my limited selection of professional clothing. But I
needed his help, which I'd take even out of pity, so I remained in leggings and a knee-length sweater. After stepping into my snow boots, I sailed out the door.

"In the neighborhood" was a solid forty-five minutes
from my apartment. By the time I parked and picked up my
pass at the security desk, an hour had zipped by.

I don't know if it was standard procedure or if I had crazy
eyes, but a security guard rode with me up to Nolan's floor.
I muttered thank you—hopefully I wasn't supposed to tip
him—and stopped at the receptionist's desk.

She smiled. "How may I help you today?"

"Are you Nolan Lund's secretary?"

"I wish." She laughed. "I'd say kidding, but I'm not. I'd
love to work directly for the man known around here as 'The
Prince.'"

Weird response.

"I'm the receptionist for this floor. Mr. Lund's private

office suite is through the last door at the end of the hall-way."

"Thanks."

I walked alongside a wall of frosted glass, which muted the shadows of the workers in their cubicles. The closer I got to the end of the hallway the harder my heart pounded. I paused to take a breath before I turned the handle . . . and half stumbled into the room.

Another secretary, this one male, seemed surprised to see me. "May I help you?"

"I . . . ah . . . I'm . . ." *Settle down.* "Gabi Welk. Here to see Mr. Lund."

A door that was part of the wall opened and Nolan saun-tered out, eyes on his phone. "Zach is lined up for Saturday. Still looking for more volunteers—"

"Your visitor is here, sir."

Then he glanced up from his phone and noticed me. "Ga-briella."

Act cool. "Hey, Nolan."

Silence.

His gaze encompassed my entire head. "What did you do to your hair?"

Shit. I hadn't seen him since last week. "You must mean what did *Dallas* do to my hair in a show of drunken camara-derie?"

He backpedaled. "What I meant to say is, it looks great. Really brightens up your face."

"Thanks." I looked around. "Am I interrupting anything important?"

"First thing on a Monday morning?" He smiled. "Nah. Come on in. Sam, please hold my calls."

I followed him. His office wasn't as big as I'd expected. But it had been decorated like I'd imagined with a retro vibe straight out of *Mad Men.* Skirting the couch, I headed for the bank of windows. Another gray day in the Twin Cities to match my mood. Slightly depressing that Nolan didn't have a great view that rose above the gloom.

"Would you like coffee or something?"

"Coffee only if whiskey's not an option."

Pause. "Two coffees coming up."

The coffee machine whirred, and I stayed in place trying to organize my thoughts.

Nolan handed me a mug.

Murmuring thanks, I immediately set it on the window-sill. With the way my hands were shaking I'd probably spill it all over myself.

He joined me in staring out the window. "What's on your mind?"

"Do you remember when you were a kid and you had that nightmare of showing up to class naked?"

A moment passed as he processed that off-the-wall start to our conversation. "Sure. Why is that relevant?"

"That'll be my reality if I can't convince you to help me."

"That wasn't cryptic at all, Gabriella."

"Sorry. I'm just trying to convince myself that I can trust you."

Mr. Suit and Tie slurped his coffee. "On some level you're here because you trust me."

Or I'm desperate.

Admitting that wouldn't win me any brownie points.

"I'm not going to try and coax this out of you," he warned. "You came to me, remember?"

"Yes. First, I need assurance that this conversation is confidential?"

"Absolutely."

I faced him and blurted out, "On Friday I have a job interview that can change the entire trajectory of my career, and I need you to help me choose a killer interview outfit, given that I have zero fashion sense."

"What's the job?"

"Not in coaching. It's a TV sportscasting job."

"You'd have to quit at Lakeside."

"Most likely."

"And I'm supposed to keep this from my brother. Your boss."

"Pretty much."

"Is this a joke?"

"No. Can you see why I had to ask for this favor in person?"

Carefully, he set his coffee mug next to mine. "Why me?"

"Because you're a fashion expert. You dress for success every damn day of your life, Lund. Doesn't matter if it's for the office or a kid's hockey game or if you're out clubbing. You look amazing. I need that mojo for a couple of hours. So please. Say you'll help me."

"Can't you get someone else to go with you?"

I threw up my hands. "Who? Liddy was supposed to be here, but she's stuck in London. My sister is even more clue-less than me when it comes to clothes, so she's out."

"How about—"

"Your cousin Dallas? She's on sabbatical. My mother lives hours away and she's a farm wife. I'd ask Margene for fashion advice only if I was going to a *Murder, She Wrote* fan conference. And lastly, there's Lucy, who would agree to help me if I begged her . . . until she learned of the conflict of interest. Then she'd tell Jax and I'd get fired. But the basic problem wouldn't have changed. That without your help, I will bomb the in-person interview because I didn't have any-thing to wear!"

"Easy." Nolan set his hand on my shoulder. "Drink some coffee."

Now I was definitely too jittery and didn't need to add to it.

Then he sort of pushed me toward the couch. "Sit."

Thankfully the sofa wasn't one of those marshmallow types that swallowed you as soon as you dropped your butt on the cushion.

After handing me my mug, he chose the chair opposite the couch and studied me over the rim of his coffee cup.

I practiced not fidgeting. Go me.

"Tell me about this job. Be as specific as possible."

"Does that mean you're going to help me?"

"How about if you answer my question first."

I exhaled. "The position is at Wolf Sports North."

"How'd you hear about the opening?"

Meaning . . . how long had I been seeking out other employment opportunities that would put his brother in a bind? "An acquaintance of a friend mentioned it to her, and she brought it up with me. I barely got in under the deadline. I passed the first two rounds. I don't even know if this is the final round or if there's more."

"What were the requirements for rounds one and two?"

"First one was filling out an extensive application. The second was calling a live college hockey game and submitting an audio file of my commentary."

"What team did you choose to provide commentary on?"

I smirked at him. "Since I'd planned to watch the games anyway, I did play-by-play of the U of M women's hockey team versus University of Wisconsin and the UND men's hockey team versus Denver University."

Nolan smirked back. "Aren't you the little brownnoser, handing off not one, but two game tapes."

"Maybe it was extra, but I believed it'd be better to showcase my skills for both men's and women's hockey. While I love women's hockey, it's time a female sportscaster changes the mindset of the networks and the fans that women sportscasters don't belong calling men's games."

"Obviously it worked."

"To this point. Now it's all about how I present myself in person."

His gaze narrowed. "Is this an on-camera position at a sports desk?"

"I'm not sure. They've been specific about certain things

and vague about others. Vague about applying for a 'winter sports' correspondent position. Then they're specific about which winter sport. I don't know if they're looking to fill multiple broadcasting positions, or if the person they hire needs general knowledge. And before you ask, I don't have any idea how many applicants have made it to this third round."

"So it could be two or it could be twenty-two."

"Yes." I leaned forward. "That means I need to knock it out of the park with all aspects of this interview. Impressing the interviewers with my sports knowledge should be the core of the interview, but clearly it isn't. I have to show them my physical appearance isn't an afterthought. That I'm fierce and feminine. The clothing has to be just flattering enough to prove I care about personal maintenance and fashion trends but nothing boob-baring like I'm some damn puck bunny."

Nolan whistled. "That is a very tall order, Gabriella."

"Which is why I'm here."

"And I can't tell Jax about this?"

"You can't tell *anybody* about it. I don't think I was supposed to reveal the name of the cable network. I'm pretty sure there was an NDA in the paperwork."

"They're definitely the big dog of the Upper Midwest cable networks." Then he gave me that lazy grin. "You realize if I agree to help you, I'll expect something in return."

Took every bit of willpower not to say *anything you want.* "Such as?"

He set his coffee cup on the table between us. "Off the top of my head, I need volunteers for my LCCO project, which also happens to be this weekend. Saturday at Rosewood Bowling Alley. It's an LGBTQ mixer for Twin Cities high schoolers."

"I'm in."

"That fast?"

"Yes. Look at me." I held my hands out. They shook like crazy. "You are my last hope, Obi-Wan Kenobi."

He grinned. "I told you before . . . I'm Lando."

"He was the ultimate fashion plate too. So are we doing this thing?"

A beat passed and he drummed his fingers on the arm of his chair. Then he pulled out his cell phone from the inside pocket of his jacket and dialed.

Keeping his eyes on mine, he said, "Sam. Please cancel all my appointments for the day." He frowned. "That was today? No matter. Reschedule everything else, I'll handle that one. Also, add Gabriella Welk as a volunteer for the LCCO mixer on Saturday. We'll stop by your desk on the way out and give you her contact details."

"Nolan. I can't thank you enough."

"You might rethink my help when I sic my sadistic stylist tailor on you." He turned his speaker on and set his phone on the coffee table.

The line rang three times before a snippy voice answered, "Mr. Lund. I'd nearly abandoned hope I'd hear from you. The new lines have been out for weeks and you haven't shown the slightest bit of interest." A pause. "Are you ill?"

Nolan laughed. "No. Just busy."

"Well, you are in luck. I had a cancellation for next Friday."

"Here's the thing, Q. I'm gonna need you to clear your schedule for today. And before you get huffy, I will also say that I'm not the one in need of your fashion expertise today. I have a"—his eyes twinkled when he said—"female friend who you'll be advising."

"Funny. A little drop-everything-for-a-Lund joke to start my week off in a total panic."

"I'm not joking. I have a couple of things to wrap up here at the office, but we can meet you anywhere in the next hour."

"Do you have any idea how much havoc this will wreak on my schedule?"

"Please don't make me play the 'I spend a fuck-ton of money with you every year' card."

A heavy sigh. "FINE. Is this consult only clothing?"

"It's the works: clothing, shoes, accessories."

"Since my showroom is not in any state to entertain clients with such short notice, we'll have to do this at the design studio. It's at D.NOLO. In the North Loop."

"I've been there, remember?"

"Oh, I haven't seen you in *so long* I assumed you'd forgotten where I do all my best work."

"Nice one," Nolan said dryly.

"See you in sixty. Ta."

Dial tone.

"Okay. That . . ."

"Went better than I'd anticipated." Nolan pocketed his phone and stood. "I need to make a couple of calls. Sam, my PA, will fill you in on the LCCO event and I'll be out shortly."

For the first time since I'd stormed in here, it occurred to me that maybe I should've waited until the end of the business day to approach Nolan for help. He had a high-pressure job. Who was I to barge in and expect him to ditch all his responsibilities and take me shopping?

God. Sometimes I was so damn self-involved.

I stood and walked over to the front of his desk.

He'd already taken his seat and was on his computer. His eyes scanned the screen, but he spoke to me. "Don't get cold feet now, Gabriella. It's a done deal. You waffling and feeling guilty will just piss me off. So head out and talk to Sam. He's waiting."

Wow. Brusque businessman wasn't a side I'd seen of this man. What did it mean that I found his large-and-in-charge persona . . . seriously hot?

Means your sense of relief is making you delusional that your attraction is mutual.

I exited his office.

Sam, a sharp-dressed man around my age, had already pulled a chair up opposite his desk. "You are an angel for helping with this event, Gabriella."

"Most people call me Gabi."

He frowned. "Nolan knows that?"

"Yes. He insists on using my full name."

"Hmm. Usually he's not so contrary."

"Yeah. Usually he's much worse."

Sam laughed. "No comment. I am curious how you and the boss man know each other."

"I work for Jax at Lakeside. I'm a hockey coach and program coordinator."

"Wait. You're the infamous Coach Welk?"

I rolled my eyes. "Infamous. Typical. What has Lund been saying about me?"

"Nolan hasn't said much. Mimi, however, believes you're secretly hiding a superhero cape under your hockey jersey. You're her coach, right?"

"Yes. I love that kid. It's hard to keep a straight face with some of the questions she asks."

"I hear ya. I swear everyone knows when she's in this twenty-two-story building. She insists on visiting her favorite uncle and I get a kick out of seeing her. Kids are just so . . . pure."

"Until they hit twelve with all the hormones and they're pure evil. Anyway, what do you need from me?"

I started paperwork while he explained the goal of the event. When he finished talking, I said, "This is an awesome way for older kids to actually see the positives of adults who've been through what they're going through now, living on their own terms."

"Every little bit of hope helps. Now all I need is to get the *L* covered in LGBTQ."

"Low on lesbians?"

He nodded. "None of my lesbian acquaintances are comfortable interacting with a group of teens that hit all the letters, not just the *L*."

"I might have a solution. You okay with a lesbian athlete?" I snickered. "She'll tell you herself that she has no issue being a token."

"God. Yes."

I called my former teammate Mariah, putting her on speaker as I finished the paperwork.

She answered, "Gabi Welk. Please confess you're calling because you broke it off with your boyfriend and you've been thinking dirty thoughts about me."

"You're too high maintenance for me, Mariah. And Tyson broke it off with me, but that's another story."

"Good! Then you should definitely come play for the other team on a trial basis. Not only do we have cookies on the dark side, we'll eat yours."

I laughed. "Damn, I miss you. But here's a chance for us to see each other for a good cause. And BT-dubs, you're on speaker." *BT-dubs?* When did I start channeling Dallas Lund?

I'd barely ended my spiel when she said, "I'm in. These girls gotta hear there's nothing wrong with likin' ladies and their delicious lady bits."

"You are da best, M. Is it all right if I give Sam, the coordinator, your contact info?"

"Sure. This Sam . . . is she hot?"

"*He* is listening in on this convo, but yes, he is hot. Wrong bits for you though, chickie."

"Amy would get jealous anyway. Hey. Can she come too?"

I looked at Sam and he nodded.

"Of course. I gotta go. Thanks, and see you Saturday morning."

Sam grinned at me. "I can't wait to meet her."

"Meet who?" Nolan asked.

"The woman who rounded out our alphabet soup," Sam said. "Now I have to do actual work today instead of fretting about this LCCO event. Unless . . ." He spun in his chair to face Nolan. "I can go home since you won't be here?"

"No. But nice try."

I noticed he already had his coat on. When I stood, he'd taken my coat off the rack and held it out for me.

Ooh. Gentlemanly Nolan gave me a little tingle too.

Stop it.

"I'll check in before the end of the day. Any crises arise . . . kick it upstairs to Britt."

"Will do, boss." Sam mouthed, *Thank you*, before Nolan herded me away.

He didn't say anything as we rode his private elevator to the parking garage.

A *chirp chirp* sounded, and the lights flashed on a white Porsche Cayenne.

"No super-fancy sportscar today, Chewie?"

"Nope. You'll have to make do with this one."

Somehow, I didn't think he'd appreciate it if I confessed I preferred this car anyway.

I waited for him to remind me he was Lando, and that retort never came either.

We'd barely buckled up when the center console in his dash lit up with an incoming call.

He sighed. "Sorry, I have to take this." He poked a button on the steering wheel and said, "Nolan Lund speaking."

Maybe I should've listened. But corporate doublespeak bored me. Who cared about risk assessment ratios and frequency markers?

But within fifteen seconds of ending the first call, another came through. This time he didn't apologize, he just launched into another conversation that I tuned out.

Meanwhile, I scrolled through my bank accounts, trying to assure myself this shopping excursion wouldn't bankrupt me.

We pulled up to the valet stand while Nolan was still on the phone. "No, Gerry, the numbers don't lie despite you trying to convince me otherwise. Yes, Brady has seen them. *I'm* the one who brought the discrepancy to his attention. Have the revised proposal to my assistant on Wednesday morning. LI is done dicking around with this. Oh. And don't ever question my right to speak on behalf of the company that bears *my* name." He hung up and muttered, "Fucking amateurs," as the valet opened his door.

Yikes.

Had Nolan realized he hadn't spoken to me at all in the past thirty minutes?

He held the building door open for me and I paused inside the entryway. The place looked like a mall with an open corridor and the stores branching off from the center. Airy. Lofty. Expensive.

A door—polished honey oak, grooved panels inset below the milky glass—was centered between the exit to one store and the entrance to another. Déjà vu hit me. I remembered a door exactly like that in my elementary school in North Dakota.

That line, *You're not in North Dakota anymore, Gabi,* nearly caused hysterical laughter to bubble up.

Nolan strode right through that door and I followed.

We'd entered a workspace with tables covered in bolts of fabrics. One seamstress ran a sewing machine while another cut pattern pieces—both of them ignored us. Nolan just kept dodging and weaving around dressmaker dummies, equipment and furniture until we were in a center room again. A room that looked like a cross between a tea shop and private study. A split staircase off to the left with twisted wrought-iron railings created a focal point.

At the center of that focal point stood a man. Tall. Burly. Sporting a full dark beard. Big square frames seemed to cover half his face. He had a measuring tape draped around his neck and a pincushion attached to his wrist.

He growled, "You're late," as he stomped down the stairs.

Nolan glanced at his watch. "Four minutes is all."

"Follow me."

We entered a large dressing area with an enormous three-way mirror. The man faced us. "Given this is an emergency, I won't invite either of you to sit."

Nolan nudged me forward with a hand on my back. "This is your client today, Gabriella Welk. Gabriella, this is Jacques Andres."

This guy was Nolan's stylist?

His hands looked better suited to cracking skulls than crafting suits.

Offering my hand, I said, "Nice to meet you. Please call me Gabi."

"Call me Q."

"Q . . . like in *Star Trek*?"

"No, Q like the gadget designer in the James Bond movies," Nolan replied. "I started calling him that because his first name is too close to my brother's and he doesn't like being called by his last name. We compromised on Q."

Q didn't add commentary. He just demanded, "Well, Gabi, what's the fashion emergency?"

I bet he got a huge kick out of saying that. "I have an in-person interview on Friday for a position that could change the course of my career. I need next-level styling."

"What's the position?"

When I hesitated to answer, Nolan said, "Client confidentiality isn't an issue, is it, Q?"

"With me? Never an issue."

"It's a sportscasting position at Wolf Sports North. Regardless if it's doing on-air analyzing or if I'm commentating for games, my look needs to be camera ready."

"What sport?"

"Women's hockey."

That's when he sized me up. "You play?"

I nodded. "And I coach."

"And she's won Olympic medals, international and national championships. Come on, Gabriella, don't sell yourself short. Sell yourself."

"Why would she need to when you're doing it for her?" Q said.

Yeah. This was going well.

Not.

Nolan's phone rang. He swore under his breath and said, "I need to step out for a moment," and then disappeared.

Jerk.

Q studied me and I sensed he didn't like what he saw. Too bad. I met his hard stare straight on.

"So how long have you and Nolan been together?"

I leaned forward. "Let's be honest with each other, okay? Nolan and I aren't involved. I'm sure that doesn't come as a shocker to you, as I am not even freakin' close to Nolan's type."

"You think I would know Nolan's type . . . how?"

That surprised me.

"I spend a lot of time with Nolan during the course of a year, yet I wouldn't call us friends. In the years I've been his stylist, he's never once brought a woman with him. Not for her opinion on his clothes. Not to help her choose clothes. So the urgency in this visit has me scrambling for a number of reasons. I'd appreciate it if you'd finish filling in the blanks."

"I work for Jax at Lakeside Ice Arena and know Nolan by default. He has the kind of style that money can buy and the type of class that can't be bought. I needed his style expertise because my other fashion-conscious friends were unavailable, and I sort of . . . bulldozed my way into his office and demanded his help."

"And he just agreed?"

"He agreed to swap favors. I'm helping him with his LCCO mixer for LGBTQ youth on Saturday and he's helping me with this." I rubbed my sweaty hands on my sweater. "You should also be aware that I have a budget."

He smirked. "A foreign concept for Mr. Lund."

"Exactly. So I'm asking you, Q, to make sure that Nolan doesn't try and pay for anything else."

"Else?"

"I'm guessing he's paying your hourly rate as his part of the favor."

"You guessed correctly." He cocked his head. "What's your budget, dear?"

"No more than one thousand dollars."

"That changes a few things."

Dammit.

After a pause, Q said, "You asked for honesty, and here it is." His eyes gleamed. "I love this challenge. While I adore working with clients who don't bat an eyelash at the cost of fashion, your monetary constraints will force me to get creative."

I blinked at him. "And that's good?"

"Very good. Plus it'll be fun."

"Thank you. Seriously. I've been worried about this money sitch." I pulled my wallet from my purse and fished out a credit card. "Payment in advance?"

"Not necessary. I'll give you an itemized bill after we've made final selections. But I'd like for you and me to strike a deal also."

"What kind of deal?" I asked, returning my wallet to my purse.

"If you get this job, I want to be named your stylist, officially credited at the end of Wolf Sports North programming— Gabriella Welk's wardrobe courtesy of Jacques Andres Designs. I realize this is all a bit premature, but that is one career bucket list item I haven't attained."

I offered him my hand. "You have a deal."

"What kind of a deal?" Nolan asked as he strolled back in.

"Just finalizing the payment option for Miss Welk." Q gave Nolan's outfit a once-over.

Today Nolan wore a dark gray suit paired with a black shirt, and topped off with a silver tie dotted with tiny red diamonds. A little more somber than his usual attire, but the man looked delectable, like James Bond—the Brosnan years.

"There's lots more color in men's summer fashion than in years past," Q continued. "Trend is to match the socks to the shirt. Which won't affect you."

"Since I don't wear socks with my suits during the Minnesota winters, I won't wear them in the summertime." Nolan's gaze zeroed in on me. "You ready?"

Hell no. "Yep."

Thirteen

NOLAN

Gabriella's nervousness surprised me.

She oozed confidence in every situation. Even after her boyfriend had dumped her.

I'd intended to ease her into this process of getting styled, but now I decided the fewer decisions she'd have to make, the better it'd be all around.

"Do you need her to strip to get her measurements?" I asked Q.

"No. That's the benefit of ready-to-wear."

She relaxed slightly.

"But I will need a 360-degree view of her form as I'm making notes." He pointed. "Please stand over there, facing the mirror."

Gabi hopped up on the platform.

Q walked around her. "Pants size?"

"Eight. But they're usually too big in the waist so I have to belt them."

"Blouse size?"

"Solid medium for T-shirts. Button-down shirts . . . it depends. I've got wide shoulders. Anything with tight arms and chest, I tend to Hulk out and seams get ripped."

I snickered at the image of Gabi in a Hulk-like rage.

"Bra size?" Q asked.

Perfect, my mind supplied.

Then I gave myself a mental slap.

"Thirty-six C right now."

Surprised, Q said, "It changes?"

"Yes. I drop to a 34B if I'm in competition shape."

"Fascinating. I can't imagine my male clients telling me that their dicks get smaller when they're in competition shape."

Gabi flashed him a quick grin. "I promise you their dicks are smaller if they're doing 'roids. Their balls too."

"This conversation has deteriorated," I said. "To get back on topic . . . do you have any issues wearing heels?"

"*That's* on topic?" she demanded.

"Yes. I've never seen you in a pair of heels. If you have a sports injury that prevents you from wearing them, that's one thing. If it's a personal 'I hate heels' thing, we need to know that too."

"You usually see me in skates, Nolan. Off the ice? I rarely wear heels since it's not necessary. But I *can* wear them and walk in them just fine."

"Shoe size?" Jacques asked.

"Eight."

"All right, we're done with that. Now onto the fun part."

"Yay," she said without enthusiasm.

"You're not excited about this at all?"

"I am. Yet . . . I'm unsure if I should even go through with the interview if I'm having this much anxiety about what to wear. Say all the stars align and I get the job. I will have to wardrobe plan. And probably keep track of which day I wore what, so I don't wear the same outfit too often."

I set my hands on her shoulders and peered into her face,

which had become flushed. Her eyes didn't want to meet mine. "Hey. Look at me."

She did.

"Listen." This close to her, I caught that warm-cookies scent and it totally derailed my thought process. That, along with the fact I hadn't noticed her eyes were silvery-blue.

Eyes that held absolute trust and that threw my thoughts into further chaos.

"Nolan?" she prompted softly. "You were saying?"

"Don't borrow trouble. One step at a time."

"Okay."

"That said . . ." I cleared my throat and looked at Q. "Let's assume this won't be Gabriella's last interview."

"So we're looking for a singular outfit with wow factor and multiple pieces."

"Yes. However, this doesn't need to be a mix-and-match situation. The interview clothing is the priority. After that we should focus on an outfit that plays up camera readiness, as well as rinkside commentary and studio interviews, and a cocktail dress."

Q tapped his chin as he studied her. "Gut instinct is to put her in the cranberry color palette. Mulberry is too muddy for her complexion, yet, I'm not ruling out the right hue of plum."

Circling Gabi, I felt her eyes watching me in the mirror as I contemplated the shape of her body. "Nothing boxy on the top. I'd suggest skipping the traditional suit jacket and skirt set."

"Agreed." Q held a piece of white cashmere next to her face. "White isn't flattering to her coloring."

"Is that bad?" she asked.

"No, sweetheart, it just means we'll have to substitute warmer tones. And thankfully, this time of year there's an excess of color." Q looked to me. "Ready?"

"Let's do it." I smiled at Gabi. "Time to be a walking clothes rack."

"You're making me come with you?"

We both gave her a stern look.

"Fine. But are you letting me choose any items? Or am I not allowed to pick anything?"

"Fair question. Unless a piece we choose has some kind of violent trigger reaction for you, you don't get to nix anything before you try it on," Q said.

"Understood."

Q looped his arm through hers. "Don't look like we're dragging you to the gallows, darling."

"I'll try. But no promises."

Two hours and five stops later we were back in the design showroom.

Q shooed us away as he grouped the items together to create his magic.

Gabi paced the perimeter of the room. Finally she said, "How often do you do things like this?"

"You're the first woman I've ever brought to my stylist," I replied.

Her eyes met mine. "Really?"

"Really."

"That is flattering. But I guess my question wasn't clear. I meant how many times a year do you meet with Q?"

"Four. During each change of seasons."

"Do you shop on your own? Like . . . hey, I feel like hitting the mall today for some new jeans. Or does he procure your entire wardrobe?"

"The truth is, I don't enjoy shopping. My style would be much different if I had to find pieces at menswear stores. I'm aware how fortunate I am to be able to outsource that task. Q has full access to my closet. Before we meet, he goes through my clothes and pulls the pieces that have outlived their usefulness or are out of style. Then he finds replacement pieces or full outfits and I try them on to check fit, et cetera. I choose what to keep and he returns what I don't buy. All my suits, and shirts for those suits, are custom tailored, which is different than ready-to-wear, because creating a look from scratch takes more time."

"What happens to your old clothes?"

"Higher-end pieces he consigns with a boutique group that operates all over the U.S. The rest are donated."

Gabi stared at me.

"What?"

"This is just a whole other level. I mean, I work for Jax and I can be at ease with him now and think of him as just Jax, not THE Jaxson 'Stonewall' Lund. I know he has money, but besides his penthouse apartment and his various businesses, I don't see his wealth. But seeing you with Q? That's when it sinks in that you are part of one of the wealthiest families in the country. This is normal for you. It won't ever *not* be normal for you."

I wasn't sure how to respond. Her tone hadn't been accusatory or laden with jealousy. Either of those attitudes I could deal with. What had thrown me? Was it the sense that this was the first time she'd had to remind herself today that she'd stepped foot into my world, and that made her see me in yet another light? And she'd yet to decide whether that was a favorable light.

Q returned with clothes draped over his arm. "All right, Gabriella. Into the dressing room with you."

"I'm fine stripping where I stand."

What the actual fuck? Was this her way of poking me for asking earlier if Q wanted her to strip?

That even caught Q off guard. "I assumed—"

"Let's clear those assumptions up. Does this place have walk-in clientele?"

"No. The side entrance you two initially used has been locked." He sent me a reprimanding look.

"Then we're good. It'd be a waste of time for me to troop into the dressing room, get dressed, troop back out here so

Nolan can weigh in, then return to the dressing room out of some false sense of modesty. I've been on hockey teams since I was eight years old. The one issue I don't have is being undressed in semipublic. Since I won't be getting totally naked at any point, then I don't have to worry about either of you leering at my lady bits. Doing all of the outfit changes right here will save a ton of time. I know you're both very busy men and I've already wreaked havoc on your schedules today. So let's do this." She paused. "Oh, and by staying out here I have the added benefit of hearing firsthand anything good, bad or indifferent about how I look and not whispered behind my back."

Guilt prodded me but I managed no reaction.

Q clapped his hands. "Excellent plan. Nolan, you take the chair on the right."

Turning, I walked to the sitting area as she started to peel her leggings down her legs. After adjusting the chair, I plopped onto the cushy seat. Now I had a much clearer line of sight.

And what a sight it was.

Holy shit. I'd known Gabi had curves; I just hadn't known they were like *that*.

Ka-fucking-pow curves that knocked my damn brain offline.

Muscled quads. Delineated calves. Her powerhouse shoulders, carved biceps and triceps rippled as she tossed the sweater she'd just removed onto the floor.

Thankfully Gabi was chattering to Q, which meant she couldn't see that my focus had gotten stuck on the bands of black lace underwear that hugged those firm, round cheeks. When I looked away, my gaze snagged on the three-way mirror that showcased the front of her body. The swell of her hips. The flat plane of her stomach, which boasted a six-pack. And those lush breasts.

Not in competition form anymore, my ass. This woman had *no* competition. I'd never seen a body that equaled hers.

Never. And I'd been up close and personal with my fair share of scantily clad females.

"Right, Nolan?"

I glanced up, guiltily apparently, because Q harrumphed.

"Were you even listening?"

"No, I wasn't aware I was part of the conversation."

He started to chew me out further, but something stopped him and he spoke to Gabi. "Let's start from the top. I'll hand you the pieces."

Gabi slipped on the first outfit. A short corduroy skirt in cranberry with navy buttons down the center and a light-weight cashmere turtleneck in dark blue.

"Do I need to put on the tights to get the whole effect?" she asked.

Q shook his head. "Love this on you. Add a patterned scarf and you'd turn heads. But for your interview—"

"It's much too casual," I supplied.

"Who picked this one?" she said.

"I did," Q admitted. "Some women pull off casualwear as if it's couture. I needed to see where you landed."

Gabi untucked the sweater and yanked it over her head. "Where am I putting the discard pile?"

"On the chair by Nolan."

She'd be strolling over and stripping right next to me? Or she'd strip in front of the mirror and then stroll in her bra and panties right next to me? So either way she'd be half-naked right next to me?

I should get a freakin' Oscar if I could pull off unaffected with Gabriella "The Body" Welk whipping clothes on and off *within touching distance* as if it was no big deal.

To her credit, she acted as if I wasn't even there. She removed the outfit, draped it across the back of the chair and moved to stand next to Q.

"You know, since I want to see shoes with these upcoming outfits, maybe you should slip on a pair of nylons."

"No problem, but I'm not shimmying into the nylons out here because that is the definition of undignified."

"Then you might as well put on the next outfit in the dressing room." Q bent down and pulled out a shoe box. "You carry these, I'll grab the clothes."

I had to give Gabi credit; she didn't dawdle. She strolled back out of the dressing room and stopped in front of the three-way mirror.

The expression on her face? Stunned.

"What?" I said. "You don't like it?"

"No. I love it. That's why I'm so surprised. I never would've picked this for myself."

I'd chosen these clothes for her. A pair of wide-legged gray pants that skimmed her ankles. The fabric tied at the waist gave the illusion of a skirt until the side slits revealed her legs. Subtle, sexy and sleek, especially paired with the simple cream-colored lace blouse that boasted a keyhole neckline and sheer chiffon sleeves. The ensemble was tied together with black-and-cream-checked cloth pumps, the toes and heels of the shoes highlighted with gray suede.

"Wowza," Q said. "That one is definitely a contender."

"I think so too."

Gabi spun around with the grace of a runway fashion model. "Thank you, Nolan."

"You're welcome. I suspected it'd be a fantastic look on you."

"I'm beginning to suspect our Gabriella will look fantastic in everything," Q gushed as he grabbed outfit three and thrust it at her.

"How many outfits have you assembled for her?"

"Twelve. More if I can mix and match. Why?"

Because seeing her nearly naked every five minutes is making me hard. "I just wondered if you planned on working through lunch or if we were taking a break."

"How about we decide after outfit six?"

"Perfect."

Gabi made a sound and I refocused on her, seeing her totally bewildered by the shirt she had on. "This is weird. Is it supposed to be tucked in? Or left out?"

"Both. That is what we call a half tuck." Q took the bottom of the shirt hem and tucked it neatly inside her ankle-length pants the color of tobacco. "Voila. Now you're on trend." Then he circled her with a critical eye. "Love the window-pane pattern and fit of this blouse, but it might be better to replace the shirt with a sweater in the same pattern." He snapped his fingers. "If we switched these slim-cut pants to looser velvet pants in the toasted-chestnut color and added fur-lined boots, she'd be ready to rock rinkside interviews."

"Sounds doable, but I need to see all of it on her, not just a description of it."

While Q muttered and slid hangers on the rack, Gabi stood in front of the mirror, turning this way and that.

I couldn't look away.

Huskily she whispered, "You like?"

"Very much. But you're supposed to be taking it off."

Keeping her eyes on mine, she slowly undid her blouse.

One.

Fucking.

Button.

At.

A.

Time.

I ground my teeth and said, "Gabriella."

Her little smirk indicated she liked torturing me.

My balls were sweating by the time she sauntered past me to drape the shirt over the clothes rack.

Then she bent over after she'd shimmied the pants down her legs and reached for the sweater Q had mentioned.

That ass—that goddamn smackable, bitable, perfect ass was right fucking there, just twitching for a sharp nip of my teeth.

Lund. Get your shit together.

My thoughts scrolled back to her text from last week, when I'd jokingly called her a pain in my ass and she'd retaliated by threatening to send me a pic of the *real* pain in her ass, which was a bruise the size of an orange.

Maybe if I squinted, I could see the mark on her skin through the nylons and those black lace panties. I could offer to kiss it and make it better.

Then Gabi was nearly nose to nose with me. "Were you really eyeballing my butt, Lund?"

"You were shaking it in my face," I said smoothly. "Where else was I supposed to look?" I gave her a tiny head-butt and whispered, "Besides, you started it, Miss Striptease."

"Fine. I'll behave if you will."

Not a chance, sweetheart.

"That ship has officially sailed for us." My eyes searched hers. "Or am I wrong?"

"No. But I'm not having this convo with you when I'm half-naked." Gabi snagged the pants from Q and she had to hop to get them up over her muscular thighs.

Hopping caused her breasts to bounce beautifully, sexily— even when she wasn't trying to be sexy.

Well, at least you aren't staring at her ass anymore.

Not that I could point that out as a victory.

She slipped the sweater on and my focus returned to styling her.

"Nope. I don't like that, too bulky. Can't see her shape at all. If we paired the windowpane shirt with that longer open-cut shearling vest and those pants, still keeping with the half-tuck style on the shirt, she'd throw off a professional-chic boho vibe."

"Marvelous idea, Nolan."

Gabi huffed.

I withheld a snicker. She had stuck to the parameters by not commenting on the outfit when it was obvious—maybe only to me—she didn't want to try it on.

But she did put it on without complaint.

And she looked freakin' fantastic.

I knew it, she knew it. She said, "This goes in the *yes* pile for sure. Can I take this off now?"

"Yes," Q said to her. "This one next. I need to see it on before we can discuss shoe and accessories options." He leaned in and whispered to her.

A long sigh. "I'll get dressed in there and take the shoes in with me. If you don't like the pair I choose, I'll switch."

"Fair enough."

She plucked up two boxes of shoes and stuck her tongue out at me before she disappeared.

Normally Q and I chatted during our appointments, but it seemed we both had other things on our minds.

The instant Gabi rounded the corner, before she said a single word, I knew.

"This outfit," she nearly shouted to the rafters. "This is *it*. From the moment I tried it on I felt confident. Like me . . . a better-dressed me, to be sure, but it doesn't feel as if I'm playing a role."

Q had kept the ensemble he'd chosen a surprise. An olive-green pantsuit, sleeveless, cut fairly low, ruched at the waist with a wide belt. The style of the trouser section of the pant-suit wasn't cut slim or wide, but a flowing cut, somewhere in between. A silky gold camisole beneath the top gave a sensuous movement to her breasts, so I knew she wasn't wearing a bra. She carried a brown leather bomber-style jacket, but even without Gabi wearing it I could tell it was a fitted cut. On her feet were suede brown fringed booties that matched the belt.

"Gabi. Darling. That is perfect. *Perfect*," Q declared. "I've got just the purse for that and we'll do understated gold-toned accessories."

"Okay." She gave Q an unsure glance. "You are writing all of this down for me, right? Which pieces go together? Because I'll get this stuff home and I won't remember."

"Of course."

"What's left to try on?"

Q cocked his head as if he didn't understand. Then he did the Vanna White sweeping gesture with, "All of this."

The look on her face . . . I knew we'd lost her. Personally, I'd stick it out until I'd exhausted all options, but Gabi wasn't like me.

I pushed to my feet. "Frankly, Gabriella's chosen what she needs."

The relief in her eyes made me feel like I'd slayed a dragon for her.

"With the exception of a dinner dress." I walked over to the rack, plucking off the cerulean-blue cocktail dress I'd chosen for her, and moved to stand in front of her. "Try this one and I promise we're done."

She nodded and sidestepped me.

But Q stopped her to hand over a box of shoes. "That dress is plainer than I'd pick, so your shoes have to make a statement."

Miss "I Can Strip Naked in Front of Anyone" had gotten more modest during the fashion show-and-tell—which I found fascinating as I watched her duck into the dressing area.

As soon as she was gone Q glared at me.

"What?"

"She—"

"Doesn't enjoy this," I supplied. "Not like I do."

That's when I realized I'd played right into his hands.

Q smirked. "If she's finished and your day is cleared for a few more hours, we have time to look at spring styles. Sam sent me your appearance schedule for the month. The only event I'm concerned with is the Grant Foundation Gala. Not black tie, but it will require a new suit. The fabric I've chosen is this gorgeous . . ."

Right then Gabi sashayed past us.

Speaking of gorgeous. The woman was stunning. The harsh line of the dress left her right shoulder bare as it swept up into an open, diagonal slash from between her breasts to the left side, revealing a peek of her skin. The skintight cut of the fabric showcased her physique—from those broad shoulders and muscular arms down to the nipped-in waist and the flare of her hips, ending right below her knees. The pumps she wore were a shade of blue darker than the dress, with silver studs outlining the sole and smaller rhinestones creating a starburst effect on the toes. The stiletto heel was shiny silver.

My damn mouth went so dry I couldn't speak, so I merely motioned for her to turn around.

The back of the dress mimicked the front except the diagonal slash was wider, revealing more skin.

And that ass. Wrapped in silk . . . the only way it would be better was when that ass was wrapped in my hands.

Gabi spun back to face us, and I blanked the lust from my face. "God. I love this. But I peeked at the tag, Q, and this one dress is my budget for this entire shopping spree. So I'll have to pass." She glanced over her shoulder at herself in the mirror and sighed. "Too bad."

"Darling, the reason I told you not to look at the tags is so you wouldn't misread them. That dress is one hundred dollars, not one thousand."

She studied him—and then me—with skepticism. "Really? How convenient. What about the shoes?"

Q laughed. "Oh, *those* are five hundred bucks . . . if you buy them outright. But we picked up all these accessories at Cindi's Attic—the couture rental store."

"Rental? I don't remember it saying that on the sign."

"It's not advertised on the marquee but that's what it is."

That stubborn jaw notched higher in disbelief. "That's a thing?"

"Yes. How many working women can afford to buy special-occasion accessories outright? They do a booming rental business. Cindi's Attic is the owner's tongue-in-cheek reference to Cinderella, the ultimate borrowed-clothes girl."

"So I can afford this?"

WANT YOU TO WANT ME   137

"Absolutely. I'll find a purse to go with this ensemble. I'll accessorize all of your outfits from Cindi's Attic, giving you a separate list of rental pieces and return dates. But usually, the rental is for a full month."

She jumped up and down—in heels—she was so excited. "This has been amazing, guys, thank you."

Her joy was infectious. Q and I high-fived, grinning like idiots.

"Okay. So I'm set. I'll just change out of this."

Wasn't until she was out of sight that I could breathe again. I leaned over to Q and whispered, "Bill me the difference for that dress. I'll handle the accessories, but find a 'rental' deal on a silver mink cape and bill me for that too."

He nodded.

"Whatever fabric you've picked for my suit for the Grant Foundation Gala better match that dress."

"I thought you weren't together," Q said slyly.

"We're not." I flashed my teeth. "Yet."

After Gabi dressed, she received a phone call about filling in for a sick referee for a high school playoff game ASAP, so she called an Uber to take her back to LI and we skipped lunch.

Q showed me the fabric for the suit and I approved it. Then we agreed he'd do the quarterly purge of my closet on Thursday and I sent him the updated security code.

I finished earlier than I'd planned so I called my cousin Zosia, who was in town for other LI business.

We met at Spoon and Stable in the bar, since the restaurant didn't open for another hour.

The first thing that popped into my head after my cousin demanded, "What the hell is going on at LI?" was she and Gabi would get along great. They were both strong women, working in what was typically considered a male-dominated field.

Both liked to poke my buttons. And I loved it when both of them did it.

"What do you mean, what's going on at LI?"

"You cancelled my meeting with you."

"Postponed," I corrected. "But I thought you'd planned to meet with Ash today too?"

She rolled her fingers on the bartop, waiting to speak until the bartender delivered our mugs of Utepils Skölsch beer. Mugs held aloft, she said, "*Skål*."

"*Skål*." I swallowed. "Now start talking."

"I'll ask you a random question. Did you know that in addition to getting the fisheries licenses grandfathered in, that we still have a commercial distillation permit from after prohibition ended?"

I blinked at her. "What?"

"Exactly. I checked the permit with the city, county and state. It is still legal and valid. License is assigned to Lund and Sons."

"Zoz, where in the hell did you find that information?"

"In the abandoned building that used to serve as the north branch of Lund and Sons, before it was Lund Industries. There's an interior room that's literally a walk-in safe, locked and chock-full of paperwork."

"How long has it been abandoned?"

"Since prior to the computer age."

"All the information is just sitting there?"

"The small brick building was shuttered after daddy-o let the business go tits-up. There's a chain-link fence around it that deters vandals. Although no one from LI has stepped foot in it for years, it still gets a biweekly security sweep. Which is what got me to wondering about it in the first place." She paused to drink again. "What could be in there that requires security LI is willing to pay for? Especially after you bailed us out and then bailed."

"No excuses, but I had nothing to do with that decision."

"I know. We've rebuilt the charter boat business and restructured the fishery. But I'll remind you, Lake Superior freezes over. We've got a helluva lot of free time on our hands that we could be using to rebuild the Lund name in Duluth/Superior, not just one business."

I forced myself to unclench my jaw and take a slow sip of my beer. Part of what I'd been doing at LI the past two years was revisiting existing LI subcompanies and properties to see what could be salvaged from within. Dealing with acquisitions remained my least favorite part of my job. But anytime I'd brought up options, such as beefing up the businesses we'd already invested years in, suggesting our investment money would be better spent there than literally buying a whole new set of problems, I'd been summarily dismissed.

Zosia set her hand on my forearm. "I see your frustration. We've talked about this before—you, me and Zeke. The truth is Zeke is capable of running the fishing/shipping/charters side himself. The timber side and the mining side have mostly been sold off, not a ton of paperwork or profit there for me to work with. The ag side of the Lund family is a separate entity that sells to LI, and I know no one at corporate deals with Thomas and David Lund, but both those families have things well in hand with Lund Farms. They keep in touch with me. What I don't like is when I have to hear from the damn chamber of commerce that a Lund subsidiary purchased one of the heavy equipment companies in my town."

I narrowed my eyes at her. "You heard this thirdhand?"

"That's why I was so pissed and wanted to talk to someone in the big three chairs at the home office. Did *you* know?"

"Maybe. What's the name of the company?"

"Equipment Service Products. They make the specialty equipment for the telecommunications industry like cable rollers, boom cranes, articulating cranes and digger derrick trucks. Rumor was they were headed toward Chapter 11 and then LuTek bought them out." She scrutinized me. "LuTek rings a bell?"

"It's a subsidiary of LI. I'm surprised *you're* familiar with it."

"I wasn't until someone outside the family told me about it," she retorted.

"The LuTek subsidiary is on the software side, or at least, that was the category the company was *supposed* to fall into."

"So you didn't know about this acquisition?"

I shook my head. Fuming. Embarrassed. Trying to pretend I was neither.

Zosia drained her beer and signaled for another. "If you don't know about this kinda shit as CEO in training, then I'm screwed."

Christ. I'd bite. "Screwed as far as . . . ?"

"Getting anyone on the LI board to reinvest in some of the smaller ideas I've been kicking around to ramp up revenue. The distillery for instance. Big market for artisanal spirits."

I groaned. "Please don't tell me you want to open a damn bar too?"

She laughed. "No way. I aim to own the creation aspect of the liquor business, not throw people out on their asses at one A.M. every weekend after they've had too much to drink."

"What else?"

"I've got ideas that'll capitalize on the resurgence of manufacturing up here, but to be frank, after the chilly response I got today, I don't know that I want to share those ideas with LI. They'll get passed on and passed over. We don't owe LI anything except gratitude for keeping us afloat when we needed it—but as of last year, we've repaid our debt. That building, and everything in it, belongs to me, Zeke and Zach. We can do whatever we want with it and we can procure our own investors."

"Your brothers are on board with this?"

Zosia nodded. "Like I said, Zeke loves the charters and fisheries stuff. Zach hates it. I'm . . . meh. It's provided us a decent living, but it's never been my dream job."

A decent living. At that moment I hated my grandfather

Jackson Lund for cutting off his youngest brother, Grover, and casting him out of the family business, and doing the same thing with his other brother, Lincoln, who'd ended up with the ag side of Lund Brothers. Our family fortune should be shared with these Lunds. Did I have an idea how to do that? No.

She squeezed my wrist. "What's going on in that head of yours, Nolan?"

"Guilt, mostly." I sighed and ran my hand through my hair. "I don't remember the last time we saw Thomas or David and their families. A hockey game probably. If not for you, we wouldn't have any contact with your branch of family."

"It comes from being the middle child. I'm the peacemaker and brutally honest. None of us have any misconceptions about what kind of man our dad was. He was a mean, drunken asshole. Hell, I'd've kicked him out of the family too."

I snorted.

"His shitty nature was why he didn't start having kids until he was in his sixties—my mom was a last resort. I'm glad that Zach doesn't remember much about him. Dad would've beaten him down just because . . . he doesn't fit a mold." She smiled at the bartender when he slid another beer in front of her. Then she looked at me. "Thank you so much for asking Zach to be part of your LCCO event on Saturday. It means a lot to him."

"Happy to have him. Will he get pissed off if I ask about his plans after he graduates from UMD this spring?"

"No. I'll be honest . . . the reason I've been pursuing these other options is because I don't want Zach to leave after he graduates. I get it if he wants to move away and do something on his own to make his mark in the world. But as he and I have discussed, he'd stay if he had the right opportunities. So I'm trying to find a way to provide that for him. For all of us." Zosia smirked at me over her beer. "Fair warning, I will tell Zach that we talked about this so when he sees you this weekend, he won't be blindsided if you ask him a bunch of questions."

"No problem. And be assured that what we've discussed won't go any further than us."

"I appreciate it."

"I will presume to ask one thing, though."

She cocked a brow at me.

"Don't go after any investors before letting me sort though some of your ideas. I'd like to see all of the things you've found as potentials. Then I'll run some numbers—all on my own time."

"You can do that?"

I tried not to bristle. "Just because I don't have fifteen finance degrees doesn't mean I can't figure out positive and negative correlations in the business world."

"I never said you couldn't, Nolan. If the other three big chairs at LI are making you feel that way, it sucks for you, but they're wrong. There's a reason I brought this to *you*. I'm just surprised you have time."

"What I've been doing at LI seems like busywork. More so this year than any others. I'll make time to do this because I know you're interested in what I have to say."

"Always. Now. Tell me about this barcade Dallas designed . . ."

We ended up eating dinner, drinking more than we'd planned, laughing a bunch, arguing even more, and it was one of the best evenings I'd had in a long time. So after I got Zosia settled in the Lund corporate apartment, I hired a car service to take me home.

Fourteen

GABI

I wasn't surprised to see Jax on Wednesday night; he usually watched Mimi's skills class. Nor was I surprised when he hung around after the start of my 14U class. However, I was surprised when he approached me to come into his office and tasked Margene with supervising my girls' practice. It had to be important if he expected me to take off my skates.

My stomach knotted at the thought of him finding out I was seeking other employment.

But how would he have heard that? Unless Wolf Sports North had contacted him for my references. Yet, that didn't make sense since my interview wasn't until Friday.

The other possibility? Nolan had spilled his guts. But again, I didn't buy that scenario. I'd like to think he'd fire off a warning text if Jax was gunning for me.

Once I ditched my skates, I had no choice but to show up in my sock-clad feet for the meeting.

Jax's door was open, but I knocked anyway.

"Hey. Come in and close the door."

I forced myself not to blurt out apologies and explanations when he subjected me to that cool-eyed stare. Throat dry, I swallowed once and managed to get out, "What's up?" without my voice wavering.

"Remember our conversation a few months back about my interest in playing hockey occasionally with other retired NHL players?"

"You got a line on making that happen?"

"Could be. A bunch of guys will be in town for the Hockey Legends exhibition prior to the Wild game tomorrow night."

I frowned. "I hadn't heard anything about that."

"Exactly. It's a surprise for fans. We'll only play one period, divided into two, with a ten-minute break in between. Doesn't add any additional time to the length of the event time for attendees, since there won't be any of the pregame stuff before the Wild take the ice."

"Bonus for fans, fun for you. Win-win. Congrats."

Jax drummed his fingers on the desk as he studied me. "You're wondering . . . what does this have to do with me?"

"You want me to referee? Since I did such a bang-up job when you and the Hammer went one-on-one?"

"No. I want you to play on my team for the exhibition."

My entire body went still. "What?"

"Lemme backtrack. I'm captain for the Western Conference and Griz—Lucas Griswold—is the captain for the Eastern Conference, since the Wild are playing an Eastern Conference team. When Griz and I agreed to do this last week, it was only on the condition that we could pick our teammates. A total of twelve, including ourselves."

I whistled. "Even with it only being one period, your lines will have to do ninety-second shifts."

"Yeah. So while it's a shortened game, it'll still be as grueling for us. I picked my teammates based on their current level of fitness." He flashed a sharklike grin. "Just because it's for fun doesn't mean I won't school those fuckers on the other team."

"Agreed. But where do I come in?"

He ran his hand through his hair. "I know it's short notice, but Drakken has a conflict and can't make it. Griz and I agreed that we didn't have to share our teammate lists with each other. So today, not only did I get a call from Drakken that changed my lineup, but a source who shall remain anonymous let me know that Griz has a woman on his team."

"While I should be flipping cartwheels that a woman is finally playing in an NHL exhibition game, that won't be the case when I find out who it is, will it?"

Jax shook his head.

"Who?"

"Amelie SanSimeon-Wipf."

Fuck me. "Seriously? Of all the fantastic women players Griz could've picked, he chose *her*?"

"I'm guessing it's because they're both Canadian. Griz also selected her brother, Gerard SanSimeon, for his team."

I flopped in the chair. "So . . . what? Griz was just gonna spring this on you?"

"Apparently. My source also claims he wants to show support for the Canadian Women's Ice Hockey Team, and he knows that a female Olympic-winning medalist playing in the NHL exhibition will get big buzz once the media gets wind of it."

"While I find that admirable for women's hockey as a whole, Team Canada *lost* the gold medal to the U.S. team, so he's essentially downplaying *our* win in *our* country by not inviting one of *our* players to participate."

"My thoughts too. Which is why I want you on my team tomorrow night, Gabi."

"I appreciate that, Jax. But like I said, you should ask a member of the U.S. Olympic Women's Ice Hockey Team to play. I can give you a list of names, three of them are even local."

Another cool stare from the man known throughout the league as Stonewall.

"What?"

"You've won two silver medals in the Olympics. SanSimeon-Wipf has won one. That's a better matchup in this case."

I leaned in. "Jax. I fucking hate her."

"I know." He grinned. "Here's where I remind you that you'll be playing in a men's hockey league, so you're not expected to abide by that asinine 'no checking' rule like in women's hockey."

Holy shit. I could fuck up her world as payback for the "accidental" hit she put on my teammate Bethany that literally knocked her out of the World Cup.

He laughed. "*Now* she gets it. So are you in?"

"Totally one million percent in."

"Awesome. We're having team skate here tomorrow morning at nine. You'll meet the guys, we'll discuss game strategy, and go over last-minute details regarding the exhibition."

"Sounds good."

"One other thing. You can't tell anyone about this. I'm locking down this facility tomorrow all day, so if staff asks you what's going on . . ."

"I'll say I don't know."

"Given the shit the last owner pulled, I hate keeping them out of the loop. But it's only for a few hours. I plan on leaving them all tickets for the game at the box office." He paused. "Do I need to have them hold any tickets for you?"

I oughta give Dani the chance to attend, even if she passed on it. It'd be a dick move not to include a ticket for Tyson. My former teammates Mariah and Amy would love to see me give trash-talking Amelie SanSimeon-Wipf—aka Asswipf—an ice facial or ten. "Four tickets would be great."

"Done. Now finish out your class. If I send you home, Margene will get even more suspicious and she'll be plenty pissed tomorrow when I give her the day off without explanation."

A million things danced through my mind as I reentered the rink, but foremost was checking my stick stash and my game skates before practice in the morning. I'd just laced up my right skate when someone plopped down across the aisle from me.

"Heya, Coach," Nolan said nonchalantly.

My head swiveled around. The instant my eyes met the intense blue of his, I felt a flutter in my belly and a warm tingle in my chest.

Which immediately morphed into panic when he said, "Everything okay? Margene said Jax called you into his office. He didn't find out about your . . . Friday thing, did he?"

Friday thing. The interview.

Shit. How had I forgotten about the most important thing in my life of late?

I cleared my throat. "No, it wasn't about that."

Nolan relaxed. "Good."

I noticed he still wore office attire. A trendy maroon-colored wool suit with wide plaid stripes a vivid blue that matched his shirt, and a vest that accentuated his blue-and-maroon-checked tie. His suit pants were the slim cut he favored, and he wore oxblood-colored oxfords and no socks. The man looked as if he'd walked off the set of *The Bold and the Beautiful*.

Not fair really.

"Gabriella?"

I'd secretly started to love the husky way he said my name. "Did you just finish working?"

"Yeah. Long day."

"And you stopped by here . . . why? Mimi's class is over. Are you meeting with Jax?"

"No. I'm here to ask if all went well with the handoff for the outfits today."

I filed away that "he's here to see me!" giddy feeling for later. "No issues, but I wasn't expecting any given Q's iron fist."

"I warned you he's a tyrant."

"Hmm. He reminds me of someone else I know." I tapped my chin in mock thought. "Who could that be, I wonder."

"Guilty. Along those lines I came to make sure you plan on taking it easy tomorrow night before your big Friday thing."

Uh no, I'm not. Actually, I'll be playing hockey in the men's league, a game which will likely be broadcast, as Amelie SanSimeon-Wipf and I break gender equality barriers and try to break each other's bones.

Not that I could tell him any of that.

How pissed off would Nolan be tomorrow night when he saw me suited up in hockey gear and not at home pressing my interview suit, and shooting bullets at the net instead of going over the bullet points of my last questionnaire?

Plenty pissed off.

I didn't answer; I focused on lacing up my left skate. Then I pushed to my feet and sidestepped onto the rubber mat. I smiled at him. "Thanks for checking on me, Nolan."

"Are you sure you're okay? You seem off."

"I am. I hate lying. I'll just be glad when this is over." I patted him on the knee before I stepped onto the ice. "Get some rest, Fancy Pants. You look like you could use it."

Fifteen

NOLAN

Fancy Pants.

And a fucking *knee pat*.

Gabriella Welk was the hardest goddamned woman to read that I'd ever met.

On Monday, when we'd found the clothing she needed to give her a visual edge for this interview, she'd shown me a vulnerable side of herself I hadn't expected.

She'd hugged me before she left.

And she'd held on.

And on.

During that wonderfully impromptu physical display, with her wrapped in my arms, her cheek to my chest, her hair tickling my chin, I was enveloped in the sweet cocoa bean, vanilla aroma that was all her.

I'd been thankful for the wool and down coats between us or she would've known how thoroughly her scent had aroused me.

Literally a dick move.

Not the first one I'd made one around her, probably wouldn't be the last. The more time I spent getting to know her, via our crazy text messages and her in-person antics, the more I realized my dickish diatribe about her not being my type had been completely true.

Had been.

Because that brash, crude, hard, unforgiving, judgmental Gabi . . . wasn't the real Gabi at all. Sure those attributes were part of her, but not all of her. Not even freakin' close. She'd shown me the loyal, funny, honest, playful and dare I say . . . sweet? side of her that was at the core of who she was. I found those characteristics appealing as hell.

So lack of attraction wasn't the issue for me now. Now I had it bad for her.

Real bad. Like show-up-at-the-damn-ice-rink-after-a-fifteen-hour-workday-just-to-see-if-I-could-get-her-to-smile-at-me kind of bad.

And when she had? I felt like I'd accomplished something monumental today.

This was after I'd negotiated a million-dollar discount on a software prototype LI was bidding on.

Just when I'd scrapped my idea to wait around and ask Gabi to dinner, my phone buzzed.

Caller ID read Ash.

I answered, "This is Nolan Lund."

"Why do you insist on doing that when you know damn well it's just me?" Ash complained.

Standing, I hustled up the incline that led out of the rink. "Maybe I'm someplace where I need to present a professional tone."

"Wrong. You're at the ice rink. I can hear the blowers going."

"I stopped in briefly to get verbal confirmation for a snag I'd hit for my LCCO event this weekend," I lied. "But it's all good. So what's up?"

"Honestly? I'm sick of my own company. Wanna grab a beer and some wings?"

"No work talk?"

"None."

"Excellent. Where do you wanna meet?"

"The only place to have wings: Branyon's."

"See you there in twenty." I wouldn't have time to go home and change. But my motto had always been better to be overdressed than underdressed.

I cranked on my audiobook for the drive, letting it distract me from my day.

Branyon's was busier than I expected for a Wednesday until I realized it was ladies' night. Luckily Ash had already snagged a booth in the back corner.

"Hey." I hung up my topcoat and then peeled out of my suit jacket before I sat down.

Ash eyed my shirt, vest and tie combo. "I'd look like a clown if I wore that. Looks great on you, however."

"Thanks."

"I ordered the appetizer platter, a dozen wings and a pitcher of Leinie's."

"Sounds good."

The waitress showed up with two frosted glasses and a pitcher. She filled our mugs and bailed.

"So you're sick of your own company, huh?"

"I've gotten into a rut." He swigged from his mug. "I'm partially blaming you for that."

"Me? What did I do?"

"Nothing. That's why I'm blaming you. We used to hang out all the time. Then Jax returns to town—"

"And yanks us both up short for using his failing bar business as our personal Cheers when we were supposed to be acting like the businessmen we are and helping him make it profitable?" I took a drink. "I'll take half the blame and the guilt."

Ash ran his hand through his blond hair. "Wow, you're really getting the hang of that."

"The hang of what?"

"Of breaking something down to its basest level to root out the problem."

I stared at him. "Jesus, Ash. Is that a compliment? Or an insult?"

"Both. Since I'm on the receiving end of both from you."

"What? Right now? You're not making any sense."

"Never mind."

Leaning in, I said, "Fuck that. I'm here. Tell me what's on your mind."

After a moment, he said, "It's embarrassing."

I didn't cajole him; I merely waited.

"Fine. I'm jealous."

"Of?"

"Of you and Jax spending more time together now that he lives here. Brady, Walker and Jens . . . you and me. We've hung out as a group our entire lives. For a while Brady and I were tight. Same with you and Walker. The three of them as brothers—no need to explain that. As the only girls, Annika and Dallas are more like sisters. Jax was an island of his own in Chicago. Which left you and me. Then when our cousins stared pairing off, we ended up hanging out more often. Which was cool, because we always got along. So like I said, now that your brother is back, it's just me by myself, and it sucks." He made rings on his bar napkin with the bottom of his glass. "I miss us doing shit together, cuz."

Not what I'd expected. Since he'd bared all, I could too. "I won't lie, it's been great having Jax back in the Cities. Sober, he's not a bad guy."

Ash snickered.

"But the brotherly camaraderie I'd started to establish with him faded awful damn quick when he and Lucy decided to give it another go. Don't get me wrong; I couldn't be happier for them. But at the same time, I'm aware that if I don't

WANT YOU TO WANT ME   153

make the effort with Jax, he won't. That doesn't mean he doesn't care. Oh, he'd realize after a couple of weeks that he hasn't really talked to me, then he'll try and make up for it." I paused. "Kinda like I'm doing now with you."

"Nolan. Just—"

"Let me finish. After Jax took us to task for our lax handling of his bar, we avoided hanging out together for a while out of guilt. For me, it seemed that translated into a tense work situation between you and me at LI, especially after being named future CEO. You treated me differently, so did Brady. I've been careful to stay in my own lane since then. That's not an excuse, Ash, it's the truth. I hadn't figured out a way to bring it up, so I just—"

"Decided working seventy-plus hours a week would prove your company loyalty?" Ash interjected.

"You know about that."

"Christ, Nolan, I *am* the COO, it's my job to make sure all the individual operations are running smoothly as part of the whole."

My neck flushed crimson and I reached for my beer. After a big gulp, I said, "So is this where you tell me to cut back on my hours? That you trust me not to make another huge financial mistake?"

He shook his head. "You need to be able to trust yourself. If that means you put in a shit ton of hours learning and discarding methods to earn that self-confidence, so be it. I've been there. So has Brady. It won't last forever, but man, when you're in the thick of it, it might seem like an eternity." He blew out a breath. "I thought we agreed not to talk about work?"

I shrugged. "We're in a family business. But on the personal front, I'll just say I'm glad you had the balls to bring this up and I'm sorry I've blown you off. I'll do better." I held my mug up and we toasted on it.

The food arrived. We jumped on it like hyenas so there wasn't much conversation.

After the plates were cleared, we both switched to soda.

Ash sighed. "When'd we get so old that we stop at one pitcher of beer?"

"Sad, ain't it."

"Next we'll be popping Viagra."

"I wish Dallas was here to demand you counteract that suggestion you just sent into the stratosphere, lest the universe believes it's a wish we want to come true," I teased.

Ash looked at the ceiling. "I retract that popping Viagra joke, universe."

"She is rubbing off on us."

"Tell me about it. I've agreed to try yoga with her when she gets back from belly dancing in Bali or whatever she's doing. I haven't seen her since the night of the pre-party. Speaking of the party . . . after my mom busted me lying about having a date, I never found out why you were minus a hottie on *your* arm?"

My brain conjured Gabi's image from that night. Not what she'd worn but the dismay on her face when she'd admitted she'd overheard the conversation at Buddy's. I wanted to crawl in a hole after that. But she'd accepted my apology with more class than I deserved and then we'd had a great time. So technically, I did have a hottie on my arm that night—she'd just been twisting it instead of hanging from it.

"Nolan?"

I looked at my cousin. "Sorry. I've been reassessing that aspect of my life too. Let me ask you this. Do you think I have a specific type of woman I'm attracted to?"

Ash blinked at me. "Whoa. Really? You want my honest answer to that?"

"Yeah."

"Okay. You like 'em easy. Tall and leggy. Hair color doesn't matter. Bra size doesn't matter. Age doesn't matter. Ethnicity doesn't matter. Most often intellect doesn't matter. You definitely don't like them pushy. You've been like that kid at a birthday party, who sees all these beautifully wrapped boxes of presents lined up and you open them one right after another, not caring what's inside because the next present might be better, it might have what you really want. But at the end of the day, you're just sitting amid empty boxes and you can't remember opening any of them."

I think my jaw might've hit the table.

Ash backtracked. He set his hand on my arm. "It's not like you're an asshole to them or anything. You're just up-front about them curbing their expectations when it comes to what you're willing to give them. They get one night, maybe two, but that's it. And a date doesn't necessarily mean they'll end up in your bed." He paused. "Am I wrong?"

"No. For some reason I thought that honesty would make me seem less shallow. But when I see it from a different perspective, it appears I have the depth of a sidewalk puddle."

"So make different choices going forward. Or don't. This wasn't a judgment call from me. You like what you like."

The question was . . . why did I prefer women like that? Had it always been that way?

No. I clearly remember dating the cute, funny, clarinet-playing geeky girl in high school. I'd also spent the first few weeks of college crazy about an in-your-face theater major.

I vaguely recalled a dormmate, a guy I'd thought had serious game, telling me to level up. To date girls worthy of my stature.

Then I remembered Jax had given me advice—aim high. Don't pick the low-hanging fruit because I'd develop a taste for them.

Apparently, I hadn't taken his sage advice. Then again, neither had he until he'd gotten back together with Lucy.

"Nolan. I didn't mean to piss you off."

"You haven't. It's hard to hear the truth."

"Tell me about it."

My gaze zeroed in on him. "Not that I'm deflecting, but what is going on with you? Since when do you have trouble getting a date?"

Ash blushed. "Since the only woman I'm interested in is the *last* one who should ever be on my radar."

"Why?" Several years ago Ash had gotten involved with his secretary and it hadn't ended well. I hoped for his sake he wasn't headed down that slippery slope of mixing business and pleasure.

When he leaned in, his eyes were a little wild. "I can't talk about it because it makes me crazy. So I'll just continue trying to ignore it. And her." He exhaled. "But goddammit. Some days—some nights, I'm like . . . but what if I'm missing out on something great?" He lifted his hand from the table in a stop gesture. "See? Even *I* can't believe the mixed signals I'm sending. How the hell is she supposed to react?"

I reached over and squeezed his hand. "I'm here whenever you're ready to be less cryptic, okay?"

"Well, well, what do we have here?" a deep voice sneered above us. "A couple of queers holding hands. How romantic. Oh, my bad. I meant how *disgusting*. Why don't you take your perverted PDA someplace else."

I glanced up at the guy—late twenties, big and bulky, obviously used to pushing his weight around.

I'd been bullied growing up. Now, I pushed back. "Nah. We're good."

"I don't think you understand, *homo*. I wasn't asking. I'm telling you to get the fuck out. We don't want your kind in here."

"What kind is that? The minding-our-own-business kind?" I asked.

He bent down close to treat me to a nose full of his onion breath. "You're about to get your sorry ass kicked."

"This tough-guy bullshit doesn't work on me. Back off now and I won't have to embarrass you."

"You? Embarrass me? That stupid-looking suit you're wearing is already embarrassment enough. Did your boyfriend make it for you? Did you suck his dick to say thank you?"

The scene played out in my head, me grabbing him by the

hair and smashing his face into the table. Could an EMT tell the difference between dried ketchup and dried blood?

Guess we were about to find out.

"I can't exactly get out of the booth with you standing there, can I?" I'd been so focused on him that I hadn't paid attention to his friends. Friends who stood behind him.

He took one step back, keeping his fists clenched and ready at his side. Eyes burning with the need to prove he wasn't all talk.

Great. I wouldn't get out of here without physical contact.

As soon as I stood, he punched me in the mouth.

And it was on.

His second punch grazed the side of my head and I was able to grab hold of his wrist. I brought it down hard, spun and turned his arm into a chicken wing, tucking it tightly against his back and using it to propel him forward, smashing his face into the table.

He howled.

His friends ran.

"Not so easy to spew hatred when your mouth is full of blood, is it?"

He whimpered, "Let me go."

"Nah. I'm happy to hold you until the cops show up."

"No! Don't call the cops!"

I looked at Ash. He nodded and pointed at the waitress.

"You took the first swing. Got a restaurant full of witnesses to attest to that fact. You were verbally abusive before that."

He thrashed hard and I dug my elbow into the side of his head to keep him still.

The manager shooed other patrons away.

Ash hadn't moved from his side of the booth. Cheeky bastard.

The cops arrived way sooner than I'd expected and took the guy off my hands.

I gave my statement, but the situation was pretty cut and dried. Bully loses and everybody wins.

"I oughta tell you, cuz, your lip is bleeding," Ash said.

"Shit. Did I get any on my shirt?"

His gaze swept over my top half. "Not that I can see."

"Good." I'd just slipped my suit jacket on when the manager returned.

"I'm really sorry this happened. Your meal is comped."

"Thank you."

Ash held out my topcoat and shoved my arms in.

The manager cleared his throat. "Just so you know, we pride ourselves on diversity in our waitstaff and our customers. Please come back."

"Just keep the bullying assholes out and we will."

As soon as we were outside, Ash threw his arm over my shoulder. "We should do this at least once a week. That was fun."

"Says the man *not* bleeding."

"I would've jumped in if you needed it."

"I know." I touched my hand to my mouth. I'd definitely be sporting a fat lip tomorrow.

When we reached the parking lot, he stepped back. "All the punching and bleeding and name-calling aside, I'm glad we met up tonight."

"Me too." I held my arms open. "We cleared the air. Now we hug it out."

He laughed and he returned my hug in that manly back-slapping way of his.

"Drive safe. See you at the office."

Sixteen

GABI

Skating with former NHL players was massively good for my hockey ego.

Even before we'd cemented the nitty gritty of the game plan for tonight, I'd had three of my new teammates tell me they'd watched me compete in the Olympics. And Rexall, the oldest man in the group, a player I'd grown up watching who was now a private skills coach, gave me props for sticking to my principles and walking away from my assistant coaching position at UND.

Then there was Matt "MM" McCoy, the hot, single goalie from Winnipeg who flirted with me incessantly.

That was good for my female ego too.

Rexall would serve as our coach. As team captain, Jax worked us hard. Since he and I were both centers, we wouldn't be on the ice at the same time during the game, but during practice, line one—his line—played against line two—my line—and we raced up and down the ice.

After a two-hour practice, we were dialed in as much as we could be.

I removed my helmet and peeled down my outer layer, which was soaked in sweat. I snagged a bottle of water and drained it, then grabbed another and plopped down at the end of the bench.

Jax remained on the ice, holding a clipboard. "Listen up."

Chatter stopped.

"Tonight at Xcel we're in the smaller locker rooms designated home. Eastern Conference players, EC for short, will be in the visitors' overflow locker room." He looked at me. "Will it be an issue for you, being in our locker room?"

"Nope."

"Good." Jax moved on to the next item on the agenda. "The uniforms aren't done now, but they will be hanging in your locker spaces by game time. Just a reminder that we don't have equipment managers, so bring your own gear: sticks, tapes, wax, et cetera."

"Yeah, don't forget your skates, Nils, like you did on that trip to the kids' hockey camp in Calgary."

Connor "Nils" Nilsin flipped off John "JK" Kingston and I remembered they'd been teammates for a time in Anaheim.

"The official program inserts will also be done by game time. During both breaks between periods, we will be set up to sign autographs on the inserts and provide photo ops for game attendees."

"Does that mean we're expected to wear our team jersey for the photo ops? Or are we expected to be in game day attire?" McCoy asked.

"Better be two sets of jerseys in that case, 'cause ain't no one wants to get close to us after we've played in them," Patrick "Parn" Parnell said.

"Eh, spray a little Febreze and they'll be just fine," Rexall said.

I snickered. He sounded just like my former teammate Dixie.

"You'll be in fresh jerseys." Jax grinned. "You'll also be on club level during the game."

That was a bonus.

"That's all I've got," Jax said. "If anything changes, I'll text you. So I'll see you at the Xcel players' entrance at five."

The guys headed to the changing room.

I stood. Before I made it halfway across the ice, Jax said, "Gabi. Hold up."

"Yes?"

"Look, you being in the men's locker room isn't ideal. But the other option was to have you share another locker room with SanSimeon-Wipf."

"Hard pass. I'd rather be stark naked center ice of the Xcel Center with a sold-out crowd than spend one second in an enclosed space with Asswipf."

"I figured. But to be honest, I'd feel more comfortable if there was another woman in the locker room looking out for you."

"You probably have a point." I thought about it for a moment. "How about Margene?"

"Perfect. I'll tell her."

I spent part of the afternoon prepping for my Friday interview and the remainder indulging in my pregame ritual of playing solitaire games on my phone.

On a whim and since the weather was decent, I decided to wear one of my new chic outfits to the arena. The gray wrap pants, paired with a peach-colored lacy camisole layered under the cream blouse with the sheer chiffon sleeves and the split ruffled collar. Since I probably wouldn't be in regular shoes for very long, I tossed the pumps in my travel bag to change into in the parking lot.

I'd packed my gear bag as soon as I'd arrived home from practice. Unlike NHL players, more often than not, women hockey players were in charge of hauling our own equipment. Several years ago I'd customized a suit bag for my gear. Long enough to contain my sticks with a separate zipped compartment on the bottom for my skates, tape and wax. Pads, socks, helmet and gloves filled the remainder of the bag space with one small slot in the top for a purse. It was heavy, but I'd added a wider, stronger metal hook on the top for ease of carrying.

Jax and Margene waited at the entrance for me with my stadium pass.

Margene whistled. "Lookit you, hot stuff. Damn, Gabi. You're quite the fashion plate."

I laughed. "This old thing?" But I was pleased that she'd noticed.

"Give Margene your bag."

"That's fine, Jax, I can haul my own gear." Even if I was wearing heels, I was still twenty-five years younger than Margene.

"As I'm aware. But Channel 9 Sports wants to interview you."

"Now?"

"Right now."

My stomach tightened. "Why me?"

"You're the first woman playing in a sanctioned NHL exhibition." He smirked at me. "Although you don't look like a hockey player right now."

"Har har."

"Come on, they're set up over here."

I followed Jax around the corner.

Lucas Griswold, who was currently in the hot seat, stumbled a bit over his words upon seeing me.

Jax snickered beside me. "Yeah, surprise, motherfucker."

We waited until the interviewer finished with Griz before we approached her.

"Pashma?"

A luminous Indian woman who I recognized as the core sports anchor for Channel 9 News, turned and beamed at

Jax. "You weren't just yanking my chain about giving me an exclusive, were you, Stonewall?"

"Nope." Jax turned, silently urging me to walk forward. "Pash, this is Gabriella Welk. She's part of the Western Conference team for tonight's Hockey Legends exhibition game."

I offered her my hand. "Pleased to meet you. I loved the piece you did on the growing popularity of girls' cricket."

That surprised her. "Thank you. I'm sorry to admit that I don't know a thing about you."

The man behind her leaned over her shoulder and read my entire, full-length bio from his phone. Out loud.

"Now I have a basis for this interview." She cocked her head, allowing a quick perusal of me. "You are interview ready, so have a seat."

Two high-backed stools faced each other in front of a white screen, with lights and other equipment overhead and an enormous camera in front.

Pashma handed me a microphone. "We can edit this, so no worries if you get stuck. That said, it's usually best to get it in one take."

"Understood."

"Talk to me, not to the camera. We're in our own bubble, just having a friendly conversation."

I nodded.

She perched on the edge of her chair, keeping her right foot on the floor and hooking the heel of her left shoe on the chair rung. Neat trick. That positioning gave her great posture and kept her clothes from bunching up. I'd have to remember that if I got an on-air position.

The stealthy assistant handed Pashma an index card and she scrutinized it before glancing up at the cameraman.

"Ready, Pash?"

"Ready." She smiled. "I'm at the Xcel Energy Center in St. Paul with an exclusive on tonight's pregame entertainment before the Wild take the ice. With me is my very special guest, Gabriella Welk. If that name sounds familiar to you, it should. Gabi is an icon in the world of women's ice hockey, having won two silver medals with the U.S. Olympic Women's Ice Hockey Team, two Four Nations Cups and three World Cups with the U.S. Women's National Team. She was also the first woman to be named assistant coach for a men's college hockey program. Tonight, she's making history again by playing in an NHL-sanctioned exhibition hockey game as a member of the Western Conference team. So welcome, Gabi, I'm thrilled to get to share this good news about your participation in this event."

Look at her, don't look at the camera. "Thank you, Pashma. I'm beyond excited to be here."

"What is the most exciting aspect of playing in tonight's game?"

"It's the opportunity to compete against, and partner with, some of the best male hockey players in the league. To be seen and treated as an equal."

"You've won international championships. You've played in both the National Women's Hockey League and the Canadian National Hockey League. You've coached on the college level. You even coached your younger sister Dani into a spot on the 2018 U.S. Olympic Women's Ice Hockey Team. Coming on the heels of their gold medal win, what do you see as the future of women's hockey?"

"Historically, more girls get interested in hockey after a major event like the Olympics. What I'd like to see is more women who grew up playing the game reactivating their interest and participation in it. The only way there will ever be any female coaches in the NHL is if hockey players and fans see women in all roles in the hockey world. Then they'll also realize that gender isn't as important as skill and passion for the game. We're still waiting for a female referee in the NHL and I can only hope team owners will give women a chance to prove themselves as coaches as well."

"Agreed one hundred percent. So back to tonight's game . . . you've never played together until today's practice.

How does the Western Conference team's talent stack up against your opponent's?"

"To be honest, the only player I know for the Eastern Conference is the team captain because Jax told us at practice. I have no idea who else we're facing on the ice, but regardless, I'm confident that we'll come out on top."

"Score prediction?"

"Two-one, Western Conference."

"Okay, you heard it here first, folks. Last question. Who do you consider the most influential female athlete in history and why?"

I said, "Billie Jean King," without hesitation. "Because she had the skill and the championships, but she also forever changed the way fans saw women's tennis and she fought for equal rights and equal pay for female players."

"Thanks for stopping by, Gabi."

I kept a smile on my face as Pashma faced the camera and finished the wrap-up. When the cameraman said, "Cut," I jumped up.

"Thanks for this. It was fun. But I've gotta get ready to play."

Jax fell in step beside me. "You are a natural in front of the camera, Gabi."

Here was a natural segue into a "funny you should mention that, Jax, but I have an interview tomorrow to try and make that a reality" type of comment.

Alas, I said nothing besides, "Thanks."

There weren't a bunch of people hanging around outside the locker room yet, so maybe we'd have a little time to get prepped in peace.

The guys were in various stages of undress as I walked in. I didn't gawk and neither did they. They gave me a rash of shit for being a camera hog, and I volleyed it right back at them—none of their faces were pretty enough for prime time, which just proved a locker room was a locker room regardless of gender.

Margene had found a semiprivate corner for me to change in, which I figured was as much for the guys as it was for me.

After I donned the underlayer, I ducked around the opposite corner to warm up with cardio. Jumping jacks first, which morphed into jumping frogs. Twists, toe touches, deep knee bends, ending that circuit with high-kneed running in place. Then I worked on upper-body strength. Pull-ups, push-ups, plank, downward-facing dog, which I transitioned into a handstand, followed by handstand push-ups with my toes touching the wall and my spine curved. A few more stretches, then I concentrated on neck and head rolls while I breathed to get my heart rate back into the normal range.

Then I joined the guys with my sticks, tapes and wax.

"So what's your tape job style, Welk? Ovie? Pasta? Orr?"

"Full blade. White tape," I said. "White with twisted gray sticky for the butt end. Boring."

By the time I'd readied both sticks, we had to warm up.

I walked across the rubber mats that stretched down the hallway until I felt that first blast of cold air that indicated we'd reached the arena. I took a deep breath and hit the ice.

I loved this sense of anticipation. The hard pull of my muscles that burned as I moved, no matter how much I'd stretched beforehand. The chill and the sounds of blades gliding and slicing across the ice. All familiar even when I was in a new place.

Then the Eastern Conference team emerged to skate.

I concentrated on doing my own thing and not tracking where my nemesis was, but she didn't grant me the same courtesy.

She skated around me. "Get used to that, Welsher."

"What? You always being a step behind me? Newsflash, Asswipf, I'm already used to it."

"No, me skating circles around you." Then she leaned over with her stick across her legs as if we were in a face-off. "Finally get to make you bleed tonight."

"My ears are already bleeding from the shrill sound of your voice." I skated off with my teammates.

In the locker room we listened to last-minute strategy. Made final adjustments to our gear.

My nerves didn't kick in until the announcer singled me out. Spotlight in my eyes, crowd roaring in my ears, I skated forward out of the lineup and waved. Then the announcer did the same for Asswipf.

MM got into position in front of the net. The first line spread out around the face-off circle and our second line returned to the bench.

Wipf didn't skate first line, which meant we'd be on the ice at the same time.

We'll see who draws first blood, bitch.

Jax won the face-off, sending Parn the puck. He wove through the EC defenders and passed the puck to Knight, which was intercepted by an opposing player. Then all the action moved down to the other end. MM saved a shot and then a rebound shot.

I got so engrossed in watching these guys play—hard to believe they were all retired—that I hadn't watched the clock to see my shift was up.

"Line two. Give 'em hell."

Jax was first in and I was first out. Parn passed me the puck and Nils took his place on the ice.

I had the puck across the blue line until a check on my left side caught me off balance. She stole the puck, passed it to a dude roughly the size of a bear and they hustled toward the opposite net.

Asswipf had turned this into a physical matchup ten seconds into us sharing ice time.

You want it that way? I'm in.

So I stayed in my lane down the center until I saw the forward looking for an open teammate. Wipf was open—until I checked her and reclaimed the puck.

My sprint across the ice earned me another hit, not from Wipf this time. But checking me just sent the puck to Nils and he took a shot.

Defended. No goal.

I zipped around to the corner and Wipf crashed me into the boards from the other side. I elbowed her hard in the gut, flipped the puck to the WC right wing. He was covered on both sides, sticks smacked and scuffed and then the EC center had the puck again.

We gave chase. When the EC center missed the shot on goal, I saw our forwards hanging behind the net, which meant shift change.

I wasn't tired but I breathed hard as I hopped the barricade onto the bench.

Nils panted, "Chick on other team. A friend?"

"No. I have better taste in friends than assholes like her."

He did a spit-take.

Our team had ramped up their aggression and they'd kept team EC on defense rather than offense.

Seemed by the time I caught my breath my line returned to the ice.

Wipf tried to welcome me back with a sneaky high stick, but I stiff-armed her.

While we were in our little skirmish, Wipf's brother Gerard passed her the puck but it sailed past her. Nils got it and took off toward the goal, with Wipf's brother hot on his heels and Asswipf on mine. Nils's shot was blocked. I rebounded and skated back to pass it to Knight. He didn't hesitate. A quick wrister and he lit the lamp.

A group hug, high fives down the line and we were in the face-off circle.

Me against Wipf.

"Gonna stuff you, Welsher."

I said, "Eat a bag of dicks," before I shoved my mouth guard in.

But that motherfucking smug bitch got me to jump and kicked out of the face-off.

Knight lost the face-off and we chased after the defenseman.

Or should I say, one moment I was eating up the ice and the next thing I knew, I was facedown and skidding on my belly across it.

The refs weren't looking at me, so they didn't see Wipf hook my skate with her stick and send me sprawling.

No matter. I popped up fast and rejoined the game. As much as I wanted to beat the fuck out of her, I couldn't let her distract me.

Even when she slammed me into the plexiglass hard enough to rattle my bones, I didn't retaliate.

The hits kept coming—not just from her. And these were big goddamned guys. By all rights I should've been lying on the ice clutching my cracked pride.

But I refused to give anyone that satisfaction.

After team EC scored on a freak breakaway and we were down to the last minute before the break, I zeroed in on Wipf as she cleared the backside of the net. I bodychecked her with enough force to knock her on her ass.

She sputtered at the refs about unnecessary roughness, but they'd moved on.

The buzzer sounded, signaling the end of the first half.

In the locker room I did some deep stretches. There wasn't much discussion on strategy—mostly the guys talked among themselves about the players they knew on team EC.

Jax sat next to me as I checked the tape on my stick. "So Wipf really has it in for you."

"And vice versa."

"What's the story between you two?"

I ran my finger over the tape lines on my blade. "Different philosophies. She's a dirty player and she pushes that hockey style on her teammates, regardless if it's on the Canadian national stage or on a women's team. She injured a teammate of mine, knocked her out cold during a semifinal game . . . but there's no checking in women's hockey, right? So she wasn't penalized at all. Plus when she is in the media spotlight, she never says anything positive about the sport, it's pure negativity about the opposing team. The final straw for me was last year when all of us on the Women's National Team threatened to boycott the World Cup if USA Hockey didn't provide us with better compensation, health insurance and per diem. Amelie spouted off to the *Toronto Star* about whiny American players believing they deserved more and acting like bratty children until we got it." I ground my teeth together. "She could've kept her mouth shut. Even that little sound bite she provided cast doubt about our intentions. But she just kept blathering, pretending to be the spokesmodel for female hockey players."

"Yeah, I can see that. When Griz introduced me to her before you arrived, she reminded me of the type of women Nolan used to date."

I snorted. I could see a leggy, vapid blond like her on his arm.

Type. Wait. Jax had said *type*. That was a very specific word choice.

I looked up. "Nolan *told* you about that?"

"I didn't give him a choice. I could see you were upset with him about something—you flipped him off during the eight-year-old skills practice, Gabi. That's not like you."

"Sorry." I picked at the tape. "When did he tell you?"

"The day after the Full Tilt pre-party. He indicated he'd apologized and you two mended fences. I was relieved to hear it."

"Do you and Nolan tell each other everything?"

He laughed. "Not on your life."

Whew.

"I'm just here to suggest, as team captain, if you wanted to give Asswipf a taste of her own medicine, don't be stealthy." He walked away.

Huh. First time I'd ever been encouraged to stir some shit. Guess that's what the hockey stick was for.

Rexall moved to address us. "You all looked good out there, but not great. Let's give these fans a show. I wanna see a faster pace, more aggressive playing and some hotdoggin'."

I leaned toward MM and whispered, "Is that even a term applied to hockey players?"

"Nope. Like most coaches, he pulled something out of his ass and hoped it'd be inspirational to us."

Dammit. Did my players think the same thing about my pep talks before they played?

"Let's get a move on, people. One minute to ice time."

We had two minutes to warm up and the first line faced off. Wipf kept coming for me and I kept pushing back.

EC responded to our speed and pressure just the way we'd wanted them to: Gerard SanSimeon got called for tripping and we had the first power play of the game.

Jax sent a beautiful slap shot right into the back corner of the net.

With three minutes to go and after an icing call, the second lines faced off.

And Wipf's mouth started running.

"Your sister couldn't beat me in a face-off during the Olympics, remember?"

"All I remember was the light reflecting off all of those gold medals from Team USA. Oh, and you bawling and acting like a bratty kid with your silver. Embarrassing for you, Asswipf."

"At least I made the Olympic team representing my country. Wait, you were your sister's coach. No wonder she didn't do anything memorable during the games. Must run in the family."

I lunged at her, knocking her on her back. We slid out of the face-off circle with me on top of her, my gloves thrown behind me so I could rip her helmet off and punch her stupid face.

She shrieked after my first punch landed. Then she reached up and yanked my helmet off; her fingers clutching the wires of my face guard allowed her to smack me in the face. With my own goddamned helmet.

My helmet went flying and she threw an elbow into my mouth. I felt that popping gush of blood on my bottom lip, courtesy of my teeth breaking the skin. She followed that up with a head-butt that knocked me onto the ice.

I saw red. Not just the blood pouring out of my mouth. But the color of rage because this bitch was clearly winning this fight.

Then we were each hauled upright as the refs tried to break it up and separated us.

That gave me the chance I needed. I jerked free of the ref's hold and swung at her, my fist connecting with her jaw.

She went down.

I pounced on her.

She got one more good elbow shot to my cheekbone before she curled into a ball on the ice, her arms attempting to protect her head from further blows from me.

This time when the refs separated us, they kept a much tighter grip on our jerseys.

The head ref spoke into his headset and it connected with the stadium loudspeaker system.

"Players Welk and SanSimeon-Wipf are ejected from the game for unsportsmanlike conduct."

Cheers rang out.

We didn't have the luxury of escaping to opposite ends of the arena. But I'd be damned if I'd go first. I didn't trust her not to attack me from behind.

She bumped her shoulder into mine as she strolled past. I lunged for her, determined she wouldn't get the last jab in.

My captain held me back. "Easy," Jax said in my ear. "Let her go."

"But—"

"We'll talk later."

I left the ice to chants of "fight, fight, fight, fight."

Margene met me in the doorway to the locker room with a wet towel. "Gabi, what am I gonna do with you?"

"Point me toward the shower and get me an ice pack."

Despite the adrenaline rushing through me, I slumped back against the wall and attempted to calm down. Time passed in a pulsing blur as my injuries began to throb. I'd just yanked my jersey over my head when I heard a familiar voice yell, "Margene! Where is she?"

Fuck. I did not need this right now.

Nolan stormed around the corner and stopped.

"Jesus Christ, Gabriella, what the hell were you thinking?" As soon as he loomed over me, he seemed to take a moment to compose himself. He gently curled his hand below my jaw, tilting my head to inspect the damage. "Does it hurt?"

I snorted. "Ya think?" Then my gaze narrowed on his mouth. "What the hell happened to your lip?"

"Bar fight." He snagged the towel from me and started blotting my face.

"What? Since when do you—"

"You're not the only one who can take a punch when you're pissed off, Welk," he said with annoyance. "Hold still."

I jerked away from him. "Stop poking me."

He didn't. He kept wiping the spots of blood on my neck. "What are you doing here?"

Nolan grabbed my hand and cleaned the blood off of there too. "Jax gave me a ticket to the game, only telling me he was part of some NHL Hockey Legends pregame exhibition. When I got here, I saw you were on the player roster." He paused in his fussing over me. "Why?"

"Why what?" I sidestepped him and sat on the bench. Bending over to undo my skates hurt my damn ribs and I sucked in a loud breath.

Nolan tossed the towel aside and crouched down, batting my hands away to loosen my laces himself. "Why would you agree to play in an exhibition hockey game tonight, of all nights, when you have"—he briefly glanced over his shoulder, looking for Margene—"the interview tomorrow?"

I lowered my voice. "What was I supposed to say to *my boss* when he gave me this opportunity? Sorry. No can do. It conflicts with my new job interview?"

"Fine. I'll give you that. But how long had you known about this exhibition?"

"Jax told me last night. I didn't even consider saying no. It's a huge deal for me, Nolan."

"You think I don't know that?"

"Then why are you so furious?"

"Because you're bleeding."

"You didn't fuss this much over Mimi when she lost a tooth and was bleeding," I pointed out.

Those fiery blue eyes connected with mine. "This. With you and me? Not even fucking close to the same situation. Tell me you understand that."

Yikes.

I nodded.

Muttering, he pulled my skates off and set them aside.

I stood on the mat. When he pushed to his feet, the top of my head barely grazed his chin.

"And the fight?" He ran the backs of his fingers across my swollen cheek and jaw, studying me with such intensity that I shivered. "Did you consider saying *no* to getting involved with that?"

His touch was so soft it took all of my willpower not to lean into it and purr.

Okay, so maybe I did angle in a little.

"Gabriella?"

"No regrets about the fight. That's been a long time coming between her and me." I started to peel off my padding when Margene returned.

"Uh, Gabi, maybe Nolan oughta go while you get undressed."

"It's nothing he hasn't seen before." I made a *rowr* sound. "Right, tiger?"

He rolled his eyes. "Deflect. Distract. I'm telling you those won't work. We *will* finish this discussion." He spun on his heel and disappeared.

"Shower is warmed up for you. It's the only private one in this locker room so maybe you wanna get a move on before the team gets off the ice and tries to commandeer it."

I stripped and wrapped a towel around myself.

Margene walked with me to the shower. She held up a baggie of ice. "Nolan got this for you and said to use it."

Bossy man.

"I'm supposed to tell you from Jax to skip the jersey for the photo op. Wear street clothes instead. The fans will have some kind of sign to hold up that gives the event info, since none of your names are visible on the front of the jerseys anyway."

After stepping into the cubicle, the warm water hit me like a lover's caress, and I groaned.

"Everything all right?" Margene asked.

"Great. Except I didn't bring a bit of makeup with me and I have to stand in front of those bright lights for the photo ops. All you'll see on my face are bruises after I get the blood washed off."

"Nolan got you mostly cleaned up." Margene paused. "Why did he come down here?"

He hadn't considered how people might find it odd that he'd rushed to check on me. I found that unsettling and a tiny bit thrilling. Still, I had to deflect. "Probably my sister sent him."

"Oh. That makes sense. Anyway, I've got face powder. That's it."

"That'll work." I stood on my tiptoes and grinned at her over the top of the door. Fuck. Smiling hurt. "Thanks, Margene, you're a lifesaver."

Seventeen

NOLAN

Talk about losing your shit.

I'd lost mine in a big way when I watched Gabi pounce on the other player and start pummeling her.

It wasn't the fighting that got to me; I'd attended hundreds of hockey games and understood anger could overtake common sense in competitive situations.

But when I saw the blood spurt from Gabi's lip like some slow-motion horror movie, rage and terror consumed me in equal parts.

Everyone in the skybox jumped to their feet when the fight broke out. Behind me Gabi's friends yelled, "Go, go, go," and beside me my mother said, "Oh dear," but any other reactions didn't register as the blood rushing in my ears blocked everything else out.

The fight seemed to go on and on.

Even after both women had gotten to their feet, Gabi was on the receiving end of a haymaker that only caught her off guard for a millisecond before she retaliated.

The crowd went nuts.

Fucking vultures.

Before Gabi even left the ice, I'd bailed out of the skybox.

The elevator would take forever, so I flashed my all-access pass to the security guard and hoofed it down six flights of stairs. Then I hustled to the backside of the arena and took the stairs down to locker room level.

Of course upon seeing me, Gabi had acted more annoyed than injured.

As she bled.

While attempting to give her the TLC she deserved, I matched her brusque attitude and made it appear my concern for her was really admonishment for how busted up she'd be for tomorrow's big interview.

Such a fucking lie.

What I'd really wanted to do instead of taking her skates off was to sit in the corner of the locker room with her curled into me, holding her until she stopped shaking.

Instead I'd filled a bag with ice and passed it to Margene after she'd kicked me out.

Now here I was, lurking outside the locker room. Listening to her male teammates—including my damn brother—giving her kudos for getting tossed from her first NHL game.

There's something to be proud of.

But maybe for her . . . it would be.

Jax barreled out of the locker room and almost mowed me over.

"Nolan? What are you doing down here?"

As far as Jax knew, Gabi and I had declared a tentative truce after I'd apologized for the Buddy's incident. I couldn't tell him why I was concerned, so I picked a plausible reason for my presence. "Mimi saw the fight and the blood, and she asked if I'd come down and check on Gabi."

Jax's eyes narrowed. "Really? Because I just got a text from Mimi asking if Gabi could teach her to fight like that because it was the coolest thing she'd ever seen."

Jesus.

"So you wanna try again?"

I shoved my hands in my pockets and gave him my slickest smile. "Actually, no, I don't. See you upstairs." I strode off.

The perks of the skybox were comped food and drink, but I needed a shot to calm down before I returned.

Standing in line at the scotch bar, scanning the options of the twenty different varieties they offered, I heard, "Nolan?" from somewhere behind me. I turned and a brunette with big brown eyes smiled at me.

She sauntered closer; her two-sizes-too-tight GO WILD! T-shirt left the strip of skin above the waist of her skinny jeans completely bare. "I thought that was you." She gave me a once-over, from my Hermès tie to my royal-blue custom-tailored suit jacket and pants to my Tom Ford loafers and back up to meet my eyes. "You look good, but you don't look much like a Wild fan."

I'm not. "My brother, a former Blackhawks center, played in the exhibition game."

"Oh. Right. Can you believe what happened near the end? Crazy to see those two chicks fighting." She leaned closer, letting her breast graze my forearm. "You know they only did it for attention since no one really cares about women's hockey and they finally had people watching them."

It wasn't the first time I'd heard that type of comment and I hated that Gabi and other female players had to deal with this attitude—especially from other women. I flashed her a fake smile. "We'll agree to disagree on that point. Enjoy the game. I've got to get back."

She frowned. "But I thought maybe we could have a drink and catch up. It's been a while."

Not only did I *not* have a clue who this woman was, I couldn't remember if I'd slept with her.

There's something to be proud of.

Guess I'd be having that shot of scotch in the skybox after all.

I started to walk away and heard her shout, "I'll catch you later."

As I returned to club level, the oddity of our other Lund family members not being in this skybox occurred to me. Since my cousin Annika's husband, Axl, played for the Wild, she'd scored her own box. I assumed that's where my cousins and aunts and uncles were.

When Jax had told me about this exhibition this morning, he'd mentioned the Wild organization had donated one of the corporate boxes for the Western Conference players, their friends and families. So I'd walked in only knowing my parents, Lucy and Mimi and the instructors from Lakeside.

Then I'd recognized Tyson and assumed the blonde with him was Dani, Gabi's sister. Two other women were in the back getting their drink on. From their expert commentary and their acquaintance with Dani, I suspected they were Gabi's former teammates.

I'd been so pissed off that Gabi hadn't told me about her participation in the exhibition that I hadn't spoken to anyone while the teams went head-to-head.

But now that I'd returned and the Wild game had started, I had no choice but to be social.

After a shot.

I waited at the bar for the pour, and Gabi's sister moved in beside me. "Is Gabi okay?" she asked, which threw me, because how had she known that's where I'd gone?

After tossing back the shot, I chased it with a drink of water.

Dani said, "Tyson recognized you as Gabi's friend, so I figured you'd gone to check on her."

I faced her, allowing a moment to look for her resemblance to Gabi, but found none. This woman still had the baby-faced features of a girl, with her big brown eyes and long blond hair. Whereas Gabi was all woman.

Then she offered me a shy smile. "Oh. I'm Dani Welk, by the way. Gabi's sister."

"Good to meet you, Dani. I'm Nolan Lund, Jax's brother and Gabriella's . . . friend."

"How is she?"

"Fuming, mostly, with a side of indignant."

"Sounds like her. She and Ass"—she cringed—"I mean, she and Amelie have hated each other for years."

"Don't editorialize her nickname on his account," a husky voice said behind me. "He's Stonewall's brother and the Hammer's cousin by marriage. He understands bad blood in hockey, am I right, Lund?"

Then the voice turned into a body that moved in on my other side. I turned my head and we were eye to eye, which put her in the six-foot-two range. She pointed at my empty shot glass and said, "Two more," to the bartender.

"I'm sorry, have we met?"

"Nope. I'm Mariah Aguirre. Gabi's former teammate and longtime friend."

"Nolan Lund. But you knew that."

"Yep. Gabi roped me'n my girlfriend, Amy"—the woman she gestured to next to her offered me her hand and a shy smile—"into helping out with the LGBTQ mixer on Saturday. Then we got the invite to this and I'm like . . . hot damn, we're movin' on up in the world."

I laughed. "I'm glad you're here to support Gabriella and I'm really happy you're helping out on Saturday."

Mariah handed me a shot.

My protest, that I didn't need another shot, died when she said, "To Gabi."

"To Gabi." I touched my glass to hers and knocked the booze back.

She said, "Whoo-ee. You and me could get into some trouble. None of these pansy-asses appreciate good scotch."

I snagged a bottle of water. "Somebody please fill me in on the bad blood between Gabi and that Amelie chick."

"We call her Asswipf—*ass whiff*—not only because she's a stanky asshole, but her damn initials are right there in the name; *A*melie *S*an*S*imeon-*W*ipf. Get it?" She laughed. "Gabi came up with it. She's clever with words like that. Anyway, Asswipf is Canadian, which means we've played against her a bunch of times internationally. She's whiny, entitled, a dirty player out for her own glory and not what's best for the team or the sport. Gabi had a chance for some payback tonight and she grabbed it with both hands."

"I just hope she didn't spill blood because of me," Dani said quietly.

Mariah leaned across me. "Girl, that high stick you took from her at the Olympic games was some serious bullshit since the goddamned refs didn't throw her sneaky ass in the sin bin for it."

Ah. So Gabi was still looking out for her little sister.

"Gabi always has my back, even to her own detriment sometimes," Dani said. She paused. "What'd you think of the interview?"

Christ. Gabi hadn't told her sister about tomorrow's interview, had she?

"Gabs was fucking eloquent. As always," Mariah said.

"Wait. What interview?"

"The one Gabi did for Channel 9 Sports today," Amy piped in. "It aired during the six o'clock broadcast. It'll be interesting to see if they try and re-interview her since she ended up in a fight and what she'll say about it."

Dani laughed softly. "It'll just be one long bleep."

Now I was anxious to see that interview. "Ladies, if you'll excuse me, I need to check on something."

Both Lucy and my mother arched questioning brows at me as I exited the box again. I scrolled to the Channel 9 News website on my phone and pulled up the interview.

Holy hell. Gabi had nailed it. If her interview tomorrow went anything like this, she'd be golden.

Unless . . . they took the brawl on national TV into consideration. Then she might be screwed.

After I returned to the box, I had a restlessness the scotch hadn't tamed. The last thing I wanted to do was sit through a hockey game. So I took Mimi off her mother's hands and we shed our excess energy by running sprints down a deserted hallway. I didn't do half-bad for wearing my office clothes and competing against a nine-year-old.

My niece kept me occupied through the break between periods one and two. The second period had just started when the players from Jax's Western Conference team poured into the skybox.

My tongue nearly did a cartoonish flop out of my mouth upon seeing Gabi in the classy, sexy outfit she'd worn for the Channel 9 interview. She looked hot as hell.

But more importantly, the manic look I'd witnessed in the locker room had calmed.

Good.

After she'd filled a plate with food, she turned, and her gaze connected with mine.

Locked on mine.

Neither of us looked away.

The woman was something.

I stood and started toward her.

Then some handsy hockey player slithered up beside her and put his arm around her, leading her to a table in the corner. A cozy table for two.

She didn't look back at me.

Because she didn't care?

Or because she thought I didn't?

Fuck. My head was spinning, and I'd only had two goddamned shots.

Let it go, Nolan.

But I couldn't. I wondered if I'd gotten to her first, if she'd be sitting with me at that cozy table instead of him. If she'd be laughing with me rather than him. If I could coax her to eat something because all she was doing was pushing her food around on her plate. She finally took a bite and winced. That asshole was too busy trying to fucking *charm* her that he'd missed it.

"Why so glum, chum?" Margene asked and then saw where my focus was. "Our Gabi looks amazing tonight, doesn't she?"

"She should be icing her mouth. She's clearly in pain. And chucklehead there clearly hasn't noticed."

"Thanks for the ice earlier," Margene said. "Gabi kept it on until she left for the first photo op and autograph signing."

"There's more than one?"

"Yep. The second one is the break between the second and third period. The players can leave after that."

Which I had no doubt Gabi would, since she had the interview tomorrow morning.

So if I wanted to talk to her, I had to do it now.

Before I'd taken a single step, Dani and Tyson stopped at their table. Gabi popped up to give Dani a hug. Their conversation was a series of whispers and squeezes of their joined hands while both men looked on awkwardly.

Then Gabi set her hand on hockey douche's shoulder and introduced him to Tyson, angling her body closer as if she and the puckhead were a couple.

Tyson seemed super uncomfortable.

Gabi's smile appeared forced. Then I got it. She was using hockey boy to show Tyson that she'd moved on.

Wrong. If Gabi planned to use a man to show she'd moved on, it would be *me*.

Without tearing my gaze from the situation, I reached down and touched Mimi's shoulder. "Hey, sport, you wanna go say hi to Coach Welk?"

"Yes!"

Perfect little ruse. No one would suspect it was my idea.

Mimi popped up, snagged my hand and dragged me over to the table. "Coach Welk, that was awesome seeing you play! You did so good."

"Thank you, Mimi."

"Well, except for you didn't make a goal."

"I tried, though. That's what matters, right?"

Hockey guy—who I now recognized as the goalie—offered his hand. "Matt McCoy. Is this your daughter?"

"No, this is Jax's daughter, Mimi. I'm Nolan Lund. Jax's brother. Mimi is one of Coach Welk's students at Lakeside."

"I'm very happy to meet you, Mimi."

But like mine, Mimi's eyes were solely on Gabi. "You look all fancy tonight."

"You're used to seeing me in my coach or ref uniforms, huh?"

"You're pretty."

Gabi's eyes softened. "Thank you, sweetheart."

"I heard Uncle Nolan say you looked pretty too."

What the hell? That little liar. I'd never said that. But denying it, yeah . . . not going there.

"Well, I agree with both of you," Matt said, smiling at her. "She does look fantastic."

A smile Gabi didn't return because she was too busy trying to fry my face off with her laser death glare.

"Gabriella, I need a word with you."

"How coincidental that I have a word to say to you too, Lund." She stood. "Mimi, why don't you sit here and keep Matt company?"

"Sure." Mimi scrambled into the chair. First question out of her mouth? "Have you won as many Stanley Cups as my daddy?"

God, I loved that kid.

Gabi bobbed and weaved through the people like she was on the ice.

I snagged an icy cold can of Coke before I followed her into the foyer.

She'd ducked into an alcove that separated the skyboxes on this level, and paced in the small area. As soon as she saw me, she opened her mouth.

"Ice that lip while I'm talking. You should be trying to keep the swelling down."

"Don't boss me around. What makes you think I want to hear *anything* you have to say?" She put her hands on her hips and stared me down. "Especially after that bullshit flattery you fed your niece and then you used her to tell me."

"I didn't. That was all Mimi. She just repeated what everyone else had been saying about you." I kept my eyes locked to hers. "But that doesn't mean it's not true. You are hot as fire in that outfit and you know it."

"Omigod, Nolan Lund, you are the *worst*. You admitted that I'm not your type. Then you apologized for it. But you never claimed you changed your mind about finding me attractive until I showed up at a party, in an outfit *you* picked out for me. To add further insult to injury, when another man acts like he's attracted to me, you decide that I'm not so bad after all?"

For fuck's sake. Did she really think I was like that?

"Yes, Nolan, I do."

This woman tied up me up in knots so completely that I don't know when I was talking to myself or out loud.

"Well, you're wrong. Completely, utterly and totally dead fucking wrong." I crowded her against the wall. "You weren't wearing that sexy outfit an hour ago when I was in the locker room cleaning the blood off your face, were you?"

That stubborn chin went higher. "That doesn't count."

The hell it didn't. "Fine, you wanna back up? We'll back *way* up. To the night at the barcade when you admitted you overheard things at Buddy's I'd said that upset you. You let me apologize, and what's more, you saw I was sincerely sorry about hurting you. You could've walked away at that point and left it at that."

"I should have."

"But you didn't," I reiterated. "You wanna know why I said you weren't my type at Buddy's that night?"

She opened her mouth. The look in her eyes suggested she was about to let a zinger fly.

So I warned, "Consider your words carefully."

She did. Then she grudgingly admitted, "Because you didn't know me."

"Exactly. The best part of my night at the Full Tilt opening was *getting* to know you." My eyes searched hers and I moved in close enough to catch a whiff of her warm and sweet scent. "I seem to remember you didn't try to run away screaming from me that night after we cleared the air."

"I didn't. But—"

"Huh-uh. We're past the time for *but*s, aren't we?"

After a moment, she nodded.

"I'm going through the order of events so when I get to my final point, you're not gaping at me in shock that how I feel about you isn't such a goddamned surprise after all."

Gabi swallowed hard.

I gently pressed the soda can to her lip and this time she held it there, watching me with those ridiculously beautiful eyes. "In the first four months of our acquaintance I only saw angry, hurt, nervous and indignant Gabriella." I took a chance and slowly moved my hand to her cheek to push a stray section of her hair behind her ear. "In the past few weeks, I've seen funny, sly, kind, sweet, tipsy and thoughtful Gabriella."

"And?"

"And . . . I like you. After that night at Full Tilt I realized you were one hundred percent the type of woman I wanted to be more than frenemies with."

She blinked at me and lowered the hand holding the Coke to her side. "But that was—"

"Before I saw you half-naked while I helped you find a killer interview outfit? Yes." I canted my head so my mouth was right above her ear. "So you don't get to blame my interest in you on lust either."

"Nolan."

I let my breath drift across her damp skin. "Know what really cemented my crush?"

"What?"

"The first random text you sent me. Christ. That might've been the corniest joke I'd ever heard, but I laughed my ass off for like five minutes. I'd had a shit day, I was still at work, feeling alone and pissy, and then your text pinged. For a brief shining moment, I knew someone in the world was thinking about me."

"For real?" she whispered.

"Absolutely for real." I let my lips brush the top of her ear. "I kept it casual and friendly. Biding my time until . . ."

"Until what?"

"Until I could make it clear to you that I intended to take friendly to a whole new level with us." Feathering my mouth between her cheekbone and her ear, I murmured, "So tell me, Gabriella, when was I supposed to do that this week? When you came to me in a panic on Monday? When I texted you and asked if you had time for lunch on Tuesday and you turned me down? Or when I stopped by the rink last night and you sent me packing? Or tonight when I stormed into the men's locker room because I worried you were really hurt?"

"You . . ." A shiver rolled through her. "Stop whispering in my ear, goddammit, it's making it hard to think."

She rolled her shoulder—to get closer or to get away from me? I froze. Waiting. When she stayed put, I had the answer I needed.

And looky there, she'd also given me better access to that tempting neck. "Jesus, you smell good."

"It's just lotion."

"It's just you," I half growled. "Have I mentioned that you were fucking magnificent on the ice tonight?"

"No . . . Oh god, that feels . . ." She moaned as I planted soft kisses down the front of her throat.

"Mmm. I want to do this all night. But I won't, because you have a big day tomorrow. And I won't add to your stress of that by keeping on about *this*, but we both know it's been building toward *this*." I nuzzled the skin below her ear. "Am I wrong?"

"No."

I eased back and said, "Look at me."

Gabi gave me that slow sexy blink that would've had my mouth on hers instantly—if not for her busted lip.

And mine.

"Once you're through your interview, call me." I gently stroked her cheek. "I won't wish you luck, because I have a feeling you won't need it."

After I stepped back, she said, "You're leaving?"

"I might pop upstairs and bug my cousins before I go. Why?"

"I have something to say." She winced when her teeth rubbed on the inside of her lip. "Thanks for tracking me down after the game. It was . . . romantic in a bizarre way."

I smiled at her. "I might've freaked out a little."

"A little?"

"Fine. A lot."

"I was still in that adrenaline rush stage, so sorry I snapped at you."

I shrugged. "Not the first time, probably won't be the last."

Gabi smirked.

"What?"

"We have a unique way of sharing our feelings, don't we?"

"It works. When it doesn't, we'll adapt." I forced myself to take another step back. "Good night, Gabriella."

"Night, Nolan."

Two hours later, as I was getting ready for bed, my phone pinged with a text.

GW: What's worse than raining cats and dogs?

GW: Hailing taxis 😊

GW: That joke, courtesy of your niece.

I laughed.

ME: Sounds like Mimi saved the best one for you tonight.

GW: Timing is everything. Speaking of timing . . . for me, it's easier to say this over text.

I tried not to panic.

ME: Say what over text?

GW: When my crush on you started.

ME: When?

GW: After you apologized for the not-my-type thing. I realized I'd been wrong about you. But you'd been wrong about me too. So I took a chance and let my guard down. I can't honestly remember the last time I wanted a man to see the real me. It scared me to think you liked what you saw. But it hasn't scared me enough to put that guard back up.

ME: I'm so glad to hear that. But I need to ask . . . am I just your rebound guy?

The . . . started and stopped three times before I got a response.

GW: No. This feels . . . different. I've decided to shitcan my fears and go all in to see where this takes us.

ME: Then we ARE on the same page. Just wanted to double-check.

GW: 😎

ME: I'll look forward to talking to you tomorrow.

Eighteen

GABI

I woke up feeling like I'd been beat to shit the night before.

Oh right. I had.

Groaning, I forced myself out of bed to start coffee and pop some Aleve.

I shuffled into the bathroom and avoided looking at myself in the mirror. Once the heat from the shower warmed up my muscles, I performed a few slow stretches. That loosened me up enough to get my hair washed and conditioned, my body parts shaved.

Needing that blessed hit of caffeine so bad, I didn't bother putting any clothes on; I just wrapped my hair in a towel and ventured into the kitchen naked.

Mug in hand, I checked my phone for messages.

None.

I didn't have time to dwell on my disappointment I hadn't heard from Nolan because, looking at the time, I realized my interview started in two hours.

The steam had cleared out of the bathroom, leaving the

mirror fog-free. When I got the first glimpse of my face, I stared at my reflection with utter dismay.

My bottom lip stuck out so far that I appeared to have a permanent pout. The gash probably should've had stitches. I had a bruise on the edge of my jawline. And on my forehead. And on my cheek. Oh, and a great big black eye. I couldn't even muster up an "it could've been worse" scenario by telling myself at least Asswipf hadn't broken my nose.

Christ. I wasn't sure I even owned enough foundation for a job of this magnitude. Besides, if I couldn't figure out how to mask regular dark circles under my eyes on a daily basis, how was I supposed to know how to contour and blend to hide bruising?

You can't.

Fuck.

Now I wanted to cry. But then my eyes would be red, my face would be blotchy *and* bruised and wouldn't that just add a lovely touch.

I fussed with my hair while options to fix this crisis came and went.

Ultimately, I realized if I couldn't hide it, I might as well flaunt it.

I dressed in the olive jumpsuit, adding jewelry, the leather jacket, the matching purse, marking off each item on the "dress for success" checklist Q had given me. I shoved my phone in my pocket, my feet into the fringed booties and hit the highway.

I believed I had a handle on my nerves . . . until I pulled into the Wolf Sports North complex. Would this be the first of many times I parked in this lot? Or the first and last time all rolled into one?

You've got this, Gabi. Go in there and show them why you're the best person for the job.

I strode into the reception area. All very sleek, chrome and glass, a retro '80s "mod look" design magazine. At the desk, I said, "Hi. I'm Gabi Welk. I have an appointment with Dahlia Switch."

"One moment please." *Clickety clack* as she typed. Without looking up at me, she said, "I've let Dahlia know you're here. There's a coatrack to your left if you need one."

Well, okay then. Not exactly personable. But still I said, "Thank you."

After I hung up my coat, I had too much nervous energy to sit, so I wandered around, stopping to check out a piece of artwork.

Entwined stripes of silver and gray paint flowed from one corner of the canvas to the other, thicker at the bottom, thinner as it reached the top. In the center of the piece was a black box with two slashes of charcoal on each side, and two lines beneath. Shiny screws, rusted washers and bits of wire were randomly glued around the box, splotches of red paint trailing behind it. Jagged horizontal lines scratched out in pencil stretched above, the images within the lines blurred with streaks of pastel-colored chalk.

What a powerful piece. I leaned down to see if the artist had signed it but there were only the initials T.A.L.

"It's remarkable, isn't it?" a female voice said behind me.

"Very. I don't always 'get' art, but this piece . . . I do."

"What do you see?"

"The box is an athlete. The lines on the top are bleachers with spectators, but it's all a blur to her as she races past, not realizing she's falling apart, or losing pieces of herself she's so focused on the finish line . . . but looking at the horizon, there is no end goal in sight."

When the woman didn't respond, I figured I'd shown my ignorance. Maybe the box was nothing more than a stylized television in a stadium since this *was* a TV studio.

"It amazes me that the artist's intent is understood by athletes, and others see a dancing box with unseen forces pulling the strings."

I murmured, "That analogy works too," and turned to look at her.

A woman with a tousled blond bob, roughly a decade older than me, offered her hand. "Dahlia Switch."

Her smile faded as she saw the state of my face.

I didn't babble an explanation. I kept my smile in place even when it hurt like a bitch, and took her hand. "Gabi Welk."

"Welcome to Wolf Sports North. If you'll come with me, we'll head back to the business offices." She swiped a badge over the card reader by the door.

I followed her down a long hallway. Some doors were shut, some open. She didn't explain where we were in the building, or indicate where the studios were located, which honestly didn't bode well for me. Especially since Liddy had mentioned the staff here were very friendly.

Dahlia stopped outside of a closed door and faced me. "Do you need to ah . . . freshen up or anything before I take you to meet Mr. Mayes, the VP of Programming?"

Wait. I was meeting the VP of Programming? Today? "I'm sorry. I thought I was meeting with you."

"Goodness, no. I'm Mr. Mayes's liaison from Personnel."

Maybe this did bode well for me. "Well, Dahlia, I'm as ready as I'll ever be."

She knocked twice and opened the door, standing aside to let me enter first.

The man, much younger than I expected, moved from behind his desk and crossed the room to shake my hand. "I'm Alan Mayes. We're so pleased you could meet with us today, Gabriella."

"Please call me Gabi. It's a pleasure to be here."

"Won't you please have a seat?" He gestured to a sitting area.

Four high-backed library chairs in coffee-colored leather were spaced around a kidney-shaped coffee table. A woman my age rose from one of the chairs and offered her hand. "Lovely to meet you, Gabi. I'm Minka. Production manager for *Minnesota Weekly Sports Wrap-Up*." She gave my outfit a thorough scrutiny. "Fantastic pantsuit. That color is perfect on you."

You rocked it, Nolan and Q. "Thank you. I wasn't quite sure if it would clash with or complement the bruises on my face."

Silence.

Then Alan chuckled. "Maybe I should offer you a cold drink instead of coffee to ice down that lip."

I sat in the chair closest to Minka and set my purse on the floor. "Ice helped a little last night after the game, but not much. I know it's not ideal to show up to a job interview looking like this, but I'm a hockey player. It's a part of the gig."

He took the chair opposite mine. "I watched the exhibition."

"Really?"

"I found it interesting that both captains added a woman to their roster, but it wasn't promoted until a few hours before game time."

"From what I learned during practice on game day, all the parties involved—including the Wild organization—kept the exhibition as a surprise for game attendees. No one on either team knew specifics on who we were playing against."

"Quite a bonus for game goers. There were ten Stanley Cup winners, Olympic medalists, and NHL conference champions on the ice last night."

"It was an honor to play with all those guys. Sort of feels like last night was a dream." I didn't add that my aching body attested to the fact all those body checks had really happened. Wouldn't want to overdo the self-deprecating humor.

"We saw your pregame interview with Channel 9 News," Minka said. "I assume you had the questions for that ahead of time?"

"No. Actually, I had no idea any news organization would be interviewing me."

"Really?" Alan said skeptically. "It was a historic moment, two women playing in an NHL exhibition."

"That was not a sound bite to make myself look humble, Mr. Mayes. I truly was not expecting it."

"Then please tell us how it came about."

"Immediately after I showed up at the arena, my boss, Jaxson Lund, took me over to where a news crew was already set up. I figured he just wanted me to wait with him until Lucas Griswold, the other team captain, had finished his interview. So I was shocked when Stonewall informed me that Pashma would be interviewing *me*."

Minka and Alan exchanged a look that wasn't lost on me. I'd nailed that Q&A. The fact I'd had no prep time and nailed it? Big bonus points in my favor.

"We usually have pregame and postgame coverage," Alan said. "Our crew asked for an interview with you after the game, but they were denied. Was that because you'd already agreed to an exclusive follow-up interview with another network?"

"No. I left at the start of the third period." I smirked. "Had to get to bed early since I wanted to be bright-eyed and bushytailed for this interview. Not that a solid ten hours of sleep helped my hockey souvenirs heal any faster."

They both laughed.

Then Alan asked, "Who in your life is aware of your ongoing application and interview process with us?"

"Just my friend who learned about the openings here and urged me to apply. I've not shared with my family or friends, including my boss at Lakeside or my supervisor at the Minnesota Youth Hockey League, that I'm looking at other career options."

"Right. I remember from your application that you're currently a referee with the MYHL."

"Yes. I also run coaching workshops and coordinate teambuilding exercises for girls' teams."

"Is that time consuming?"

"While I'm running the events? Yes. But I don't have to

do the paperwork or the legwork setting things up. I am able to tailor my workshops on the fly when I hit the ice that day."

Minka jotted something down on her notepad before she said, "You do all of these projects and classes because of your love for hockey?"

This was the type of question I hated because my answer could skew the interview. Should I be honest? Or give them the answer that would sound better?

"It's a combination of love of the game and economic necessity. Last year I needed flexible paying positions that allowed me to train and coach my sister. Now that the Olympics are over and the current hockey season is wrapping up, I decided to pursue other avenues. Does that mean I'll just abandon my positions if I am offered opportunities that are more in line with full-time employment? It depends."

"On?" Alan prompted.

I let my gaze move between them. "What this interview is for. I've fulfilled all of the requirements, but I still don't have any idea what specifically this job entails."

"I'll bet you have a guess or two what we're looking for."

"My first guess would be a game commentator, but that test could've just been to judge my verbal abilities and limitations, regardless if it's on-air."

"And your second guess?"

"An analyst to dissect the weekly games played and to make predictions for upcoming games."

Alan watched as Minka wrote something else down. Then he looked at me. "You're the only applicant that turned in game tapes for both men's and women's games. Why did you deem that necessary?"

I gave myself a moment before I spoke. "Because the most logical slot to shove me in is women's hockey. Which I obviously love. But I was hired as an assistant coach for a men's college team, and I didn't want that achievement to get overlooked. Not to denigrate any applicant's preferences, but I will point out that most female hockey players prefer to stick with what they know, which would be commentating on women's hockey. I believe I'm more versatile."

"You feel you'd work well on-air as an analyst with either a man or a woman offering opposing commentary?"

"As long as the person was respectful to both genders of players, I'd be fine with either."

"Would you also be fine working with someone you might've had a personal conflict with in the past?"

"Meaning, would I take issue if you expected me to work with, say . . . Amelie SanSimeon-Wipf as my co-commentator?" I paused. "Yes. I would have a big problem with that."

"Why?"

"Her specifically? She's a glory hound. She's divisive. She's not a team player." And those were the most flattering things I'd ever say about her.

"That's it?"

I wasn't surprised that Alan pushed the issue about potential personality conflicts. "That's all I'm willing to say during an official interview that impacts my future."

"Fair enough." Minka passed Alan her notebook. He scanned what she'd written, added something and passed it back.

While I should've been happy they weren't whispering back and forth, it still felt rude.

Alan studied me. "You've already signed confidentiality paperwork so I can tell you that we're hiring for two positions. The first one is for the weekly wrap-up show."

I smiled. I guessed right. Go me.

"The second position is brand new, created to diversify our broadcast team. We intend to strengthen our brand as the go-to place for local sports, which means we want our viewers to be familiar with their broadcasters. The commentators for men's and women's college hockey will be a two-person team; a man and a woman. This concept will launch in the fall, so there are months to build buzz about our new streaming service. The position will entail travel, both preseason and extensively during the hockey season."

"Which local college teams? You're already the official broadcast for all the U of M sports programs."

"We'll officially broadcast U of M Duluth—UMD— hockey starting this fall. Previously we used their local affiliate as our broadcast, but we are replacing that with our own on-site broadcasting team."

"When you say travel, and yet you also say local, are you talking about traveling in a vehicle with a news team and the co-commentator?"

"That will be our first choice for events within driving distance."

I tried to wrap my head around the logistics, but I couldn't.

Minka cracked open a bottle of water. "If you have questions, please don't be shy."

"*Shy* is rarely a word attributed to me. So you are suggesting that your new co-commentators will cover all of UMD women's and men's hockey games. I'm not being flip when I point out that's thirty-four regular season games—per team, only half of which are played on their home ice."

"As we're aware."

Then it hit me. "Your broadcast team would need to live in Duluth during the season."

"Yes. We've prepared a contingency plan for when the men's and the women's teams will be playing simultaneously. Our plan for the first year is to have a secondary unit from here cover whichever game is played on home ice. The broadcasters will travel to the away game . . . unless—"

"The men's team is playing at home, and the women's team is playing in Wisconsin, the secondary unit will travel there. Because the goal is making sure whichever team has the winningest record gets the best coverage."

"Yes."

Now that made sense. The UMD men's team had just won the Frozen Four. If Wolf Sports North owned the broadcasting rights, that meant if the team made it back to the finals, the big sports channels would have to pay Wolf Sports North for the right to broadcast. However, it didn't mean that as a local commentator I'd get a chance to call the games for the biggest championships in college hockey. But both UMD men's and women's teams were NCAA champions—the women's team were five-time champs—so I would have visibility and that could launch me into an even bigger market.

"Like we said, we've been vague about this position because it'll be new to us as well."

"Does that mean you've already decided on the male half of the broadcasting team?"

Alan nodded.

"Does he have any input on who is selected as his co-commentator?"

"Outright? No. We'll review the short list with him."

I knew they wouldn't tell me who they'd picked so I didn't ask.

"Gabi, while we can't disclose how many applicants we're currently considering, we do want to let you know that you are being considered for both of those positions."

Be cool. Don't tell them which position you'd prefer.

"That's exciting."

By their blank expressions . . . had I been too blasé?

"Do you have a time frame on when you'll get back to applicants . . . win or lose?"

"Honestly? Nothing solid. Right now we're in the middle of a merger, which is how we're picking up UMD broadcast rights and diversifying into a streaming service."

"So you're aware," Minka inserted, "the merger is not public knowledge so anything we've discussed here today . . . it's vitally important nothing is disclosed to anyone outside this room."

"Understood."

"Anything else you have questions on?" Alan asked.

"Yes. To start . . . salary, benefits, travel per diem, as well as wardrobe expectations and compensation. Now that I know moving is a requirement, relocation expenses as well as potential housing allowances."

Minka smiled as she handed me a stapled set of papers. "We've prepared the benefits package information, which includes the housing allowance. The relocation expenses are reimbursable at one hundred percent but aren't included at this time."

I scanned the first page. Flipped to the second. And wanted to flip a damn cartwheel when I saw the base salary—more money than I'd ever made. More than I'd hoped for. Somehow, I played it cool as I speed-read through the rest of the information. Finished, I glanced at Alan. "May I keep this?"

He shook his head. "This is a preliminary interview. If you're hired, you'll have immediate access to the financial benefits package being offered in the contract."

Which meant the numbers were negotiable. I'd need to research starting salary in the industry and not assume it was the best they would offer. I handed Minka back the packet.

"Is there anything else we can go over with you?"

"Not right now."

"All right." Both Minka and Alan stood. "Thanks for coming in today. We'll be in touch."

I snagged my purse before I got up. "I'll hear from one of you? Or Dahlia?"

"From here on out you'll be dealing directly with us," Alan assured me.

Another round of hand shaking and then I was returned to Dahlia's care.

Once again, she didn't speak as we hustled through the hallways. This time she didn't escort me into the reception area.

The receptionist didn't even glance in my direction when the door closed behind me.

But the blonde flipping through the magazine in the corner looked up.

A beautiful blonde I recognized.

There was only one reason she'd be here; she was interviewing for the job too.

I felt my hope start to slip away.

She stood and sashayed over to me.

Maybe it was petty, but her outfit wasn't as stylish as mine. *But her face isn't bruised . . . oh, and she's gorgeous. And smart. And experienced.*

"Gabi Welk? Is that you?"

"Yes, Jubilee, it's me."

She stopped and gasped. "Omigod. What happened to your face?"

Yep. She was still a total bitch.

"Hockey."

Her red lips curled up. "You're not supposed to try and stop the puck with your face. I thought you would've figured that out by now."

"Really? Wow. Great tip. But now that you mention it . . . they *did* teach us that in 2010 at the U.S. Women's Winter Olympics training camp, don't you remember?" I paused. "Oh right. You weren't there. My bad."

"Yes, that's the year you lost to the Canadians. Again."

And . . . I was done. I walked over to the coatrack for my jacket. When I turned around, Jubilee was right there.

"Sorry. That was uncalled for. I know you girls tried your best. Anyway, what are you doing here? It's strange to run into you at a broadcast studio, of all places."

She fucking *knew* why I was here. She just wanted me to ask why *she* was here.

How fun to deny her the chance to brag.

"Oh. I played in an NHL exhibition game last night at the Xcel Center before the Wild game. They caught my interview with Pashma Patel on Channel 9 News . . . did you see it?"

Her blond mane brushed her shoulders as she shook her head.

"I guess the Wolf Sports North news crew tried to find me after the game to do a follow-up interview on being the first woman to play in an NHL-sanctioned matchup, but I had so much going on that I had to postpone until today." I smiled. "Take care."

I walked off.

Ultimate mic drop moment and no one there to see it.

I didn't call Nolan to tell him how the interview went until I got home, changed into my real clothes and flopped on the couch.

He answered, "Hey. I was starting to get worried that I hadn't heard from you. How're you feeling?"

"Fine. Sore. My face is a train wreck. But I think I pulled off the 'semi-charming rapscallion hockey player' in the interview so they overlooked the bruises."

"How did it go?"

I told him about meeting with the VP of Programming, and the production manager, and the kudos I'd gotten on my outfit. I rambled a bit about the actual job, that it was an on-air position, but I kept the rest to myself.

"Nolan?" He'd been quiet for so long I thought we'd lost the connection.

"Sorry. Today is the definition of a shit show. I'm trying to do ten things at once—"

"That's fine, I'm sorry I interrupted you. I'll go. We can talk about it later."

"Gabriella. Don't you dare hang up."

Just because I'd let him get all bossy last night did not mean I'd let him get away with it today.

"Hold on one second. Please."

Okay. The *please* worked for me.

Who are you kidding, Gabs? There's so much about this man that works for you.

So. Much.

"All right. Now I have a moment to talk. And by talk, I mean demand to hear what you're not telling me." He paused. "Because I know there's something."

Shrewd man. "Two things. You're a businessman. What employment website gives the most accurate info for salary and benefit packages? I need to make a comparison analysis of what they offered me versus industry standard in case an offer does come through."

Silence. Then, "That might be the sexiest thing you've ever said to me, Gabriella."

I laughed. "I'm serious."

"So am I." Then he gave me the names of three websites. "Now, what's the next thing?"

My smile faded. "I honestly thought I did great in the interview. Asked insightful questions, reiterated my experience and passion for the game. Naturally they wouldn't tell me if they planned to offer me the job, and then they also couldn't give me any idea of when I'd hear back from them."

"If you're feeling confident, what's the problem now?"

"I *was* feeling confident . . . until I returned to the reception area and saw someone I knew. Two guesses why she was there."

"She was interviewing too."

"*Ding, ding*, we have a winner."

"Who is she?"

"Jubilee Jones."

Nolan snorted. "That's her name? For real?"

"Nolan, that's a *great* name for someone in broadcasting. Can't you just hear it? 'Now from Studio B, Jubilee Jones, senior analyst for Wolf Sports North news.'"

"I disagree, it sounds like a stripper's name. Is she a hockey player?"

"No. A figure skater who got fifth place at Nationals."

"See? Then she's no competition. Why did you let her torpedo your confidence?"

I sighed. "Because she *is* my competition. After she didn't make the Olympic team, the PR department hired her to do 'slice of life' type stories of other Olympic athletes on TV. She lived in Olympic Village with us."

"So?"

"So Jubilee is beautiful and graceful and smart and experienced, and they'd be stupid not to hire her because she's the whole package."

"Welk, *you're* the whole package. You're not a bit of fluff. A flash in the pan. You are the real deal."

I closed my eyes for a moment and just basked. "Thank you."

"Look, I can meet you tonight. It'd be much later because I have no idea when we'll get a handle on all that needs to be done here at the bowling alley before tomorrow, but I will make it work if you need me."

"I am grateful for the offer, but I have to ref at four and then I have my 14U class to teach after that and I know I'll be tired. So you do you tonight."

Nolan groaned. "Are you trying to get me to admit that I'd like to do *you* tonight?"

Would you? hung between us.

"Say the word, Gabriella."

"Yes. But we'll talk more about this tomorrow after your event."

"I'm holding you to that."

Nineteen

NOLAN

Sam and I showed up early Friday at the bowling alley to set everything up for Saturday's LGBTQ mixer sponsored by LCCO. Unfortunately I hadn't realized how run-down the place was; I wished I'd done a more thorough inspection before we finalized the mixer.

I couldn't blame the condition of the building on Jax's neglect. He'd ended up buying Lakeside Ice Arena and Rosewood Bowling Alley as a package deal. Not only had his focus been on dealing with staffing issues at the ice rink, he'd spearheaded a complete renovation of the former Boundary Waters bar into Full Tilt Barcade. Plus, in his personal life, he and Lucy had reconciled, moved in together with their daughter, Mimi, and tied the knot the day after Christmas. It'd been a busy few months.

Rosewood Bowling Alley had thirty-six lanes with automated scoring machines on each lane, which was the only decent thing about it. The building still reeked of smoke from three decades of Salems, Lucky Strikes, and Pall Malls.

The décor retained that '60s vibe, Danish modern minimalism meets the Jetsons, from the curved bright orange bench seats to the scoring tables accented in pale teal to the odd placements of the decorative spindles throughout the space.

A standard feature in a bowling alley was the shoe rental counter, where the casual bowler paid three bucks to rent the most hideous-looking shoes known to mankind. Here, the entire area and all the shoe cubbies had been upgraded to carpet. Too bad they hadn't upgraded the shoes themselves. There were maybe . . . fifty pairs total, from the 1950s if my estimate was accurate.

Sam and I explored the men's and women's locker room areas with twin expressions of horror. There was one bench in the center of each of the rooms. We couldn't get ten kids in here at one time, say nothing of the one hundred and fifty we were expecting.

But at least there were bowling balls of every weight and color everywhere we looked.

The restaurant had closed years ago, and in an effort to be more family friendly, the previous owner had sold the liquor license. The only food available was from the ancient popcorn machine—which I was pretty sure used the same oil for the butter topping that the janitor used on the bowling lanes—plus jars of Tijuana Mama hot meat sticks and even bigger jars of gigantic dill pickles. And the soda machine wasn't working.

No food. No drinks. No place to change. I had the sinking feeling that my first solo LCCO project was about to be an epic failure.

Amidst self-recrimination that I should've prioritized this project among the twenty other irons I'd had in the fire the past month, I was sorely tempted to send out an SOS to Aunt Priscilla, Aunt Selka and my mother. But as far as I knew, none of my other family members had been bailed out. I was competitive enough that I would *not* throw in the towel and ask for help.

I could fix this. With LCCO funds at my disposal, I called in an industrial cleaning crew. Pay the emergency fee and a dozen men will show up in thirty minutes.

Luckily Sam had hired four food trucks for Saturday, so lack of kitchen equipment wasn't a problem. Actually, everything he'd been tasked with was done. I was the one with no follow-through.

That'd been a favorite taunt from my grandfather. *Second born, second string, second best—you'll coast through life and let everyone else pick up the slack. There's a word for that boy, and it's lazy. That's what you'll be known as: No-Good Nolan, the lazy Lund.*

Even if I dropped the ball sometimes, I was always the first person to pick it back up and run with it until I crossed that goal line.

Another perk of having the last name Lund? Businesses wanted our business. I put calls in to two sporting goods stores and within three hours Rosewood had one hundred new pairs of bowling shoes in various sizes. Not only that, the manager promised to drop off a banner with the store's name as a proud sponsor of the event.

Because the cleaning crew had needed six hours to finish, Sam and I didn't get started setting up the registration tables until eight o'clock. I sent him home at ten and I locked up at eleven.

Now today was the big day. I thought I'd vanquished all my nervous energy yesterday, but it was right there waiting for me first thing when I pulled up to Rosewood Bowling Alley.

Fortunately, so was Gabi.

My double take at seeing her must've been funny because she laughed so hard, she almost dropped the coffee she'd brought me.

"That was definitely worth getting up early for, Lund."

"Speaking of early . . . you don't have to be here for another hour."

"I know. But you seemed really stressed yesterday when we talked. I thought I'd come early to see if you needed extra help."

That was thoughtful of her. I loved that she showed me her sweet side. "And extra caffeine?"

"That too."

I ambled closer to her. "I think you missed me."

"Yeah? You're the one who's stalking me like a big jungle cat right now."

"Guilty. Are you afraid I'll pounce on you?"

"No."

"Then hold still."

She blinked at me, but she didn't move.

Interesting. She'd worn her hair in a high ponytail, allowing a clear view of her face. I ran the back of my knuckles down the side of her jaw. "Any new bruising?"

She shook her head.

Her right eye had a black, raccoon-like ring around it. The swelling on her cheekbone looked the same size as Thursday night, except now a dark purple bruise bloomed beneath her pale skin. I touched it with just the tips of my fingers, and she jerked back. "Sorry. Did that hurt?"

"It just surprised me. It's okay though."

Taking her jaw in my hand, I tilted her head slightly. My stomach bottomed out when I got an up-close look at her lip. Still split, still puffy, a dark mark below it and bruising above it. However, it did look a little better. "How bad does it hurt?" I murmured, softly stroking the skin between her jawbone and the bottom of her lip.

"It smarts when I smile. So I'm smiling less than normal."

"You've been icing it properly?"

"Last night I held a quart of Häagen-Dazs raspberry chocolate on it until the ice cream melted and I had to eat it."

I grinned at her. "That's an excellent example of dual-purpose thinking." I forced myself to stand back, even when I wanted to continue to hold her battered face in my hand.

Gabi handed me a cup of coffee. "I didn't bother with makeup today. You think I'll scare any of these kids away?"

"No." Impulsively I leaned down and kissed her forehead. "And you're not scaring me away either, Gabriella."

I strode to the front entrance and shoved the key into the lock. No security system. Then again, a brick through the glass door or any of the multitude of windows would render any security system worthless.

After passing through the outer entrance, we were in a glass-walled entryway with another glass door that opened up into the bowling alley proper. Most places in Minnesota had this feature, giving customers a place to keep out of the elements while waiting for a ride or for their vehicle to warm up. Didn't make economic sense to me, though, trying to heat spaces that were mostly glass walls.

The tiled floor that led to the counter was pitched at an odd uphill angle. I wondered how many bowling balls had careened down that incline.

"Wow. This is totally retro. I'd love to see what magic Dallas could work with a place like this."

"It'd need a lot, but it looks a million times better than it did yesterday. Amazing what gallons of bleach can do. The only place we didn't allow the industrial cleaning crew was the mechanical area behind the lanes." I frowned. "I hope Curtiss shows up today because I have no earthly idea how to turn any of the pin setting machines on. That'd be just my luck—"

Gabi gently placed her fingers over my mouth. "Stop obsessing. It'll be fine. If Curtiss doesn't show up, then we'll YouTube it. You can learn how to do anything on there."

I started to respond, but her thumb was lightly sweeping over the swollen spot on my bottom lip and I sort of forgot how to breathe.

"This looks better too." Then her blue-gray eyes met mine. "Have you been icing it properly?"

"Yes." I puckered up and kissed her thumb. "With a tumbler of scotch on ice."

"Whatever works."

She retreated and sipped her coffee, but I felt her watching me.

Which made it hard to focus. My phone buzzed and I answered it without checking the caller ID. "Nolan Lund."

"Morning, boss. I'm headed to the bowling alley. Just wanted to make sure you're on your way since you're the only one with keys."

"I'm already here."

That surprised Sam. "Oh. Aren't you an eager beaver this morning?"

"Are you even using the phrase 'eager beaver' in the right context?"

Gabi blushed.

Why did I find that so damn cute?

Sam sighed. "Since you're so contrary, I'm eating your muffin."

I snickered. My mind was on one track today—I didn't dare look at her again.

"Never mind. See you in fifteen." He hung up.

"Sam is on his way. I don't know what I'm supposed to do because he's got the lists."

"I don't want to *bowl* you over with my suggestions, but we could go back into the mechanical room and flip some switches."

"Hilarious. Let's put a *pin* in that idea for now."

She smirked at me.

"Come on, I'll let you watch while I find some lights."

"I never asked how many kids signed up for the event."

"A hundred and fifty. Above our initial projections."

Gabi continued to stroll around, checking everything out. "Since this is a LCCO event, will there be media coverage?"

I shook my head. "Strictly a private mixer. I wasn't certain we could skip the parental permission forms since the attendees will all be minors, but Sam assured me it wouldn't be necessary since it's not a school-sanctioned event." That little niggling ball of doubt started unraveling in my chest. "I hope kids show up. My fear is that they'll wake up today and think . . . *No one will ever accept me, so I'll just stay home.*"

"That is a possibility. But there are also those kids who will be nervous as hell to come, but they'll do so anyway and maybe for the first time ever, they'll be surrounded by people who accept them, and they'll see they're not as different or alone as they'd thought."

"I hope you're right."

"Why'd you decide to do an event like this?"

"I wish I had a great, uplifting story as an inspiration. But I'd been waffling on two other ideas when Sam suggested this. I immediately got on board." I swigged my coffee. "Why?"

She shrugged. "I would've guessed you, as a member of the Lund family, would host a sports-themed event."

"I'm sure Jax will do that once he's caught up building his business empire. As far as my cousins, we all do our own thing when it comes to LCCO. Annika sponsors a coat drive. Brady and Lennox host tutoring classes. Walker and Trinity build and paint sets for community theater. Jensen and Rowan run a summer camp that focuses on music, dance and art." I smiled. "After today? The pressure will be on Ash and Dallas to get their projects lined up."

"Woo-hoo!" sounded from the entryway. "The star power is here, baby, so light 'em up!"

"Back here," I shouted.

Gabi's friends Mariah and Amy wandered in.

"Write it on the calendar, Mariah is early for a change!" Gabi said.

"What do you mean, early?" Mariah whirled on Amy. "Woman, did you *lie* to me about what time we were supposed to be here?"

"Yes. How was I to know you'd actually listen to me for a change and we'd be nearly an hour early?" Amy smiled at me. "Hey, Nolan."

"Amy. Thanks for coming."

"What do you want us to do?"

Sam hustled in, laptop bag dangling from the crook of his arm as he carried in two boxes. "I'd love for one of you to grab the other box of volunteers' T-shirts in the back of my car while I set up the coffeemaker."

"You bought a coffeepot?"

He looked at me over the tops of his sunglasses. "*You* bought a coffeepot. You know I don't function at all without massive amounts of caffeine."

"Yes, we agreed not to discuss the Miami incident ever again."

Mariah and Amy returned, and introductions were made. Then Sam's friends Markus and Edison arrived.

Sam clapped his hands to stop the chattering. "I have two boxes of T-shirts for volunteers so please find a size that fits and put it on. If someone approaches you claiming to be a volunteer, send them to me. Since we are dealing with minors, I have a list of *officially* recognized volunteers."

While Sam passed out other assignments, I snagged the bright blue T-shirt off the top of the pile that had my name on the sticky note. I checked out the design as I walked to the locker room area. VOLUNTEER in big black letters across the front, curved over a rainbow. The LCCO logo on the back. Perfect. Simple with clear sponsorship.

I'd just removed my button-down shirt, when I heard, "Nolan?" I turned around.

Gabi stood there, gaping at me. "Oh. I, ah . . . sorry."

The way her eyes devoured me didn't say "sorry" at all.

So I flexed my arms and tightened my abdomen as I leaned over to pluck the T-shirt off the bench. "Did you want something?"

"I . . . ah . . ."

Erasing the distance between us allowed her a better—closer—view of my torso, because she hadn't looked me in the eyes since she'd walked in. "Gabriella? Are you okay?"

She blinked and tilted her head back to meet my gaze,

then jammed her finger into my sternum. Hard. "No, I'm not okay, you sneaky jackass."

"Excuse me?"

Another poke, harder this time. "I really thought the reason you wore such fancy-ass custom-made clothing was because you're the brainy type, not the athletic type . . . kind of like when that super-nerdy character Chidi from *The Good Place* whipped off his shirt after being doused by sprinklers and everyone was like . . . whoa, *he* is built like that? Now I see that you had *this* kind of a dream body underneath those ridiculously trendy clothes the whole goddamned time I've known you. What the fuck?"

"Why are you pissed off?"

"Because how is that fair? Seriously. You've got this beautiful face, and a stupidly charming personality, and you're smart, and disgustingly rich, and freakishly stylish, and now I find out you are sporting a ripped and toned physique too? You suck, Lund."

How could she throw out such a flattering list of compliments and make them sound like insults? Jesus. What was wrong with her?

What is wrong with her? What is wrong with you*? Since that is one of your favorite things about her.*

I couldn't help it: I laughed.

"It's not funny." She got this gleam in her eye that scared me a little.

"What?"

"Level with me, sport. Do you have a big dick too?"

What the hell? "No. I think it's about average."

"Oh. Well . . . that's good. There's still a chance for us then."

And . . . I was fucking gone for with this woman. Crazy, mad about, completely wild for her.

Before she retreated, which I sensed she was about to by her body language, I circled my hand around her wrist and brought it to my mouth to nip at the finger that'd been poking me. "Now you know how bowled over I was when you stripped down to nearly nothing to try on clothes on Monday. Every inch of you is utter perfection, Gabriella, which you cover up in hockey gear and tracksuits." I pressed my lips to the top of her head. "You are glorious and I'm obsessed."

We stared at each other and I swore the temperature of the room went up fifty degrees.

"Nolan."

"Yes?"

"Are you ever gonna kiss me?"

Angling my head, I bussed her cheek. Then dragged my mouth to her ear. "Yes. But not until that lip is healed."

She muttered something about me being a sadistic cock of the walk.

I nuzzled her temple, inhaling the sweet warmth of her skin. "Harsh words from a woman who smells like god-damned cookies."

"Boss . . . Oh, crap, sorry, I'll come back."

Sam's interruption snapped Gabi out of it, and she stepped back. "Put a damn shirt on, loser." Then she turned and stormed off.

I never did find out why she'd tracked me down.

I needn't have worried about no kids showing up for the event. We were absolutely slammed from a half an hour before we were set to start.

Not all the attendees wanted to bowl, which actually worked out because the lanes could only accommodate 144 bowlers at a time. The food truck meals were complimentary, but the attendees had to sign in and get a ticket before jumping into a line.

The "alphabet" volunteers wandered among groups of kids, talking to them, answering questions, just hanging out, being their authentic selves.

Gabi and I weren't working together, but I'd catch a glimpse of her ponytail bobbing as she cut through the crowd. It soothed me to know she was here.

Sam and I were dividing up the prizes for the bowling tournament winners when I heard a familiar voice.

"Nolan, darling, this is amazing."

I got up and skirted the table to hug my mother.

Edie Lund was a stunning woman; ageless, her asymmetrical bob complemented her strong jaw, high cheekbones and wide smile. I'd inherited her eye color and her fashion sense. Although she'd dressed down in navy-colored silk harem pants, an emerald and navy plaid jacket over an ivory lace blouse that matched her navy cloth pumps trimmed in ivory, her style screamed classy. A sapphire necklace, emerald earrings and pearl bracelets rounded out her look.

She gave me that raised Mom eyebrow. "Do I pass inspection?"

I grinned. "Always. Great weekend outfit."

"I tried to get her to wear jeans," my dad complained. "No such luck."

This had been an ongoing joke for years. My mother never wore denim out of the house and my dad would live in jeans on the weekend if Mom let him. Besides, I really didn't need to hear Dad going on about how fantastic her ass looked in jeans anyway.

He held his arms out. "No comment on my great outfit?"

Dad had refused to wear "fancy" jeans, meaning ones he couldn't get at a sporting goods store. He preferred the Levi's 501 shrink-to-fit, button-fly style, which he wore with Orvis oilskin leather hiking boots. Beneath his brown leather bomber jacket, he'd donned a hunter-green waffle-weave Henley. I hid a smirk that mom had coordinated his outfit to hers. "You look outdoorsy, Dad. Fit as the proverbial fiddle."

"Perfect for hiking in the mall, eh?"

I took in his dark hair, streaked with gray. "Did you get a haircut?"

WANT YOU TO WANT ME   217

"Yes, but I swear this is the last one. I'm thinking of growing my hair out. Past my ears at least."

"Dude. You're almost seventy."

"Still younger than Jagger and Clapton and they've both got flowing locks." He threw back his shoulders. "I could pull it off." He winked at me. "My old man is breathing fire in hell at the idea of 'any son of his' contemplating hippie hair."

"I say you oughta do it."

Then Dad noticed my assistant. "Sam! I almost didn't recognize you."

"And why is that, sir?" Sam asked.

Mom and I exchanged a look—sometimes, despite his being CEO, what came out of Archer Lund's mouth wasn't PC.

"Because you're usually rocking those suits that cause envy throughout the office," Dad added as clarification. "Love the casual look."

"Thank you, sir," Sam said. "I'm pleased you decided to see LCCO at work, especially on your day off."

I squinted at my mom. "Are you checking up on me?"

"I'm here offering my support to my very capable son, nothing more." She gestured to the wall-to-wall people. "This all came together very well."

"We weren't sure yesterday if it would. Sam has gone above and beyond."

Sam blushed. "I'm just the idea man, boss."

"Hey, Sam, do you have any more volunteer T-shirts? Nolan's stylist, Q, and his husband, Elton, are here." Gabi froze when she saw my parents. "Oh. Sorry to interrupt."

"No, dear, it's fine." My mother's too-shrewd gaze winged between us. "I didn't realize Coach Welk was helping you out with this, Nolan." Her head tilt indicated she'd found it intriguing that Gabi knew the name of my stylist and his husband.

I wasn't getting anything past Mom.

"If you're here, who's running the rink?" my dad asked Gabi.

She laughed. "I think you know Jax is cracking the whip on all my classes today, so feel sorry for the kids. They will be thrilled to have me back Monday."

"Maybe we oughta swing by there, Eeds."

Eeds. Dad shortened everyone's name. An annoying habit he'd passed on to my brother. My mom swears I believed my name was Nol until I started kindergarten.

"Before you go . . ." I ripped off four meal tickets for the food trucks. "I've heard the bratwurst is good. So's the Purple Rain ice cream. Help yourselves."

"Thanks. You've done good work here, son." Dad snatched the tickets. "See you Monday." He wrapped his arm around my mom's shoulders and steered her away. When he leaned in to whisper in her ear, she threw her head back and laughed.

"My god. Those two are the cutest thing *ever,*" Sam said with a sigh. "Hashtag couple goals."

"Did you seriously just hashtag my parents?"

"Darling, *everyone* should hashtag your parents," Q said behind me.

I turned to face him and his husband, Elton, a Korean man who literally was a rocket scientist at U of M.

Q said, "Gabriella invited us. She said these kids needed to meet people who are happy and successful and uniquely themselves. I told her to sign us up."

"I'm thrilled you're here. I'm embarrassed to admit I should've thought of you and issued the invite myself." I handed Q an XXL T-shirt and Elton a medium. "We're about half-done with the event so get T-shirted up and jump right in."

Although I didn't get out to the food trucks, two street tacos and a bratwurst with mustard appeared at my spot at the registration table right as the event wound down. In my gut I knew Gabi had gotten it for me. Not that I'd seen her recently to thank her.

Sam was off . . . doing Sam things, leaving two seats open at my table.

Mariah plopped down next to me, and Amy sat on her lap. "So, big boss man . . . let's talk about Gabi."

I indicated that I was chewing.

"You like her," Mariah said.

"We can tell," Amy added.

"Yeah?" I glanced up. "How?"

"You went racing out of the skybox right after she got injured."

Now I wondered how many people had noticed that. I thought I'd been circumspect.

"Oh, then you two hustled out of the skybox together, although she didn't look happy to leave that other hockey dude sitting there with one of her students." Amy tapped her chin. "But I'm pretty sure *you're* the reason she seemed so huffy in the first place, so does the chasing-after-her thing count as a romance angle?" she asked Mariah.

"Yes, because Gabi was much calmer and happier when she returned to the skybox."

Amy said, "Cool beans."

"So you like her, we like you, we like the idea of you two together, so we've decided to give you a crash course in romancing Gabi," Mariah announced.

I took a swig of water. "What makes you think I need that?"

"Because it's Gabi."

"Fair point." I lowered my voice. "You know she'll kill you both if she finds out you're doing this, right?"

Amy lightly punched Mariah in the arm. "I told you."

"So let me save your lives and say thank you, I appreciate the offer. But if I can't figure out how to romance Gabriella on my own . . . I don't deserve her. I've already screwed up more times than I care to admit to, but each time it happens, I learn something important about her." And myself, but they didn't care about that.

Mariah harrumphed. "This was a bust." She lifted Amy off her lap. "Call us if you get stuck and maybe we'll help you."

After the food trucks pulled out, the kids started to go too.

We got a lot of questions about when we planned to do this again. While I appreciated that they had a good time, we wouldn't make any future decisions until we'd crunched the numbers. While LCCO didn't only do fund-raisers, an event where we footed the bill entirely wasn't the goal either.

I gathered the volunteers around. "Thank you, everyone, for coming today. It meant a lot to the kids and it meant a lot to me too. So give yourself a round of applause."

I waited for the whistling and commotion to fade before I spoke again.

"And because I'm an astute people manager and I noticed the looks of envy you all gave the bowlers today, I'm now giving you the chance to hit the lanes. Free bowling for all volunteers!"

They acted way more excited about it than I'd imagined. Even Q and Elton went to dig through the boxes of shoes so they could bowl against Mariah and Amy.

Gabriella tracked me down as I restacked the tables that'd already been stacked. She said, "OCD much?"

"Only about some things."

"Why aren't you bowling?"

I shrugged. "Not really my thing." I looked at her. "Why aren't *you* bowling?"

"Everyone is partnered up already." She sighed. "Now I know what it feels like to not be picked for a team."

"Pretty sure you're full of shit, Welk." I tugged on her ponytail and bent to whisper, "You told them that we'd agreed to bowl together so you could get out of it, didn't you?"

"Yes."

"Why?"

"I hate bowling."

Did she? Or was she trying to get me to challenge her to

a game because she was a damn ringer? Gently, I cupped her chin in my hand and titled her head up to meet my gaze.

The woman had a killer poker face. I had no idea if she was bluffing.

Only one way to find out.

"Well, I can't have you lying to my volunteers. So find some shoes and a ball because we're going head-to-head on the lanes."

"I can't."

I cocked an eyebrow at her. "Because?"

"Because I'm . . ." She dropped her gaze. "Still sore from the hockey game."

"Maybe you should show me exactly where it hurts." I lowered my voice. "I'll kiss and make it better."

Her gaze snapped up to mine. "Nolan."

"Your ribs, right?" I slid my hand down and curled it around the left side of her ribcage. "Here?"

"Uh. Yeah."

"Lemme see."

"No. It's okay."

"I'll be gentle. I promise."

"It's not that. It's just . . . I don't want to lift my shirt. There are people around."

This, from the woman who stripped down to her skivvies in front of me and Q, and only two days ago was buck-ass naked in an entire locker room of hockey players? If I hadn't seen that behavior with my own eyes, I absolutely would've believed her shyness.

"No worries. I'll block you from view." Then I hooked a finger beneath the hem of her T-shirt and started to peel it up.

"What are you doing?"

"Helping you." I held fast when she tried to jerk away. "Now, hold still. I wouldn't want you to further *injure* yourself."

"Omigod. You don't believe me."

"I'll believe it when I see it."

"You are such an ass." She stepped back and pulled her T-shirt up to the bottom of her sports bra band. "See?"

I bent down to get a better look. "Nothing here," I said after placing my thumb on her sternum and stroking my fingers across the soft skin on the left side of her torso.

Skin that immediately rippled into gooseflesh.

And I might've lost my head for a moment, getting caught up in the cocoa vanilla sugar scent of her skin. But I snapped back to reality when I saw the two big bruises on the right side of her ribcage.

Gabi wasn't moving at all. I think she might've quit breathing. Which quickened my breathing considerably.

Ignoring my need to kiss down that rock-hard belly, I pressed my lips on the bruises . . . and blew a raspberry.

She shrieked. "Stop! That tickles."

I straightened up. "That's what I think of your 'I'm too sore to bowl' excuse. Nice try, though."

She yanked her shirt down and harrumphed. "What gave it away?"

"You'd have to be near dying to admit that you hurt too much to compete with me." I locked my gaze to hers. "So why don't you want to bowl?"

"Because I was trying to do something nice."

I frowned at her. "I'm confused."

Then she poked me in the chest. "I said I didn't want to bowl with you because I was saving you from embarrassing you in front of your friends, okay?"

"Wait. Are you claiming that you will beat me so badly that I'll hang my head in *shame*?"

"Pretty much."

Was she bluffing?

Christ. I couldn't tell by her smirk, but no fucking way was I letting this slide.

I loomed over her. "Find a ball, get your shoes on and meet me on lane seven."

She shrugged and sidestepped me. "Don't say I didn't warn ya."

"Wait." I put my hands on her hips and spun her back to face me. "How about we have a little side wager on this game."

"Like?"

"Like the winner gets to choose what we do tomorrow on our date."

"We have a date tomorrow?"

"We agreed after the hockey game that once our favor for a favor was done, we'd continue to explore this thing between us." My eyes searched hers. "Unless you've changed your mind."

"I haven't."

"Good." I trailed my fingers down her face. "Let's make it official and go out on a date."

"Okay." She gave me the sweet, shy smile that just slayed me. "Can't wait until I get to tell you what I've got planned." She mock-whispered, "It might involve glitter glue and pipe cleaners."

"Gotta win first."

She rolled her eyes. "See you down there, loser."

By the time we were ready to bowl, everyone else had finished. And they all decided to stick around and watch our game.

I half expected Gabi to stroll down to the lane with a mono-grammed bowling bowl and her own shoes, such was her confidence level.

"Ladies first," I said and sat at the scoring console to watch her do her thing.

First frame she left a ten-pin, but she picked up the spare.

My turn. I held the ball close, pushed out, swung back and smoothly released it down the lane.

Strike.

I kept my face neutral as I turned around.

Sweetly, she said, "Beginner's luck?"

"I never said I was a beginner."

"But you said bowling wasn't your thing."

"It's not. Doesn't mean I can't do it."

She groaned. "I'm gonna regret taunting you, aren't I?"

"Probably." I tugged on her ponytail. "You're up."

We stayed neck and neck until the tenth frame. I left a seven-pin, but I picked up the spare. A strike would win the game. Anything less . . .

The ball left my grip a little wonky and I held my breath until all the pins were down.

I'd only beat her by one pin.

But a win was a win.

Gabi offered me her hand. "Good game."

I didn't care that we were in plain sight of our friends. I clasped her hand and pulled her body against mine. "The victor demands a hug."

She melted into me. With her cheek against my chest, she could hear how fast my heart beat and I could feel her smile when she said, "You really do like me, don't you?"

"Yes, Gabriella, I really do." I kissed the top of her head.

"What's the dress code for our date tomorrow?"

"Casual."

"Ugh. That tells me nothing because I know we have different definitions for casualwear."

"When I pick you up, I'll tell you if you're not properly attired for our outing. Deal?"

Gabi tipped her head back and looked at me. "You wouldn't rather meet?"

"It's our first official date, so you deserve the full date treatment."

"What time are you picking me up?"

"Eleven?"

"That'll work."

Just then Mariah and Amy butted in. "You've had your

turn with her, Lund, now it's ours and we have plans for the *center* of our universe." Mariah's fingers circled Gabi's wrist and she forced her to wave. "Bye-bye, this was great fun and I hope we can do it again sometime."

Gabi mouthed, *Help*, and I laughed. "Not a chance."

Twenty

GABI

Sunday morning I cursed Liddy and Dallas for being MIA when I needed their style advice.

I cursed Mariah and Amy for plying me with tequila shooters and sending me to bed without my usual dose of pre-hangover killers.

I cursed the fashion industry for making me question if leggings were pants or if wearing them was a dating faux pas.

I cursed the universe for the exciting hockey game on TV that distracted me right after I'd dabbed Preparation H on my lip to try and reduce the swelling.

Which meant I'd totally forgotten about the goop when I answered the knock on my door.

Nolan said, "What's on your mouth?" three seconds after I'd let him in.

And I also cursed Jensen Lund for giving his cousin my apartment number so I didn't have any warning before my date showed up.

"It's to reduce swelling."

He leaned closer to scrutinize my messed-up face.

It took everything inside me not to tuck my chin to my chest to hide from his scrutiny.

"What did you put on it? Vaseline?"

"A form of it."

"Does it still hurt?" he said softly.

"In some places more than others."

"I'd offer to kiss and make it better, but I see that's still not an option."

Deflated, I didn't move when he retreated and smiled at me.

"You ready?"

That's when I noticed the whole put-together package that was Nolan Lund.

Mr. "Casual" arrived wearing a gray-and-black pin-striped sport coat over a cream-colored cashmere turtleneck and black jeans.

I might've . . . sorta . . . growled at him.

"Uh-oh. That's an angry Coach Welk noise. What's wrong?"

"Fancy Pants. In what context is that outfit you're wearing considered casual?"

He looked down at his clothes and then back at me. "'Brunch with the Lund Collective' casual? I just came straight from there."

"Did you bring other clothes to change into?"

"What's wrong with what I've got on?" When I continued my hard stare, he added, "I'm wearing jeans, a sweater and a coat. Same thing you are."

My Lucky Brand dungarees and gray fisherman's pullover sweater were in the same category only insofar as they were cloth that covered body parts. I looked down at my socks that were decorated in flying pigs, because I knew I'd beaten him on the cool socks front, but even they couldn't bring a smile.

"Gabriella." Nolan gently trapped my face in his hands and forced me to look at him. "I'll say this once. How *I* dress has no bearing on *you* or on what *you* wear. None. I don't expect you to change anything about yourself to accommodate me."

"But I—"

"No *buts*. You are unlike any woman I've ever known. I like you just the way you are."

That Billy Joel song started playing in my head, and yeah, maybe it warmed my heart a little.

"You know that I'm a 'fancy pants' clothes hound and you've accepted that about me, right?"

I nodded again.

"So chances are high that our daily styles won't be in alignment. I won't take it as a personal affront that you didn't dress up for me if you don't take it as judgment that I have a different idea of casual than you."

Right then, I fell a bit more for this man.

Okay. A lot more.

We'd misjudged each other based on appearances and here was an explanation—not an excuse—that I could agree with.

"You just destroyed any argument I might've had with logic. How dare you."

He smiled.

"My only request is if we decide on dinner or drinks or whatnot at a place that has a dress code, you give me advance notice."

"How far in advance?"

"An hour? I should be able to pull something together in that time."

"Done." He pressed his lips to my forehead in a lingering kiss. "You ready for our day?"

Wait. We were spending the whole day together? Did that mean the night, too?

Good thing I'd shaved.

"I'm hoping wherever we're going has food. I'm starved."

"There's food."

"Cool. Then let's roll."

Full-date-treatment Nolan held my hand as we walked to his sportscar.

The music in the background during our ride changed from rap to rock to country. I thought it was sweet he'd shared his "favorites" playlist with me. Kind of like giving a girl a mixtape back in the day.

When we pulled into the Topgolf parking lot in Brooklyn Park, I smiled at him. "This is awesome, Nolan."

"So I get positive marks for our first date activity?"

"Yes. I've always wanted to come here." I leaned over the console and mock-whispered, "Just because I haven't golfed *here* doesn't mean I haven't golfed. See how that full disclosure thing works?"

Nolan turned his head. We were face-to-face. Almost mouth to mouth. His gaze dropped to my lips and then crawled back up to my eyes. "Stop it."

"What?"

"Tempting me with those 'please kiss me' puppy-dog eyes."

"But don't you want to kiss me?"

"You really want me to kiss you for the first time in the parking lot of Topgolf?"

"Yes please," I breathed.

He shifted slightly so his lips grazed my cheek. "Nope."

I might've called him a vile name.

As usual, he chuckled.

Nolan kept hold of my hand as our host took us to the second level. "We'd appreciate a server coming over right away."

"Not a problem."

Nolan passed me the menu. "I ate a substantial amount at brunch, so I'm not hungry, but you go ahead and get whatever you want."

I ordered an appetizer snack platter of fried pickles, mozzarella cheese sticks, fried mushrooms, cheese curds and seasoned fries. He ordered us both a margarita.

I wandered to the edge of the platform to check out the place. Although we were outside, we did have another level above us, so it didn't feel as if we were out in the elements. Each table had a pair of gas heaters and there were signs around that more heat could be provided if the guest requested it. I must've been navel-gazing for a while because when I returned to the table, the food and drinks were there.

Sliding into my seat, I said, "Do you come here very often?"

"Maybe twice a year. Have you ever been to one of these?"

"A couple down South but I didn't think they'd be open up here in the winter."

"It is. And winter is almost over."

I shook my finger at him. "No. I am not getting sucked into a discussion about the weather on our date, because that's a sign things are going bad."

"Agreed. So what shall we discuss?"

"I wanna know why they call you 'the Prince' at LI."

His eyes narrowed. "Where did you hear that?"

"Around." I dipped a fry in ranch dressing and it stung the shit out of my lip when I popped it in my mouth. I'd overdone it since my injury with all the talking, using my whistle during games, drinking and eating. Inactivity was the only way to heal faster. I looked at all the crunchy fried food I'd ordered and realized I probably couldn't eat any of it. Awesome. Maybe Nolan wouldn't notice.

"The optimistic me would like to think the employees consider my dad the king, so I'd be the prince."

"Dare I ask what pessimistic Nolan thinks?"

"That I'm lucky not to be nicknamed the joker."

"Ooh. Harsh." I picked up a mozz stick. The breading scraped against my lip. I set it down and shoved three cheese curds in my mouth whole because I was starved.

"Annika is known as the 'Iron Princess' for being straightforward."

A swig of my margarita washed down the cheese, and the salt stung my lip. "It sounds like a literal definition. So you're definitely 'the Prince' for being the most charming of them all."

He smiled. "Total optimism, Pollyanna."

I ate a mushroom whole and that seemed to go okay so I ate two more.

"We've never talked about your Welk family name. Jax mentioned your relation to the famous Lawrence Welk, but he didn't specify how."

"His youngest brother, Mike, was my great-grandfather. I never knew him. My grandpa was actually an 'out-of-wedlock' baby, raised alone by his mother, who was a Lutheran woman, which was a cardinal sin in a German Roman Catholic family like the Welks. They were basically ostracized, so she relocated them to Grand Forks, but funnily enough, she gave him the Welk name."

"How many new people you meet ask about that family connection?"

"In the Midwest? Everyone." I attempted another fry.

"Does it bother you?"

I looked at him. "No. Unless people are being mean and say *an-a-wunna-an-a-tuua* because they think he's a joke. Uncle Larry—that's what I've always called him in my head, BT-dubs—was a *wunnerful, wunnerful* man who never forgot his roots. He brought joy to a lot of people. It's a legacy to be proud of."

He studied me. "You're not being facetious."

"Not a bit." I found a small fried pickle and chewed it slowly to see if it'd sting. It did.

"I wish I could kiss you right now."

And . . . the pickle got stuck in my throat. I sputtered, coughed and managed to choke it down. "Dude. Don't *say* things like that when I'm eating."

"Are you done chewing for a moment?"

"Yes."

He leaned forward. "You have the sexiest mouth."

"Even with a boxer's lip?"

"Even then."

I made the time-out sign.

"What?"

"I think before you try and melt my damn panties while I'm scarfing down appetizers, we should review our dating ground rules."

"Jesus. Of course she has rules." He knocked back a large drink of his margarita. "Hit me with rule one."

"We're exclusive."

"Kind of a no-brainer, Gabriella."

I ate another mushroom. "Rule two. STDs. We exchange health histories ASAP because I'm allergic to most condoms. We could use a spermicide if you want, even when I'm on the pill."

Nolan's eyes flashed with heat. "This matter-of-fact discussion of us fucking is turning me on. Was that your intent?"

I rolled my eyes. "You won't even kiss me, so no."

"I don't have an STD, despite my manwhore past. I had a physical mid-January. All clean." He pulled out his phone and started swiping through apps. Within a minute, my phone pinged with a text message. "My latest test results. I haven't been with anyone since New Year's Eve."

"Not being sarcastic, but is that unusual for you?"

"Very. I wanted my personal life to go a different direction this year and it has." He stole a fry. "How about you?"

"I also had my yearly physical in January, as required by the Minnesota Youth Hockey League. Clean test results, which I'll send after I piss and moan about the fact I can't remember my damn log-in for the health site."

He snickered.

"The last time Tyson and I had sex was like . . . December."

"It's April."

"Yeah, so? Like I told you earlier, I was a shitty girlfriend to him. But I promise, Lund, I will be the very best girlfriend to you."

"You're already the best girlfriend since you'll be the first woman I've ever slept with without wearing a condom."

I fake gasped. "I get to be a first for you for something?"

"The pressure is on, baby." He grabbed my hand and kissed my knuckles. "I wanna be a first for you for something too."

"Maybe you'll be the first guy who can beat me at golf." I stood. "Let's play."

He frowned at all the remaining food. "But you barely ate anything."

"I was a dumbass ordering what I did, since it's all breaded and salty and impossible to eat. I'll be fine."

"Wrong. I'm not taking a chance you'll topple over the edge, so I'll find something on this menu you can eat while you figure out your password and send me your health history."

Okay then.

By the time I found the information, copied it and texted it to him, the fruit and protein smoothie he'd ordered had arrived.

"Thank you, Nolan. This is really sweet of you."

He messed with the digital screen, adding our names. "What game do you want to play first?"

"What are the choices?"

"Basic high score out of nine balls, or accuracy hitting four targets, or farthest shot and closest to the flag shot."

"Nine balls."

As he relayed our game choice, I wandered over to choose my club. All of them were kind of crappy choices. I lifted the one I wanted out and spun around.

Nolan took one look at me holding the 9-iron and began to laugh. Hard.

"Wanna share what's so gut-bustlingly funny?"

"Happy Gilmore."

"Excuse me?"

"This reminds me of *Happy Gilmore*."

"Because I'm a hockey player about to play golf?"

"Yes! I freakin' love that movie. And now I'm annoyed with myself for not naming it when we were texting about comfort movies."

"You're weird, Lund."

"Not a surprise to you, Happy."

I lowered the golf club. "Did you just call me Happy?"

"Yep. I've decided that'll be my pet name for you."

"No."

"Yes. Come on. It's perfect. And that means you get to give me a pet name too."

I opened my mouth to say something rude, when he stopped me. "Something *nice*, Happy."

Christ. He'd nicknamed me Happy.

At least he wasn't calling me Crabby Gabi.

Think, Gabi. Something clever. Something to do with a prince . . .

Aha.

I smirked at him. "Okay. Got one."

"Tell me."

"You have to earn it. So quit stalling and let's play. You can even go first."

I realized he really knew how to play golf after I witnessed his Tiger Woods–worthy swing.

Jerk.

So, looking around to make sure no one was watching me, I went for comedic relief, racing up to the ball sideways, swinging my golf club like a caveman the way Happy did in the movie.

Nolan laughed so hard he was crying.

To see him let go so completely with me . . . that was heady stuff.

When the man trounced me in all three styles of games, I

couldn't even be mad about it. I couldn't remember the last time I'd had so much fun on a date.

Yes. You can. At the barcade.

But that hadn't been a date.

How about at the bowling alley yesterday?

Technically, that hadn't been a date either, but why had it felt like one?

Because every time you're with him it feels special, and yet at the same time . . . familiar.

I felt the press of his body behind mine and his hands squeezed my hips. "Whatcha thinking about so hard?"

"What game I could beat you at three times in a row for our next challenge."

"We don't have to compete with everything, Happy."

"Yes, we do, Ozzy. It's what we do."

Nolan went still behind me. "Ozzy is the nickname you came up with? As in, Ozzy Osbourne, Prince of Darkness?"

"See what I did there?"

"Babe. The woman who created *Asswipf* can do better than that."

"Fine," I huffed. "I'll just call you Charming."

"That'll work." He tugged on my ponytail. "Come on. Our time here is up. Onto our next dating adventure."

Our next stop was Izzy's Ice Cream. Nolan didn't even make fun of me for mostly holding the plain vanilla malt cup against my lip until it'd melted enough that I could drink it.

He drove us to a parking lot, demanding I let him cover my eyes as he directed me forward, laughing as we duckwalked with his arms wrapped around my chest and his rough-skinned hands covering my face.

Then he whispered, "Okay, open them."

We stood in front of the Riverview Theater, a movie house that'd been in business since the late 1940s. I'd wanted to come here for ages, not solely because they had cheap ticket prices, but because it'd retained that classic old-movie-theater vibe.

But when I saw what was playing on the marquee, I spun around, my mouth open in total shock. "*Ladyhawke*? Is this a coincidence?"

"What do you think?"

When I narrowed my eyes at him, he laughed.

"I called in a favor. No big." He pointed to the line of people waiting to get in. "As you can see, this will be profitable for them too."

"I want to kiss you so badly right now it actually hurts."

Nolan lowered his forehead to mine. "I know."

I covered my sappy moment with a flip, "Well, you'll get off cheap at the concession stand, not having to buy me popcorn since I can't eat it."

After the movie, I figured Nolan would take me home. But we ended up at the Hi-Lo Diner. He ordered soft scrambled eggs, white bread, not toast, and plain oatmeal—for both of us.

"You don't have to suffer just because I am."

"It's killing me not kissing you so I figured we could suffer *all* things together."

This man. I was half in love with him already. On our first damn date.

He threaded our fingers together across the Formica tabletop. "What?"

"Will you freak out if I tell you this is the best date I've ever had?"

"Ever?"

"Ever."

"We're on the same page, Happy, because it's the best date I've ever had too."

Happy. He killed me.

"What's on the tycoon's agenda this week?"

"Headed out of town on Wednesday. Business trip that I've been putting off."

He swept his thumb back and forth over the inside of my wrist. Natural affection was another surprising reveal about Nolan Lund.

"What about you?" he asked.

"I'm doing season wrap-up stuff. Then I'm holding an out-of-town clinic. Although the last class doesn't end until eight, I'll probably come home Saturday night. I'd rather sleep in my own bed."

He sighed. "Juggling 'opposite schedules' is part of the dating gig with business professionals, isn't it?"

"Unfortunately, yes. I'm glad we can text." I lifted our joined hands and looked at his long fingers. He had nice hands.

He has a nice everything.

"That's not an accurate gauge, you know."

"What?"

"A man's hand size in relation to the size of his dick."

"Umm, dude, that's not what I was contemplating at all. Since you already told me your dick is average sized."

He lifted a brow. "What if I lied?"

"Telling me it was a monster cock would've indicated that you were attempting to overcompensate, so I believe you that it's average."

"Jesus, Gabriella."

"Besides, it's not like I'll find that out firsthand tonight."

Our food arrived and we didn't say much as we dug in.

After we cleaned our plates, we both ordered coffee.

Nolan leaned back in the booth, looking at me curiously.

"What? Do I have egg on my face or something?"

"Hilarious. But no. I'm wondering why you think I don't plan on ending our date with a bang."

I squirmed at being put on the spot.

"Tell me."

"You've mostly been a 'one and done' or 'two and through' guy. You don't want that with me. You want our relationship to be different from the start."

"How can you know me so well in such a short span of time?"

I shrugged. "I pay attention to body language. I'm a good listener. Maybe I've been comforting myself throughout this date with the knowledge that even if you could kiss me breathless, we still wouldn't end up naked together at some point tonight."

"That bothers you."

"Of course it does." Leaning closer, I rested my forearms on the table. "Why do *you* get to decide that? It takes two to tango, Charming. My lust for you should get a vote."

"Gabriella."

God. The sexy, raspy way he ground out my name scraped along my nerve endings like a rough caress across my skin.

"But the truth is . . . I get it. It's probably a good thing we're not making out like fiends. I doubt I could come without being kissed anyway."

Nolan choked on his coffee. "What the hell is that supposed to mean?"

"Kissing is . . . intimate. Or passionate. Or sweet. It sets the tone for sex. Without it? No real intimacy. Or passion. Or sweetness. I can't come without those sensations being in play."

He met me halfway across the table, eyes flashing fire. "I can make you come, harder than you've ever come in your life, without putting my lips on yours even one time."

I laughed.

"I'm not even close to joking, Gabriella."

"Well, it's a moot point." I signaled for the check. He'd become so broody he hadn't objected when I paid for our meal.

Nolan continued to mutter on the way back to Snow Village. Once there, he parked sideways in front of the row of single-car garages.

When he still didn't speak after shutting off the car, I'd reached my limit.

"Look. I don't know what crawled—"

"Under my skin and into my thoughts to the point I can't think of anything else?" he supplied. Then he faced me. "That would be you, Gabriella. Specifically the challenge you threw down that I can't show you intimacy without us being in a liplock. I want a chance to prove you wrong."

"Wait a sec. You mean you want to do this *now*?"

"Yes. Right here, right now." Then he eased his seat all the way back and patted his thighs. "Come sit on my lap."

"B-but . . . my apartment is right there."

"We both know what'll happen if we're in a space with a bed. So let's mess around, pace ourselves and not race to the finish line." He reached over and curled his hand across my throat. "I want to make you mindless from just my touch, my whispers in your ear and my mouth on your skin."

That might've been the hottest thing any man had ever said to me.

He kept that sexy gaze on mine as his thumb stroked my neck. "What do you say?"

My body screamed YES! But reluctantly, I replied, "No."

Shocked, he echoed, "No?"

"I don't want pieces of intimacy, Nolan. I want all of you, all of us, touching and kissing without limitations. Not only can't I kiss your mouth, I can't kiss you anywhere else. So as anxious as I am to explore this heat between us, I'd rather wait until I can get you as lust-drunk as I know you will make me."

After a moment, he sighed. "Fair enough."

My gaze fell to his perfect, pouting mouth. "I really want to kiss you good night."

"You'll have to settle for this." He kissed my cheek. Then my temple. Then the corner of my eye. Then my ear, where he growled, "Fucking cookies," before he nipped my lobe and retreated.

Then a beep and his car doors slid up.

I was surprised to see him get out of the car too. At my quizzical look, he said, "I'll at least walk you to the door."

"Not necessary." I smirked at him. "I might be tempted to invite you in. You can watch me from here. Good night, Charming."

"Good night, Happy."

I wrapped my coat more tightly around me as I walked to my building. I turned and blew him a kiss after we were safely separated by a locked glass door.

Twenty-One

NOLAN

I hadn't seen Gabi yesterday. Nor had we exchanged more than a quick text or two.

That worried me. Had I pushed her too far Sunday night? Even when all I'd done was suggest we mess around, mostly clothed, in a parked car like a couple of horny teens?

Way to bring your A game, Lund, when it really matters.

So yeah, I felt a bit stalkerish parking in the Lakeside lot, waiting for her to lock up for the night. But I needed to see her in-person reaction to me, so I hadn't texted her that I'd planned to stop by after work.

The last student had left ten minutes ago. Finally the interior lights in the building clicked off and Gabi pushed through the door, pausing outside to set the alarm.

As soon as she turned around, I flashed my car lights to get her attention and held my breath for her reaction.

She lifted her head and stopped on the sidewalk.

I'd rested my backside against the driver's side door of my

Bugatti, trying to look casual and cool, but my heart skipped. I managed a smile and a dorky, "Heya, Coach."

Gabi's face lit up and she ran toward me.

Ran.

Okay, then. Guess that answered that question.

I caught her, giving her a full-body hug, which she fully returned.

Everything inside me settled.

"I was just about to call you and see if you wanted to meet up," she said against my chest.

I kissed the top of her head. "Where did you have in mind to meet?"

Gabi tipped her head back and looked at me. "My bedroom."

For once, my focus didn't get ensnared by her twinkling silvery-blue eyes. My gaze fell to her mouth.

Her mostly healed mouth. Her busted lip looked . . . nearly normal.

"How?"

"After you dropped me off Sunday, I knew if I wanted it to heal faster I'd have to rest it fully and do nothing to agitate it. Which meant no talking. At all. No eating besides drinking protein drinks. No constantly blowing a whistle. So I didn't work yesterday or today. I came in half an hour before class ended to close up so Margene could go home. I kept the cut dry, using gauze and cotton—even when I slept, which was a lot—and that allowed me to use ointment to speed up the healing process."

"You needed the rest. I'm glad you took it." I scrutinized the rest of her face. The bruises looked more colorful, but that meant they'd be gone soon too. "Is it still sore?"

"Only one way to find out," she whispered huskily.

I curled my hands around her face and lowered my mouth to hers.

We'd both formed our lips into an exaggerated pucker, and we remained like that for several long moments, just because we finally could. Then we smiled simultaneously, and our lips started to move against each other's. Tentatively at first, not out of fear of reinjuring her lip, but to drag out each breath-taking second of our first kiss.

I willed time to stand still so I could remember every teasing glide of her soft flesh against mine. Every soft breath. Every gentle lick. Every needy moan rumbling between us. Her sweet taste on my tongue. The fervent sucking as she tasted me. The pliant give-and-take.

We were explorers, eager to experience each sensation until we were ready to move on. Greedy for the next one as we gorged on it in a dizzying rush of desire. Soul kissing. Openmouthed and hungry. Our heads in a constant state of movement as we attempted every angle to find the perfect fit of our lips. Our tongues twining, stroking lazily, teasing and retreating. We were lost to everything except sating this endless need for more.

Gabi shivered and I forced my mouth from hers, although not entirely as I continued to give her soft smooches as the fog of pleasure began to clear.

I opened my eyes to see her staring at me with the same awe I knew was reflected in my eyes.

"Nolan."

"Mmm?"

"Did we just reinvent kissing?"

"Sure seems like it."

"Come home with me. Now."

"Yes." I swept my lips up the strong line of her jaw to her ear. "But you have to let go of my jacket first, sweetheart."

"Oh. Damn. Right." She released her death grip on my lapels and stepped back. "Uh. See you there."

But she didn't move toward her truck.

"Gabriella? Are you okay to drive?"

"Not right at this second. Are you?"

"Not even fucking close."

She made the time-out sign. "We need to stay in our separate corners to get our heads on straight before we hit the road, okay?"

I nodded.

In my car I turned the air conditioner on full blast, as well as Eminem to clear away the lust long enough to operate a damn vehicle.

When Gabi honked twice to get my attention, I shoved the car in gear and followed her.

The instant we'd closed and locked her apartment door, we were on each other. Mouths sneaking kisses as our coats and shoes littered the floor.

Clamping my hands on her ass, I lifted her and demanded, "Bedroom."

"End of the hallway. Hurry," she said, her fingers diving into my hair as she attacked my neck with her teeth and sucking kisses.

Her bedroom wasn't totally dark, but lit by a lone lamp that gave me enough light to admire her by. I let her body slide down the length of mine before I put a few feet between us.

I shrugged out of my suit jacket, draping it over a chair. As I undid my cufflinks, I said, "Get naked for me."

She yanked her sweater off, letting it fall behind her, leaving her in a see-through nude-colored stretchy sports bra.

"Christ. Lookit you. C'mere."

"Nope. Your turn."

"First time I've ever regretted wearing a three-piece suit," I grumbled. I loosened my tie, ditched it and my vest before unbuttoning my dress shirt and chucking the pile toward my jacket, leaving me in just a T-shirt.

Next, instead of unhooking her bra, Gabi peeled her leggings and underwear off.

"Gabriella."

"We're taking turns. So drop your pants, Lund."

I undid my belt, unbuttoned and unzipped, shucking my

boxer briefs and pants to the floor, all without taking my eyes off her chest.

She was quiet a beat too long and I chanced a glance at her. "What?"

"Nice manscaping. Oh, and, Charming? That's definitely above average."

"Glad you approve. Get those sweet tits over here."

"The last of our clothing off at the same time."

I said, "Fine," and whipped off my T-shirt so fast that I wouldn't miss a millisecond of my first glimpse of her unfettered breasts.

Gabi popped the front clasp on her bra and then she stood before me, gloriously naked, eyes blazing as her gaze worshipped me as thoroughly as mine worshipped her.

"This body," I groaned. "Gimme all of it."

"Same."

I molded her flesh in both hands, then bent down. Faced with all that abundant skin, I feasted on her breasts, sucking her nipples, kissing the valley of her cleavage, over and over as she writhed against me.

Jesus. The sweaty, musky, salty taste of her kicked my greediness to an epic level and I couldn't stop.

Her soft plea of my name brought me back around, when I realized I'd reverted to grunts as my only manner of communication.

Nuzzling the soft swells of her breasts, I reached for her hands and flattened her palms on my pecs. "Your turn. Touch me, Gabriella. Please."

She ruffled her fingers through the hair on my chest, lightly dancing the tips of her fingers over my nipples until they were hard nubs. She bent her mouth to them.

I hissed with unabashed need.

Instead of continuing in a southward progression, she glided her palms up. Smoothing them over my shoulders, squeezing and sighing as she mapped my biceps and triceps with her strong grip. Then she pressed a singular kiss to my

Adam's apple as one hand cupped the back of my neck and the other hand sneakily slipped between my thighs to cup me there.

I circled my hand around her wrist, stopping her. "Let's finish this on the bed."

In one fast move, she sidestepped me and pushed all the pillows and the comforter to the floor. Then she crawled to the center of the mattress, making sure I got an eyeful of her luscious ass.

Which I obligingly sank my teeth into since she'd presented it to me so blatantly.

She squealed and I flipped her onto her back, pressing my body over hers, silencing her protest with my mouth.

We kissed for an eternity.

Kissing Gabi when we were clothed was spectacular.

Kissing Gabi when we were naked was the ultimate intimacy. Yes, there was urgency, but there was also sweetness. And trust. And tenderness. And an understanding even before our bodies connected that this was special. Nearly sacred. So we weren't in any rush.

Until we were.

I slid my hand up the center of her body and planted kisses across her neck, stopping below her ear. "Open your mouth for me."

Before she did as I'd asked, she said, "Your bossy side in bed does it for me in a bad way, Lund."

"Good to know." Keeping my focus on the split spot on her lip, I eased two fingers inside her mouth. "Suck on them. Get them nice and wet."

"Is this where I confess you won't need the extra lube because I'm completely soaked?"

I nipped at her closest nipple.

She gave me a helluva show as she tongued and sucked on my fingers.

Gently I eased my fingers out of her mouth. Then I shifted my arm down to slowly push them inside her as I kissed her collarbone. "You weren't kidding. I love that you're hot and wet." My voice became a rough whisper against her skin when I said, "Smooth and silky and perfect."

"Nolan. Please."

I switched to barely there butterfly kisses on the most sensitive part of her neck as my fingers and thumb began to work her over faster.

Gabi tried to ride my hand, but I stopped it with a firm, "No," rasped directly in her ear. "My pace. You like me bossy."

When she whimpered and swore at me, I rumbled out a low laugh against her throat that caused gooseflesh to break out across her entire body.

Her breathing quickened so I sped up my movements between her legs.

And I watched every emotion on her face as she came undone. Arching, gasping, giving her pleasure over to my keeping entirely.

I murmured, "Beautiful," and she blinked her eyes open.

Her answering smile managed to be both soft and sexy.

Her eyes went back to lustful when I slid my fingers out and rose onto my knees between her thighs. She watched as I wiped her wetness on my shaft. "It's killing me not to shove my fingers in my mouth and suck them clean, but the first time I taste you will be directly from the source."

"God, you dirty-talking bastard. You're killing me. Fuck me already."

I grinned. "You ready for this?"

"Bring it, Charming."

I stretched my body over hers, propped up on my elbows as she reached between us to guide me.

Her breath was hot in my ear as I pushed inside her. Slowly.

Holy hell. This was . . .

Everything.

I closed my eyes and counted to ten. To twenty. To fifty.

Soft hands brushed over my ass. "Nolan?"

"Give me a moment to savor doing this with you with no condom." My teeth sank into my bottom lip. "This is the most epically amazing day of my entire existence."

She snickered.

"You won't be laughing when I confess this won't last long. It feels so fucking insane that I'll probably forget about touching you, so you'll have to help me out."

"I'm already halfway to coming again so we're good," she murmured huskily and scraped her teeth down my throat. "Move this hot body and show me whatcha got."

A quick thrust up as I pressed my groin into her core. After hitting her hot spot, which elicited her sexy groan, I pulled out and immediately slammed back in with a fast snap of my hips.

"Yes. Like that."

"This is next level," I grunted as I ramped up my pace.

Her tits bounced as I drove into her.

The heat from her body and mine created a slick friction, surrounding us with the new scent our bodies created together. I wanted to stay right here, in our hot, dirty sex cocoon, forever.

I realized the guttural sounds of need were coming from me when that familiar tingle started to build. But it was fast. Too fast that I couldn't hold back.

So by the time her rhythmic pulsations were viselike around my shaft, I was flat-out gasping as I came harder than I ever had in my life, pouring myself into her while she whispered wicked encouragement in my ear.

Finally I couldn't hold myself upright anymore.

Brain fuzzy. Quads quaking. Biceps shaking. She'd spun me into that place where even my hearing had deserted me, and I melted on top of her.

Gabi's mouth sought mine. I found the strength to roll onto my back, keeping her stretched out on top of me while we caught our breath between lazy kisses.

My hands shook as they stroked her spine.

She nuzzled my jaw sweetly, peppering my chest with kisses as she ran her hands through my hair.

With every shift of her body across mine, that warm, cocoa butter, sugary vanilla scent wafted up.

I continued to hold her, just breathing her in, basking in her—in us. However, I did rouse out of my languor to lightly whap her butt when she snickered at me, muttering, "Fucking cookies."

Her shiver brought us back to reality.

She pushed away from me and leaned down to grab a blanket.

When our eyes met, I reached out and curled my hand around her face. "Saying thank you seems inadequate for what just happened between us."

"I know. But I'm thankful too."

"I wish I could stay with you tonight. But I've got a six A.M. flight."

She sighed. "How long will you be gone?"

"I get back Thursday night."

"Of course you do because I leave Thursday afternoon to drive to Rice Lake for a hockey camp."

"When will you get back?"

"Late Saturday night."

"Then I'll be here Sunday morning at nine so we can spend at least one day together this week."

She turned her head and kissed my wrist. "I'd love that."

"It sucks that we've got opposite travel schedules."

"It does. But like you said one time, we'll adapt. We can always sext."

"No offense, Happy, but even sexting ain't gonna cut it when now I know it's like *this* between us."

Gabi smirked. "We do have killer chemistry. And just think . . . sex will only get better between us."

I groaned. "You just had to point that out."

Twenty-Two

GABI

It started out as a typical Tuesday morning at Lakeside.

Except I was dragging ass into work because Nolan had kept me up late last night "saying good-bye" since he had business meetings out of town again the first part of this week.

We'd been dating for two weeks. Most of that time we'd spent apart but when we were both in town, we spent our time together, usually in my bed.

So while both Nolan and I wished our relationship allowed us more time together, we made the best of those moments we had. Plus, we'd gotten incredibly good at sexting.

After brewing a pot of coffee, I opened my laptop. While I should've been going over Jax's questions on our revised summer schedule, my thoughts drifted. Nearly three weeks had passed since my job interview with Wolf Sports North. Maybe it was time to accept that I hadn't been chosen for either sportscasting position. But I knew I couldn't continue to languish at Lakeside either—a decision that would be harder to follow through with now that Nolan and I were in a relationship.

The alarm to the front door dinged, startling me out of my melancholy.

Probably just UPS. Or maybe Margene had come in early. Still, I hopped up because I should've locked the main door behind me after I'd arrived. I'd just cleared the edge of my desk when Edie Lund walked into the office.

She looked outstanding in a flowing cream shirt, beautifully patterned with pastel flowers, paired with ankle-length trousers the color of lemon sorbet and raffia wedges edged in gold trim that matched her handbag and her gold jewelry. The chic shades covering her eyes probably cost more than my LASIK eye surgery. Even after she pushed them on top of her head, her hairstyle wasn't mussed at all.

"Good morning, Gabi."

"Good morning, Mrs. Lund." I paused. "Is everything all right?"

"Yes. Please call me Edie. If you're not too busy, I'd like a word with you."

"Sure. Come in. Would you like coffee?"

"Desperately, but no need to wait on me. I'll get it and be right back."

I flopped in my chair, half-afraid that I was about to get the "you're no good for my son" warning.

She paused in the doorway and looked nervously over her shoulder. "You're sure you're the only one here?"

"Yes."

"Good." Then she shut the door.

My panic climbed about fifty levels.

After she glided into the chair opposite my desk, she set her enormous purse on the floor and met my gaze as she sipped from her cup. After that first drink, she sighed. "I wouldn't have survived parenthood if not for unhealthy amounts of caffeine. It's a habit I've never broken."

"Are you just a coffee drinker? Or are you into energy drinks?"

"I've tried them, the crash is just too severe. With coffee, I can dose myself all day long and no one has any idea how much I consume." She smirked. "You won't tell on me, will you?"

"Of course not."

"So I imagine you're a little unsettled that I just popped in unannounced, when we don't really know each other."

"I'll admit . . . it is kind of freaking me out."

"Well, the situation I've found myself in is freaking *me* out and I need your help."

I blinked at her. "My help?"

"It's come to my attention, that you . . ." She snapped her mouth shut.

Silence settled between us and it took all of my willpower not to confess that yes, I was currently sleeping with her son and loving every moment of it.

"I'm making this harder than it has to be, but I came here to warn you." Then she blurted out, "Lucy has decided she needs to bond with the women employees here at Lakeside, in keeping with the 'family' vibe Jax is trying to create. Yesterday I picked Mimi up from school and brought her to hockey practice. Lucy had mentioned wanting to talk to me, so I tracked her down and she was sitting over there"—she pointed to the loveseat and chair lounge area in the corner—"with Margene and Connie."

"Connie the office manager? What had she been doing here that late?"

"I wondered that too. While I was standing there, awkwardly I might add, your co-coach, Anna, bounced in, and said, 'Oh good, we're all here, now we can start.'" Edie took another fortifying drink of coffee. "That's when I noticed a pile of yarn on Lucy's lap. My first thought was selfish. I'd hoped her knitting baby booties was a clever way of sharing that she and Jax were expecting."

"Is that why you need my help? To throw a baby shower?"

"Heavens, no. I'd jumped to the wrong conclusion. Then Anna plunked herself right next to Lucy and pulled out her own ball of yarn. In one of those slow-motion 'I can't believe what I'm seeing' moments, I realized everyone held yarn balls. *Everyone*, Gabi. Then Lucy handed me a bag and welcomed me to the first meeting of the Lakeside Craft Club."

"*Noooo*," I gasped in horror.

"Yes! Lucy started a craft club and she expects me to be in it. Me." She thumped her chest. "Do I *look* like I enjoy crafting?" She paused. "No, don't answer that. I'm not being disrespectful. While I appreciate that women love crafting and kudos to them for being so passionate about it, I am *not* one of those women."

"Me neither."

"I suspected as much. Which is why I'm here."

My brain scrolled back to something she'd said when she first walked in: "*I came to warn you.*"

"Oh, *hell* no."

"They have a bag like this"—she reached down and pulled out a canvas bag with an iron-on transfer of an ice skating pond, with EDIE in red sequins across the top—"literally with your name on it."

"You're joking, right? This is some prank you and Lucy are playing on me since I'm dating Nolan, to see if I have a sense of humor off the ice."

Those eyes, so much like Nolan's, widened. "You are dating my son?"

Damn. "I thought you knew." I forced myself to breathe and my heart to slow down.

"Nolan has been scarce lately on the weekends. Even Archer mentioned they hadn't played racquetball recently." She sat back and studied me for a few beats before she smiled. "Now it makes sense. You and Nolan. Interesting."

What was interesting to me was he hadn't told his parents

about us. Then again, I hadn't told my parents about him, so we were even on that front.

She said, "How long?"

"We had our first date the day after his LCCO event. But we'd been talking for a few weeks before that."

"I'm thrilled for both of you, but it'll be our secret, okay? I'll wait for him to tell me. Now back to the crisis at hand. When your name came up during crafting club, Connie, Anna and Lucy said they were scared to approach you, but Margene said she'd handle it. Today."

Scared. I snorted. "A crafting club. Why not a book club or a wine club or a—"

"Strip club," we said simultaneously.

We both laughed.

"I'm guessing because *they* all like to craft. And what's worse? They're all doing the *same* craft, so they can—"

"Compare?" I supplied with dread. "Omigod, no freakin' way."

"There's no possible way we can get out of this."

I could get out of it if Wolf Sports North offered me a position. But that'd leave poor Edie alone—a non-crafter in crafter club. I couldn't do that to her; hell, I couldn't do that to anyone, but especially not to Nolan's mother since I wanted her to adore me.

"What if . . . we got kicked out of the club?"

Edie's eyes flashed surprise, then hope. "That is brilliant! How would we go about it?"

"My first thought as a hockey player would be to pick a fight."

"Sorry. My brawling days are over." She frowned and pulled her phone out of her purse. After reading the screen, her face held an expression of dismay.

"What's wrong?"

Edie flipped her phone around so I could see it.

It was Connie: 40% off yarn sale at Hobby Lobby! No coupon needed!

My eyes met Edie's. I whispered, "Are you in a crafting text message group now too?"

"Yes. Lucy gave them my number, Gabi."

I circled her wrist. "I'm gonna get you out of this, Edie. I promise."

"Thank you."

The outer door dinged again and we both froze.

Margene's distinctive whistle echoed down the hallway.

"She can't catch me in here," Edie said in a panic, shoving the craft bag back into her oversized purse. "She'll know that I warned you."

"She always goes to the break room first. Hide behind the door. When I open it, I'll keep you hidden and her busy while you make a break for it." I gripped her arm again. "Don't look back. No matter what you hear, make a run for it and don't look back."

Edie nodded.

I was up, out of my chair and opening the door before Margene could reach us. "Hey, Margene. You're early today."

"Gotta get some stuff done. Where're you going?"

"To get more coffee. That's where you were headed, right?" I said a little louder than usual as we continued walking.

"Yep. After that, there's something I wanna talk to you about." She stopped and grinned at me when we were in the break room. "Something fun."

The door chime dinged.

Margene whirled around. "Wonder who that could be?"

"No one," I lied. "Probably just the wind. It's been a phantom menace lately."

Blank look.

Nolan would've laughed at my *Star Wars* pun.

Margene shrugged and I relaxed that Edie had gotten away.

I wasn't so lucky.

LATER THAT NIGHT . . .

ME: I accidentally outed us to your mother today.

NL: Good.

ME: Nolan, you have to tell her we're together and act surprised when she acts like she doesn't know or karma will make us break up over something stupid.

NL: DALLAS GIVE GABRIELLA BACK HER PHONE THIS ISN'T FUNNY.

ME: Ha. Good one. I'm serious though.

NL: No prob. I'll tell her when we go over the LCCO event numbers Friday morning. What did you and my mom talk about?

ME: It's a secret. But I will tell you I like her.

NL: If the two of you are already swapping secrets then she likes you too.

ME: ♡

NL: When do you get done with your hockey clinic this weekend?

ME: Saturday. Mid-afternoon.

NL: I want you to spend the weekend with me. At my house.

ME: Charming. For REAL?

NL: Yes.

ME: I'd be honored. That wasn't me being flip.

NL: I know. Sending you the address now.

ME: Does that mean I won't hear from you until then?

NL: I'll text you when I can. Think of me. Miss me. Send me tit pics. 😬

ME: NO WAY

NL: 😝

Twenty-Three

GABI

Nolan's place wasn't anything like I expected.

First of all, it was an actual house, not a luxury apartment with skyscraper views.

And it was in the suburbs—St. Louis Park to be exact.

He'd instructed me to follow the driveway up and around the back of the house since there wasn't parking on the street. The angle was so steep I wondered how he got out during the long Minnesota winters. Maybe he had one of those fancy heated driveways that kept ice from forming. Or maybe he hired a company to clear his driveway after every snowstorm. Or maybe he hired a car service to pick him up.

The fact I was contemplating the logistics of snow removal in his life indicated my nervousness at being here.

I parked off to the side of the three-car garage and looked up at the place Nolan Lund called home.

Quirky was the first word that came to mind. It wasn't sleek and modern with glass and metal architectural details. The entire place was built out of cream-colored bricks. The main entrance had a ranch house–style vibe, huge front door and a low-slung roofline that rose half a story higher than the long garage. The left side of the house, which faced the street, had been dug into the steep hillside and appeared to be two stories—but was only half a story higher than the main entrance, giving the entire structure a staggered look.

Grabbing my bag, I exited my truck and walked to the curved brick path leading to the front. Now that I was right upon the door, I could see that it was painted a vibrant blue with shiny enamel paint. On each side of the door were wide panels of square glass bricks in a milky pale blue hue that created a beautiful, funky transition between the door and house.

Before I could ring the doorbell, the door swung open.

And there was my man. Dark hair tousled and damp from his shower. Gorgeous face cleanly shaven. Wearing a slate-gray cashmere V-necked sweater that did amazing things for his eyes, and dark jeans.

"Hey, you're here," he said warmly, "please come in."

After I stood in the foyer and he closed the door, a rare bout of shyness overtook me. Nolan was sharing a part of his life that few got to see. I didn't want to say or do the wrong thing that'd make him uncomfortable in his own home, because god knew, I tended to screw up.

So I sort of froze when I looked at him.

"What's wrong?"

"I'm nervous."

"Because you think I'll pounce on you the second you walk into my house?"

"I wish you would. I can handle the 'I want to fuck you now' side of you. But this? God, Nolan, it sounds stupid, but I don't feel worthy of being here. Like you'll realize it's a mistake and send me packing. That scares the crap out of me."

He took my bag and tossed it on the floor. Then he pushed me against the door and buried his face in my neck. Just breathing me in.

That's when I realized his heart was racing too. A slight sheen of sweat dotted his forehead, leaving a dampness on my skin as he kissed my neck. He muttered, "Fucking cookies."

My heart rate launched into quadruple time when he framed my face in his hands and kissed me, delicately, as if I was spun of glass. Sweet nibbles of his lips, a soft smooch at the corners of my smile, a glide back and forth of his parted lips across mine.

Then he stopped and stared into my eyes. "It's sweet that you're nervous, my Gabriella."

Sweet?

"But you're not nervous about being invited into my home. Your nerves are because you understand after you've been in this space I only share with the special people in my life that you're special. And, Happy, this isn't a mistake, because I'm done making mistakes with you."

This man . . . when he went in, he went *all* in. I couldn't believe my luck that he wanted to go all in with me.

I pressed my mouth to his. "So do something to calm my nerves."

His answering growl sent my blood racing.

Gentle kisses vanished as he ate at my mouth. Forcing my lips open wider to take his ravenous kiss. His hands followed the contours of my body. Sliding his fingers around my hips, tucking his fingertips inside the waistband of my leggings and yanking the stretchy fabric down to the tops of my UGGs.

After he dropped to his knees, he only bothered to remove one of my boots, shoving my leggings to the side. Those rough palms were sliding up the outside of my bare legs as he left sucking kisses on the inside of my thigh.

My head fell back against the door at the first touch of his mouth to my core.

He was so so so good at this. And he loved winding me up to see how high he could make me fly.

When he started to use his tongue, I wondered if his door was electrified—my entire body buzzed like a live wire. My nerves jumped. My blood fizzed. My legs quaked.

He took me apart with precision and speed that left me gasping.

Then he did it again, just to prove he could.

Cocky man.

Nolan petted and nuzzled me as I regained my bearings.

"How are those nerves now?" he asked.

The smugness in his smile and his eyes; I just ate that up.

However, he'd awakened my competitive side. "Now that you took the edge off, let's get started." Balancing on my left foot, I kicked off the other boot and shed my leggings. "Which way to your bedroom?"

"We don't have to . . ." His voice trailed off as I pulled my sweatshirt over my head and unhooked my sports bra, whipping it on top of my clothes.

"Oh, but yes we do." I offered him my best attempt at sultry as I slowly ran my hands down my naked curves. "You really gonna turn this down?"

"Fuck. No." Without taking his hungry gaze off my body, he pointed to the left. "My room is that way. Last door on the right."

"Lead the way, Lund."

"I'll follow you and enjoy the view."

Maybe I did a little more high-stepping, ass wiggling as I sashayed down the hall. I'd never had a man appreciate my body the way Nolan did.

We entered a cool, dark space. No natural or artificial light, just an odd arc of pale sunlight from the hallway that bounced off the door and across the carpet. I stopped so abruptly that Nolan ran into me inside the doorway.

"Sorry. Lemme turn on a light."

Turning, I flattened my palm on his chest to keep him in place. "No. I like it dark." I inched my fingers under his soft sweater, loving his sharp inhale when I touched his nipples.

I kissed the hollow beneath his Adam's apple and whispered, "Off. All of it."

After Nolan ditched his sweater, he teased me with flirty kisses as he shucked his jeans. I could taste myself on him and I swayed closer to feel the heat of his bare skin on mine.

His restraint vanished. He fastened his mouth to my neck, biting, licking, kissing, building a frenzy in both of us.

It was glorious being on the receiving end of that passion.

In a move worthy of an MMA champion, he took us to the floor.

As soon as all that hard, heated muscle covered me, I wrapped my legs around his hips.

My back arched off the floor when he drove into me.

There were no words between us. Just sweat and heat and friction in the dark.

And passion. God. The passion this man showed was staggering.

The blood racing through my body sizzled like I was burning up from the inside out. I couldn't get close enough to him. I couldn't touch him enough. Every breath I took was saturated with his scent. Wherever I kissed his skin I tasted salt and musk and Nolan. I rubbed my face against his flesh, bathing in him.

His mouth was on my jaw, then my neck, then my breasts, and he kept a steady rhythm that seemed in perfect sync to the pounding of my heart and the rapid breaths whooshing from my lungs.

I never wanted this to end but at the same time I knew I couldn't spend another minute this close to the edge.

He slowed down just enough so he could push my legs to the floor, spreading me open, so each grinding thrust was exactly where I needed it.

My body responded immediately.

Tingling pulses rippled from my core outward and I let the pleasure wash over me, not chasing it, but feeling that connection with Nolan strengthen as he gave it to me.

When he buried his face in my neck as he found his own release, his deep groan vibrating against my skin sent chills racing through me again.

Spent, breathing hard, still joined together, I reached up and twined my arms around his neck, keeping him in place in case he got the idea to get up because he thought he was squishing me.

When he lifted his head, I trapped that beautiful face in my hands. "Nolan. That . . ." I saw such satisfaction in his eyes, and I wanted to be the only one who put it there. Forever. "That was everything."

A smile curled his lips, which he lowered to mine.

Neither of us wanted to be the first to break the bubble we'd created. We didn't speak, we just existed in this new intimacy.

Nolan kissed my temple. "You're shivering."

"So are you."

"Let's go sit by the fireplace."

"You have a fireplace?"

He pushed to his feet. "I'll give you the tour. But please get dressed or else we'll never make it out of the hallway."

"Same goes. But you'll have to bring me my clothes since I stripped in your foyer."

"Which makes you the best houseguest I've ever had." He handed me his robe to wear.

I decided my clothes could stay on the floor after I'd wrapped my naked self in the fluffy comfort of his robe that smelled like him.

In the main body of the house, a freestanding wall provided a focal point across from the entryway. Walking to the left led into the living room, and to the right into the kitchen, but the space behind it was open from one end to the other. The shiny gray lacquered kitchen cabinets complemented the white countertops, swirled with gray and black and dotted with tiny bits of silver. Here and there were items the same glossy blue as his front door.

Wood flooring—a pale ash gray—stretched throughout these two rooms. Again, his living area wasn't the leather-furniture, chrome-and-glass bachelor pad I'd seen in every other single guy's house. His living room looked cozy and inviting with wide-wale corduroy couches in navy blue. Two bookshelves crammed with books rose to the ceiling on either side of the mosaic-tiled fireplace. A large ivory-colored wool rug covered the floor and he'd placed a funky antique coffee table in the center of it all. What surprised me was that all the windows had been changed to the same milky pale blue glass bricks like by the front door.

Nolan saw me studying them and shrugged. "There's no view, so I just switched them out for something that gives light and interest."

"It's really cool, Nolan. Your home feels lived in, not like a decorator's experiment."

He seemed pleased. "Jensen's apartment was like that and he hated it. Right after he sold it, he bought Snow Village."

I ran my hand across the sofa table made of iron with an inset mosaic tile in various shimmering hues of metallic blue. "I figured you'd have one of those fancy high-rise luxury apartments."

"I did for a while. It felt like I was living in a hotel. Since I've got a great view of the Cities from the Lund building, I decided I didn't need that at home. This house is an oddity. It's not big enough to be a family house and there's no yard, which is unusual given it's in the suburbs. Plus the spiral staircase that goes to the lower level is problematic for most people."

"You have a spiral staircase?"

He grinned. "It's cool. Come take a look."

The staircase wasn't a basic metal one, but wood with wide steps and a curved bannister with twisted metal. The thing was a work of art. "Omigod, I love it!"

"It's one of the things that sold me on the house. Downstairs has the media room, the second bedroom and guest bathroom."

"This house only has two bedrooms?"

"It had three, but I converted the one upstairs next to the master into my closet."

"I love that you personalized this house so it works for you now, not the you in a few years when you might be married and want something bigger with different amenities."

When he didn't answer right away, I thought maybe I'd said the wrong thing.

But he pulled me into his arms and hugged me tightly. "Thank you for saying that. I don't think my family gets it, except maybe for Jensen. A big space when you live alone just feels ten times emptier."

"I think Dallas gets it." I wasn't sure if I should mention her ghost issue with the house she owned. "Plus, you don't entertain so why would you want anything more than this?"

"Along those same lines, if I had a bigger place would I be expected to have people over?"

"So you really don't socialize here?"

Nolan tipped my head back and looked into my eyes. "No. There's so many of us in the Lund Collective, when we get together we're usually at one of our parents' houses."

"What about friends?"

"Socializing to me has always meant going out. So even when I had what my family called my flavor-of-the-week years I never brought them to my home."

"You went to their place for hookups?"

"Sometimes. LI has a small studio apartment downtown for out-of-town business associates that's rarely used on the weekends. It was easiest to go there."

"Handy if you were drinking. And for parking. But I imagine some of those women were expecting you'd take them to the Ritz or someplace since you're a gazillionaire."

His eyes searched mine. "You really aren't jealous, are you?"

"No." I snaked my arms around his neck. "We've both got pasts. So what if you dated the beautiful people. They're not here with you now. I am." I kissed his surprised expression. "Any doubts I had about your attraction to me have been more than satisfied, Nolan, and I hope I've given you that same confidence."

"You have." He rested his forehead on mine. "Do you know how crazy I am about you?"

"Maybe." I nuzzled his cheek, just because I could. "But maybe you'd better prove it to me again a little later. In front of the fireplace on that soft-looking rug."

"Done." Another smooch to my mouth. "But I believe I promised you a late lunch."

I cut back through the foyer to grab my cell phone out of my bag. The only seating in the kitchen was one of four chairs tucked under the long side of the marble counter opposite the prep area. "Weird question, do you have a dining room?"

He shook his head. "That was another plus about this house. However, I did add another garage bay after I bought this place. The builder created a laundry room / storage area / mud room between the garage and the house. Made more sense to me than having the laundry room in the utility room downstairs." He pulled a covered bowl from the refrigerator. "The one thing I kept was the double deck." He pointed out the French doors. "On this level there's a bistro table and a small grill. On the bottom level there's a hammock. That's about as much outdoor space as I wanted."

"This is honestly one of the coolest houses I've ever been in."

"You have been in Jax and Lucy's eight-thousand-square-foot rooftop apartment, right?" he said dryly.

"Yes. That is a fantastic space for them. This place is just . . . you. I get why you keep it to yourself. I wouldn't want to share it with anyone either."

Nolan reached across the counter and tugged my hair.

"Careful, or I'll think you'd never want to move in here with me."

Did he mean that? This was one of those times I didn't know how to respond so I tossed off a flip, "Well, I don't know, Charming. I would need *some* closet space."

"For you, my Gabriella, I'd make space."

"Nolan."

He grinned. "No need to give me your answer now. I'll wait until after you've seen my bedroom with the lights on. And the master bathroom. It has a Jacuzzi garden tub and a steam shower."

Once again, I was speechless. Then my phone buzzed on the counter, startling me.

Caller ID said: Wolf Sports North.

I just stared at it until it nearly vibrated off the countertop. Nolan said, "Babe. Answer it."

"Why are they calling me on a Saturday afternoon?"

"You won't know if it goes to voice mail."

I hit answer call and said, "This is Gabi Welk."

"Gabi! Alan Mayes from Wolf Sports North. How are you today?"

"Good. Curious." I couldn't believe I was basically taking this call naked.

"I imagine so, so I'll get right to the point. We want to hire you as our co-broadcaster for the UMD college hockey TV program."

"Are you serious?"

"Yes. You were the best qualified candidate and we saw an enthusiasm for the game that transcended our expectations. We'd love to have you as part of the Wolf Sports North family."

I paced to the French doors. "I am in a happy shock right now, so excuse me if I'm coming across like an idiot. But yes, I am one hundred percent on board."

"Excellent. We're keeping this on the down low until we

get a few more details finalized. But we will be in touch with you on a weekly basis to keep you in the loop as far as start dates and preproduction."

"Do you have any solid dates in mind? Because I do need to let my boss know he'll have to find someone to fill my position."

"I understand. But if you could hold off until you get the all clear from us, outside guess is maybe two weeks?"

"Okay. That seems doable. As long as I have access to the financial details of the proposed contract for my attorney to look over."

"Of course. We'll send the links to your email. Congratulations and have a great rest of your weekend."

"I will, sir. Thank you."

I ended the call and stared out the window, not really seeing anything, the buzzing in my head was so loud. Had that really just happened?

So when Nolan came up behind me and set his hands on my hips, I jumped.

He murmured, "Easy." He stayed warm and solid and strong behind me until I leaned back into him. "You all right?"

"In shock. I got the job."

He squeezed me and kissed the back of my head. "I figured. Are you happy about it?"

"Yes. But it sucks because I can't talk about it with anyone."

"Not even to me?"

Especially not to you. After you practically invited me to live with you and now . . . I'll be moving to Duluth.

God. How could I be so excited and yet so . . . unhappy at the same time?

"Gabriella?"

"No, I'm sorry, I can't tell you either. My new boss reminded me I signed a bunch of NDAs and until they're ready to announce this, I have to keep it under wraps." I groaned. "I hate that I can't tell Jax. Or Lena at Minnesota Youth Hockey

League. And now, there's no way I can try out for the new NWHL expansion team here in the Twin Cities."

I spun and wrapped my arms under his, grabbing onto his shoulders and squeezing him tight. "Sorry to babble. Thank you for listening."

"What is this about? Because there's something you're not telling me."

"The truth? I'm crazy about you." I nuzzled his chest and pressed a kiss to his heart. "While maybe you're thinking this job is the greatest thing for me, the truth is . . . you're the best thing that's happened to me in a long time. Maybe ever. I've never said that to a guy because I've never felt it before."

"You . . . It's . . ." He laughed softly. "Christ, I can't even think straight after hearing that." He pressed his lips to the top of my head. "Being with you has filled me with joy. I've tried to contain it around you because I wasn't sure if you were there yet with how you felt about me."

"But you didn't doubt that I'd get there, right?"

"I was prepared to wait until you realized we're right for each other regardless of how wrong we started out." The way he gazed at me . . . stole my breath and weakened my knees.

"Let's go to your room right now." I tried to catch his marauding mouth, but he dodged me.

"Food first. We're both gonna need to keep up our strength to make it until morning."

Twenty-Four

NOLAN

Waking up with Gabi in my arms might've been one of the best mornings of my life.

And that wasn't solely because she blew my fucking mind in the shower.

Although she had done that.

My thoughts scrolled to the heat of her mouth enveloping me. The scrape of her nails up the outside of my legs. The little nuzzle across my abdomen before she reached her ultimate destination. The push and pull of her teasing. Her eyes dark with playful passion as she gauged my every moan and grunt of satisfaction before she sucked me into that morass of orgasmic ecstasy.

A loud smack sounded and my ass stung. My gaze followed her as she moved to stand beside me at the sink while I brushed my teeth.

"You were thinking about that blow job again, weren't you?"

I spit and rinsed. "Yes. Every time I have a dopey look

on my face, it's because I'm reliving our epic fuckfest last night."

"And this morning." She kissed my sternum and plucked my toothbrush out of my hand.

Normally I'd be grossed out by her using my toothbrush, but we'd forged an entirely different path last night where I wanted to share everything with her.

I left her in the bathroom while I dressed in khakis and a white T-shirt.

Ten minutes later she emerged still wearing just my robe.

I'd toasted two English muffins and filled them with scrambled eggs, sharp cheddar cheese and a piece of Canadian bacon. I added sliced bananas and strawberries to the plate and slid it in front of her.

"This looks delicious. Thank you."

"You're welcome. Coffee?"

"Yes, please."

Just then, my phone buzzed with a text message from my dad.

AL: You coming to brunch?

ME: No. I'll explain later. Meet me at the club at 3?

AL: See you then.

She looked at me curiously over the rim of her coffee cup. "What?"

"Isn't Sunday brunch with the Lund Collective mandatory?"

"No. I haven't been there the past two Sundays because I've been with you."

"Which I've been happy about."

"But?"

"But nothing. I was just making sure I'm not keeping you from seeing your family."

"You're not." I shoved my hand through my hair. "Up until the last year or so I had a different woman to brunch damn near every week. Maybe it seems stupid, but by *not* taking you to brunch, I'm keeping our Sundays private until we're ready to let my entire family know that you'll be a permanent fixture at brunch with me."

"You don't owe me an explanation, Nolan."

"I owe you the courtesy of making sure you understand I'm not hiding this relationship. Besides, I know you have to work today and I wanted to spend as much time with you before you have to go."

She smirked at me. "Good answer. I wouldn't have had the right clothes with me to wear to brunch anyway. It'd be the ultimate walk of shame."

"Brunch has gotten chaotic. Jax and Lucy and Jensen and Rowan letting Mimi and Calder run around. Walker and Trinity's kid crying when Trinity leaves him to go throw up in the bathroom because she's pregnant again. Brady and Lennox keeping their baby in the stroller, practically wrapped in plastic against germs. Aunt Cilla looking longingly at Selka's grandbabies and Annika avoiding her mother's questions about when she and Axl are starting a family. Ash, Dallas and I have skipped brunch more often than we've attended since the first of the year."

"Yikes."

"Our cousins Zosia and Zach used to come down sometimes while their brother Zeke ran the fisheries, but even they've avoided it." Although, to be honest, I doubted it was the family aspect that was keeping them away.

"You're frowning. What's wrong?"

"Just thinking about some corporate issues that you don't give a crap about."

"Hilarious. I only said that at Buddy's that night because being contrary used to be my default response to you. But you can talk to me about business stuff. I can't promise to understand it, but I am a good listener."

"I know you are. I'll probably take you up on it when you're not dealing with other secret job stuff."

"Speaking of job stuff . . . I have to take off in an hour since I'm refereeing two games at two different rinks. Then Dani wants to get together and talk, which I don't want to do, but I've been putting her off for a while."

"You never mentioned what your parents think about Dani and Tyson."

"They weren't super shocked. It was a pretty short conversation."

"They didn't ask if you've become involved with a sexy, well-dressed businessman who adores you?"

"Oddly enough, that didn't come up." She paused. "You think Jax knows about us? Or maybe I should ask if you've told him anything?"

I shook my head. "He's dealing with four projects right now, so I don't know if seeing us together more often has registered. Who have you told?"

"Besides accidentally spilling the deets to your mom?"

"She gave me an 'atta boy' for that, which was weird."

"I'll bet. Oh, speaking of weird . . . Dallas knows about us. I didn't tell her though. She said she saw it in the stars."

I snickered. "Of course she did."

"This is super bizarre. I can't believe I forgot to tell you. Remember I told you that she, Liddy and I had that girls' night before they both skipped town, forcing me to ask you to help me with interview outfits?"

"Can't say I'm sorry about them not being around since it led us here."

"Me either. But when Dallas came back from Bali, she popped by and asked how it was going with us. The question flustered me. Then she told me to look on the top shelf where I keep my spices. She'd placed a note there, the night we were drinking together, that said, *You and Nolan will get each other in all the ways that truly matter.*"

"Jesus. That is spooky."

"But entirely true."

"Mm-hmm."

I sat next to her and we devoured breakfast.

Afterward, Gabi pointed at yesterday's newspaper on the coffee table. "You still get daily delivery?"

"I'm a throwback. I know most people read news online, but I like the paper version."

"Me too! Did you get today's *Star Trib*?"

I got up and snagged it off the catchall table in the foyer. "Right here."

Gabi curled up in the corner of the couch with her coffee. "Can you pass me the sports section?"

In that moment, I could see us reading the newspaper together every morning while we fortified ourselves for the day. She'd gotten a panicked look in her eyes last night when I'd mentioned her moving in, so I'd have to be patient before I brought it up again. But she belonged with me.

After she left, I cleaned up the kitchen and made a grocery list for my housekeeper. Rather than go into the office, I logged into the LI server on my laptop and read through the million reports that defined my professional life.

At two thirty I changed into basketball shorts and a T-shirt, loaded my bag into my SUV and drove to meet my dad. I couldn't wait until the weather warmed up and we could play racquetball at their outdoor home court rather than at the country club, which wasn't my favorite place. But he'd been a member for years and we never had to wait for a court.

He'd booked enough time for us to warm up. He walked in, tossed me a towel and a bottle of water. "Go easy on your old man today, eh? I think I overate at brunch. Got some indigestion going on."

"You wanna postpone?"

"Nope. We've already skipped two weeks." He started stretching.

I grabbed a ball and bounced it on my racket, rotating it forward to back as a wrist warmup.

"So we missed you at brunch again. You said you'd explain why."

"Don't pretend that Mom hasn't already told you."

He raised his eyebrows. "Told me what?"

"That Gabriella Welk and I are in a relationship."

A grin appeared. "Eeds did tell me. Sounds like it's been going on a couple of weeks so it's more than a one-off?"

"It's the real deal, Dad. She's just . . . it for me. I know it seems fast—"

"It's not the length of time that's the test, it's the depth of the feeling in that time."

I stared at him. My dad never said stuff like this.

"I like her. Is there a reason you're keeping it under wraps?"

"Besides that it's new? Not really." I nudged him with my elbow. "Done stalling, old man?"

"Yeah, yeah, yeah. You're so damn competitive. No idea where you got that from."

I laughed.

We'd been playing racquetball since my early teens. For a while there we'd been evenly matched. But the older Dad got, the slower he got, so our games weren't as rigorous as in years past. After I trounced him the first game, and he was sweating and had lost some color, I'd made him sit and hydrate.

Of course, he grumbled the entire time. "You don't have to treat me with kid gloves, kid. I get enough of that at LI."

I snorted. "After the last round with Ash and Brady *I'm* the one walking around on damn eggshells."

He mopped his face with the towel. "I know we have a policy of not talking business outside of work, but I get the feeling you're really unhappy with some of the recent decisions."

"Any disagreement I've had with decisions stem from the full autonomy the executive board has been accorded. I've made some mistakes, but I've owned up to them and dealt with the backlash. As far as I can tell, Brady and Ash don't believe they've made wrong decisions. When I bring up the financial facts, then I'm told I don't see the whole picture. If I'm wrong, I'd like someone to explain to me why, and so far, no one has bothered."

"Nolan, why haven't you come to me with this?"

"Because I don't want to be the guy who goes running to Daddy when I don't feel like I'm getting a fair shake. I've tried to fight my own battles. I've given detailed financial rebuttals for recent acquisitions decisions I've vehemently opposed. But the fact you don't know anything about all the work I've put in means they aren't taking my concerns seriously enough to bring them up with you." I swigged from my water bottle. "And I get that this situation is somewhat of my own making, given that in the past I haven't been as dedicated to the company as I should've been. Again, this is not an excuse, but everyone assumed Jax would come back and learn the ropes to take over the CEO position when you're ready to retire. Only I knew you had doubts about Jax's interest in that. But I felt like you had doubts about me too."

He sighed. "I get where you're coming from. And maybe I have rubber-stamped some of their recommendations because Brady and Ash aren't usually wrong." He stood and spun his racquet around, ready to play again. "Tell you what. Send me everything you've considered a red flag. I'll look into them."

Another pat on the head. I half wondered what he was hiding. Opting to ignore the convo, I got back to my feet. "Thank you, sir."

"Sir. Ha. Serve, smartass."

We'd played five points when Dad lowered to his knees. At first I thought the ball had struck him. But when he crashed to his side on the floor, I knew something was wrong.

I dropped beside him. "Dad!"

His face had gone gray and he was clutching his left side. His eyes were wild and he tried to speak.

"Don't move. I'm getting help." I tried to remember every-thing I'd read about what to do when someone was having a heart attack but my mind went blank.

I hit the emergency button on the speaker for the intercom system. "Call 911 and an ambulance. My dad is having a heart attack or a stroke or something."

Several excruciating long moments passed before I heard, "Ambulance is en route."

"Thank you.

By the time I'd returned to my dad's side, he'd gone limp. Fuck.

I searched for—and found—a pulse in his neck. He was breathing. We were in a metro area so he had a good chance at survival. I kept telling myself that because I couldn't ac-cept anything else.

"Dad. Stay with me. Help is on the way."

Nothing.

I grabbed his hand. "I'm here. Just hold on." I kept talking to him, watching for changes in his breathing, keeping my fingers over the pulse point in his wrist to assure myself his heart hadn't quit.

Time didn't register and then the ambulance crew was there, loading him up. I yelled at the country club attendant, "Call Edie Lund. Her name is on file. Tell her to meet us at"—I looked at the paramedic—"which hospital are we go-ing to?"

"Good Hope Hospital has a cardiac emergency center."

"Is that closest?"

"It's the best."

"Take us there." Then I yelled down the hallway as we exited the building in case the guy hadn't heard me the first time. "Call Edie Lund. Tell her Nolan said we're going to Good Hope Hospital."

On the ride to the emergency room, the paramedic asked me a bunch of questions I couldn't answer.

Dad still hadn't regained consciousness, but his color

looked less gray after they'd placed him on oxygen. As I stared at him, I couldn't believe my strong, larger-than-life father was in this state. He'd always been healthy. Taken good care of himself and enjoyed things in moderation. Had I pushed him too hard in the game? Did he feel he needed to prove himself to keep up with his son, half his age?

The medical staff whisked him away as soon as the ambulance doors were open. A nurse took me to the emergency room desk to fill out paperwork, but I could only answer the most basic info: name, address, age and insurance provider.

My mom arrived ten minutes after we did. I couldn't imagine how fast she'd driven to get here so quickly.

I'd never seen her so panicked. "Where is he?"

"He's with the doctors."

"What happened?"

I explained and directed her to the front desk so she could finish filling out the medical portion of the admissions forms.

As soon as she finished, she demanded to see him. We were told to wait.

She paced, her high heels clicking across the tile. She had her arms crossed over her chest and she was shaking so hard the bracelets on her arm rattled.

Without a word, I moved in front of her and wrapped her in my arms.

"I c-can't lose him, Nolan. I c-c-can't imagine life without him."

"Me neither. I got him help as soon as I could."

"You didn't call me. You had the club call me."

"It was the fastest way to let you know. My cell phone is still in my bag at the club." I looked at her. "Who else did you call?"

Horror crossed her face. "No one. I grabbed my keys and slipped my shoes on and left. I don't have my purse or my phone. We have to call Jax. And Ward and Monte."

"I'll call Jax." At the front desk, I said, "Can I use your phone please?"

"Sure. Dial nine first."

I was half-afraid Jax or Lucy wouldn't pick up, believing it was a spam call, but after the second time I called, he answered with, "What?"

"Jax. Mom and I are at Good Hope Hospital. Dad had a heart attack."

"Jesus. Is he okay?"

"He was unconscious in the ambulance but we don't know any more than that right now. He's with the doctors."

"I'm on my way." He hung up.

Mom had returned to pacing.

"Jax is on his way."

She nodded.

I stood by the door and waited for my brother. It seemed to take him longer to arrive than I thought it should.

Jax clapped me on the shoulder and went straight to Mom.

We relayed the information to him. After another hour of waiting, we'd hit the wall of politeness and demanded to know what was going on.

A woman in scrubs approached us and took us back to where they'd isolated Dad and run tests.

Mom gripped both mine and Jax's hands hard at seeing Dad unconscious and hooked up to machines and an oxygen mask strapped over his face.

Then we were directed to a small room where we were told to wait for the cardiologist.

The woman who introduced herself as Dr. Curran appeared to be Jax's age and she got right down to business. "Is there a history of heart disease in your family?"

"Not that I'm aware of."

"Unfortunately I didn't see anything in Archer's medical records that he had any recent tests that would've given him a warning to his condition."

"What condition?" Jax asked.

"He's got four heart blockages. He looks fit for all intents and purposes, but I suspect, given the damage to his heart, he's been masking his symptoms for at least a year. The good news is he is healthy enough for us to do the surgery. The bad news is he needs to have this surgery tonight."

"What surgery?" Mom asked.

"Quadruple bypass surgery. We've got a team in place and as soon as we have your permission, we can get him prepped." Then the doctor went into an explanation that should've come with a PowerPoint presentation. I got lost after the description of the purpose of removing an artery from his leg to use for blood flow to his heart. Mom was rapt and asked question after question that never occurred to me. I looked at Jax and in that moment I knew we both felt like little boys again, hoping Mom could make everything better.

But *we* were supposed to be the strong ones. She needed to believe she could lean on us.

Jax made the time-out sign. "Look, Dr. Curran. I'll be blunt. We won't settle for just *any* cardiac surgical team. We require the best team, with the highest patient survival rate because we're not going to fuck around with his life. We have the means to take him anywhere in the country, or to bring the premier surgical team here. So before we continue this conversation, we require the names of your medical team members so we can have them vetted immediately with our medical experts."

"Understood, Mr. Lund. I'll get that information to you straightaway. But please be aware we are the highest-rated cardiac care hospital in the Midwest. And being equally blunt, we are aware of the Lund name. Dr. Lee, the head of the cardiac and thoracic surgery units, has already been apprised of the situation. I have his direct number if your medical expert needs to speak with him."

"Thank you."

She left and came back with the list.

Jax took over from there, partially because he was the only one with a cell phone. After talking with Monte and Ward, who consulted with the Lund family medical team, they agreed that Dr. Lee's team was the best option.

Plans were finalized and we got to go in, one at a time, and spend a few minutes with Dad.

Mom had tears streaming down her face, and an angry set to her jaw to keep her chin from wobbling after she left him.

Dr. Lee arrived and gave us the final rundown of the procedure and sent us out to the waiting room.

Enough time had passed since Jax's phone call to the family that Monte and Priscilla, Ward and Selka, Brady, Ash and Lucy had arrived.

While I was thankful for my mom's sake that she had family supporting her and Dad, I felt disconnected. I'd never felt so acutely alone.

Twenty-Five

GABI

After the second game I refereed ended, I stopped in at Lakeside and gathered up all my practice clothes from the week, my water bottles and my coffee mugs. I had a tendency only to notice things I needed after I'd run out of them.

It surprised me that Margene was still there. There'd been a birthday party scheduled during open skate time, but I would've thought she'd be long gone by now. I snagged my stuff out of my locker before I went looking for her.

She was leaving the office and did a double take when she saw me. "Gabi? What are you doing here?"

"Had to get this stuff cleaned up before the week starts. Why are you here so late?"

"Lucy called and asked if she could drop Mimi off and have me wait with her until her aunt picked her up."

That was weird. "Is Mimi still here?"

"No. Her aunt came about ten minutes ago. Poor Lucy was frantic to get to the hospital."

My stomach bottomed out. "Hospital?"

"Evidently Jax's dad had a heart attack. Lucy said he has to have emergency surgery and she wasn't sure how long they'd be at the hospital, so she needed her sister to take Mimi for the night."

"Omigod. When did this happen? What hospital?"

"No offense, sweetie, but I don't think you should just show up. I'm sure Jax and Lucy know you're thinking about them."

I tried not to snap at her. "Nolan is my concern—we're together now."

Margene opened her mouth. Closed it. "After seeing his behavior at the NHL exhibition after you were injured, I'm not surprised."

"When did this happen? I left Nolan's house before noon and he and Archer were supposed to play racquetball today."

"It happened at the club."

"Nolan must be losing his mind. What hospital?"

"That cardiac one off of Central Avenue. Good . . . Hope."

"Thank you." I raced to my truck and threw everything in the passenger's seat.

I tried to call Nolan twice, but it went to voice mail both times. Then I called my sister and cancelled our plans—she wasn't happy, especially when I didn't explain.

Finally, twenty minutes later I pulled into the parking lot at Good Hope. I didn't waste time looking for familiar cars, I just headed to the emergency entrance. "Lund family? Probably in the surgical waiting area?" I added.

"Second floor. Elevators are to the left."

I tried to be patient, but it might've been the slowest elevator ever. I burst out of the doors when they opened, my shoes squeaking loudly on the tile. Everyone in the waiting room turned and stared at me. But I was only looking for one person. "Nolan?"

He spun around from where he stood alone by the windows. "Gabriella?"

And I beelined toward him.

He caught me and squeezed me tight.

I buried my face in his neck and didn't want to let go.

He set me on my feet, and I curled my hands around his face. "Are you okay? Is he okay?"

"How did you find out?"

"I had to stop at Lakeside and Margene told me. I got here as soon as I could."

Nolan pressed his mouth to mine and the kiss lingered. "Thank you for coming. I wanted you here so badly, but I didn't have my phone and it's been hectic."

"Tell me what happened."

While he filled me in, our bodies just naturally gravitated toward each other.

The soft touches and gentle caresses between us relayed our familiarity, our intimacy, more than a passionate kiss would have.

A loud throat clearing had us breaking apart.

No surprise that everyone stared at us, mostly with shock.

Jax approached us first. His gaze winged between us. "How long?" He paused and answered his own question. "Since the exhibition hockey game. Christ. I didn't even notice when she stopped flipping you off, did I?"

Nolan flashed him a fast smile. "Nope."

"To be honest, I still flip him off more than is probably healthy," I said with obvious affection.

Jax snorted. "Am I the only one at Lakeside who didn't know?"

"No one at Lakeside knew. Including Margene. She's the one who told me you were at the hospital."

"As you've probably heard, there's not much to tell at this point," Edie said behind me.

I faced her and hugged her. "How are you holding up?"

"As well as can be expected." She straightened the collar of my T-shirt. "I'm glad you're here for him."

"I'm here for you too." I clasped her hand in mine and squeezed. "Three years ago my dad had this same surgery. I understand how scary this is. My dad pulled through and he's better than he was before. Archer will be too."

"I wish I had your confidence."

"I have enough for both of us."

She leaned in and whispered, "Now I wish we would've stuck with the crafting thing. I need something to do with my hands besides pray."

"I can sit beside you and hold your hand for as long as you need, Edie."

Edie patted Nolan's cheek. "Keep her." She walked over to where her brothers-in-law stood.

I took my first look at Nolan's outfit; he was wearing athletic shorts, shoes and a baggy T-shirt. "You said you don't have your phone. Don't you have other clothes?"

"I left everything at the club when I jumped in the ambulance."

"I know you can't leave, but do you want me to go to the club and get your stuff?"

"And Dad's. And yes, that would be great."

Jax said, "I'll call them right now and make sure someone has it ready for you."

"Perfect. Thank you." I smoothed Nolan's hair down. "Do you want me to pick up food for everyone?"

"We'll order in if we need to. After you get my car keys, can you get my other bag out of my car? It's got a change of clothes in it."

"Of course."

Nolan kissed me. "Hurry back."

"I will."

The country club was officially closed, but someone had stayed to hand off the Lunds' items. I grabbed the other bag out of Nolan's car and returned to the hospital within an hour.

Nolan's uncles had taken him aside and were talking to him intently as Jax, Ash and Brady looked on across the room. Lucy, Edie and the other Lund matriarchs were sitting in between the two groups, eyeing each group warily.

As soon as Nolan saw me, he excused himself to meet me.

Jax came over too. "Thanks, Gabi. I'll get Dad's bag to Mom. At least she'll have his phone until we get hers."

"No problem."

Then Jax looked at Nolan. "What's that about?"

"Some crap that I absolutely don't want to deal with right now." He sighed and grabbed his bag, pausing to give me another kiss. "Thanks for this. You know I loathe being in these types of clothes longer than necessary."

"It's the first time I've ever seen you dressed like that."

"Don't get used to it," he warned.

As soon as he was out of sight, Jax said, "So you and Nolan. I didn't see that one coming."

"Us either."

"Is there a reason neither of you told me?"

"Why? Do you disapprove?"

"Are you kidding? I think it's great."

Lucy called him over just then.

Rather than try and make small talk with the other Lunds, I headed down the hallway to wait for Nolan.

He emerged from the bathroom wearing gray fleece sweatpants and a long-sleeved black shirt. He said, "Better?"

"You look warmer." My gaze searched his face. "You okay?"

"Not really. If it's not enough to deal with Dad being in surgery, my uncles would like LI to put out a press release tomorrow that I'm 'acting' interim CEO."

"That seems . . ."

"Premature? Or like they're not hopeful the surgery will be successful?" he said tersely.

"Neither of those," I said soothingly. "That seems like something your dad would expect from them because he'd do the same thing if he were in their shoes."

"Except they're not. Their sons are in charge. And my cousins have both made it clear they're against the announcement."

My mouth dropped open. "Why?"

"Perception or some such shit. I don't know. But to be honest I really can't think about any of that now anyway." He took my hand. "Have I mentioned how glad I am that you're here?"

"A time or two."

His stomach rumbled.

"You haven't had anything to eat since breakfast, have you?"

He shook his head. "I'm fine though."

"No, you're hungry. At least let me get *you* some food."

"I'd like that."

"I'll be right back."

Nearly four hours after I arrived, the doctors came into the waiting room.

Jax and Nolan stood by their mother's side while the rest of us hung back. Somehow Lucy and I ended up holding hands as the doc delivered the news that Archer had survived surgery and was resting in ICU.

Not long after, everyone left. I managed to sneak down to the cafeteria before it closed and grab a few sandwiches. For them claiming not to be hungry, they sure devoured everything.

When it came time for Nolan to visit his dad, I got ready to leave.

He tried to get me to stay, kissing me in that slow, druggingly sweet manner that usually left me clinging to him and begging for more. Despite the tingling in my body and the buzzing in my head, I managed to extricate myself from him. And I'll admit, when he murmured, "Please. Don't go. I need you," I almost gave in.

"Your mom needs you. I'm a phone call away. I don't care what time it is, if you need to talk, call me. Promise."

"I promise." He brushed his mouth across my ear. "I'm crazy about you, Gabriella. It seems as if I've always felt this way about you."

"Don't you dare make me cry, Nolan."

He kissed me again. "I'll see you tomorrow."

T he next day, I had a million things to do at Lakeside, including fielding phone calls from people offering to help after word got out about Archer Lund being hospitalized. Even in such a short amount of time Jax had created a family vibe at Lakeside. I knew I'd miss that.

A tired-looking Jax showed up right before closing time. "Hey. Any fires I need to put out?"

"Just the usual ten thousand people asking . . . are you starting club hockey teams for next season?"

"Christ. The season barely ended."

"Parents and students want their names on the list even if there's only a slim chance Stonewall is coaching club hockey."

He snorted. "I have no idea what the hell I'm doing next week, let alone months from now." He sorted through his messages without looking at me. "Have you talked to Nolan today?"

"We've texted a few times. I suspected he was swamped when he went into the office this afternoon. Why? Is something going on I need to know about?"

"They named him acting interim CEO. And he doesn't seem happy about it."

"Probably because it feels disloyal to your dad. Archer hasn't even been out of surgery for twenty-four hours and LI already named his replacement."

Jax's laser-eyed gaze pinned me in place. "Did Nolan tell you he felt that way?"

"No. But I know him, Jax. Anyone who thinks he wants this right now doesn't understand him at all."

"So you think that's why Ash and Brady were so against Nolan being named acting interim CEO? They knew he didn't want that added pressure?"

I shrugged. "Nolan doesn't talk to me about his work."

"What *do* you two talk about?"

"Maybe we're too busy fucking to talk," Nolan said as he walked into the office. "Isn't that what you really want to know? If there's anything more substantial than just sex between Gabriella and me?"

"Whoa." Jax held up his hands. "Where did that come from?"

"Have you forgotten you warned me off Gabi?"

I hated when Nolan called me Gabi. I'd gotten so used to that deep, sexy, drawn-out *Gab-ri-el-la* that it almost seemed sarcastic when he called me what everyone else did.

"Yeah, I had forgotten that, because it was out of line. *I* was out of line." Jax erased the distance between them. "If you think I'm anything less than ecstatically happy about you finding a woman who is worthy of you, then you don't know me at all, brother."

They glared at each other—which made no sense.

"Well, good," Nolan finally said.

"Dumbass." Jax looked at me. "If he gets out of line? He's really ticklish below his ribs."

"Jesus, Jax. You had to tell her that?"

"Yep. See you both tomorrow." He paused in the doorway and turned around. "For real, Nolan, if you want to talk about any of the LI stuff, I'm here."

"Thanks."

Nolan didn't move until he knew his brother was gone. Then he came up behind me, banding one arm across the front of my body and tilting my head to get at my neck.

The feeling of his warm mouth and the nip of his teeth made my knees weak. "God, I love the taste of your skin after you've been on the ice. The salt of your sweat turns your sweet scent into this warm musk that drives me fucking insane. I want to strip you down, bend you over, drive into you when you're still wearing your skates." He nuzzled my damp hairline and the air from his rapid breaths sent shivers flowing through me. "You'd have to rely on me to keep you balanced. You'd have to trust that I could wring every bit of pleasure out of you with my fingers between your legs, my mouth on your skin and my cock buried deep inside you."

"Nolan."

"I've been fantasizing about that a lot. One of these days? I'll make it a reality. But for now . . ." He spun me around and clamped his hands on the sides of my head, smashing his lips against mine. This ravenous kiss proved how perfectly we meshed; how I needed this verbal and physical reminder of who we'd become to each other.

Everything.

He slowed the kiss gradually, then kissed my chin, my jawline, my temples, my eyebrows, my forehead, all while holding me in a way that felt like he needed me to hold him up too.

"You all right?"

"Been a surreal day."

"How's Archer?"

"Better than yesterday. He hates being seen as weak, so he refused all visitors after his brothers left this morning. He wouldn't even let Mimi come." Nolan stepped back and ran his hand through his hair. "Is it asking too much if I want you to stay with me tonight?"

I hadn't slept well last night, and Nolan had stayed at the hospital, so I wondered if he'd slept at all. "I'll need to borrow your toothbrush again. And your robe."

"Of course."

After a long shower, Nolan barely lasted long enough to eat an omelet.

I crawled in bed with him until he fell asleep, then got up and worked on my coaching strategy. No rec team from Lakeside had ever been invited to the Cities' End of Season Invitational Tournament, so my girls were pumped to compete.

As excited as I was to start a new challenge, I wondered how much I'd miss coaching.

And refereeing.

And teaching workshops to girls who acted like I was a rock star.

And watching the newbie players become seasoned.

And the time I spent alone on the ice. And the time I spent on the ice with players who loved the sport as much as I did.

I'd miss Margene.

And learning from Jax.

And how was I supposed to walk away from Nolan now that I'd found him? When I finally mustered the guts to tell him about the required move that went along with the job, would he accuse me of putting hockey above everything else?

If he asked me not to take the job, what would I say?

He'd say you should've told him the job required you moving to Duluth as soon as you knew that was a stipulation.

Sleep was pretty damn elusive for me after that.

Nolan woke up energized.

Very energized.

He hadn't let me out of bed until he'd "made up for" his neglect last night.

By the time he finished with me I decided being on time for work was overrated anyway.

Still, I couldn't help but tease him. "So as the acting interim CEO, you can just show up whenever you want?"

He swatted my ass. "I'm large and in charge, baby—and don't you forget it."

"Mmm. You reminded me of that very thoroughly this morning, Mr. Lund."

His smirk was entirely justified.

"What is on your agenda for today?"

"There's a board of directors meeting on Thursday. I'm sort of treading water until then." He drained his coffee. "How about you? Any more news from Wolf Sports North?"

I shook my head.

He glanced at his phone. "I've got to run but I wanted to give you something first." He pulled his keys out of his pocket and unhooked one key from the rest of the ring. "I want you to come and go as you like. Naturally, I'd prefer you to be here all the time, but I won't push." Then he held the key out.

The key dangled between us for a moment. I curled my fingers around it and was tempted to clutch it to my heart. "Thank you."

"There's an alarm code to open and lock the door: 8532. That's mine. We'll set you up with your own as soon as you decide on one. The security box is identical to the one at Lakeside so you shouldn't have a problem. Any questions?"

"No. I'm actually a bit speechless."

Nolan kissed me. "I'll call you later."

I watched him walk off and wondered how I'd gotten so lucky.

And I worried that the other boot would drop and my luck would run out.

Twenty-Six

NOLAN

Acting interim CEO.

Didn't feel good.

Didn't feel right.

On Monday we'd waited a full four hours after sending out a company-wide memo about my change in title before PR sent out the press release. It hadn't gotten much notice from the mainstream media.

The announcement hadn't changed anything for me.

I still worked from my same office.

My uncles had handled the phone calls, reassuring investors everything was running smoothly.

Monte had called a board meeting.

Part of me had silently wondered if that should've been my responsibility.

The fact that Monte ran the board of directors should've put me at ease, but it just drove home the point the *acting* CEO title was an honorarium and nothing more.

All my Lund cousins who were shareholders were in

attendance. No one congratulated me; I hadn't expected it because I didn't deserve it.

Britt, the floating admin who worked with me, my father's secretary and Sam, handled rescheduling appointments and filled me in on little things that were vital to running a company.

Problem was, I already knew most of what she'd deemed necessary.

This was more busywork. I wasn't finding answers to what I really wanted to know.

I had Sam call Kayla, head of IT, into my office.

She popped in within five minutes since we were on the same floor. "How may I help you, sir?"

"I'm getting access denied on a bunch of files."

Kayla came around my desk and stood over my shoulder. "Can you show me which files?"

"Sure." I relogged in to the cloud and clicked through security screens until I reached the executive file section. "See?" I put in the password, which changed every day, and the access denied message appeared.

"No wonder. Those files can only be accessed on the executive floor."

"Since when?"

"It's an additional security system failsafe installed about six months ago. Do you have problems logging in when you're on the CEO's floor?"

"Not that I can remember. But I guess that makes sense." I sighed and rubbed my eyes. "Were you taking bets in IT how long I'd stay on this floor after I learned about lack of access to the executive files down here?"

Her lips twitched. "No. But if I may be honest, I advised against that system change."

"Why?"

"It's a pain in the ass for us too. Unless LI is suddenly dealing with government contracts that require another layer of security, it's redundant."

"Who made the change?"

"Your father."

I slumped back in my chair and Kayla returned to her seat in front of my desk. "So let's say I haul my laptop up to his office. What are the chances of me gaining access to any of those files?"

"Zero. Before you ask, I can't get you access in terms of resetting passwords. It'd have to be a system change and that . . . would be a bit of an undertaking."

"But you could do it?"

"Yes, sir."

"To countermand his initial order, I'd need to sign off on a confidential work order," I muttered.

"Yes, you would," Kayla said. "But as you are acting interim CEO, other signatures from the executive branch aren't necessary. Once we have the work order, we can jump right on it."

"What's the time frame for this?"

Kayla tapped her finger on her lips as she thought about it. "A week if you want me and two others. Three days if I put a team of ten on it."

"I'm for the smaller team." I hit the intercom button on my desk phone. "Sam. Can you rustle up a confidential work order?"

"I'll bring it right in, boss."

I felt Kayla studying me. "Something else on your mind?"

"If I say we all hope your dad makes a speedy recovery . . . will you take that as your employees would prefer him to you in the big chair?"

"I honestly don't know how to deal with most of this. It's been a blur."

"I can't imagine."

Two knocks sounded on the door and Sam entered. He handed me a piece of paper. "There are about five different confidentiality work orders. Please read through this one and make sure it's comprised of the language you require before signing it."

I might have grunted my response as I scanned the document. Then I saw the differentiation I needed. "This form doesn't go to operational until *after* you've signed off and your team has completed the order, Kayla."

"That works for me."

"Great." This way no one would be aware of the change until after it'd been implemented, so the work order couldn't be challenged or outright denied. I signed, dated and handed it over to her. She had to have it within her possession if anyone questioned what she was doing. "Please bring it back once the work is done and we'll file it from here."

"Will do, sir. Have a great day."

Sam and I watched Kayla leave. After she'd closed the door, I filled him in on the access issues I was having.

"So that means we'll be moving upstairs?" he asked.

"No. Soon enough I'll be able to get into those files here. I doubt anything in them is pressing, but that doesn't mean I don't need to know."

"Understood. But speaking of pressing . . . the Grant Foundation Gala is Saturday night."

My eyebrows rose. "This Saturday?"

"Yes, sir. Are you taking Gabi?"

We hadn't spent time together because she'd called extra hockey practices in the evenings due to the tournament happening . . . this Friday and Saturday. "No. Her 14U team is in the city rec tournament. Which means I can't be there to support her either."

"What about asking—"

"Don't even suggest I show up with another woman on my arm, Sam," I growled at him. "Gabriella and I are officially a couple—and I'm pretty sure that's against the rules in the couples' handbook."

He rolled his eyes. "Calm down. I was going to suggest you ask your mother. It'll be win-win for you, her and LI."

I stood and clapped him on the shoulder. "Excellent thinking. I'm headed to the hospital now. I'll ask her after we meet with the doctors."

"What time will you be back?"

"It'll be a couple of hours at least. Call Q and apologize for the late notice, but I'll swing by for my final fitting."

"Yes, sir."

A rcher Lund was in a foul mood.

And he took it out on everyone.

Except his wife.

Lucky for him because by the time the doctors left, Jax and I were both seething.

After bidding Dad a curt good-bye, Jax and I stopped down the hallway from his room.

"What the fuck was that?" Jax asked me.

"I'd say Dad is scared, but he's got that glint in his eyes that suggests he's just pissed off."

"At who? Us?"

"At anyone who's keeping him in the hospital. At himself for landing in the hospital in the first place."

"I get that. But Jesus, Nolan. Chewing the doctor's ass because the need for bypass was undetected? When the man absolutely refuses to go in for regular checkups?" Jax shook his head. "I seriously wanted to take the 'subpar' sock Dad was bitching about and shove it in his mouth. Who bitches about socks, anyway?"

I snickered.

"How are you not bothered by his attitude?"

"Because I deal with Archer Lund, CEO, every damn day, Jax. It's just a more extreme version of him."

"Can I remind you how happy I am not to be in your position?"

"Yes, please, rub it in that I'm completely unqualified to be even a placeholder for that man."

Jax loomed over me. "Since when do you talk down about yourself?"

"Just forget it. I'll see you later." I turned and walked off. At least the trip wasn't a total wash; my mom had agreed to attend the Grant Foundation Gala as my date.

"Nolan. Wait."

I kept walking.

My brother fell into step with me. "What is going on with you?"

"LI stuff. Don't worry. I'm handling it."

"I'm not being accusatory. I'm genuinely worried about you." He paused. "I have been since before Dad's heart attack."

"Great."

"Why won't you talk to me?"

I poked the button for the elevator. "Because I don't know what the fuck to say, all right?"

We stepped inside the elevator doors. I was grateful we weren't alone because I knew Jax wouldn't continue our conversation in front of strangers.

As soon as the doors opened, I made a beeline for the parking lot and my freedom.

But Jax's long stride kept up with mine. When we reached my car, he leaned against the driver's-side door, denying me access. "I'm done being patient and hoping you'll confide in me. Neither of us is going anywhere until you talk to me."

I shoved my hands in my pants pockets and glared at him.

"Every time I've brought up how things are going at LI, since I walked away from there months ago, you either A) make a self-derogatory comment about your position in the company, or B) you ignore it and me and blow me off. Why?"

"Lemme ask you this. Didn't you assume all the years that you played hockey that when you were done, you'd take your place at the helm? Everyone knew you, as the oldest Lund in this generation, would be named CEO. When did that change?"

Jax studied me for a moment before he spoke. "It changed

when I realized I didn't have the skill set to run the company."

I nodded. "Like any faith in your business acumen had been misplaced."

"How did you know . . . ?" He shook his head and vehemently said, "Fuck that, Nolan. You are in a different place entirely as far as understanding the business than I was."

"No, I'm not and that's the reality I'm facing now."

"Who made you feel like this? Brady? Ash? The uncles? Because I will kick every one of their asses—"

"Goddammit, will you just listen to me? If you want to know where my mind's been, then you need to shut up so I can tell you."

"Shit." He scrubbed his hands over his face. "Sorry."

I moved to stand next to him, resting my backside against the car. "I hadn't realized how much I'd counted on you being named CEO . . . until you decided you didn't want that."

He didn't respond.

"It caught everyone off guard, but me more than anyone else. Especially when Dad named me as second choice almost right away." I crossed my arms over my chest. "I've had to pretend that decision had made me happy, when the truth is . . . I'm really far from qualified."

"How do you figure?" Jax said tersely. "You've been working there since you graduated from NYU with a damn business degree."

"But how much work did I put in? Nothing like Ash, Brady and Annika, who worked there while they earned their degrees. I lived in NYC and had the full college life experience away from home. I even took a gap year after college to travel around the world—the stereotypical rich boy request of needing freedom before settling into the daily grind of a family business. Walker's the only other one who didn't stick around following high school graduation and follow the Lund family college plan. Even Dallas did more—

part time at LI while she was in school—than I'd done as a full-time employee."

My brother had no response for that.

"I've had a lot of time to think about this, and trust me, it stings like a motherfucker to realize I *am* the lazy Lund. The No-Good Nolan that Granddad accused me of being. I've always gotten by with the minimum amount of work and yet reaped the maximum amount of financial benefits. I've been able to cultivate my reputation for charm because I worked at it. Much harder than I did at any job I was assigned at LI. While I basked in seeing my name mentioned in the society pages of the newspaper, always with a beautiful woman on my arm, reveling in being named one of Minnesota's most eligible bachelors, Brady and Ash were busting their asses learning the company from the inside out. I let them. I justified it by believing my less-than-obsessive need to prove myself made me a more well-rounded man. So when they did pop their heads out of these offices, I could show them what they'd been missing. I could caution them not to work too hard, there was more to life than spreadsheets and counting coin—me, who had the money and lifestyle they were too busy to enjoy.

"It's mortifying to realize I would've gone on with that attitude permanently, if not for a couple of things that yanked me out of believing my own press. First, when Brady met Lennox and started to work less, it became apparent how much those extra hours and his meticulous ways meant to our bottom line. If he wasn't working ninety hours a week . . . someone had to pick up the slack. I tried, but like most things, I did a half-assed job."

"Why?"

I shrugged. "Because I knew deep inside it wouldn't matter because you'd come on board as CEO-in-waiting and I'd be the charming colonel to smooth things over after General Stonewall Jackson stormed through. I'd follow your lead."

"Second-in-command? Is that always how you've seen yourself?"

"It's never bothered me to play second fiddle to you, Jax. In fact, that's what I was counting on. Then you threw a wrench into the whole works by leaving the company. Then Dad and the uncles were looking at me, thinking I'd been involved long enough, and they had enough time to get me in a position to take over when Dad retires. But guess who wasn't on board with that school of thought? Brady and Ash. With good reason." I sighed. "I haven't invested enough of myself or my time into LI. It's hard not to take it personally, knowing they love me as a family member but don't trust me as an equal in the business that bears our name."

"Have they told you this?"

"Have we had an honest discussion about it? No. I think it scares all of us about what'll happen to our family relation-ship. They've gotten used to sweeping the 'he's inadequate' fears aside. Now, with Dad in the hospital, they can't do that anymore. So even if I'm acting interim CEO for a month, it's a month of them babysitting me because I was too busy screwing around when I should've been learning this shit. They know it. What's more, they know *I* know it."

"Jesus, Nolan."

"Even when the opportunity presented itself to me to change, I didn't. You handed me control of your bar for two years and in that time, I did nothing but show up, drink and treat it like my own personal club."

"I handed the club over to you *and* Ash," Jax retorted. "He could've kicked it in the ass at any time. The responsibility didn't fall solely to you."

"Ah, but it did. Because Ash already had his hands full with LI. I haven't confirmed this suspicion, but I think he purposely stepped back to see if I'd step up." I swallowed hard. "And I didn't."

"So what are you saying?"

I sighed. "Besides that I'm unfit for this job? Talk about having the shittiest timing in the world for that kind of reali-zation. Although, to be honest, my screwup with Digi-Dong really drove home that point for me. Failure is a great teacher. I'd never failed before because I hadn't tried. So now, I'm putting in the work I should have from day one. But that doesn't change the fact that my knowledge about LI isn't close to what it should be after nearly a decade. I think Dad is terrified I'll fuck up while he's convalescing. I think Brady and Ash are terrified that Dad *won't* come back to work and they'll be stuck with me as CEO."

Jax went quiet for a while. He didn't offer platitudes, which I appreciated.

Finally, I said, "Just say it. At this point, whatever ego I had has been decimated."

"Because I'm the type to kick my brother when he's down. Christ. I really wanna clock you if you believe that."

"I don't," I said evenly. "It's just a chance for you to weigh in without fear that my feelings will get hurt."

"Fine. I think you're being too hard on yourself, little brother. Maybe your time at LI has been the Peter Principle at work, but you've already made steps to change that. Dad is sixty-four. This health situation might slow him down temporarily, but he'll be back, more determined than ever to prove he's still up for running the company. He took over the reins of LI when he was forty. By my estimation, if he's healthy he won't retire for another six years, so you've got that long to refocus on what you missed when you weren't focused on how to run a multi-billion-dollar conglomerate."

I didn't deserve his faith in me even when I was happy to have it.

My phone buzzed. I pulled it out to read a message from Gabi.

GW: Total Dallas moment, but I just had the weirdest feeling about you. You okay?

Grinning, I replied.

ME: Just having an existential career crisis. The universe is a tattletale. It was supposed to be on the down low.

GW: Now I'm worried.

ME: Don't be. Chatting with Jax helped. I'm about to head back to the grind. Everything okay with you?

GW: Yeah. I'll be glad when this week is over.

The . . . started and disappeared three times before her words finally appeared on-screen.

GW: I miss you.

I looked up and whispered a silent thanks to the sky for bringing this woman into my life.

ME: I miss you like crazy too. Can I come by your place later?

GW: YES.

ME: It might be late-ish.

GW: I don't care what time. I'll wait up.

ME: Should I bring anything?

GW: Simply your sweet, sexy, smiling self.

ME: Sweet talker. See you soon.

"Only texting with Gabi puts a smile on your face like that," my brother commented.

I returned my phone to my pocket and gave him the side-eye. "She makes me happy."

"Have you talked to her about any of this LI stuff?"

Tempting to say that we didn't give each other career advice. But that'd be an outright lie, so I hedged. "I'm sure she'd listen if I brought it up. Seems we have other things on our minds when we're together."

Jax smirked. "I'll bet."

My smile faded and I swallowed hard again.

"What?"

"This is scary shit with her. I just want to be around her all the time. Even when I'm with her I'm thinking about how we can spend more time together. It's like a damn obsession." I ran my hand through my hair. "I'm sure I sound like a lunatic."

"No, you sound like a man in love."

"Well, I wouldn't know."

"You're telling me that you didn't feel that way about even *one* of the women you paraded to family events or social gatherings the past decade?"

I shook my head. "Literally they were the flavor of the moment to me. Now I can barely recall any of their faces, say nothing of their names."

He whistled. "Not a good feeling, is it?"

"No, regardless if it comes from apathy or booze, the end result is that sinking feeling that you wished you would've stopped it sooner."

"Does Gabi know how you feel about her?" Jax said softly.

"She knows it's never been like this for me before. She says it's the same for her."

"My only advice is if you're sure you love her, tell her." He pushed away from my door. "Grab that happiness and make it yours. Don't wait."

Halfway to his car, he stopped and turned around. "I've

learned to be a good listener, Nolan. Anytime you need to talk, day or night, I'm here for you. Always."

"Thanks, Jax."

I returned to the office after my suit fitting. Thankful for busy-work, I hadn't looked at the clock until Sam threw in the towel at eight P.M. Normally, I'd hoof it to the gym, regardless of how exhausted I might be. But tonight . . .

Tonight I drove straight to Gabi's, with a short stop at a C-store to pick up a couple of pints of ice cream.

I knew she'd finished her last practice at seven thirty, since she'd texted me, but I didn't let her know I was on my way. I still had a gate pass to access Snow Village from when Jax lived here, so the guard waved me in.

After exiting my car, I realized in my haste to leave the office I hadn't put on my topcoat, but thankfully the weather had warmed up enough that I didn't need it. Too anxious to wait for the elevator, I took the stairs to the third floor. I couldn't keep the grin off my face when I knocked on her door.

The door swung open.

Gabi's gaze moved over me from head to toe and back again. "What the hell are you wearing?"

Frowning, I glanced down at my three-piece custom suit in a patternless gray-black wool. The trousers were slim cut. The vest had an unusual, low oval cut, curved with a row of buttons on each side. The jacket was also slim cut, with slightly shorter sleeves, which revealed the white shirt cuffs that matched the white collar on my pale-gray-striped dress shirt. The jacket had wide lapels with no notches, no match-ing hankie. I'd finished off the ensemble with a dark gray silk tie with small white polka dots. "You don't like this?" I man-aged before I looked up at her.

The raw lust in her eyes as she stalked forward nearly

buckled my knees. "Are you kidding me right now? That might be my favorite suit you've ever worn. You look ridiculously fuckable."

"Gabriella," I murmured.

"Shut up and get in here before someone else sees you dressed like this." She grabbed hold of my tie and pulled me into her apartment, muttering, "Jesus. No wonder they call you the motherfucking prince of LI."

Once we were inside, she slammed the door and pushed me against it. Using her grip on my tie, she brought my mouth to hers. She kissed me with every bit of blistering heat I'd seen in her eyes. This onslaught of passion fired every nerve ending in my body. My heart raced, my blood roared, my dick got hard—all within about a minute of her lips on mine.

She kissed a path to my ear, her tongue leaving a trail of fire in its wake.

I shuddered helplessly. Happily.

"Nolan," she practically growled. "Let me have you." She brushed damp kisses over my ear, stopping only to suck in a quick breath, which she knew made me crazy. "Please."

"Baby, you own me." I tried to reconnect our mouths, but she evaded. So I said, "Whatever you want from me. Take it. It's yours."

Her triumphant smile flashed before she reclaimed the kiss. As soon as she released my tie, both her hands were on my waistband, unfastening and unzipping my pants in record time.

I literally had to lock my knees when she dropped to hers in front of me.

Whoosh. My pants and briefs were around my ankles.

Then she took every inch of me into the hot, wet suction of her mouth.

My head thunked back in total surrender. The bag containing the ice cream hit the floor, allowing me to curl my hands around her head.

Gabi didn't tickle or tease or torture. She showed me that her need, her passion for me, equaled mine for her. She kept a punishing grip on my quads with the tips of her fingers as she wound me tighter and tighter, driving me toward that apex of pleasure without pause.

The more she worked me, the more heat her body created, and her warm sugary scent wafted up, making me harder yet.

My wordless response—a drawn-out growl and my thumb moving to the corner of her mouth to feel the wet glide of her taking me deep—caused her to moan around my shaft and sent electricity straight to my balls.

Good thing she didn't need direction in this because I couldn't have formed a coherent sentence if my life depended on it.

And when I reached the point of no return, she tipped me into the abyss, swallowing my release as my shaft pulsed and jerked on her tongue.

Black glittery dots danced behind my closed lids. I might've groaned. I definitely babbled, but the words were unclear since she'd sent my brain completely offline.

I gasped at the sharp sting of her teeth into my thigh that brought me out of my blissed-out state. I managed to open one eye and look down to see the top of her head as she whispered soft kisses across my quivering flesh.

At some point my hand had slid down from her face and circled the front of her throat. I squeezed slightly to get her attention.

Those sexy, slumberous eyes met mine.

"I'm glad you like the suit."

She smiled. "I like *you*. The way you fill out a suit is just a bonus for me."

"I missed you."

"Obviously I missed you too."

"We seem to have a thing for doing it against doors, don't we?" I murmured as I caressed the hollow of her throat with my thumb.

"No complaints from me about that." After giving my softening shaft one last teasing lick, she rolled to her feet. "I'll let you put yourself back together while I pour you a drink."

Since I hadn't brought other clothes, I slipped my pants back up, kicked my shoes off, hung up my suit coat and snagged the ice cream before I went looking for her.

She had her back to me in the kitchen as she tipped tequila into two margarita glasses.

I put the ice cream in the freezer. Then I moved in behind her, kissing the curve of her neck, from the base of her hairline to the slope of her shoulder. I loved the loose sweatshirts she wore that were always slipping off one shoulder, providing me the perfect access to one of my favorite parts of her. "Thank you," I murmured as I tasted her skin.

Gabi turned her head and nuzzled into me. "I love unraveling you as much as I love winding you up."

"Mmm. Same. I'm looking forward to the drink, but I did bring ice cream." I nipped her earlobe. "You unraveled me so fast it didn't even have time to melt."

She snickered. Then she sidestepped me and turned to hand me the glass.

The drink was perfectly tart, sweet and cold. "Delicious drink, Happy."

"It's one of the few things I've mastered."

"I can think of one other thing you fucking rock at too."

That brought a cocky curl to her lips. She snagged her glass and said, "Let's sit in the living room."

We sat side by side on the couch and she snuggled into me. "How's your dad?"

"Better. They're letting him out tomorrow. He's still being an asshole about the whole thing."

"I think that's a default reaction. I remember my dad being the same way. I thought he'd be thankful to be alive, but he was pissy because he wasn't aware his body had reached the point of failure."

"That sounds about right." I took a sip. "How was your day?"

"Follow-up tourney meetings for the state refs at HQ. Then training and teaching. Same old, same old."

"For now. Any word from Wolf?"

Gabi shook her head. "I'm guessing it's because they know I'll be out of reach the next couple of days. This is the last tourney, so I imagine they'll get with me first thing next week."

I twined a section of her ponytail around my finger. "If your team makes it to the finals . . . that game is the last one on Saturday night, right?"

"Yes. While I'm hopeful, we've got about a twenty percent chance of that happening. Why?"

"There's this Grant Foundation Gala on Saturday night. Attendance is required for me so it sucks I can't come and cheer you on *when* your team makes the finals."

She snorted.

"That said, since I knew you had a conflict and couldn't attend the gala as my date, I'm giving you a heads-up that I did have to arrange to take someone else."

Her entire body stiffened.

"Don't be mad, this is one of the unavoidable CEO things we talked about."

"Who?" she demanded.

I don't know what tempted me to mess with her, other than I liked seeing her jealousy. "I've known her for a long time. She's been to a bunch of these events so she's familiar with them."

"That is not easing my mind, Nolan."

"I'm sorry. I wish I could skip it."

"Me too," she retorted. "I hate the idea of some other woman having your undivided attention all night. Seeing you in yet another one of those fuckable suits you own. Touching you. Makes me wanna rip her hair out by the roots."

I smiled against her ear. "I don't think my mother would look good bald. Then again, maybe she would."

She froze.

I laughed. "Yes, I'm taking my mother to the gala. Dad should be going, but since he's not, and I have need of a date, and she has a dress . . ."

"You jerk." A hard punch landed near my ribs. "That's for making me believe I could be so easily replaced in your life."

Grabbing her chin, I forced her to look at me. "You can't. Ever. I don't even want to try."

She blinked at me.

"I had this whole . . . scenario in my head of how I'd do this. There might've been wine. Roses."

"Weeping violins?" she teased.

"Perhaps. I definitely needed more time to craft romantic words to tell you—"

"Holy shit, Nolan, you're not kidding."

"No."

"But you don't have to—"

"Yes I do, so please listen to me." I stroked her cheek. "I wanted it to be special when I talked about how this seems to have happened so fast between us. Yet, maybe that's why I know it's real, because I've never felt this way about anyone else."

"How do you feel?"

My heart pounded like thunder when I said, "I love you."

A pause and then she said, "I know."

"You do?"

"Well, yeah. You told me like three times when I was blowing you."

My jaw dropped. "Are you messing with me right now?"

"Nope." She set our drinks on the coffee table and returned to straddle my lap, facing me. Keeping our eyes locked as she brushed her soft lips across mine, she said, "You don't remember?"

"Of course I don't remember," I half scoffed. "Christ, I lose all brain synapses when your mouth is anywhere near my dick."

"So you didn't mean it when you said, '*Fuck me, I love you so much*.'" Her mouth gravitated to my ear. "Or when you said, '*Love you, baby, that's it, take me all the way*.'"

I groaned. Half-mortified / half-turned on.

"Or when you said, *Goddamn woman, I love love love you*."

"Yes, I meant it. all of it."

"Oh good." She looked me in the eyes. "Because I love love love you too."

Then she kissed me softly. Sweetly. Thoroughly. Giving me the heart-melting moment I'd wanted to give her.

She paused long enough to whisper, "Stay with me tonight."

"Yes."

The kiss heated up, our bodies began to move together . . . and then my stomach growled.

I tried to ignore it, but Gabi wouldn't let me.

"Nolan. Did you eat tonight?"

"No. I was busy and then I was anxious to get here."

"But you stopped for ice cream."

I kissed her nose. "I didn't want to show up empty-handed."

"Instead you show up with an empty stomach." She pushed back to her feet. "I can make you an egg-white omelet with ham and veggies or heat up a frozen dinner."

"You don't have to—"

A quick kiss shut me up. "Yes, I do want to take care of my man. So let me. Choose."

"Omelets."

"On it." As an afterthought she said, "If you'd like to change out of the fantastic suit and want to wear something besides your equally fantastic birthday suit, there's a robe hanging on the back of my bedroom door."

"Is it pink and fluffy?" I said with a quick grin.

"Do I *look* like the pink and fluffy robe type, Lund?"

"Point taken." I headed down the hallway to her room. After I stripped to my boxer briefs and T-shirt and hung up my clothes, I checked behind her bedroom door for the robe.

My eyes narrowed on the plush fabric—the plush familiar fabric.

What the hell?

I snatched the robe off the hook and headed for the kitchen. "When did you get this?" I demanded.

"Today. Surprise."

"How? This is the exact same robe I have at my house."

Gabi smirked. "I know. I called Q and made him tell me where to get one for you."

"Why?"

"Because I know you're particular about that stuff. I want you to be comfortable when you're with me."

I was at an utter loss of what to say.

Thankfully she took pity on me, crossed over and hugged me. "It's just a robe, Nolan."

No. It was so much more than that. It was everything.

Just like her.

Twenty-Seven

GABI

T he final buzzer sounded and my girls' team jumped the
wall and raced onto the ice.

Anna and I hugged, exchanged high fives and basked in
watching the team's exuberance at coming in third place in
their division.

"This is all you," Anna said loudly. "If you hadn't taken
over and pushed them, they wouldn't have believed this was
possible."

"Two coaches on this team, Anna. Never sell yourself
short. We did great." Another hug, a couple more fist bumps
and we turned to watch the girls skate across and congratulate the opposing team members.

We waved to the crowd of parents in the stands, who were
almost as giddy with excitement as their daughters were.

Anna said, "I'll head to the locker room with the team if
you want to deal with them and make sure they all know
where we're going."

"Sure. I won't be long." I glanced at the clock. Seven thirty.

When I reached the group of parents, I was surprised to see Jax there with them.

He grinned at me. "Congrats, Coach Welk, on a well-played game and a great season. I'm thrilled this is Lakeside's first trophy under this new ownership."

"Thank you. The girls worked hard, all year. So to say they're pretty pumped right now is an understatement." I focused on Parker's mom. "We've reserved the back room at Marco's for the pizza party. And just to be clear it is the Marco's closest to this rink, not the one by Lakeside. That locker room isn't big, so I expect your daughters will be out shortly."

"Coach Welk, will you be at the pizza party?" Keena's dad asked.

"I wouldn't miss it for anything."

While they returned to talking among themselves, Jax took me aside. "I admire your dedication, Gabi, but isn't tonight the Grant Foundation Gala Nolan's attending?"

"Yeah. He knew I had a game so he's taking your mom since your dad can't go either."

Nolan had attended the game last night. His in-person support meant everything to me, especially when I understood how much pressure he'd been under since his dad's heart attack.

After we'd won and shared congratulations and I'd dealt with excited teens and parents about what to expect playing in the consolation round, Nolan had been my calming sea. Treating me to a lingering hug, a chaste kiss on the cheek, a quick peck on the mouth and sweet praise murmured into my hair.

Suddenly we'd been on the receiving end of wolf whistles.

Parker, the nosiest kid I'd ever met, had gasped after seeing Nolan so openly affectionate with me. "Coach Welk! Is Stonewall Lund's brother your *boyfriend*?"

"As I'm sure *you* wouldn't like to be referred to as Abbie's sister, he has his own name other than Stonewall Lund's brother."

"But that doesn't answer my question."

"Yes, Parker, I'm very, very lucky that Coach Welk calls me her boyfriend," Nolan had inserted smoothly.

Even my heart sighed at his confession.

"Gabi?" Jax prompted.

I blinked, clearing the memory. "I'm sorry. What?"

"I'm not telling you what to do, but if you make an appearance at the pizza party and stay for a slice or two, there's still time for you to get to the Grant Foundation Gala. Nolan will squire my mom around for a while; I'd be shocked if she stayed past ten. I know she doesn't like leaving my dad, even if he isn't alone. Nolan will feel compelled to stay at least until midnight."

"If you're here, and Nolan is at the gala, who's with Archer?"

Jax smirked. "Lucy and Mimi. Meems brought every board game she owns and a tub of crafts."

"If nothing else, she'll tire him out," I said dryly.

"True. So I am headed over there after the pizza party."

"You're coming?"

"Hell yeah. Someone's gotta pay for the free food."

Of course the man would pay for the party, rather than everyone chipping in as Anna and I had planned.

"That also leaves you no excuse not to show up at the gala fashionably late. Besides, if you'd planned on attending before everything happened this week, I know you've got something to wear, so that ain't gonna be an excuse for you not to make my brother's whole night."

I studied him. "You really are happy that Nolan and I are together."

"Very. From the moment we met it's felt like you were part of the family. You make Nolan happy, Gabs. I see that he does the same for you."

"Don't you make me cry, asshole."

He laughed. "Heaven forbid." From inside his sport coat, he pulled out an envelope. "This is literally an engraved invitation that'll get you into the gala. Doesn't matter whose name is on it as long as you have it."

I hugged him. "Thank you so much, Jax. I hope Nolan doesn't mind me showing up late."

"He will be thrilled. Mark my words."

"But don't tell him, okay? I'd like it to be a surprise."

I returned to my apartment by nine fifteen.

In lieu of a shower, I rubbed on lotion since that's the scent Nolan preferred on me anyway.

Once I'd reapplied my makeup, using a heavier hand on the eyeliner and lipstick than usual, I pinned my hair into a messy bun. For once, it looked great on my first attempt.

The dress fit beautifully. I scarcely recognized myself. I still had a few days before I had to return the accessories I'd borrowed and when I opened the case where I'd stored them, there was a jewelry box I hadn't noticed before. A jewelry box with a big bow on it and a tag that read:

To wear with the blue dress, no peeking beforehand—Nolan

When I opened it, I nearly blinded myself from the jewels' shininess.

This was no costume jewelry. Only real gems shone that brightly.

The earrings were chandelier-style. Platinum inlaid with diamonds until the last stone, which was a very round, very blue, very big sapphire.

My hands shook when I put them on. They were really heavy, but damn they were exquisite.

Next I donned the necklace. It was every bit as modern and abstract as the earrings were traditional. With the diagonal strip of fabric across my chest, I worried that anything would look off. But I needn't have worried, the heaviness of the metal, coupled with the weight of the diamonds, sapphires and blue topaz added interest to the lines of the bodice rather than detracting from it. The last item in the box was a bracelet. Two ropes of pavé—platinum inlaid with diamonds—that looked like four strands of diamonds when clasped around my wrist.

I took one last look at myself in the mirror. No surprise that Nolan knew his jewels too.

After calling for an Uber, I placed the invite, my cell phone, lipstick, house key, ID and credit card into the small satin-covered purse. I slipped on my heels and the silver fur cape and took the elevator to the main floor to await my ride.

The Uber driver wasn't chatty, which sucked when I needed a distraction. The venue was a private country club I'd never heard of, but that wasn't saying much since the only country club I'd been to in the Twin Cities was the one Nolan's parents belonged to—and only the parking lot of that one.

Although this club didn't appear fancy on the outside, I guessed it'd be crystal chandeliers and polished marble on the inside.

A young man wearing a full coat-and-tails-type tuxedo helped me out of the car. He immediately escorted me to the concierge.

"Good evening. How may I help you?"

"I'm here for the Grant Foundation Gala. My previous event ran late." Ooh, didn't I sound posh? I handed him the invitation. "Hopefully I haven't missed too much."

"Just the dinner and the speeches. The silent auction is still in progress. Dancing started half an hour ago."

I glanced at the clock behind him. Ten thirty. I hoped Jax was right and Nolan was still here.

"Coat check is on your left inside," the concierge continued. "Then follow that hallway until you reach Ballroom A."

"Thank you."

After I ditched my wrap, I headed to the party, which I heard as soon as I entered the building.

The people who passed by smiled quizzically, as if trying to place me.

Good luck with that. I'm so far out of my realm I'm in another world.

The doors to the ballroom were open, the lights were still up on high. No shadowed corner for me to lurk in and get the lay of the land, so to speak.

Inside the ballroom, I snagged a class of bubbly from a passing waitress and roamed the periphery of the room. Did I see anyone I knew? Not a single soul—including my boyfriend. So I kept moving. It took an entire glass of champagne to navigate one quarter of the massive room. If I kept up this drinking pace, I'd knock back four glasses before I finished where I'd started.

Tempting. Especially when I reached the halfway mark and still no sign of Nolan.

I had attracted two male admirers, who approached me as soon as I quit moving.

"Hello there. How did we miss such a ravishing beauty at dinner?" pseudo-charmer number one asked.

"I'm afraid I missed the dinner. Previous engagement."

"I can hope you were breaking it off with your boyfriend. You'll crush me if you admit you're not single," guy number two said with mock sorrow. "Not a good end to the evening."

The nerve of these guys. And this forced charm . . . not charming at all.

"Please at least tell us your name."

"Gabi." I glanced away from my would-be paramours and finally saw my man across the room.

Women hanging on his every word. Some men too. Quick with a smile. Quick to toss off some comment that had his groupies laughing again.

Breathtaking was the only way to describe him. His custom-tailored suit stood out and was the perfect complement to my dress. I muttered, "You sneaky bastard."

"Who?" guy number two asked.

Then he saw where my focus had strayed.

"That guy is a total sneaky bastard, from what I've heard. He has a one-and-done rule."

"Ironclad," guy number one added.

"Do you know him?" I asked.

"I know *of* him. I mean, I know his name—everyone does." He paused. "Do *you* know him?"

I said, "Nolan Lund."

That's when Nolan went still. Almost as if he'd heard me. His gaze scanned the room until his eyes landed on me.

He treated me to a once-over. Then another.

I hid my smirk behind my champagne glass when he completely abandoned his conversation, booking it in my direction, nearly plowing over a waiter and a couple exiting the dance floor in his haste to reach me.

My two new pals had gone silent.

Especially after Nolan arrived, swept me into his arms and kissed me squarely on the mouth. "I can't believe you're here."

"Good thing my champagne glass was empty or I'd be wet."

He plucked it out of my hand and held it out; within two seconds a waiter appeared to take it from him.

"Neat trick."

"Did your team win?"

I nodded. "Third place."

"Congrats, Coach."

"Thanks."

"God, you look stunning." He ran his finger along the upper curve of the necklace and the skin beneath. "I knew these would be perfect on you." His dark eyes met mine. "Were you surprised?"

"Very. They're beautiful. Thank you for lending them to me."

His mouth opened. Closed.

"Tell me you borrowed them from your mother or the Lund family jewel vault."

"I promised never to lie to you, Happy, so the truth is . . . they're yours. As is the entire outfit."

"Nolan. You can't just—"

"Yes, I can." He put his mouth on my ear. "Say, *Thank you, Nolan.*"

"It's too much."

"Say, *Thank you, Nolan*, or I'll be forced to buy you even flashier pieces because I'll worry you didn't like these."

"You're ridiculous, Lund, but thank you."

He kissed me again, the type of kiss that wasn't a make-out session, but an intimate brush of lips that conveyed more.

When he retreated, he noticed the two guys who'd stuck around but had hung back to give us privacy.

Nolan offered guy number one a smile. "And you are?"

"Rupi Gilroy." He nudged his friend's shoulder. "This is Cooper Winchell."

"Good to meet you both." Nolan slipped his arm around my waist. "I see you've met my girlfriend, Gabriella."

I gave them a finger wave.

"If you'll excuse us . . ." He steered me away.

"That wasn't subtle."

"Wasn't meant to be. I've done my social duty tonight. I'm debating between ignoring everyone so I can have you to myself and introducing you to everyone because I want the world to know we're together."

"Can't we find a happy medium?"

"Mmm. Maybe." He led me out of the ballroom into a hallway that had a long red-carpet runner covering the floor. The backdrop was the Grant Foundation Gala logo on portable walls, which reminded me of the sponsorship signs at an ice arena—albeit classier promotion, but paid advertising, nonetheless.

Before I could ask him where we were going, a man wearing two cameras stopped us.

"Lund. That area is off-limits."

"Hey, Barnes. I was looking for you."

His eyes narrowed. "Why?"

"My girlfriend arrived late, and I wanted a pic of us at the gala together."

"Are you drunk, man?"

Nolan laughed. "No. I'm serious." He practically presented me with a flourish. "Gabriella, this is Barnes, a freelance photographer I've known for a very long time. Barnes, this is Gabriella Welk, my girlfriend."

"You were already here with a date—your mother—so nice try," Barnes sneered.

"I'm trying to give you an exclusive."

"So Notorious Nolan has settled down?"

"Yes. You know how many dates I've brought to these types of events over the years and how many times I've referred to said dates as my girlfriend." He paused. "Zero."

Barnes considered him. "You know I'm gonna sell this pic to the *Trib*'s society page."

"Which is why I'm here. You get an exclusive and I get a formal pic of us looking hot together."

I elbowed him.

"Deal. Stand over there."

We trooped to the backdrop.

"What's the deal with her?" Barnes asked, fiddling with his cameras. "Gotta have the story and not just a couple of pics."

"The deal with her? What's that supposed to mean?" I demanded.

"I'm not doing the work for you, Barnes. Google her name. That's all you're getting from me except a promise I'm not messing with you. She and I are together and it's serious."

Nolan kissed me softly.

"No kissing shots. I can't see your faces." He gestured and Nolan tugged me beside him. "Pose like it's prom, kiddies. Or *RuPaul's Drag Race*."

I snorted.

"Be serious," Nolan whispered in my ear.

When Barnes dropped his lens cap and turned around to pick it up, giving us a glimpse of his butt crack, I cracked up.

Nolan tried to stop my laughter by kissing me, but I dropped my chin, and his lips smacked into my cheek. Then we were both busting a gut.

Somehow, we managed to get a couple of killer shots.

"Email those to me ASAP," Nolan said. "Don't make me track you down."

"Yeah, yeah, yeah." Barnes ignored us so we walked away.

"Do you trust him?" I asked when we were out of earshot.

"I trust his greed."

"But you want a pic of us to be in the paper."

"Yes. I haven't been in it for months and this is an opportunity to let the world know we're a couple."

"While I know we are, do you worry that others might interpret it as a maneuver on the part of LI to put the rumors to rest that you're still too much of a playboy to run the company?"

That question brought Nolan to a complete stop.

"I guess if PR had put me up to that I might see it that way. But I had no ulterior motive besides wanting to have a happy end to what was one of the roughest weeks of my life."

I reached up and caressed his face. "If that put a smile on this handsome mug, then I'm happy to've been part of it."

Nolan kissed me. "Thank you. Now will you dance with me?"

"I'm kind of a lousy dancer, but sure."

But come to find out, I wasn't terrible if I followed his lead.

The man could move on the dance floor. I found myself monumentally turned on with every precise snap of his hips.

With each grind of his body against mine. With each soft kiss he teased me with. I'd only had one glass of champagne . . . so why did I feel light-headed?

Because you are intoxicated with everything about this man.

Nolan could see my hunger, my restlessness growing. After the song ended, he towed me off the dance floor, smiling at acquaintances, but not making a point of introducing me like he had for the past hour. The only official good night was given to the members of the Grant family after Nolan thanked them for a remarkable event and evening.

As he led me toward the exit, his deep voice tickled my nerve endings from my ear to my toes. "You're coming home with me."

I handed him my coat-check tag and he made a brief call while he waited for our coats.

He seemed to take great pleasure in swinging the cape around and buttoning it. "This looks amazing on you. The way the fur catches the light and changes the color from silver to different shades of gray reminds me of your eyes. Shining one moment, dark the next."

"God. Stop with the sweet-talking words. You're making me wet."

He raised an eyebrow. "And that's an issue because . . . ?"

I stood on tiptoe to reach his ear. "Because I'm not wearing any panties." I wheeled around, letting the soft edge of the cape flap against his chest before I sauntered outside.

Less than a minute later, his hands rested on my hips and he planted a kiss on the side of my neck.

I smiled. "Are you going to torment me the entire time we're waiting for the valet to bring your car around?"

"No, smart mouth. I'm going to torment you until the car service arrives."

"Did you hire a car service before or after you saw me here?"

"Before." He traced the shell of my ear with the underside

of his bottom lip, eliciting my shiver and moan. "But I up-graded it after I saw you."

Just then a glossy black limo pulled up.

I whirled around. "Did you really order us a limo?"

"Yep." He smiled. "You seemed excited about that idea the night you rode home with Jensen, so here's your ride, baby."

"You are ridiculously awesome, man of mine."

A valet stepped over and opened the limo door for us. Nolan palmed him a bill as I tried to get in gracefully, without tripping. Once my ass hit the seat behind the driver, Nolan slammed the door shut.

"Good evening," the driver said. "Still headed to the address in St. Louis Park?"

"Eventually. I'd like it if you drove around some first. I'll let you know when to head to our destination. Oh, and engage the privacy window, please."

"Certainly, sir."

While I watched the glass change from clear to reflective, Nolan pulled the champagne out of the ice-packed silver cask and gently worked the cork free. He poured the bubbly into one glass and said, "We'll share."

He offered me the first glass.

I downed it.

Not to be outdone, he poured himself a glass and downed it too.

We shared the third glass. Then he set the bottle and the glass back in the ice.

"Have you ever ridden in a limo?"

"Yes." I rose to my knees on the seat—whoa, plenty of headroom—and straddled his lap. "But I've never been fucked in one."

After he unsnapped my cape and set it aside, his teeth were on my neck and his hands cupped my ass. "I intend to make all your fantasies come true." His fingers found the hem of the dress and he began to slide it up. "I should hoist you up on the seat and spread you out so I can gorge on you, but I need inside you first." He groaned when his fingers met bare skin and then proof of my desire for him. "Christ. You weren't kidding about no panties."

"I never kid about VPL," I whispered before I crushed his mouth beneath mine.

We kissed ravenously as he got his pants undone and his dick freed.

The fact we both needed this right now, without foreplay, just intensified the effect of the champagne—my head spun, my breath caught when he aligned me over his hardness and slammed home.

"God. Yes," I moaned and let my head fall back as he thrust up into me.

We moved together with a synchronicity that would've scared me had it not been everything I'd ever dreamed of. If it hadn't been spontaneous. While Nolan obviously had mad bedroom skills, I considered myself lucky that all that expertise was now solely focused on me.

All. The. Time.

He traced the cord in my neck with his nose. "I think I could come just from the scent of your skin. Drives me fucking insane."

Bracing myself with my hands on his shoulders, I let the sensations roll through me. The friction of his suit pants on the backs of my thighs. The heavy breathing that'd already fogged up the windows. His hands squeezing my hips as he drove into me.

And his scent, skin-warmed wool, cotton and piney cologne. I already felt that tightening in my core, that tiny tingle that lit the fuse toward detonation. Swiveling my hips, I ground down every time he rocked his pelvis up.

"Like that. Just like that," he panted against my throat.

"Yes, I'm almost there."

"Give it to me. I wanna feel you come around me." His lips found mine again and he interspersed kisses with words.

"Nothing is sexier than that. Nothing gets me off faster than that."

"Say it. I wanna feel the rumble through my body when you say it."

His mouth returned to my ear. "Gabriella. My Gabriella." The low-pitched near growl reverberated through every nerve ending, every skin cell, every synapse, and I flew apart.

Nolan didn't kiss me as I came. He kept his mouth on my ear, saying such dirty, delicious things that it made me shiver and tremble.

Best thing ever that he'd figured out my trigger point without me having to tell him.

Then he said, "Fuck," his quads tightened and he was there too. I matched his frantic race to the finish line, but managed to angle my head so I could watch his beautiful face awash in pleasure.

In the aftermath we clung to each other. Bodies still. Breathing labored.

His voice was ragged when he said, "How can it get better every time?"

"I've been wondering that myself."

He framed my face in his hands. "I love you."

"I love you too. But don't you dare make me all teary eyed after you just fucked me stupid."

He laughed. "Never a dull moment with you, Welk. Let's finish the champagne."

I found tissues and we cleaned up, setting our clothes to rights again. "Love that suit on you too. Total coincidence it matches with my dress?" I teased him.

"Not even close. I knew that we'd have an occasion to wear them, I just didn't know when."

"That was before . . ."

"I kissed you or touched you or had any idea whether you'd laugh in my face at the thought of us being more than friends." He grabbed my hand and kissed my knuckles. "And look at us now. Getting tipsy in the back of a limo after you rocked my world."

I didn't know how to respond to that, so I let it stay as the last word.

We drained the champagne, classily passing the bottle back and forth, laughing—about what, I had no idea, but we were just two happy, silly fools in love. That would've been the perfect end to our night . . . except the limo driver informed us he couldn't make it up Nolan's driveway.

"That's fine, we'll walk." Nolan helped me out of the car and tossed me my cape. I teetered dangerously on my stilettos as I caught it.

I squinted at the Mount Everest of driveways. "Dude. There's no freakin' way I can walk up that in these." I pointed at my feet.

"Take 'em off and walk up barefoot."

"It's thirty fucking degrees out here."

"I'm not sober enough to carry you." Then a gleam entered his eyes. "However, I could give you a piggyback."

"What part of 'no panties' is confusing to you? You want me to flash your entire neighborhood?"

Nolan laughed so hard at that I feared he might've pulled something since it took him forever to quit holding his stomach.

Or what forever felt like to a very tipsy woman, tipping over in her high heels.

He wiped his eyes. "Okay, leave it to me."

His grin just . . . god. Filled me with joy because this playful, sweet, carefree Nolan was only mine. No one else got to see this side of him.

"Take off your shoes. I'll take off my jacket and you put it on, it'll be long enough to cover your girlie bits when you hop up on my back. We'll go slow and you have to promise me to stay bent forward over me like a turtle, so we don't get off balance."

I slipped the jacket on under the cape. My purse and my shoes dangled from my left hand. "Ready?"

"Climb on, hot stuff."

It only took one try until my body was curved high over his back, with my knees bracketing his hips and his hands cupping my feet.

Nolan made a run for it and I half expected to hear his war cry too. I bit my cheek to keep from laughing about how crazy we must've looked. But his plan worked, and we were at the top of the driveway.

I kissed his ear. "My brave man. You're breathing a little hard. You'll have to get into better shape if we ever want to compete in that wife-carrying contest."

"Probably. I'd have to add ax throwing to my workout regimen too." He carried me to the front door and punched in the alarm. Then he gently set me on the floor, shut the door and reset the alarm.

Then he stalked me.

"What?"

"It freaks you out if you're not wearing the right clothes, but the thought of being my wife someday doesn't?"

I shrugged. "You fit me no matter where we go or what we do. Unfortunately that's not the case with clothes."

"Well said," he whispered against my cheek. "Let's go to bed where clothing doesn't matter at all."

Twenty-Eight

GABI

My week had started out great. I spent all day Sunday lazing, laughing and loving with Lund.

On Monday Liddy had returned from her long trip to London, so we spent the evening catching up until jetlag caught up with her.

Since hockey season had ended, I didn't have many responsibilities at Lakeside, teaching wise. Jax had already started pushing for a new schedule, but I couldn't discuss his options until I received the all clear from my new boss to share the news about my career switch.

Last night Nolan had business to attend to, and we hadn't even texted.

This morning I wound up at TRIA—the Minnesota Wild's brand-new gorgeous training facility in St. Paul—with a few former teammates, my sister and recruits for a pickup game and to hear the final details for the Whitecaps, the new NWHL women's ice hockey franchise based in the Twin Cities in partnership with the Wild.

Then after the game, my former teammate Carly, newly named head coach of the Whitecaps, had taken me into her office for a private meeting. She'd offered me an assistant coaching position. Full time. Lots of travel promoting the team, especially in the off-season. While the money and the benefits were good, and the contract didn't exclude me running hockey camps as an extra source of income, I had to deflect on why I turned down their offer without seriously considering it. I wondered why the Whitecaps organization hadn't offered me the job earlier, because I would've taken it.

Lost in thought, I'd just pulled out of the parking lot when my cell phone rang through my speakers. The caller ID read: Wolf Sports North.

Finally. I hadn't heard from them at all last week.

"This is Gabi Welk."

"Gabi. Alan. How are you?"

"Good. And you?"

"That's why I'm calling. You're on speaker conference call with Minka and CEO of Wolf Sports North, Lance Jacoby."

Why was the big boss in on this call? "Hello, everyone. What's going on?"

"I'll cut right to it. Monday's *Tribune* had a picture of you with Nolan Lund, acting CEO of Lund Industries, at some charity event. The text that accompanied the picture indicated that you're personally involved with Mr. Lund. Is that correct?"

"Yes, sir, it is." I bit back my response to question the relevance, but if they mentioned it, it was likely why they were calling.

"That puts us in an awkward position. As you know, we've held off announcing our new programming lineup due to the merger. With today's announcement of LuTek acquiring Wolf Sports North, you can understand why the whispers of nepotism might cause us to rescind our offer of employment to you."

My feet literally hit the brakes. Thank god no one was behind me. I pulled over and flicked my flashers on. "I'm sorry, Alan. I don't follow. Why would a tech company purchasing the station affect my employment?"

"Because the acquiring tech company in question is a subsidiary of Lund Industries."

I would've dropped the phone if I'd been holding it. "And how was I supposed to know about that? Nolan and I don't talk about business."

"You're telling me that the man you're involved with, who is acting interim CEO of the acquiring company, didn't inform you of the acquisition?" His tone dripped of skepticism.

"Let's get something straight. Nolan wouldn't share classified information regarding their family corporation with me or anyone else even if it wasn't against company policy."

"So you're claiming that Mr. Lund could've known about the acquisition but didn't share job opening opportunities with you?"

"No, I'm telling you that Nolan and I didn't start dating until *after* my in-person interview with WSN. Not that it matters, because someone outside your network who also applied for the job is complaining about nepotism because they didn't get the position. If it truly was nepotism at work, then Mr. Jacoby would've been told by someone in the executive branch of Lund Industries to make sure I got hired. That doesn't appear to be the case, does it, Mr. Jacoby? Since I was offered the job *before* the LuTek acquisition announcement?"

"Was Mr. Lund aware of your application to work at Wolf Sports North?"

Deflection. No surprise. "Yes. But—"

"So he could've smoothed the path for you."

"I have no clue if he *could* have, I just know he didn't. I passed the various application levels on my own merit, *before* Nolan and I became involved." I took a deep breath. "Let me ask you something. When I interviewed, I was informed a merger was taking place. I was not given the name of the acquiring company and I didn't breach protocol by asking. But what if one of the other job candidates was somehow given that information?"

That had surprised them.

"Mr. Jacoby, with the merger in place, who do you answer to directly now? Someone in the executive branch of Lund Industries?"

"No. As a subsidiary of LuTek, I answer to that CEO."

"Is Nolan Lund now the CEO of LuTek?"

"No, he is not the CEO of LuTek. But how is that—"

"Relevant? It's the only thing that's relevant as you are attempting to deny me a job that I fought for, for myself." I paused. "Permission to be brutally honest?"

"Granted," Alan said.

"Jubilee Jones applied for the same position I did. I've dealt with her in the past and she is not a trustworthy person. So if she gained insight from one of the Wolf Sports North employees about which company was acquiring them, she *would* use that classified information to her advantage."

"Your objection is noted, Gabi," Alan said. "But for right now, until we gather more information, we're suspending the hiring process with you."

"You've got to be kidding me."

"I'm sorry, but no, we feel this is a necessary step."

I laughed harshly. "You do realize if I had the almighty power of nepotism, all it would take is one phone call to secure my employment?"

"Hi, Gabi, Minka here. We're asking you not to do that."

That's when I suspected Minka had leaked the acquisition info to Jubilee—they were two slimy peas in a pod. She would've championed Jubilee for the job over me.

"That's the thing. I would never do that. While I'm waiting for your verdict on my future with your company, might I suggest you find that leak? Someone in a position of authority spoke out of turn. It doesn't take a personal connection with the Lund family to understand that a company the size of Lund Industries takes confidentiality agreements seriously."

"Thank you for the reminder, Gabi. We'll be in touch."

After I hung up, I got back on the road and drove directly to Lund Industries.

Since I hadn't given Nolan a heads-up for the visit, I had to wait until someone secured a visitor's pass for me.

I stormed past the receptionist on his floor and booked it directly to Nolan's office.

Sam was on the phone and held me off until he ended the call. "Gabi. Lovely as it is to see you, today is not a good day to visit."

"Let me guess. Nolan had no idea about the LuTek acquisition of Wolf Sports North and he's losing his mind."

Surprise flashed across Sam's face. "How did you know?"

"It affects me too."

"How?"

"Yeah, how?" Jax said behind me.

I whirled around. "Jax? What are you doing here?"

"Nolan called an emergency board meeting. I've never heard him so infuriated. It worried me so I came to check on him. Now why don't you tell me how this affects you?"

Fuck my life. I paced to the alcove and Jax followed me. "I applied for a sportscasting position at Wolf Sports North."

"When? Why didn't you tell me?"

"Because you're my boss and we were in the busiest time of year for coaches and referees. We didn't need any extra tension between us, and we both know there would've been a shit ton when I told you I was exploring other career avenues."

"Instead, you left me in the dark and I'm guessing you're about to leave me high and dry at Lakeside."

"While I don't want to get into this here, please remember I don't have a contract with Lakeside. Working at a rink and running rec hockey programs was never on my career path.

I'd planned on sticking it out through the end of the season, which I have."

I hated how we were huffing and puffing and staring each other down.

"Did Nolan know about you applying for a job elsewhere?"

"Yes, I knew," Nolan said from the doorway.

I glanced over at him and my stomach bottomed out. I'd never seen him look like this—pinched mouth, clenched jaw, hard eyes.

"Gabriella told me in confidence. But it's no secret her talents are not being utilized to their fullest potential at Lakeside. Hell, Jax, you've even said so yourself. So don't get pissy about this. She's hated every minute she's had to keep this from you."

Jax said nothing.

"But what I didn't know, as the goddamned CEO, until I read it in the damn paper this morning, was that LuTek had purchased Wolf Sports North. Apparently LuTek had been in negotiations with All Sports Central, the parent company of Wolf Sports, for two fucking months."

Jax's jaw dropped. "Christ, Nolan, are you kidding me?"

"Not even a little. Still think I'm an LI bigwig?" he said bitterly.

Oh. My poor man. He hadn't known and that made it so much worse for him because it would make him look incompetent, not only to employees, but to the business world at large if it got out.

"Did you come to chew my ass too?" Nolan asked me.

I shook my head. "I got a call from Wolf Sports North today. A conference call with Alan, the Programming head, and Lance Jacoby, the CEO."

"What did they want?"

"To tell me that after seeing our picture in the paper, someone is crying nepotism about me landing the sportscasting job, since, as of today, Lund Industries owns the cable network through LuTek, and you're the acting CEO of LI so you must've been all-knowing."

"Jesus, Gabi. I'm sorry."

"They've suspended my employment contract while they investigate."

Nolan didn't cross over and take me in his arms. He just stared at me. Through me. "What did you say when they made that threat?"

"What could I say? Beyond we weren't involved until after my in-person interview. That it didn't matter because you and I don't discuss business. And that there's a leak in their company if the nepotism bullshit had been brought up on Monday, before the acquisition deal was publicly announced."

Panic flitted across his face. "Did you tell them that I . . . ?"

"No. I'd never do that to you," I said softly. "I came here because I wanted to give you a chance to explain if for some reason you *did* know about the acquisition and hadn't told me."

"I didn't have a damn thing to do with you getting hired, Gabriella. You did that all on your own. *You* know that. I know that. And I hate that you've gotten caught up in this too."

I clenched my hands at my sides, wanting so badly to go to him, to soothe him and in doing so soothe myself. But I stayed put. Seething for both of us.

"What's the position?" Jax asked.

"Co-broadcaster for the UMD men's and women's hockey teams."

Jax frowned. "Both teams? That's a shitload of games. A ton of travel. Were you planning on driving back and forth between Duluth and the Cities?"

Of course this would come up now. When I hadn't even hinted to Nolan I'd have to relocate.

"No. Contractually I'd have to live in Duluth during the preseason and until the end of the playoffs."

"That's like ten months. You might as well move there."

I felt Nolan staring at me, but I didn't have the guts to look at him.

Then he laughed. A little meanly. "Well. It appears not only is my family keeping me in the dark about things that directly affect my life, but my girlfriend is too."

"Nolan—"

"I don't want to hear an excuse. I deserved to know about that employment stipulation as soon as you did, because we were making plans for a future together."

"*Were?* Don't you mean *are*?"

He jammed his hand through his hair. "I don't know fuck-all about anything anymore, even things I was one hundred percent sure about this morning. This day is an example of epic failure and for once, I'm not the one who's gonna shoulder the blame for it."

My spirit, my hope . . . crumpled.

"One thing I do know is this is still my office and I'll ask you both once to get out while I prepare for the board meeting." He walked away and the door slammed behind him.

Jax swore and went after him, but Sam blocked his path. "You heard my boss. Go visit your wife, Jax. Maybe she can help you understand why *your* family shut out one of their own."

I waited until Jax had left to make my own escape.

Sam didn't acknowledge me at all as I slunk past his desk.

I managed to hold it together until I shut myself in the privacy of my truck. Then I sobbed for everything I'd lost today. But thinking about all that Nolan had lost, that's when the dam really broke. I'd caused some of his pain, instead of being his safe harbor against the rest of the tides rushing over him.

Oh god, that hurt me like a hundred knife cuts.

I hadn't told him about the required move to Duluth because I knew he'd urge me to go. He would've put a positive spin on it and assured me we'd work it out.

But I hadn't trusted that we'd built a strong enough foundation yet to withstand long periods of separation. So in my fear of losing him, I'd made the decision not to tell him something that could've given us a chance to fortify that foundation . . . and I might've lost him anyway.

I don't remember the drive to my apartment. Once inside, I turned off my phone and crawled into bed.

Twenty-Nine

NOLAN

Back when I was about five years old, I went to the office with my dad.

For some reason he'd left me with Grandpa Jackson, which was odd because Dad knew his father was a mean old man. Even more odd was that Grandpa had wanted to play a game with me, when normally, he just scowled at me and called me "the spare" or worse.

Eager to please, I listened intently to the rules of the game, which would result in five marshmallow cream eggs if I made it through all five levels—but that was the trick. If I made it through two levels, I didn't get two eggs. I got nothing. Four levels? Nothing. Only winning all five levels would earn me the prize.

Being a typical kid, I'd complained that it wasn't fair. Shouldn't I be rewarded for trying?

If he could've gotten away with boxing my ears, he would have. Instead, he'd grabbed me by the arm and jerked me close enough that I wouldn't miss a word of his wisdom.

Life wasn't fair.

Trying wasn't winning.

If you gave up you deserved to lose everything no matter how hard you thought you'd worked for it.

As an adult, I understood his message better than the young boy who'd just wanted a grandpa who wasn't a candy-hoarding, name-calling, rough-grabbing, mean-mouthed asshole.

I kept that lesson in mind as I strode into the Lund Industries boardroom. I'd intentionally showed up ten minutes late so no one had a chance to waylay me beforehand.

LI used a nondescript table for board meetings. But the chairs were comfortable for those few times a year when meetings ran long. In years past, I'd always sat somewhere in the middle of the table, usually next to my cousin Walker so I could kick his chair whenever he dozed off.

Today, even though my dad had made it to the meeting, I had the head of the table. My uncle Monte sat at the opposite end. The only unoccupied chair belonged to Dallas as she was off on another adventure. I looked at this group of people I loved and forced down the anger that had been burning in me since late last night when I'd discovered the duplicity.

"Good afternoon. I know it was sudden notice and I appreciate everyone taking time from their busy day to attend this meeting. I can't promise it'll be brief, but it will be thorough. Bear with me while I bring everyone up to speed on events that led to this meeting.

"Several weeks ago I met with Zosia Lund. She mentioned two things that disturbed me. First, that none of the LI executive officers would take the time to meet with her." I shot Brady and Ash each a look and I was pleased to see embarrassment on both of their faces. "Second, she'd learned from a Duluth Chamber of Commerce member that LuTek had recently purchased ESP, a manufacturing company in her town. I was shocked by the news for her sake since it's *always* been LI company policy to give notice to any LI business conducted in Duluth. On a personal level, I was mortified because I knew nothing about the acquisition. Nothing," I repeated. "An acquisition I've since learned cost ten million dollars." My gaze scanned the room. "Show of hands. Who was aware of the purchase of ESP through LuTek prior to it happening and not after the fact?"

Brady's hand went up.

Ash's hand went up.

My dad's hand went up.

My mom's hand went up.

"Who knew about the expenditure only after the transaction had happened?"

My uncle Monte's hand went up.

My uncle Ward's hand went up.

My aunt Selka's hand went up.

My aunt Cilla's hand went up.

"Who had no idea about this expenditure at all?"

Jensen, Walker, Annika, Jax and the three nonfamily members we were required to have on the board all raised their hands.

"The executive officers spent ten million dollars without bringing it to the board. Correct me if I'm wrong, Monte, but that's not how this is supposed to work, is it?"

"No, Nolan, we have proposal procedures to prevent this sort of situation."

The room was much quieter than I'd imagined it would be, as those not in the loop were glaring at the executive officers.

"After Zosia brought the issue to my attention, I attempted to find a paper trail so I could see if there was a legitimate reason we'd been uninformed of this acquisition. But I found nothing. As a subsidiary, LuTek's offices aren't in this building, so it wasn't like I could pop down to floor fifteen and ask for duplicate copies. Last week, right after Archer's heart attack, I stayed in the boardroom to add to my notes and I noticed a separate server listed that's only accessible on this floor to the executive officers. I'm guessing if you don't work on this floor regularly you never would've noticed it.

"Here's where my annoyance started. I don't like secret servers. I don't like locked files. Especially not when I know there's ten million dollars basically unaccounted for. Since I'm acting interim CEO, I tasked IT with getting me access."

"You had no right to do that," Brady said.

I leaned across the table. "Wrong. I have every right. Especially when I saw the other massive expenditure that Lu-Tek had already agreed to also in those files. The buyout that was announced today to the tune of fifty million dollars. To be honest, I'm pissy about the fact LuTek has that kind of money and I had no clue." I paused. "No, that's not true. I'm livid that if I hadn't accessed the files in the server late last night, I would've had to read in the fucking newspaper, like everyone else in the general public, that a subsidiary of the company where I'm currently acting interim CEO spent fifty million dollars acquiring a cable network. Let me repeat. Fifty. Million. Dollars."

Silence.

"So let's do the show-of-hands thing again. Who knew that LuTek has been in negotiations with All Sports Central for two months to purchase Wolf Sports North?"

Brady's hand went up.

Ash's hand went up.

My dad's hand went up.

"Great. Who knew about the purchase only after it was a done deal?"

Monte's hand went up.

Archer's hand went up.

My mom's hand went up.

"Awesome. Last really fun thing . . . who didn't know until today that we now own a cable network?"

Everyone else at the table raised their hand.

"Annika, none of the press releases announcing the acquisitions came through Lund Industries PR?"

She shook her head. "Frankly, on a 'don't fuck with my department' note, I'm pissed off we weren't tasked with creating a much better way to announce the acquisitions."

"I'm sure it's nothing personal, as I'm so often told."

My dad cleared his throat. "If I may."

I nodded.

"Nothing we did was illegal. We are allowed to make financial decisions in closed-door executive committee without board approval *because* LuTek is a subsidiary."

"So you don't regret your fellow board members—as well as your family—finding out about our business deals via the newspaper?"

My father looked me dead in the eye and said, "No. We did what we had to do. The cable network was a steal at that price."

"Brady? Ash? Care to share your opinions?"

"I stand by what Archer said," Ash said.

Brady said, "I concur with the CEO."

"I know that sounds like a lot of money," my dad continued, "but Brady and Ash deal with numbers higher than those every day in the buying and selling shell game. They don't always have time to call a board meeting and get approval or the opportunity is lost."

"Then why have a board at all?" Jensen asked. "Sounds to me that any objections we raise, you've already designed a work-around."

Jax nodded. "It's been a point of pride that we don't have infighting on the LI board, so maybe we've become a rubber stamp for the executive officers' decisions."

Little discussions broke out and I had to rein them back in. "I agree some of this could stand for a deeper look, but that's not our focus today. Does anyone have any questions regarding LuTek's purchase of Wolf Sports North and ESP?"

No one said a word.

That tiny kernel of bitterness arose that my two-million-dollar screwup had garnered way more criticism and suggestions. But the executive officers outright hiding sixty million dollars' worth of deals doesn't even get a *WTF* from anyone on the board?

Just proved I was about to do the right thing. "Well, I have something to say. I understand the need for covert discussions when it comes to business deals. During the past few months after I was named future CEO, I've tried to take a more positive attitude anytime I've been dismissed from a discussion due to privacy issues. I've done my research on acquisitions prospects after the Digi-Dong disaster. Anytime I've asked specifics on actions or purchases or sales that didn't make sense, I basically received a pat on the head and have been told I'd understand if I had real-world experience. Several of you have commented that my time at LI has been so insular that I'll always be two steps behind. The lack of faith in my abilities has forced me to ask some hard questions of myself.

"So since Archer is on the mend and will likely be back in the big chair as early as next week, I officially tender my resignation to Lund Industries as well as resigning my position on the board of directors. Effective immediately." I floated the typed resignation to Ash. "Sam, my PA, has agreed to stay in my office until everything on my docket has been cleared. If I might suggest adding Zeke, Zosia or Zach to fill my seat on the board, it'd show solidarity for *all* the branches of the Lund family, not just those Lunds fortunate enough to reap the rewards of Jackson Lund's machinations. Thank you."

I bailed out of the room and nodded at Sam on my way past him. He'd detain them long enough for me to make my getaway.

But where to go? No idea.

———

Gabriella wasn't answering her phone, which was just as well. I needed to think about what her omission regarding her job meant for the trust we'd begun to build.

I loved her. I knew she loved me. But I also knew that if she lost out on her dream job because of me, we might not ever get past it.

So I was wallowing. Sipping a glass of my most prized scotch, Tullibardine 1952.

The doorbell rang at nine P.M. I knew it wasn't Gabriella since I'd given her a key.

Maybe she's here to return it.

Cheery thought.

I snagged my phone and opened the door cam app.

In the image my mom and dad stood on my welcome mat.

As soon as I opened the door, my mother flung herself into my arms.

"Ah, hello, Mom." I glanced at Dad. "Shouldn't you be in bed? I'm pretty sure you've had enough excitement for one day."

"Being a bit bossy to your old man for being a *former* acting interim CEO, doncha think?"

I couldn't help it; I laughed. "Anyone ever told you you're an asshole?"

"Lots of people. Every damn day. Now, you gonna let us in, or what?"

My mom finally released me. She wiped under her eyes before looking up at me. "I'm so mad at you right now, Nolan Finnegan Lund."

Full-name mad. "Come in anyway." I shut the door and followed them into my living room. Might make me selfish, but I was happy I'd put away my spendy bottle of scotch because I didn't feel like sharing it. "Can I get you something to drink?"

My dad saw the finger of amber liquid remaining in my glass, opened his mouth to ask for the same thing I was having, but my mom shook her head at him.

Defiant, he locked his stare to hers. "Nothing for me, thanks."

She said, "Oh, don't be such a baby, Archer," and steered him to the couch. "Doctor's orders."

Mom perused my space as Dad and I avoided eye contact. "I forget how perfectly *you* this house is. I love it."

"It's funky but it works for me." I took a tiny sip of my scotch, closing my eyes for a moment to savor the complex flavors.

"Does this place work for Gabi?"

"It did. I haven't heard from her after the earlier revelations about the new ownership at Wolf Sports North."

"Son. We had no idea Gabi had gotten a job offer from them."

"Wasn't something she could share, given she already had a job with Jax."

"LuTek wasn't supposed to announce it until next week. If you want, I could—"

I held up my hand. "The absolute worst thing you could do is speak on her behalf. Current management at Wolf has already accused her of getting the job offer due to nepotism. You forcing them to hire her would just prove that. She has to live with their final decision either way, but she knows she got the position on her own merit, even if they opt to pass on employing her now."

"I wish the best for her. I really do. The only reason All Sports Central came onto our radar was because LuTek had purchased ESP. They believed we might be expanding operations in Duluth and *they* approached *us*. Initially, we turned them down. Then the LuTek financial team sent the breakdown of the increased revenue stream that could only happen with an FCC-approved merger. Brady said the numbers more than held up so that's how it came about."

"Which is why it makes no sense that you would hide that."

He sighed. "Damn, son, you should've been a detective."

"Excuse me?"

"We thought we'd buried that paper trail for the ESP acquisition, but little bloodhound you just kept sniffing and digging until you uncovered it."

Stay calm. "I don't like being locked out of information that by rights shouldn't have required me to become a goddamned cyber detective to find."

Mom put her hand on my knee. "We know. That's your dad's way of saying he's proud of you. We both are. But you are missing several pieces of the puzzle and you deserve to know the truth." She nudged Dad. "Go on. Tell him."

"Six months ago no one at LI or LuTek had heard of ESP. I received a cold call email that said I needed to buy the company for twenty million dollars. I sent the email to spam and forgot about it. Two days later, I got the same type of email, a little more strongly worded. Again, I ignored it. The next time, the email came with a picture."

"Of what?"

"Of Winita Lund. Beat to shit. It was an old picture, but it was very clear who was in it."

Winita Lund was Zosia, Zeke and Zach's mother. "Who would have that kind of picture?"

"That's what we didn't get. It was sensitive info, so I brought Ash and Brady in on it. The next thing that arrived via email was a handwritten account from some woman who we knew wasn't Grover's wife, detailing how Grover Lund had raped her."

A chill went down my spine. "Jesus. Who sent it?"

"Be patient. I'm getting there. This person claimed to have photographic evidence going back almost forty years of Grover Lund's psychopathic behavior. That's when I knew we were being blackmailed. The prevailing wisdom is refusing to give in to these kinds of demands. Normally I would've turned it over to our lawyers, but I suspected the blackmail-er's reaction would be swift and harsh. When we found out who was sending us this stuff . . . to be honest, it knocked us for a loop."

Mom leaned over and kissed his cheek. "I'll get you a drink of water. Keep talking."

"Who was blackmailing us?"

"The daughter of the woman Grover had raped. Scarlet Biersbach."

"Meaning . . . Scarlet was his kid?"

Dad nodded. "Scarlet didn't know that Chris Biersbach, the man she'd called Dad, wasn't her biological father until he told her the whole story after he went into hospice. Leda, her mother, had become pregnant and was terrified of Gro-ver, so Chris agreed to marry her and raised the baby as his."

"How old is Scarlet now?"

"Two years older than Zeke. And yes, we demanded a DNA test and it came back with the biological markers that indicated Scarlet is closely related to Grover's other kids."

My eyes searched his. I didn't know how he managed to get our cousins' blood to verify the tests, but I wasn't shocked that he'd done it. "Do any of them know they have a half sister?"

"As far as she's indicated to us? No. Chris Biersbach built ESP into a successful business. The only part Scarlet told us about her childhood was Leda committed suicide when Scar-let was eight. Chris knew Grover had married and had a fam-ily. He'd see Grover around town. Drunk. Rude. Lecherous. Since Chris was in a position of power as a business owner in Duluth, he set out to negatively affect Lund Fisheries con-tracts and covertly smear Grover's name. Grover wasn't liked in the community and didn't care about his reputation, so it was easy for Chris to obtain pictures of Grover being abusive to his own kids, his wife and even a few of the younger guys who worked for him on the docks. As well as stories of the other horrible things Grover had done after he and your grandfather had a falling-out."

"And Scarlet knew about none of this?"

"Beyond that her dad had turned bitter after her mom died? No. After his deathbed confessional, he told her where to find the files with all the pics and stories about Grover's atrocities. When she saw the phrase 'Make the Lunds pay,' she took it literally. She'd inherited ESP from Chris and was struggling keeping it afloat. She promised to turn over the file if we bought her out." He paused and took the glass of water from my mom. "LI could've weathered the storm from that information going public. But it would've been different for Zosia, Zach and Zeke. They've worked hard to earn the respect Grover never had nor cared about. That had the potential to ruin the fishing and charter business, not to mention make their lives in Duluth hellish."

Mom handed me a glass of water and it hurt as I chugged it down, my chest was so tight with anger.

"Yes, we, the executive officers, buried that information, but we had good reasons for doing so. We also felt we needed a plan for how to bring this to Grover's kids, which is why Monte and Cilla and Ward and Selka were told about the situation after we'd made the acquisition."

"That's why no one would meet with Zosia when she came to LI?"

He nodded. "She's shrewd. She'd take one look at our faces and know something was up, because some of that stuff in the file . . . Christ, son, you can't unsee it."

Mom reached for my hand. "I don't know what happened to Jackson, Lincoln and Grover Lund. Their father—your great-grandfather Magnus—amassed the wealth that built the Lund family name. They had every advantage growing up. Jackson refused to talk about him and given the fact both Jackson and Grover turned out to be nasty bitter men . . . I'm thankful every day for Alice Lund's resolve to not let *her* sons turn out like their father. They're all warmhearted, loving men, and that's worth more than the Lund fortune—in my eyes, anyway."

"Eeds . . ." my dad said softly.

At that point I had to get up, giving them a moment while I tried to wrap my head around the information. I snagged the Macallan 15, my go-to cheap scotch—which wasn't cheap at all—and poured myself three fingers.

I paced as I sipped, letting all the information roll through my head.

When I returned to my seat, I was surprised to see on the clock that half an hour had passed.

My parents looked at me, then exchanged a bemused glance. "What?"

"You have that stubborn set to your jaw that indicates we won't like what you're about to say."

I raised a brow. "And that amuses you?"

"No, son, it makes us proud. Because you're about to tell us how to fix this mess."

"You're right. I could rail at you for your stupid decision to give a goddamned *blackmailer* ten million dollars without blinking an eye, but in the years I've been at LI, you never would've given the Duluth Lunds that kind of money to improve their business or their lives. They've languished and we've let them. That's about to end. The only logical and ethical solution is to give Grover Lund's other children ten million dollars. Each."

When my dad opened his mouth, I held up my hand. "You, yourself, said that LI deals with sums much larger than fifty million dollars every day, so thirty million bucks . . . is a drop in the fish bucket, right?"

He snorted at that.

"LI will also give the Duluth Lunds financial advice—for free—on how best to protect their inheritance."

"Done."

"The LI board of directors will expand to include all three members of the Duluth Lunds. And someone from LI will contact the Lincoln Lund branch of the family to open a dialogue about some of them serving on the board too."

"I'll agree to that as long as you rescind your resignation from the board."

I tapped my fingers on the couch. "Agreed. But my resignation from the company stands."

My mom looked stricken. "Why?"

"While I'd like to believe I've been spinning my wheels at LI because the executive officers were trying to keep me from uncovering the reasons behind LuTek's acquisitions, the truth is I need practical experience running a company. Not a multi-billion-dollar conglomerate.

"Dad, you've said it yourself that you were pretty seasoned by the time you took the CEO position. You'd bought and sold and merged several businesses to expand LI's platform. I need to learn how to do that, and sitting behind a desk, double-checking all potential empire-building options that are brought to my attention by someone else, knowing that Brady will triple-check the bottom-line numbers anyway . . . renders my time there useless. So I'm taking the leap to sink or swim on my own."

"Define 'on your own,'" my dad demanded.

"I've been searching for ventures for investment, but I will focus my search for owner/operator-type businesses. I don't need to remind you my Lund trust accounts give me plenty of capital."

"You'd turn down partnerships and use your own money?"

I knew he wanted to bark at me that I hadn't learned *anything* under his tutelage; the first rule of business is to always use someone else's money to make money. "In the future? I'd absolutely be open to corporate partnerships. But to be blunt, if there's no chance I'll lose my inheritance, then how will I ever learn true risk management?"

Heavy silence stretched between us.

Then Dad cleared his throat. "I've always been proud of you, Nolan. But never prouder than this day, when you've shown you're willing to risk it all not just for yourself, but to right family wrongs we've been ignoring for years." He

WANT YOU TO WANT ME 351

stood. "Now c'mere and give your old man a hug, and promise me you won't be too proud to ask me for business advice if you ever need it."

"I promise. And I'm not saying I won't be back at LI someday." Then I found myself enveloped in a hug from both of my parents. They squeezed me tightly but for the first time today, I felt like I could finally breathe.

Thirty

GABI

I cried myself to sleep. Alone.

Even witnessing my puffy eyes and face this morning didn't keep more stupid tears from falling. I didn't want to leave my apartment, so I paced, and stopped to look out the sliding glass door, ratty Kleenex clutched in my hand, everything in my line of sight a complete blur.

The knock at my door came too early for it to be Liddy. Or Dallas.

The look on Nolan's face after he'd dismissed me yesterday . . . definitely wasn't him.

So whoever it was could just go away. I wasn't in the mood.

The interloper was persistent.

"Gabi. Open the damn door."

Dani? What was she doing here?

I unlocked the door and let her in, immediately turning around to try and get myself together.

"What is going on with you? You don't answer your phone or texts. And I get here, and you don't wanna answer the door either? Are you sick or something?"

"I'm trying to work through some things and didn't want to be disturbed, okay?"

"No, it's not okay." Grabbing my shoulder, she forced me to face her. "Are you crying?"

"No. It's allergies."

"Bull. Shit. Why is the tough-as-nails Gabriella Welk bawling her eyes out?"

"I don't want to talk about this with you, Dani. Just go."

"No, goddammit. You *will* talk to me. How am I supposed to help you if I don't know what's wrong?"

And I was tired of being a stronghold against the world. The walls cracked, the tough-girl façade came tumbling down and I didn't even try to stop it. "Everything is wrong. Somehow I managed to fuck up everything in my life all at one time."

Rather than a trickle of tears, she got a flood of them.

But my little sister took it all in stride. She didn't let go when I clung to her. She didn't ask questions, she just let me babble.

And cry.

When the biggest sobs started to subside, she parked me on my couch with a box of tissues and an admonishment not to move.

Dani returned with a tray with two steaming cups of tea. She wrapped my hand around one mug and took the second one for herself. "Now. Start from the beginning."

I started from the night Tyson dumped me—maybe as a test to see if she'd protest. But she didn't. How Nolan had hurt my feelings. I'd confronted him, we'd talked and realized that without our mutual preconceived ideas, we liked each other. I broke down again when I talked about Nolan helping me prep for the interview even knowing if I got hired, it'd put his brother in a bind. How much fun we had together. How hot the sex was. How with the perceived nepotism of an LI subsidiary buying Wolf Sports North, I might lose the job I'd fought so hard for. A job that I'd neglected to mention to Nolan would entail me moving. Plus,

Jax being pissed at both Nolan and me for keeping him in the dark and messing up his staffing for Lakeside.

Following the spewing of that word vomit, I literally felt stick to my stomach and ran to the bathroom to vomit for real.

Afterward, Dani tucked me in bed and then she lay down next to me, her body curled around mine like I used to do for her when she was upset.

That made me cry harder.

She didn't go Pollyanna on me and offer chipper advice that it'd all work out—just another sign that Dani had grown up.

"Thank you," I managed without crying.

"Anytime."

"You don't have to stay."

"Sucks for you then, because I *am* staying."

I didn't want to sleep, since it was still . . . oh, morning . . . but I dozed off anyway.

When I awoke, Dani remained right beside me.

I struggled to get up, crafting some crack about being a lazy crybaby, but she kept me in place with a simple, "Don't."

Okay.

"Now I have a few things to say."

That rarely boded well.

"You've been my role model my entire life. I could've gotten annoyed hearing, 'Wow. You're Gabi Welk's sister?' from every coach and every female hockey player I ever met. But not me. It's been the greatest thing being your sister and your protégée. I know you could've made big money privately coaching another player and she'd be the one with the Olympic gold medal instead of me. Or you could've tried out for the national team and you'd have that medal for yourself." She paused. "I know you sacrificed your dream of gold for me, no matter how you deny it by claiming you were 'too old' to train that hard."

Busted.

"I've never taken you for granted. Never expected you to do half the things you've done for me, yet you do them. You are this bright shining beacon, sis, and I'm humbled that I've gotten to stand in your light. Because you always made sure that's what it was for me—your light, not your shadow."

I was too stunned to speak.

"I also know that the past year and a half has been difficult for you. I—we—didn't want to add to that by falling in love. I'm not saying this to justify anything, but the reason you and Tyson didn't work isn't because he was supposed to be with me; it's because you were destined for someone else."

Destined. Now she sounded like Dallas.

"When you were on the ice for the NHL game and got hurt? Nolan lost his shit, Gabi. He bailed out of the VIP box and I knew where he was going: straight to you. I don't know where you were in your relationship with him at that point, but he sees everything in you that a man who adores you is supposed to see. That's what I saw in him. He loves you, Gabs. And let me tell you . . . you are a difficult person to love."

My entire body stiffened but Dani held tight.

"That's not to say you're unlovable. You love unconditionally, but you put conditions on those of us who love *you*. What we're allowed to do *for* you. What part of you we're *allowed* to see. That is some one-sided bullshit right there. No one who loves you is gonna run away in fear if you show them that you need them. I promise." She squeezed me and whispered, "This is what I've wanted, to give back the strength and love that you've always given me."

I sniffled. "You forgot patience."

"Yes! You've tried my patience for years, but it's finally paid off."

"I've tried *your* patience?"

Dani snorted. "Gotcha. Anyway, I'm here—you're letting me be here for you. This is a big moment in my life."

"I'm sorry. I'm so used to being the big—"

"Spoon?" she supplied. "It's not so bad being the little spoon sometimes, is it?"

"No." I swallowed hard. "So what's your advice, big spoon?"

"For you to look at this crisis as if I came to you with this problem. If I'd busted my ass to get the job on my own merit, and some jealous wannabe made threats of going public with accusations of nepotism *after* I'd been awarded the position, but *before* the business side had been made public. Threats that could not only mar my career but cause issues between me, the man I love and his family. What would you tell *me* to do, sis?"

I didn't hesitate for a second before I answered, "To march into that studio tomorrow morning and demand a meeting with the CEO and the president of Programming. I'd point out that not only wasn't I involved with the acting CEO of Lund Industries at the time of my interview, it's a moot point since a subsidiary purchased the media group—not Nolan Lund personally."

"Good. And?"

"And I followed the rules they required as far as NDAs— the leak in their department is not my concern. I expect them to keep their word that the job is still mine."

Dani laughed. "There you go."

I elbowed her. "Brat."

"Last thing. Nolan." She paused. "You love him, right?"

"Right."

"Then, again, I'll give you the same advice you'd give me. Follow your dream. If it's the job, then pursue it. If it's a life with him, then pursue it. If you want both, you'll have to work twice as hard and make some compromises. You both will. But you can make it happen, sis. I believe that. I believe in you. And if anyone deserves both, it *is* you."

I turned my head and looked at her. "How'd you get so wise?"

"By watching and listening to you."

"I love you, Dani girl."

"Love you too, Gabi." She sat up. "Now get yourself together, woman. We've got plans today."

"We do?"

"Yep." She stood in front of me and grabbed my hands. "None of that mani-pedi-pampering-spa-type crap. No retail therapy. No drunken karaoke. We're doing what makes you happiest. What makes you whole. What makes you . . . you."

More tears shimmered because this sweet, tough girl understood me better than I'd ever imagined. I opened my mouth to ask specifics, but she shushed me.

"Huh-uh. You gotta trust me."

Did I?

Yes.

I took her hands and let her pull me to my feet and out the door.

Dani took me to TRIA. The fact I'd been there two days in a row—in full hockey gear—didn't escape anyone's notice. Least of all Carly's, the Whitecaps' head coach. She skated over to me. "You rethinking my offer, Welk?"

"Maybe. I have something else going on as far as a career track that's up in the air right now. I'll tell you my decision just as soon as I can."

"Fair enough. But why are you here?"

"To blow off some steam, get my head straight. This is what does it for me."

We exchanged a look. As a fellow hockey player she understood and didn't prompt me for more.

"Warm up. Pickup game starts in ten. Oh, and don't go easy on these girls. They've gotta know what they'll be up against with the other teams in the league."

"Got it, Coach."

I knew about half the players. Carly placed Dani and me on opposite teams and we grinned at each other in the face-off circle.

The game was as grueling as any regular hockey game, which boded well for this team. They were fierce competitors, and it was exhilarating to be on the ice with them.

Since most of these players had already had a full practice session before the game, we cut the periods in half, so we played thirty minutes, but it felt like sixty minutes.

Must be that pesky age thing nipping at my blades.

Dani's team won 3 to 1, but I was proud the lone goal for our team belonged to me.

Exhausted, but more at peace than I'd been since yesterday, I jumped when someone beat on the glass behind me. I spun around and saw a guy in a ball cap and a bomber jacket.

My eyes narrowed; he was wearing a Chicago Blackhawks ball cap. In the Wild's practice facility.

Only one guy cocky enough to do that.

Jax gestured to the open section between the seating and the exit, so I skated over there.

Dani joined me.

Before I could say a word, Dani half elbowed me out of the way and said, "Glad you made it, Mr. Lund."

Mr. Lund?

"Call me Jax. You ladies looked great. That goalie of yours . . . she's top-notch."

"Right? Glad I'm not playing against her."

"So how many are interested in talking to me?"

Dani said, "I've kept it to two."

I whipped off my gloves and made the time-out sign. "Someone wanna tell me what's going on?"

"After our talk this morning," Dani started, "I realized I'm the perfect replacement for your position at Lakeside. Well, not your position exactly, as I think Mr.—Jax—has ideas on pursuing club hockey options."

He grinned at me. "I'm here recruiting. I'm also here to tell you there are no hard feelings. I always knew you had bigger things awaiting you out there. You leaving Lakeside forces me to get my ass in gear about making changes. Dani texted me earlier and said she'd be happy to fill in for you as long as necessary. So I went one better and hired her."

I looked at my sister in shock . . . and awe, to be honest.

"Yeah, sorry, I lifted his number from your phone. I figured the least I could do was help you clear a couple of hurdles."

"Dani." Then it hit me. "Wait. What's the other hurdle?"

A guy in a hoodie and jeans stood up and joined Jax.

Nolan.

No wonder I hadn't recognized him. He didn't look like my Nolan at all.

"For the record, I strongly object to being referred to as a hurdle," Nolan said dryly.

"For the record, Gabi needs a ride home as I will be in business meetings with Mr.—Jaxson Lund." Dani gave me a one-armed hug and leaned in to whisper, "Call me later. You got this."

Jax gave us the thumbs-up and then took off.

My eyes met Nolan's. "How long have you been here?"

"Since the game started." He smirked. "Awesome deke, by the way."

"Thanks."

He leaned closer and tucked a piece of hair behind my ear, letting the backs of his knuckles graze my cheek. "You shine out there. I love watching you play. I hope that no matter what happens, you'll never stop playing." He dropped his hand. "So I'm hoping you have time to talk."

I snorted. "I have *nothing* but time, apparently, since my sister overed on my damn job."

"It's a perfect solution. I'm thrilled she's helping *you* out for a change."

"Me too."

"She ah . . . texted me so I knew where you'd be."

"The girl's gone rogue, breaking into my phone."

"Are you upset she contacted me?"

I shook my head.

"Okay. Good."

Why was this so awkward between us?

"Umm, I'll get changed and meet you by the locker room

entrance in fifteen." Then I took a chance, giving him a bla-
tant once-over. "But before I go, I have to know . . . did you
get assaulted by a bum and he forced you to trade clothes
with him?"

Nolan threw back his head and laughed. Then he grabbed
my jersey and leaned over the partition to give me a
blistering-hot kiss that nearly melted the ice beneath me.

After he released me, he said, "Hurry. And, Happy, you
know I'd prefer it if you didn't shower anyway."

"Pervert."

He gifted me with a smacking kiss on the mouth. "Go."

After I stowed my gear, I decided to check my phone and
see who else my little sister had contacted on my behalf.

No one, thankfully. But there was a voice mail from a
Wolf Sports North ID.

My gut clenched. Better to get it over with. I hit play.

"Gabi? This is Lance Jacoby, CEO of Wolf Sports North.
We spoke yesterday. I'm calling to let you know that we've
researched the situation and found ourselves in error. It was
unnecessary to put your position on hold. As you indicated
yesterday, you sailed through the interview process with flying colors on your own merit and qualifications. We regret
our hasty response in questioning your personal relationship
rather than giving you the professional credit you deserved.
So I apologize on behalf of the entire team here if we allowed you to doubt your worth to us. We are very much looking forward to working with you and ask that you call us at
your earliest convenience to set up a time to officially sign
the contracts so we can publicly announce our coup in signing you to our broadcast family. Thank you for your understanding. Have a wonderful rest of your day."

Had to hand it to the man, that was a helluvan apology. I'd
wait until after I talked to Nolan to call him back.

As soon as Nolan saw me exit the locker room, he swooped
me up into his arms. "Just let me hold you for a sec."

"For as long as you want."

WANT YOU TO WANT ME 361

After we broke apart, he said, "Where to?"

"I've heard the Stacked Deck Brewery on the first level is great."

Nolan studied me.

"What?"

"I'm hardly dressed for—"

"A brewpub?" I poked him in the ribs. "Lighten up, Lund. I doubt the fashion police are around today."

"Hilarious."

We snagged a table and ordered two glasses of the seasonal ale.

After a fortifying sip, I said, "I'll go first. I hated how things played out yesterday. But I am sorry that I didn't tell you the job requirement was moving to Duluth. I know it hurt you and that wasn't my intent."

"Apology accepted."

My eyebrows went up. "That fast?"

"After I had time to think about it, I do understand why you didn't tell me. But going forward, I'll ask you not to keep me in the dark about things that affect both of us, okay?"

"Okay." I exhaled. "So along those lines, the CEO of Wolf left a voice mail for me today. I just listened to it."

"And?"

"And he apologized and indicated the job is still mine if I want it."

He frowned. "Why wouldn't you want it?"

I leaned closer to Nolan so we were face-to-face. "Because the man I love, the man I told I wanted to build a life with, might take issue with suddenly finding himself in a long-distance relationship with his girlfriend. So you should also know that the Whitecaps organization offered me an assistant coaching job yesterday. It is a good opportunity. I'd get to work with the best players, including my sister. There's some travel, but I would be based in the Cities, which works better for us—"

"No."

My heart sank. "No?"

"No, because you're not turning down your dream job for me. I know you love coaching, but would you be happy?"

"I'd be unhappy in any job that takes me away from you."

Nolan curled his hand around the side of my face. "Well, the man who loves you, the man who is thrilled you still want to build a life with him, is unemployed as of yesterday and is searching for employment opportunities in . . . Duluth. So it would be better for me—for us—if you took the sports-casting job."

Lucky thing he held my jaw, or it might've hit the table. "What happened?"

He explained about files that protected a Lund family secret and confronting the executive officers and the entire board about it, but he didn't get into specifics beyond it was serious enough to have him reconsider his career.

"The bottom line is I'm still on the board, but I'm no longer employed by LI. After talking with my cousin Zosia, who lives in Duluth, I started researching investment opportunities, which is fortunate since I'll need to pick one and see how strong my business acumen really is."

I couldn't remember ever seeing that glint of excitement in his eyes when he talked about work. "The business opportunities are in Duluth, though?"

"Yep. And allow me to channel Dallas for a moment and mention the fact that we're both ending up there seems like a huge cosmic sign for us."

"A big flashing neon-green cosmic sign that says, *Your life together starts here.*"

He grinned. "I'm so crazy in love with everything about you, Happy."

"I'm so crazy in love with everything about you too, Fancy Pants."

"I want us to live together. I understand you'll have to travel a lot and you'll have to put up with me either working a lot or not working at all, depending on my business situation, but I want us to exist in the same space in all our downtime."

"I can't wait. So since I'm shacking up with a billionaire heir, will we be looking at exclusive high-rise apartments with a killer view of Lake Superior? Ooh, and can we have a pool table *and* an air hockey table? Maybe a bowling alley?"

"Take your expectations down a notch, Gabriella. My billionaire heir days are behind me. I'll be a working man, on a budget, so don't get your hopes up about a life of luxury."

"Shoot." I sighed. "I'll just have to be content living with you, even if it's in a closet. Because that's truly where I'm at. At peace and excited as hell to be starting this stage of life with you, Nolan, no matter where we end up."

"Babe. I'm still a millionaire, so it's not like we'll be roughing it in a fishing shack."

I cocked my head. "So now that you're a working man, does that mean you'll start buying your clothing off the rack? Yourself?"

He literally shuddered. "God forbid."

I laughed.

Nolan pointed to my beer. "Taking your time with that."

"Beer is not really my thing." I smoothed my hand over his hair and down his neck, letting my thumb rest in the hollow of his throat. Feeling that slow, steady heartbeat and seeing the happy glow in his eyes, I realized no matter what happened job wise, he and I would thrive together. "I'm wondering why I suggested it."

"Me too."

I noticed he'd barely touched his glass either.

"Actually, I'm hungry. Wanna take a drive?"

"Sure. Where'd you have in mind?"

"A seafood joint in Duluth I know you're gonna love."

"Lead the way."

Epilogue

―――――

NOLAN

I looked at my phone for the tenth time in the past five minutes. No messages.

A shadow fell across me and I glanced up at the bartender.

"You sure I can't get you anything while you wait?"

Maybe it was ornery to say, "What do you have for nonalcoholic liquor?" but I asked anyway.

"You mean like nonalcoholic beer?" he said.

I shook my head. "No. I mean like nonalcoholic gin or vodka."

The guy snorted. "Buddy, there's no such thing."

"Not yet." But there would be, once Lund and Sons Distillery was up and running. In the meantime, we'd been granted an import license to bring in the nonalcoholic booze that was only available in Europe. And we wanted to build buzz about options for people who liked the taste of spirits but didn't want the buzz.

His eyes narrowed and he gave me—clad in my usual suit and tie—a suspicious once-over. "Who are you?"

I slid my business card across the bartop.

He read the text, "Nolan Lund. Lund and Sons Distillery." Another skeptical look. "You related to Zosia Lund?"

"She's my cousin. And one of the distillery owners."

"Ah. So you're one of them billionaire Lunds from the Cities. I've heard about you. Just here visiting?"

"Nope. Been living here for four months. I'm part of the investment group that bought the old cannery."

"The one that's been abandoned for fifteen years? Sheesh. That place is a wreck."

"It won't be when we're done with it."

"Yeah? Whatcha planning on doin' with it?"

"Half of the space will be distillery manufacturing; the other half will be retail venues."

He crossed his arms over his chest. "So you came to warn me that your investment group is putting in a bar?"

I laughed. "Not even close. We will be strictly wholesale to bars and liquor stores."

"Just the nonalcoholic stuff?"

"No. We'll be distilling our own line of regular alcoholic spirits and nonalcoholic spirits once the manufacturing side is up and running. Right now I'm just out in the community introducing myself. Letting people know that we are the exclusive distributors for Clearheaded Spirits, the only nonalcoholic brand currently available in the U.S." I pointed at my business card. "Call the number and we'll set you up with a private tasting of our products."

"You don't say." He scratched his chin. "I can see where there might be a market for it. Don't know if it'd be a big seller here, but I'd be glad to give it a try."

"Great. Like I said, we'd be happy to discuss some of the promotional opportunities we're creating just for local bars with competitive pricing."

"What's Zosia's place in Lund and Sons?"

"She's the big boss. Right now she's focused on getting

the distillery operational, so she's handling employee recruitment."

He grinned. "Everyone in this town loves that woman. I'm happy to hear things are going her way for once."

"Me too. We've talked about running a business together for years and I'm lucky it's finally a reality." Not only had she and her brothers let me become a major investor, they agreed to let Jax invest too so we had all the capital we needed to get started right away.

"If the retail space ain't gonna be a bar, mind me askin' what it is gonna be? And who's runnin' that?"

"The full concept hasn't been finalized, but the confirmed anchor stores are Duluth Clothing and the distillery. Do you know Zach, Zosia and Zeke's youngest brother?"

He nodded.

"Zach is head of property development and he's working on bringing in local, diverse businesses to round out the remaining retail spaces."

"What's your part in it?"

"I'm the numbers-crunching money guy. There are a lot of opportunities in Duluth for existing and new businesses, so I get to check them all out."

"Ambitious. What's Zeke got to say about this? He ain't hanging up his fishing hook for good, is he?"

"No way. He's invested in the businesses with us, but he's made it clear his focus will always be on the charter company and Lund Fisheries."

Just then the outer door banged open, sending a bright streak of sunlight across the dark bar. I barely contained my grin; my woman still barreled through life at breakneck speed even when she wasn't on the ice.

The bartender turned. "Gabi! Darlin'. It is good to see you."

Of course the bartender already knew her by name.

"Hey, Charlie."

"Saw your interview last night with the UMD athletic program director. You didn't pull any punches."

She laughed. "Someone's gotta hit him with the hard questions. Glad to hear you enjoyed it."

"We all did. We're ready for the damn hockey season to begin already."

"You and me both, Charlie."

Then Gabi stopped five feet away from me. "Dude. You're in my seat."

"I picked the *one* seat that's yours? Seriously? Out of all of these empty chairs you want this one?"

"Yep."

I felt the bartender watching us closely. I sighed and pushed back to stand. "Fine."

Her gaze moved over me from head to toe. "Is that a new suit?"

"Yes. You like?"

"I love it. Damn. Q gets a gold star for making you look that hot." That's when she moved in, stood on her tiptoes to wrap her arms around my neck, kissing me like she hadn't seen me in a week—which she hadn't. After she finished blowing my circuits, she put her mouth on my ear. "I missed you like crazy, Charming."

"Missed you too, Happy."

"So tell me again why we're meeting here and not racing home to get naked and sweaty in our big soft bed after you've been in the Cities for a damn week?" she demanded softly.

I tugged on her ponytail. "I have to get used to sharing you with the community—maintaining a public presence is part of your job as the newest co-anchor of the Wolf Sports North college hockey broadcast team." I'd never get tired of saying that. I was so damn proud of her.

"I know that. But it's barely afternoon and we're the only ones here." Her eyes narrowed. "Spill what you're really up to, Lund."

"All right. I'm doing recon and promo for distillery distribution."

"And?"

"And I saw your Instagram post from here three days ago. What *is* it with you and finding dive bars, Welk?"

She shrugged. "It's my thing. Plus, this is the postgame hangout for the college crowd, including the players. I'm guessing I'll be here a lot."

"So we're both doing recon."

"I *was* doing recon earlier this week. Now I'm here to drag my man home so he'll do all the dirty, wicked things to me he promised in his last text message."

Check, please.

We turned back to the bar and Charlie was still watching us. "The two of you are together?"

I grabbed her hand. Even in this dimly lit bar the five-carat diamond engagement ring on her finger flashed like fire. "Yes, this woman has agreed to marry me next spring after the hockey season ends. Why?"

He shook his head and addressed Gabi. "No offense, but he just doesn't seem like your type."

She looked at me with heart eyes. "He loves me just as I am, which means he's exactly my type."

"Perfectly said, my Gabriella." I kissed the top of her head. "Come on. I'll race you home."

LUCY

"Mommy. What time will Daddy get here?"

Whenever the hell he feels like it.

Not an answer I could give my precocious eight-year-old daughter, even when it was the truth. "He said after six. Since it's now six fifteen, he'll be here at any moment."

Mimi sighed heavily. Then she kicked her legs up and hung upside down from the back of the chair, balancing on her hands. It was obvious to everyone she inherited her natural athleticism from her father. Embarrassingly I was one of those people who trip over their own feet . . . and everyone else's.

"You sure that hanging like a monkey in a tree won't upset your stomach?" I asked her. "Or give you a headache? I'd hate for you to miss an overnight with your dad."

"I have to practice so being upside down doesn't make me sick," she replied with another sigh, as if I should've already known that.

"Ah. So what are you practicing for this week?"

"It's between a trapeze artist or an ice skater. If I decide to have a partner I'll have to be used to being upside down."

Last month Mimi wanted to be an astronaut. The month before that a dolphin trainer. While I've always told her that she can be whatever she wants to be when she grows up, it's exhausting finding an activity that holds her attention. After spending money on dance lessons, gymnastics classes, martial arts classes, T-ball, soccer club, fencing, swim team, tennis lessons, golf lessons and horseback riding lessons, I'd put my foot down and said no new organized activities. If none of those worked then she needed to wait until she was older to try others.

Still, I feared she'd play the guilt card and I'd find myself buying tickets to the circus, a Cirque du Soleil show or a Disney on Ice program. Or . . . maybe . . .

"I'm sure your dad would love to take you to a performance." Not really dirty pool—Mimi's father, Jaxson Lund, was a member of the billionaire Lund family as well as a highly paid former pro hockey player, so money had never been an issue for him. And there was nothing he loved more than humoring Mimi's requests, even if it was to alleviate the guilt that he'd missed being a regular presence in her life for most of her life.

The doorbell pealed and Mimi squealed, "I'll get it!" twisting her lithe little body sideways from the chair to land lightly on her feet, agile as a cat.

I heard her disengage the locks and yell, "Daddy! I thought you'd never get here."

He laughed. That sweet indulgent laugh he only had for our daughter. "I missed you too, Mimi."

"I got my stuff all packed. I'm ready to go now."

Without saying good-bye to me? That stung. But I sucked it up and started toward the entryway.

"Sure. Just let me get the all clear from your mom first."

Then Jaxson Lund and I nearly collided as we turned the corner simultaneously.

His big hands circled my upper arms to steady me.

I had to tilt my head back to look at him as he towered over me by almost a foot.

It was unfair that my ex actually looked better now than he did when he and I met a decade ago. His dark hair was shorter—no more long locks befitting the bad-boy defenseman of the NHL. No scruffy beard, just the smooth skin of his outlandishly square jaw and muscled neck. His eyes were clear, not bloodshot as I'd usually seen them, making those turquoise-hued eyes the most striking feature on his face . . . Besides that damn smile. Hockey players were supposed to have teeth missing from taking a puck or two hundred to the face. I knew Jax had a partial, but he'd never removed it when we were together. The lips framing that smile were both soft and hard. Druggingly warm and soft when pressed into a kiss, but cold and hard when twisting into a cruel sneer. A sneer I'd been on the receiving end of many times.

That shook me out of my musings about Jax's amazing physical attributes.

"Hey, Luce."

Jax had called me Luce from the first—a joke between us because I warned him I wasn't loose and wouldn't sleep with him on the first date. An inside joke made me feel special—he made me feel special—until I realized Jaxson Lund used that killer smile and those gorgeous twinkling eyes as a weapon on every woman he wanted to bang the boards with; there wasn't anything special about me.

I forced a smile. "Jaxson. How are you?"

He retreated at my cool demeanor and dropped his hands. "I'm fine. You're looking well."

And people thought we couldn't be civil to each other. "Thanks. You too."

"Anything I should know before Meems and I take off?"

Meems. He'd given our daughter another nickname, even when Mimi was already the shortened version of Milora Michelle. "Nothing worth mentioning. She's been looking forward to this all week."

Those beautiful eyes narrowed. "So don't disappoint her, right?"

"Right."

"Luce. I'm not—"

"Daddy, come *on*. Are we goin' or what?" Mimi demanded.

"We're goin', impatient one." Jaxson hauled her up and cocked her on his hip with seemingly little effort, because his eyes never left mine. "We can do the switch back at the Lund Industries thing on Sunday afternoon?"

"You'll be there?"

"I work there, remember?"

In the past six months since Jax had joined the family business, I'd hardly seen him hustling around the building in a suit and tie, so I had no idea what his actual job title was. As far as I could tell, he didn't "work" there like I did. Sunday's event was a retirement party for a woman I doubted he knew personally. "I'm surprised. I wasn't aware that you knew Lola."

"The poor woman was tasked with getting me up to speed on all departments when I started at LI. I'd still be aimlessly wandering the halls if not for her."

"Lola will be missed, that's for sure. So if you want to bring Mimi's things on Sunday, that'll work. I planned on going for the two hours."

"Sounds like a plan. Speaking of . . . what are your plans for the weekend?"

None of your business. "Oh, this and that. Mimi has more things planned for you two than you could fit into two weeks, say nothing of two days."

His dark eyebrow winged up. "Now I'm taking that as a personal challenge."

Mimi held her arms out for a hug. "Bye, Mommy."

"Bye, wild one. Behave, okay?"

"Okay."

"Promise to call me tomorrow sometime."

She sighed heavily. "I'd call you all the time if I had my own cell phone."

I chuckled. "Nice try. Use Daddy's phone. Or Grandma Edie's."

"But all of my friends have iPhones."

"Eight-year-olds do not need a cell phone." I sent Jaxson a stern look as a reminder not to swoop in and buy her one just because he could. Then I kissed her cheek. "Love you, Mimi."

"Love you too."

Jaxson gathered Mimi's stuff with her chattering away at him like she always did. I wondered how much of it he paid attention to.

Not my concern. I'd had to learn to let go of a lot of my issues with Jaxson's parenting style since he'd returned permanently to Minneapolis.

I waved good-bye and locked the door behind them.

As I readied myself for my first date with Damon, my thoughts scrolled back to the first time I'd met Jaxson Lund a decade ago . . .

I'd left work early to take my mother to the doctor. After I'd dropped her off at her place, I pulled into one of those super fancy deluxe car washes that offered one-hour detailing inside and out. Winter in the Twin Cities meant tons of road salt and freeway grime, and my poor car needed TLC. Not that my Toyota Corolla was anything fancy, but it'd been a major purchase for me after I'd graduated from college. My first new car, and I took good care of it.

With an hour to kill, I grabbed a magazine and a Diet Mountain Dew. The lobby wasn't jam-packed with other customers—which was a total contradiction to the lines of cars outside—but I embraced the quiet for a change and settled in.

My alone time lasted about five minutes. A guy blew in—the wind was blustery, but not nearly as blustering as the man yakking on his cell phone at a thousand decibels.

"Peter. I told you I'm happy to stay at the same salary."
Pause. "Why? Because a salary freeze for a year isn't the end
of the world for me. Especially if that means they can use
that extra money to lure the kind of D-man we need."

I rolled my eyes and wished I'd brought my earbuds.

"No. What it speaks to isn't that I'm not worth more money.
It shows that I'm a team player."

I tried to ignore the annoying man. But he paced in front of
me, forcing me to listen to him as well as watch his jean-clad
legs nearly brush my knees as his hiking boots beat a path in
the carpet. From the reflection in the glass that allowed customers to see their cars going through the automated portion
of the car wash, I knew he was a big man; tall, at least six foot
four, with wide shoulders, long arms and long legs.

And huge lungs, because his voice continued to escalate.
His pace increased. He gestured wildly with the hand not
holding the phone. He couldn't see me scowling at him, as his
head was down and his baseball cap put his face in shadow.
Not that he'd looked my way even one time to see if his loud,
one-sided conversation might be bothering me.

*Look at me, look at me! My job is so crucial that I can't even
go to the car wash without dealing with such pressing matters.*

Ugh. I hated when people acted inconsiderate and self-
important.

He stopped moving. "Fine. It's stupid as shit, but an in-
crease of one dollar if it'll make you happy to have on record
that my salary went up again this year. I'll let you keep one
hundred percent of that dollar instead of your usual twenty
percent commission." Pause. "Do you hear me laughing?
Look. I'm done with this convo, Peter. Call me after the trade
is over. Bye."

I flipped through a couple of pages.

He sighed and shoved his phone in his back pocket. Then
I sensed him taking in his surroundings for the first time.
The lack of customers, no car going through the car wash to
entertain him.

Please don't assume I'll entertain you. He was definitely that type of guy.

I silently willed him to go away. But I'll be damned if the man didn't plop down on the bench directly across from me. I felt his gaze moving up my legs from my heeled suede boots to where the hem of my wool skirt ended above my knees.

Continuing to ignore him, I thumbed another magazine page and took a swig of my soda.

"Ever have one of those days?" he asked me.

The smart response would've been no response. I'm not sure what compelled me to say, "One of those days where you're enjoying a rare moment of quiet and some rude guy destroys it with an obnoxiously loud phone conversation? Why yes, ironically enough, I *am* having one of those days right now."

Silence.

Then he laughed. A deep rumble of amusement that had me glancing up at him against my better judgment.

Our eyes met.

Holy hell was this man gorgeous. Like male model gorgeous with amazing bone structure and aquamarine-colored eyes. And his smile. Just wry enough to be compelling and "aw shucks" enough to be charming and wicked enough that I had a hard time not smiling back.

"I'm sorry. I don't normally carry on like that, but he was seriously missing my point."

"So I gathered." Dammit. I'd confessed I'd been listening in.

He leaned in, resting his forearms on his knees. "I'm serious. I'm not that annoying cell phone guy."

"Maybe not normally, but you were today."

"You don't pull any punches, do you?"

"No. Also now you've moved on from being 'annoying cell phone guy' to annoying guy determined to convince me that he's not annoying cell phone guy . . . which is even more annoying."

His grin widened. "I'm supposed to apologize for that

too? Okay. Sorry for interrupting your quality time reading"—he snatched the magazine off my lap—"*Redbook* and this article on how to prioritize organization in day-to-day life."

My cheeks flamed even as I scooted forward to snatch back my magazine. "Gimme that."

"After you answer two questions. First, are you married, engaged or currently involved with someone? And if the answer is no, will you go out on a date with me so I can prove that I'm not annoying?"

I laughed. "I actually believed you couldn't get more annoying, but I was wrong."

"Are you single?"

"Annoying and tenacious—there's a winning combo," I retorted.

"And she hedges yet again. Fine. Don't answer. I'll just read this fascinating article that's got you so engrossed you can't even answer a simple question."

"Gimme back my magazine."

He lifted a brow. "I doubt it's your magazine. I'll bet you took it from the stack over there that's for customers to share."

"Fine. Keep it."

"Let's start over." He tossed the magazine aside and offered his hand. "I'm Jaxson. What's your name, beautiful?"

Calling me beautiful threw me off. I automatically answered, "Lucy," and took his hand.

"Lucy. Lovely name. Please put me out of my misery, Lovely Lucy, and tell me that you're single."

"I'm single but I'm not interested in flirting with you because you're bored at the car wash and I'm convenient."

He flashed me a grin that might've made me weak kneed had I been standing. "I'm far from bored. Let me prove it by taking you out for dinner. I promise I'll be on my least-annoying behavior."

That's when I realized he still held my hand. That's also when I realized I was a sucker for his tenacious charm, because I said, "Okay. But if that cell phone comes out even one time I will snatch it from you and grind it under my boot heel as I'm walking away."

"I'd expect nothing less."

I tugged my hand free before he did something else completely charming like kiss my knuckles. "Are you single?"

"Yes, ma'am. And this is the first time I've asked a woman I met at a car wash for a date."

"This is the first time I've agreed to a date with a man I find a—"

"Attractive?" he inserted. "Amusing? Feel free to use any A-word except the one you've repeatedly overused."

"Calling you an asshole is an acceptable A-word?"

"Damn. Opened myself up for that one, didn't I?"

"Yes, in your arrogance."

Another laugh. "I'm definitely not bored with you. Now where am I taking you for our dinner date?"

I smirked. "Pizza Lucé."

"Hilarious, Luce."

"I'm serious. That's where I want to go."

"For real?"

"Why does that surprise you?"

"I figured you'd pick someplace more upscale."

"Sorry to disappoint, but I'm the pizza and beer type."

He leaned in. "I'd ask if this was a setup, with you being a sharp-tongued brunette with those big brown Bambi eyes, because you're exactly my type. But I stopped here on a whim, so I know my friends and family aren't fucking with me."

"Mr. Jaxson, your vehicle is ready," a voice announced via the loudspeaker.

I cocked my head. "You refer to yourself by your last name?"

He shook his head. "Long story that I'll explain over pizza and beer."

"Miz Q, your vehicle is ready," echoed from the loudspeaker.

Jaxson—Mr. Jaxson—whatever his name was—winked. "Lucy Q? What's the Q stand for?"

"Nothing."

We stood simultaneously.

"Come on. Tell me," he urged.

"Maybe, as a single woman in a public venue, I didn't use my real name or initial as a safety precaution."

That declaration—a total lie—was worth it to see his smugness vanish.

Outside, the attendants stood by our cars.

No surprise that Mr. Annoying and Tenacious drove a Porsche.

But my eyes were on how spiffy my beloved blue Corolla looked. I smiled at the attendant and slipped him five bucks. "Thank you."

"My pleasure."

I looked across the roof of my car to see my date staring at me. "I'd say the last one to arrive at Pizza Lucé has to buy the first round, but my Toyota is at a disadvantage in comparison to that beast."

"I planned on following you, in case you decided to make a detour."

"Worried that I might come to my senses and change my mind about this bizarre date?"

"Yep." He grinned at me. "Lead the way, Lucy Q. I'll be right behind you."